DARK GIFT

T.L. Jones

With

John Brightman

Dark Gift
An Independent Publication

First North American Publication October 2012

All Rights Reserved.
Copyright © 2012
T.L. Jones with John Brightman

Cover Design © Nathalie Moore at Graphic Muse
Cover Illustration © Tracy Rocca Knowles
Cover Model Amanda Borges, Cover Model

Technical Production Consultant:
Karen L. Syed at Sassy Gal Enterprises

T.L. Jones
www.tljonesauthor.com
Ladynblu1233@aol.com

ISBN 13: 978-0-9885600-0-0
ISBN10: 0-9885600-0-3

Acknowledgements:

T. L. Jones would like to thank the following people: Her husband, Dave, for always being there to support her. Maria Santos and Ericka Boussarhane, two wonderful psychic mediums that always avail themselves for information pertaining to fictional characterizations. Nathalie Moore of Graphics Muse and Sassy Gal Productions for Cover Design. Tracy Rocca Knowles for Cover Photo, Amanda Borges, Cover Model, Christine Dias for the title, Karen Syed of Sassy Gal Productions for her invaluable guidance, and last but not least, friends and family that encouraged me to keep going (you know who you are!)

John Brightman would like to thank his girlfriend, Chrissy and children, Savannah and Aaron for putting up with him for all the time spent away from them investigating and attending events. Without you all sticking by him, knowing this book was his dream and to do what he loves doing in the paranormal realm, he wouldn't be where he is today. The N.E.P.R. group, Vinny, Joellen, Kayleigh, Dave, Craig (a.k.a. Chad Davies), and Sue, for all the hard work you guys do on investigations. None of this would be possible without you and he thanks each of you for that. Marc Tetlow from Ideal Event Management for bringing him into your agency and helping him to teach some of the most important aspects in this field. As for John Zaffis, Brian Cano, Rev. Tim Shaw, Jason Hawes, thank you for being there when he needed someone to discuss a case with or seek advice, he learned a lot from you guys. To his buddy, Ken Decosta, from Riseup Paranormal, thank you for the Saturday morning talks at the donut shop, keeping him sane and all of your support when he needed it most. Tim and Matt M. from Spooky South Coast, thank you for involving John in the Bridgewater Triangle Show, as well as, other events you do.

To the rest of John's family and friends, thank you for the support you give, along with the hard times to keep him in line, even though it's in good fun, that is what drives him to push and get things in life accomplished. To all the N.E.P.R. supporters out there John would like to thank you for believing in him and his group. It means a lot knowing you want this book. Come out and see John and the N.E.P.R. gang at events across the Country. He would love to meet you and of course, sign your copy.

PROLOGUE

The Freetown Forest stood eerily quiet. The moon high in the sky, brightly lit the leave-strewn paths winding through the over-grown trees.

Blood-curdling screams pierced the silent night with horrifying intensity. The young woman behind the screams, tortured beyond anything her mind could comprehend.

Finally, the screams ceased and her mangled lifeless body lay in the center of a carved out pentagram. No more pain to feel, no more blood to give. The dirt beneath her body held no blood. The eye sockets that were once beautiful green eyes were nothing more than black holes. Her naked body, marred with holes that had held tubes to drain every last drop of her blood. The heart that once beat in her chest had been removed. Her once beautiful face, forever frozen in a gruesome contorted horror from the pain she had endured.

The killer stood back and looked upon his work with endless pleasure. She had been delightful, he thought. She had been such a fighter, and of course, her calling out to God to help her made him tingle from head to toe. Yes this one had been a good choice. He walked around collecting all his tools, making sure to leave nothing behind. After all, he still had a few more of these rituals to complete before he would be ready. It certainly wouldn't do to give the local law enforcement any help in stopping him. He had to achieve his goal, or all of this would be for nothing.

Making several trips around and around the site to check for any possible items being left behind, had him whistling to himself. He was impeccable about his rituals, and this one would be no different. Once satisfied everything was packed up he poured water on the fire. It wouldn't do to leave a bonfire burning all night in the Forest he snickered.

ONE

John Bingham and his wife Chrissy were cuddled close and sleeping soundly. The cell phone on the nightstand lit up and began playing "Ghost Busters." Blindly John reached for the phone before Chrissy woke up. He loved his new ringtone and she hated it!

"Hell," he said sleepily.

"John, wake up and listen." The voice of Mark Mason was urgent.

John sprang to a sitting position and spoke quietly "hang on a second." He looked over at Chrissy who still appeared sound asleep, and quietly crept from the room. Once in the hallway he spoke normal. "Hey ya, Mark, I'm awake what's up?" He strode further down the hallway.

"You're not going to believe this shit!" Mark sounded both agitated and excited.

"Well unless you tell me we'll never know." John was grumpy and ready to crawl back into his nice warm bed.

"We've got another one man! Another fucking naked body drained of all the blood. Site was clean and fresh, hadn't been long. Some poor campers looking for a place to pitch their tent found it. The damn wood from the fire he must've used for light still smoldered." Mark, a police officer for the Freetown Police Department and a member of John's paranormal investigative team called John, day or night, usually to vent.

"Same place?" John asked waking up fully.

"No, I mean the Forest yeah, but not same location. This makes four." Mark stubbed his cigarette out sweating even though it was cool out. Fall in Massachusetts is usually not too cold, but nowhere near warm.

John swiped his free hand over his beard stubble. "Shit."

"Another young woman, she'd been tortured just like the other ones. I'm beginning to think this killer enjoys what he does." His stomach roiled at the pictures forming in his mind of the scene. A fresh memory, he could still smell the vile stench present at the scene.

"Where are you now?"

"Sitting in my patrol unit, I wanted to let you know right away. I know you've been thinking it's a cult killer, and there isn't a doubt about it. Guess I just needed to talk." Mark rolled the window down further laying his head back.

"Wanna grab a cup of coffee?" John knew his friend, and he didn't like the sound of Mark's voice.

"Nah, go back to bed. I shoulda thought before I woke you up." He started the engine and pulled out of the station parking lot. He had to get back to work. Relieved he didn't have to participate in the police investigation of these recent grisly murders he shook the scene from his mind.

"Don't mind buddy if you need someone to talk to, I'm here for you." Not too sure he'd be able to sleep now anyway.

After a brief hesitation Mark answered him "nope I have work to do. You go back to bed with that beautiful wife of yours, we'll talk soon." He flipped his cell phone shut before John could argue with him. Feeling bad knowing John was a wake because of him, he hoped it wouldn't be long before his friend was snoring again.

Driving to his district he felt glad his young partner had called in sick tonight, definitely not a crime scene for a rookie. He hated training new, young, inexperienced officers. You never knew how they would react in any given situation.

John went downstairs and popped the top on a can of beer. Pulling out a chair at the small breakfast table he plopped himself down. Thinking about his paranormal team he wondered if he should call off the investigation planned for tonight at the Assonet Ledge. The Forest has always been a place of danger, in one form or another, but this killers striking hard and fast. He knew his team would balk at the thought of cancelling, but he just wasn't sure. Taking a long slow swig from his beer he thought about the women Mark had told him about. This killers a total wacko, for some reason he tortures, and removes body parts that apparently he takes with him. Funny, John thought, why do we always assume it's a man? Shaking his head he got up and carried his can of beer with him to peer through the window. Looking out upon his back yard he noticed how the bright moon lit everything up. He could see his entire yard, and some of his neighbor's yards. He knew the Taunton River lay just past his rear neighbor, and he tossed around the idea of grabbing his fishing pole and heading down to the river.

Finishing off his can of brew he threw it in the trashcan and headed back up to bed. He needed sleep and if Mark didn't need him that's where he was going. Turning off the light he stood still and listened. This was the first night in a while he hadn't thought about the spirits that frequently caused havoc around his house. All's quiet and he was going to take advantage of that.

Slipping under the sheet, just about home free, when Chrissy rolled over and looked at him "what are you doing?" she asked in a husky sleep induced voice.

"Sorry, hun, didn't mean to wake you. Go back to sleep, everything's okay." He slipped his arm around her and snuggled her close.

"You smell like beer." She said pushing her body back against him.

He laughed. They'd been together for quite a while now, and they were comfortable with each other. He knew he didn't have to say anything else to keep her from questioning him. She was warm, and he knew the cuddling wouldn't last too much longer because her body heat over whelmed him eventually. He needed to turn over the other way, but would wait until Chrissy was good and asleep.

They often lay like this until one or the other would get too hot then roll in the opposite direction to sleep.

John lay there thinking about Mark. He was a good friend, and John knew he had been upset about this latest murder. Mark told him a lot of things he probably shouldn't, but everyone needed someone to talk to, and Mark wouldn't tell Lilly, his wife, about the horror's he saw on the job.

He realized then what Mark had said, 'It's a cult killer no doubt about it!' Why hadn't he picked up on that during the conversation? He needed to know why there's no doubt about it now. When he told Mark what he thought Mark assured him there's nothing to substantiate that. Now he said no doubt? What had happened this time? He listened to Chrissy's even, deep breathing, and pulled his arm from under her. When she didn't move he rolled back out of bed. Pulling the covers up to keep his wife warm he looked at her, and wondered how he had gotten so lucky. Smoothing her hair back from her face he kissed her forehead.

Scribbling a quick note, he then propped it on the counter in case Chrissy got up looking for him. Taking his keys from the hook near the door, he grabbed his cell phone off the counter, and headed out.

Mark stepped up to the counter of the small convenient store, cup of coffee in hand, he didn't bother to pay for the coffee since Larry, the clerk, made it clear a long time ago, officers got their coffee free. Sick of being in the car, and dealing with his imagination he was going to talk to Larry for a while.

"Slow night tonight?" Larry asked as he restocked the cigarette shelve.

"No, not really just needed to stretch my legs for a few." He blew into the small hole of the lid, and tried for some semblance of normalcy.

"Uh huh, you just needed to stretch your legs." Larry looked at him noticing the officer didn't wear his usual smile.

"Yep." Mark leaned back against a rack filled with snacks. "Oh, and a cup of your fine coffee too, let's not forget." He tried a smile, but knew he didn't quite pull it off. Hearing his phone ring he stuck a finger up at Larry. "Hang on a se," he said to the clerk. "Mark Maso," he grumbled.

"Hey, where you at?" John's voice sounded gruff.

"I'll be right back," Mark said covering his hand over the phone, and stepping outside. "What the hell are you still doing up?"

"I need to talk to you, where you at?"

"Just stepped out to get a cup of coffee, listen man, I'm sorry I woke you up."

John cut him off "don't worry about that. I could use a cup to."

"I'm at the little Stop & Go over on Main Street."

"Be there in a few. Hang tight." John hung up.

Going back into the store Mark picked his cup up from the counter, he told Larry he better brew another pot. Sliding his phone back into his pocket he stood there and waited for John. He wondered about how much he would tell his friend about the woman tonight. He liked talking to John. He knew no matter what he told the guy it never left John's lips. He was a good friend.

Larry stepped from behind the counter and started a fresh pot of coffee. "More of your *compadre's* coming in for Joe?" he asked with a laugh.

"Nah, John Bingham."

"Good ole' John." Larry sighed.

"Yep, guess he couldn't sleep," Mark lied.

Mark's a good-looking man, mid-thirties, not quite six feet tall, slender, but with a toned body. His dark hair always cut short and his brown eyes are soulful. His wife Lilly teased him about the women that came onto him, offering a variety of colorful ideas to keep from getting tickets. She never worried about him straying though. He's as faithful as any man can be.

Larry simply shook his head, and walked back behind the counter. He had been the clerk here at the Stop & Shop for almost six years, and enjoyed the night shift. He wasn't much to look at, but always treated his customers with respect. The officers spent time in the store nightly, getting their coffee, and giving their butts a break from the long hours sitting behind the wheel of their patrol units. He'd actually thought about a career in law enforcement at one time, but decided he wasn't made for that. Looking over at Mark he wondered why anyone would really follow through, and train for a job that's so dangerous, and often unappreciated. Just as he was about to ask that very question John Bingham pulled into the parking lot. "There he is now," Larry said looking out the window.

"Yep," Mark said pushing open the heavy glass door.

Both men watched the tall, well-built man step from his pickup truck. John stood six foot four inches, with a barrel chest. His dark brown hair lay just below his ears and had a habit of curling upward. His hazel eyes could be sweet and sensitive looking, or hard and demanding, depending on his mood. John locked his truck and walked toward his friend.

"Hey," he said smiling.

"Hey yourself." Mark held the door wide.

"Whatcha know, Larry?" John asked walking over to the coffee machine.

"Not too much, you?" Larry watched as John poured a cup.

"Awe nothing you want to hear about." He chuckled.

Larry turned back to restocking the shelf.

Mark motioned to John with his head to come out side. Stepping outside he walked over and leaned against his patrol car, sipping his cup of coffee.

Larry rang John's coffee up and accepted his change. "Thank you, next cup is free John." Larry said.

"Why thank you. That's a deal." John grabbed his cup off the counter and walked out the door.

"Couldn't sleep huh?" Mark asked feeling guilty.

"Probably could've, but something you said hit me, and I need to know about it." John blew into the hot liquid.

"What did I say?"

"You said no doubt they were cult murders. What's changed?"

"Oh shit! Did I say that?" Mark looked surprised.

"Yep, so give. What's changed?"

"Not much really, except this girl was laying, dead center of a carved out pentagram same everything else!"

"A pentagram, huh?"

"Yep"

"What was it carved from?"

"Just the dirt, you know like he took his time making it all just right. We gotta catch this sonuvabitch, and fast." Mark became angry in an instant.

"Everything else was the same? That's odd don't you think?" John asked with a puzzled look.

"Hadn't really given that much thought, maybe he's just progressing using a pentagram this time."

John stood there deep in thought.

"Why so quiet? What are you thinking?" Mark asked taking another sip of the hot liquid.

"Not sure, these killings are so different than anything in the past. If it is cult related, may be more than one person. Yet, something doesn't feel right, ya know?"

"Does murder, especially gruesome murder, ever feel right?" Mark was exasperated with this whole damn mess.

"No, that isn't what I meant."

"I know it wasn't I'm just tired, and frustrated. These have been the worst I've seen yet, he, or they are animals John. I mean why remove the eyes and heart? Drain every drop of blood from their bodies, and make these poor women suffer so much their faces are left with such horror in there last expression." He shook his head, trying to dislodge the pictures still forming one after the other.

John patted Mark's back trying to comfort his friend. "I wish I knew, Mark," was all he could say in way of comfort.

The two men stood in the parking lot drinking their coffee, and bullshitting for a while about their paranormal investigative team, 'New England Paranormal Research' had been founded by John some 3 years earlier. They talked about the upcoming investigation at the Assonet Ledge, and John voiced his thoughts about cancelling. Mark didn't agree, and said so. They both went back inside for a refill, but Larry wasn't behind the counter.

"Larry? Where are you?" Mark shouted after checking the men's bathroom.

Larry strolled out of the cooler, "I was restocking, wasn't sure if you guys were coming back in or not." He said taking his place behind the counter once again.

"Shit! Don't do that!" Mark said. "You can't just disappear like that. I thought day shift did the stocking."

"They do, but I was bored, and no one was in here. I can see the doors through the glass. I figured what the hell, didn't mean to scare you Officer!" Larry laughed.

"Well, you know we've been having some pretty grisly

murders around here lately. So laugh if you want, but I was worried someone carted you out the backdoor."

"Have there been anymore?" Larry asked concerned.

"Another one tonight," Mark didn't give any other information.

"Holy shit, tonight?" Larry seemed visibly upset.

"Yep." Mark turned toward John, he wanted this conversation done and over with.

John walked over and threw a dollar on the counter. "For the coffee refill," he said.

"No, this one's on the house." Larry handed the dollar back. "I appreciate the company this time of night."

"Thanks, but think I'm going to hit the road back to my bed." He looked over at Mark. "Walk out with me." Nodding to Larry he left the store.

John climbed into his pickup truck as he watched Mark stride quickly out the door. As Mark approached the truck the engine roared to life, and John rolled the window down. "Hey, you gonna be okay?"

"Sure, sorry I woke you up. Could've waited till later today to call you, and fill you in." Mark still felt guilty.

"No problem I like having the information first hand. I have plenty of time to get caught up on my sleep." Putting the truck in gear he said. "Let me know if anything new comes up."

"Will do, go get some sleep." Mark stepped back from the truck and stood there watching until the taillights couldn't be seen. Looking at his watch he walked back in to tell Larry goodnight. He was going patrolling.

On his way home, John thought about what Mark had told him, he was analytical in his thinking. These murders seemed familiar, somehow, but he couldn't quite put his finger on it.

TWO

N.E.P.R. team members arrived at the Assonet ledge about an hour or so before sunset. Everyone pitched in to bring all the equipment out of the vehicles that would be used during the investigation. The team consisted of ten members. Of these ten only seven showed up tonight.

John Bingham of course, Craig Foster, a man of few words, average height and build, with sandy colored haircut short, his looks could still be called boyish even though he's close to forty.

Vinny Muso, a cutup, likes to have fun no matter what he's doing. He's a tall lanky fella, with dark hair just above his collar, green eyes, and a beautiful smile that he uses often.

Joellen Hanks is the group's mother figure. She's mid-fifties with a graying bob cut around her chunky face. Some people consider her a plump woman, but she doesn't care what anyone thinks about her.

Dave Dawson is the 'brains' of the group, over sixty, he's short and trim built, with white hair and round glasses accentuating his intelligent eyes. He has a stern demeanor about him, and very good at debunking non-paranormal activity.

Kaliegh Olsen is a cute and bubbly addition to the group. She's late twenties, with light brown hair that cascades down her back like a milk chocolate waterfall. Her eyes are the soft buttery-brown of caramel.

Last, but not least, is Matt Downing. Matt is thirty, and has a dark and dangerous look about him. He's tall and well muscled, with eyes so dark they could be considered black. He has a Native American background somewhere in his ancestry, and unknown to him, Kaliegh has the hot's for him.

Missing tonight for one reason or another is Mark Mason and Sue James.

Sue is the youngest of the group, just turning twenty-one a couple of months ago. She's in to fitness and her body says so. Being just under medium height with a well-toned body she spent hours, at the gym, perfecting.

Then of course, there is Christine Bingham, known to everyone as Chrissy. Chrissy is a pretty woman in her early thirties, with brownish blond hair that covers her shoulders. She has blue eyes that twinkle when she's in a good mood. Her cheeks are dusted lightly with freckles, and her smile is becoming with deep dimples. Chrissy doesn't investigate with the team she's more into the research part of it all.

John had chosen his team members carefully, each had a role to play. The equipment used during an investigation is not assigned to any one person. That would be a problem if the team member trained to a certain piece of equipment couldn't make it to an investigation. John made sure everyone on his team knew all the equipment well and comfortable using each piece.

The Assonet Ledge was one of mystery, dating all the way back to the King Phillips War. To this day, it's purported to be haunted by Indian Spirits, as some three thousand were slaughtered there. The locals refer to it as The Ledge. There are urban legends about a Lady in Black who haunts The Ledge looking for her boyfriend she was supposed to meet, and run away with, but when he didn't show, she flung herself off the cliff into the cold, rocky waters. He arrived late and found her crumpled body lying on the rocks, one hundred feet below. Or so the legend goes...

Over the years, many people have committed suicide at The Ledge. It's a place where frightening, dark, cold feelings exist, and try to pull you in.

With the Urban Legends handed down for generations, The Ledge remains a place of intrigue. Sometimes in an attempt to impress their friend's, high school kids jump off the rocky cliff into the frigid water below. It still remains a popular place for the high school kids to hang out and swim, sharing ghost stories for fear, and fun. The Ledge seems to draw people with darker, evil intentions, definitely a chilling place within the Forest.

John stood looking around, remembering back to his high school days. He thought about the campfires he and his friends would sit around late at night, drinking beer. They took turns telling ghost stories, trying to scare each other.

Growing up in these woods, riding dirt bikes, and racing along the many trails had given him an avid interest in paranormal activity. He knew every inch of these woods. He loved the sounds, the smells, energy that the very trees themselves released. He was a part of this Forest.

John shook the memories off when he heard Vinny laughing. Vinny was giving Kaliegh a hard time. Everyone knew she had the hots for Matt, except Matt.

"Come on over here sweet-thing, I'm having a craving for sugar." Vinny smiled that sexy smile at her and winked.

Kaliegh just shook her head and laughed.

"If we're all done playing around, let's get this investigation going," John said walking over to stand in the middle of the group. "We're going to be in the dark soon, so I want to remind all of you about the killer that has been frequenting our Forest. I don't want anyone to wonder off alone. Since The Ledge isn't all that big we'll stick together on this one. Grab the equipment, and let's get set up. We're losing light, and we need that advantage." He stooped down and grabbed a couple of cameras to take down the steep slope to the bottom of The Ledge. "Vinny, you gonna run the DVR system tonight?" he asked trying to get Vinny on track.

"Yep I got it. I'll get the system set up, while you guys get the cameras in place." He turned and starting picking up the heavy equipment.

"Good okay, everyone you know what to do!"

The team members began grabbing camcorder cameras, still shot cameras, along with long rolled up electrical cords. These cords had to stretch all the way to the bottom of The Ledge. Facing every direction, they would use a camcorder on a tri-pod. They were used to the setup, and didn't take long to get the equipment in place. Each taking their task seriously, they worked like a well-oiled machine.

The trek down The Ledge took a good twenty minutes to hike, no one wasted time.

When they were finished, they had four cameras at the bottom of The Ledge facing in different directions, and four on top facing different directions. One of the four being a still camera, equipped with ultraviolet/infrared capability.

With all the equipment in place, and the sixteen-channel DVR system ready, John made sure all the equipment had been plugged into the generator enclosed in the noise proof box sitting in the back of his pickup. He pooled everyone around him for last minute instructions.

"Alright we're ready. I want Vinny and Joellen to watch the DVR system, the rest of us will do our thing. Any last questions?"

Everyone looked around at each other, pretty typical for an investigation to run this way, there were a few slight shakes of their heads and they disbursed grabbing equipment as they went.

Vinny and Joellen went to the table holding the DVR system, pulled up chairs, and settled in for a long night.

Dave grabbed a thermal video camera, which they used for showing hot/cold spots around them. He also picked up one of the digital recorders used for EVP's (Electronic Voice Phenomenon).

John picked up a small handheld camcorder. Sometimes things couldn't be seen with the naked eye, but the cam picked it up if they were lucky. He also took a digital recorder and placed it in his shirt pocket.

Kaliegh took another of the small handheld camcorders. Typically they would use three regular camcorders during an investigation, but since they were shorthanded tonight, they would only use two.

Craig took the EMF detector, (Electromagnetic Field Detector), which measures electromagnetic frequencies present in the area. Spirits are thought to manifest through energy, or create energy. Natural electromagnetic fields exist, so you have to rule those out if you get a meter reading. If the energy is high enough you could feel sick, or even hallucinate.

Matt handed out notebooks and pens to each investigator, they would log all activity, and sounds during the investigations. If anyone coughed, sneezed, laughed, yelled out, or dropped anything, it had to be noted. Any and all noise had to be tagged by an investigator. Around his neck he wore a 35mm camera equipped with infrared capability. He stuffed his pants pockets full of little film canisters, and even extra batteries, preferring the old camera to the new digital types. He picked up a K-2 meter, which would be used for picking up energy in the area. Since spirits are believed to emit, or create energy the K-2 is used to communicate with them. The meter has five lights that light up if energy is present. Investigators use this meter to answer yes and no questions when talking to the spirits.

John stuffed extra batteries in his pants pockets since entities had a way of draining batteries pretty quickly.

This had not been there first time at The Ledge for an

investigation. Actually they had been here several times previously, and caught a few EVP's, even some orbs, but nothing significant. Tonight they hoped would be different. They worked with a medium by the name of Debbie Milo on occasion. John wished tonight was one of those occasions; however, Deb wasn't available tonight. They would just have to do this one without her.

The sun, completely gone, left the moon shining brightly. Not quite a full moon, but full enough. Each investigator had a flashlight, and there were lights attached to the cameras.

Dave started walking looking for hot spots. He held the thermal camera at arm's length searching. The other members followed behind quietly. Everyone's equipment had been turned on, and monitored for any activity.

It was quiet by any normal person's standards, spooky as hell in the dark with no sound emanating from anywhere, no wildlife, no wind rushing through the trees, nothing, but dead stillness.

Dave led the way, and John brought up the rear. It didn't take long for Dave to find a cold spot. Matt took the K2 up front, and walked around looking for signs of energy. No one spoke, or made any noise. They were used to working as a team, and did so without uttering a sound. John slowly moved the camcorder side to side. Vinny stood hunched over, keeping watch on the video system for movement. Everyone worked in unison, watching the equipment for any sign of activity.

Matt set the K-2 down on the ground fairly close to the tripod. The lights were flickering away. He didn't want to hold it, and have something like his cell phone interfere with the results. After stepping back a bit the lights continued to flick, he looked up at John. John nodded his head, and Matt acknowledged.

"Are you causing those lights to flicker?" Matt asked softly, and began snapping stills with the 35mm. He may not see a thing standing there, but hopefully once developed they would have unexplainable pics.

Everyone stood still watching as five lights lit up.

"Are you a woman?" Matt continued, still clicking away on the camera.

The lights stopped flashing then all five lit up quickly indicating a yes answer.

Kaliegh kept the camcorder on the K-2 while Matt spoke, John's camcorder flowing slowly over the area.

"Did you die here?" Matt asked watching the meter.

The K-2's five lights flickered again.

"Did you kill yourself?" Matt questioned calmly.

Two of the five lights lit up. This indicated a no answer. "Were you murdered here?" Matt was calm, but vigilant in his questioning.

The five lights lit quickly. Matt and John looked over toward Vinny. Vinny shook his head side to side. Nothing to see here, he wanted to shout, but knew better.

"Is there any other spirits here with you?"

Two lights lit up. Dave kept track of the questions Matt asked, and the answer given by the lights. He watched Matt closely.

"Do you want to move on?"

Two lights again. Dave busily writing the question and answer down didn't notice the K-2 jiggle then suddenly fly up, striking the side of his head, "ouch," he said dropping his notepad and pen. He reached up to feel a knot forming just above his left ear "dang it!" He snapped.

John missed seeing the K-2 in flight he was turned back toward Vinny and the video system. Kaliegh didn't get it on film either she had been sweeping the area with her camcorder. The full spectrum recorder faced the opposite direction from the K-2 meter. No one had caught this on film.

John walked over and put his camcorder up to Dave's head, shining the bright light to see the injury. There was a knot forming and a small cut sat dead center of the knot "you all right to continue?" John asked Dave.

"Of course," Dave retorted angrily. Everyone tried to stay as quiet as possible while on an investigation. Its nerve racking to be angry, and not able to vent, Dave thought to himself.

The investigation continued, while Craig turned the full spectrum video camera around to face the group.

With The Ledge not very wide the group wasn't spread out like they would've been, in a building, or someplace larger.

Matt continued asking yes and no questions once Dave threw the K-2 back to him to replace on the ground.

John walked over to Vinny and Joellen. He stood beside them to watch the DVR for a bit. He wasn't concentrating on this investigation like he should've been. He kept thinking back to his conversation with Mark, and trying to imagine where the killer would strike next. Hell for all he knew, the killer was in the brush watching them at this very moment. He turned to look behind him at the dense woods, and knew they shouldn't be out here tonight. Looking back at his team he wondered if he should call the investigation off and head home.

Everyone seemed into their duties and this investigation, except John. He decided to let it go and stay where they were for now. He would let his team finish the investigation, they had all worked hard to get here tonight, and he wouldn't deny them.

Vinny leaned in to look at the monitor. Right in front of the full spectrum / infrared camera something formed. Vinny looked over at the area and didn't see anything, elbowing

John he pointed to the monitor. John leaned down to get a closer look. Looking up at the area nothing was visible to the naked eye. Vinny called out to Matt. "Keep up the questions you have something forming right there in front of that camera." He pointed to the direction and pushed a button to tag the exact spot on the DVR system while Joellen hurriedly made a reference note in her tablet.

Matt looked over at Vinny, John made a rolling motion with his hand telling Matt to keep going. As Matt continued the questions, John and Vinny kept their eyes on the DVR. It looked like the misty silhouette of a woman. Goosebumps formed on the arms of both men. They stood there staring until the thing dissolved.

"Do you want to leave here?" Matt asked quietly. The meter flashed slightly. That was a definite no. "Do you want us to leave?" Once again the meter lit only two lights. "Do you need help?" The meter lit up. "We want to help you can you help us understand what we can do to help you?" Nothing, but darkness

The K-2 meter sat dark and quiet. Matt still tried for answers that were not forthcoming.

After several more failed attempts to get answers the group began to wander around.

They watched everything thing in sight, scribbling in their notebooks when a noise was made, or anything significant happened. Not that anything significant had happened yet... that they could see, other than the K2 hitting Dave.

They chatted quietly amongst themselves while trying for another encountered, but after several hours with nothing happening John decided to call the investigation over.

"Wrap it up folks I think we're done here." He believed they had all they were going to get tonight. Shuffling around everyone pitched in to pack up, and talked excitedly about the headache Dave was sure to have as he took a small ice pack from the cooler and placed it on his head. He hoped to get some of the swelling down while he listened to the snickering going on around him about his injury.

Trips were made down to the bottom of The Ledge to gather equipment, while others packed the already collected items into their vehicles. Vinny and Joellen had the DVR system broken down quickly, and sat sharing a cup of coffee that Joellen had brought in a thermos. They laughed and joked about Dave being hit in the head, and the fact that with all the cameras about, not one had caught the incident.

Over an hour later all the equipment had been stowed, and everyone agreed to head over to John and Chrissy's house to help unload.

The vehicles rolled slowly out of the Forest and back onto the open roadway. John led the way, as each member made their way to the Bingham house. John called Chrissy and told her they were on their way. He knew she would have hot coffee brewing and sandwiches ready.

THREE

Mark had just finished his fourth cup of coffee for the night. His shift from six P to six A was the most demanding shift. He had been training his rookie, Chad Dingler, for a while now and it was time for the kid to make it or break it. Mark had some serious concerns for this young officer.

Chad came out of the Stop & Shop and slid into the passenger seat of the patrol car. "Hey where to now boss?" he asked with a smirk on his face.

Mark started the engine and looked over at the young face that for some reason really irritated him lately. "Why don't you call us back in service and let me worry about the direction we take." He didn't mean to sound short, but he did. He put the car in gear, and pulled out of the parking lot onto Main Street.

Listening Mark heard Chad check them back into service over the car radio. He had to get himself under control. All rookies liked to play around and joke, but it seemed that Chad didn't do anything else.

"What's got your panties in a wad boss?" Chad joked.

Mark took a deep breath and pulled over to the side of the road. Throwing the gearshift into park he twisted as much as his gun belt would allow, and stared at the young man. Once he knew he could speak without ripping into the kid he said, "okay listen I'm only going to say this once." He watched Chad's face sober immediately. "I understand you're new to all of this, and right now it's all fun and games, and I hate to say it, but soon you are going to see things you wouldn't wish on your worst enemy. You're going to have to get your head out of your ass and into this job. You need to

26

understand there's a time and a place for playing and it isn't in front of civilians. If you ever make me look like an ass again in a public place I'm going to pull your heart out and stuff it down your throat!" He glared at the kid. "You got that?"

Chad sat there looking at Mark like he'd just lost his best friend. Sure he joked and played around, but everyone did. "I'm sorry I didn't mean to make you feel like that, I was just playin'." He looked all innocent and actually a little hurt.

Mark straightened his body back out and hung his head. Shit! He didn't mean to come across as such a hard ass. Sitting there for a minute he turned his head and looked at Chad. "Okay loo," he said in a resigned voice, "I understand what you thought you were doing back there, but when we play and joke around it's at the station, or in the car, not in a public forum. You need to learn what you can say and do, and where you can say or do it. I probably shouldn't have said what I just said either, but dammit you need to learn." He put the car in gear and pulled out.

The car was quiet except the radio traffic that spewed out into the tension-filled vehicle. Both occupants sat staring straight ahead and thinking their own thoughts.

Mark had the murderer on his mind all of a sudden, and decided to head toward the Forest to see if anything seemed unusual. He didn't want to think about the way he had talked to the kid. He figured it had to be said, and he said it.

Chad looked over at Mark trying to figure out what he had done to piss him off so badly. He had jokingly said something about the fourth cup of coffee and pissing out in the woods, but he didn't think that was bad enough to warrant what just took place. More than ready to be on his own he hated being trained by cops that thought just because they had a few years on the streets they already knew everything. Mark Mason was his fourth field-training officer, and would be his last. Chad just needed to keep his mouth shut and do what was expected of him and they would cut him loose.

Mark knew the area well he knew who belonged, and who didn't. He knew the local vehicles, but the Forest always brought tourist to town. He patrolled nice and slow looking at everything. He should tell the kid what he was looking for too, but he didn't want to talk anymore. He drove in silence. He knew Chad was looking around the area as well he just didn't know what he was looking for.

Mark pulled onto Copi-Cut Road and dimmed his lights then drove slowly into the Forest. Finding a small niche not too far in, he stopped and back into the tight spot. Low limbs and bushes scraped along the sides of the patrol car.

Chad looked over at his trainer as Mark killed the engine. Eerie quietness closed in. Finally he couldn't stand it any longer and blurted out "what are we doing here?"

"Lookin'," Mark replied.

After a few minutes more, Chad asked, "For?"

"Anything out of the norm." Mark's window was open so he could listen to the woods. He'd turned down the radio and was halfway sticking his head out.

Chad watched his odd behavior, but didn't say another word he simply rolled his window down too.

They sat there for about ten minutes, no talking, just listening and looking. When it appeared all was quiet Mark turned the radio back up, started the car, and pulled out of the Forest. As he drove he put his window back up and waited for Chad to do the same.

Mark's cell phone rang and he looked over at Chad. "Can you put that up so I can hear?" he asked still irritated.

Chad obediently rolled the window closed. Mark looked at the caller ID. "Hey babe what are you still doing awake?" he asked sweetly.

Lilly didn't make it a habit to call Mark at work so she was brief and to the point. "Someone was in the backyard, it

28

kinda freaked me out. If you're not busy could you swing by and take a look around?"

"Did you see someone hun?"

"Yeah, a man was standing in our backyard just kind of staring at the house. I couldn't see him very well, but I saw him none the less." She hated doing this, she knew he was busy, and now he had to deal with home stuff too.

"Be there in a few, don't open the doors, and turn the lights off." He waited for her to acknowledge what he told her then snapped his cell phone closed.

"Everything alright?" Chad asked somberly.

"Lilly said she saw a man in the backyard. We're going to swing by there and check it out real quick."

Chad grabbed the radio to advise dispatch and Mark snatched the radio out of his hand.

"What are you doing?" Mark shouted.

"I was just going to check us en-route to your place." Chad sounded offended.

"You don't have to tell them everything. We don't check out at our residence got it?" He glared at the kid again.

"Yes sir!" Chad replied shaking his head and looking out the side window. He was sick of Mark's attitude.

Mark took a minute to pull himself together he was being unduly hard on this kid, and he didn't know why. "Look Chad, I'm sorry I'm being such an asshole. I guess it's just one of those nights, ya know?"

Chad didn't know. He could see absolutely no reason for the way Mark was treating him. "Yeah sure," he said anyway.

Mark didn't say anything else, just drove as quickly as he could to get to his neighborhood. When they arrived he turned the headlights off and drove very slowly. Both officers looked between houses and in the bushes for a man that didn't belong there. Pulling into the neighbor's driveway about three houses down Mark cut the engine. They both exited the vehicle not closing the doors hard enough to make a sound. Mark nodded to Chad and they both walked toward the Mason residence.

Mark hand signaled Chad to go to the far side of the front yard and he would go up the closest side. They would converge on the backyard from different directions, and try to cut off an exit for the guy if he was still back there. Chad watched as Mark removed his sidearm and signaled for Chad to do the same. Then they both lost sight of each other as they headed towards the rear of the dark house.

Mark knew he had the easy side, it had a gate. Chad would have to jump the six- foot wooden fence to gain access to the yard. Mark waited quietly at the gate. Lifting the metal lever that held the gate closed, he silently prayed Chad wouldn't beat him into the yard. Pulling the gate open as quietly as he could, he stepped back to let the gate swing past him. He lowered his body and looked into the yard from about two feet above the grass. If someone were watching the gate side they wouldn't expect him down that low. He looked around. Chad leaped over in one fast, fluid, motion and crouched down low.

They made eye contact, and Mark pointed with his pointer and middle fingers at his eyes then back out into the yard. He was telling Chad to keep a look out. Chad nodded his head and Mark stood to walk into the yard openly, defiantly.

Nothing moved except Mark. He walked very slowly, but purposefully around the yard. Not seeing anything at all he turned back toward the house. Re-holstering his weapon had Chad doing the same. They stood on the back porch as Lilly turned on the outside light and opened the door. She had been watching from the kitchen window.

"I don't know where he went Mark. I came back to the window after calling you and he wasn't there." She looked embarrassed.

"It's okay sweetie. Tell me what you saw." He pulled her into his arms and felt her shaking.

As he rubbed his hands up and down her arms she said. "I'm not sure about anything except he stood right there, and stared at the house." She pointed past Mark to a spot just to the left of the hammock he liked to spend his days off in when possible. "I couldn't see him very well, but it was definitely a person Mark. A man and he had a cigarette I could see the red tip." She said emphatically.

"I don't doubt what you're saying Lilly. It's okay." He held her close. "Are you going to feel alright about staying here by yourself the rest of the night?"

"Of course, I'll be fine. I'm just wondering what he was doing back there." She said pushing away from his hold. Noticing Chad standing there quietly she acknowledged him. "Officer Dingler, I'm sorry you had to witness this. I feel like an idiot." She gave a tentative smile.

"Why would you feel like an idiot Mrs. Mason? We get these kinds of calls all the time, and the person is almost always gone by the time we get there." He tried to sound like he knew what he was talking about. He gave her a beaming smile.

"Babe, you sure you're alright? You're shaking like a leaf." Mark threw his arm around her shoulders.

"Yes I'm sure Mark. It gave me a creepy feeling to know he was watching, and I don't know how long he had been there. I wish he was still here so we could find out what he was doing." She looked nervously around the yard.

"Okay let's get you locked in nice and tight. Chad I'll be out in a few, can you shut the gate on your way back to the car?" He made sure Chad understood he expected him to go back to the car, and wait.

"Sure thing." Chad turned to leave. "Good night, Mrs.

31

Mason," he said as he walked away.

"Good night Officer Dingler." Lilly said quietly.

When the gate closed and Mark heard the latch catch he and Lilly went inside. He closed and locked the back door then checked all the windows to make sure they were all locked. Once the entire first floor had been secured he went through and turned all the lights off. He had left Lilly in their bedroom with her cell phone, and a revolver. She had strict orders to call if she heard anything out of the norm. He hated leaving her while she was still upset, but he had to get back to work.

"All tucked in?" Chad asked when Mark was once again seated in the driver's seat.

"Yup, thanks for your comment back there about calls like this all the time. She's feeling silly, and I can reassure her all day long, but it's different coming from you I guess." He was nice for the first time since the shift started.

"It's okay Mark, I understand. She looked pretty frightened."

Mark pulled out and drove away slowly. He wished he could stay home the rest of the night. It was only two in the morning so there's no choice, but to go back to work.

"She's going to be alright you know." Chad tried to get Mark talking. Maybe he could find out what was bothering him.

"I hope so. Guess I'm jumpy with a fucking killer running loose." Mark hit the steering wheel with open hands. He was frustrated to say the least. He drove past John Bingham's house and noticed everyone was there. Damn he wanted to stop, but with Chad there he knew he couldn't.

FOUR

Chrissy laughed at everyone as they sat around drinking ice-cold beer and eating the sandwiches she had prepared. She'd made coffee expecting them to be a bit chilled when they returned. She should've known better. They were all chatting excitedly about the misty apparition, and the fact that Dave had been dinged in the head with the K2 meter.

"Okay so the game plan is this." John stood to get everyone's attention "I have to work tomorrow evening, so I will get some of the video stuff together tomorrow, and then Matt, how about you and I get together and listen to the audio stuff? Say, day after tomorrow?"

"Sure sounds good. Can we make it at my place though?" Matt asked. "Jersey just had surgery and I don't like leaving her too long."

"Oh no what was wrong with her?" Chrissy asked. Jersey was Matt's female chocolate lab.

"Nothing wrong really, just got her spayed. She's alright and the Vet said no worries or problems, it's just so soon after, and I want to see for myself that everything is good."

"Oh for sure, poor Jersey." Chrissy sighed. She knew Matt treated Jersey better than most men treated their wives.

John gave a nod of understanding to Matt then looked over at Chrissy. She shrugged her shoulders showing she didn't care about him going to Matt's. "Okay then, I don't have a problem with that, let's say around four o'clock?"

"Yup, sounds good." Matt took the last drink of his beer. "I'm going home it's late and I'm tired." He stood stretching his long body out.

"Yeah I think that's a good idea. Come on everyone let's

get going so these folks can get some sleep. The sun will be up in a couple hours." Joellen began clearing paper plates and empty beer bottles to the kitchen.

"You don't need to do that Joellen, I got it." Chrissy jumped up to clean the cocktail table off.

John started herding people to the door. He was more than ready to call it a night. They always sat around and unwound together after an investigation. It seemed to be a part of the process. Telling everyone good night he closed the door, and locked up.

Chrissy came in from the kitchen and smiled "long night?"

"You know it. I'm gonna sleep like a bear. Come on." He headed for the stairs.

Chrissy was following when the basement door opened and slammed shut. She stopped instantly and looked at John.

Shaking his head he came back down the few steps he had made it up, and said, "You go on up, I'll check it out even though we know, there won't be anyone there." He gave her a light shove up the stairs. Going into the kitchen he flipped the light switch and looked around. The basement door was closed and everything appeared normal. They had a few spirits that liked to cause problems on occasion, and this was apparently one of those occasions. He walked over and opened the basement door. Looking down the stairs he listened for any noise at all, of course, there wasn't any. He closed the door and said quietly. "Could you please be quiet tonight? I really want to sleep!" Standing for a minute longer with nothing else happening he turned the light off and headed up to bed.

Chrissy asked nervously as he came into the room "everything okay?"

"Yep, nothing there." He gave her a tentative smile. He knew the spirits freaked her out, but it was what it was, and nothing could be done. At least not right now.

"I really wish we could do something about them." She said crawling into bed.

"I know, and we'll figure it out, don't worry." He pulled her close and cuddled with her. "At least they stopped opening the cabinets and chunking everything." He tried to laugh and make light of it.

She snuggled closer, looking around the darkened bedroom. She half expected an American Indian, or Spanish soldier to come walking through the wall.

They had a few different mediums come to the house and try to help with the issues they'd been having, and were told that there were several spirits residing in their home. Chrissy was thankful that at least they weren't malevolent spirits, and even though they seemed a bit mischievous at times they never hurt anyone. She was a bit creeped out by the whole idea.

John lay awake listening to the even breathing of his wife lying next to him. His mind was going over all the events of the investigation, and the murder victims. He knew there was something he should be remembering that was important, but for the life of him he couldn't figure out what he was missing.

He was excited to view the recordings both visual and audio from The Ledge investigation. He couldn't believe the mist that appeared, that was a first for him and his team.

As he lay there he wondered how Mark was doing. He knew his friend had been very upset the night or morning before. Mark was good hearted, and John considered himself fortunate to have him as a friend.

Willing his mind to slow down so he could sleep, he listened to the night sounds around the room. A creak here, a rustle there, nothing out of the ordinary, he sometimes wondered if that was the spirits trying to keep his attention. He knew the spirits that lived, or rather resided with them, bothered Chrissy, and he wished it could be different for her, but knew it wouldn't change.

Just on the verge of being asleep he heard a loud thud outside. Someone was in the backyard. He got up and crept to the window, looking out into the dark backyard he noticed the door to the shed was swinging. That was odd he always kept it locked. Throwing his jeans back on, he slipped his feet into some leather house shoes, and grabbed a sweatshirt on his way out of the room. Making his way quickly to the back door he checked one more time out the window before stepping out. No one could be seen, but the door moved again.

Not bothering to turn the outside light on he quietly opened the door and slipped out into the darkness. Moving stealthily toward the shed he listened for movement inside. He sure didn't want to happen upon an armed stranger.

Reaching the shed he stood off to one side, still not hearing anything at all he stepped into the dark space and looked around. His eyes had already adjusted to the darkness since he had not turned one light on, on his way out.

Hmm that was weird, nothing seemed moved, or tampered with from what he could see. He stepped out and looked at the pad lock on the door. It had been cut, no doubt. Reaching inside on a shelf near the door he removed a flashlight and turned it on. Taking a closer look he still couldn't see where anything was missing. Why would someone cut the lock and open the door, but not take anything? He had plenty in there, fishing equipment, camping equipment, two large toolboxes filled to capacity, not to mention the lawn care stuff.

He stepped into the yard shinning his flashlight around to make sure he hadn't missed someone hiding back there.

Looking around he felt sure who ever had been here was long gone. He got another lock out of a toolbox and re-secured the door.

Remaining there just a minute longer he felt a nagging tug, but decided he had done everything he could do tonight. Throwing the cut pad lock into the trashcan, he went inside.

John awoke to the smell of bacon frying and coffee brewing. He rolled over and looked at the alarm clock, eight A.M., rolling onto his back he thought about going back to sleep, last night had been a restless night.

Throwing the blanket and sheet back, he stood up stretched his big body trying to get the blood moving. Reaching for his blue jeans and sweatshirt from the night before, he made his way into the bathroom.

Chrissy was zinging around the kitchen getting breakfast on the table, and pouring a big cup of coffee for John since she heard him moving around. He would be grumpy this morning she thought to herself. It had been a late night for both, and he wasn't a morning person.

John stepped into the kitchen just as Chrissy turned with the cup in her hand. "Good morning sweetie." She smiled sweetly and handed the cup over.

"Is it?" He took it to the table and flopped down on a chair, yawning loudly. Taking a sip of the hot liquid he looked over at his wife. "You didn't by chance need in the shed yesterday for anything, did ya?" He remembered the night before and stood to look out the kitchen window.

"No why?" She brought a plate of bacon, eggs, and toast to the table for him.

Turning away from the window he said. "The lock on the shed's been cut off. I heard it flapping last night, and went to check it." He sat putting his cup on the table.

"Cut off, are you sure." She looked stunned.

"Oh yeah, very sure I thought maybe you needed in there and couldn't find the key." He knew very well she wouldn't cut the lock, but he wanted her to know about it, just not over-react about the incident. He thought he did a good job until she joined him at the table with a plate of her own and said.

"John I took the trash out last night and that door was closed, so someone did that after dark. Who would be sneaking around our property after dark?"

He thought before he spoke. He needed to make sure she didn't feel insecure, or maybe she should with the killer running around. "Chrissy I don't want you going out by yourself." He stopped, and got his voice under control, he couldn't demand it, or she wouldn't listen. "Honey you know we've had several young women murdered here recently. There's a killer running around, mutilating his victims. I don't care about the lock, and I don't believe it was the killer, but you need to stay safe." He looked at her making sure his words sunk in.

"I hardly think that killer would want someone like me. He appears to pick younger females, and single at that."

"We don't know what he likes maybe it's just females of convenience so far. I don't like the fact that someone cut that lock, but I'm also not going to jump to conclusions, and neither should you." He took a big bite of food.

They ate in silence, both were thinking about the killer. Not so much about the unknown person that had been on their property, which maybe, should've been their focus.

After breakfast John went outside to look around in the daylight. He checked the new lock on the shed, and it remained intact. He looked at the hard ground outside the shed, trampled grass, and a cigarette butt, was all he found. Even though he didn't smoke, the cigarette butt didn't seem out of the ordinary, since he had plenty of friends that did.

Chrissy cleaned the kitchen and gave John a kiss goodbye as she left for work. She was a librarian at the local public library, hence her love for researching for the team.

The house was eerily quiet now that John was home alone. He went to the closet and took out a small .38 caliber revolver, cleaned it well, and loaded it. Setting it on Chrissy's nightstand table, he wrote a short note telling her to use it if she needed it, ending the note with the statement *Don't Hesitate!* He felt somewhat better knowing she knew how to use the gun, and didn't mind them in the house like most women.

John left for work a few hours later. He worked for a big hotel chain, and liked the evening shift normally, but right now he didn't like Chrissy home at night without him. He shook off that nagging feeling that something was going to happen, and took off for work. Just as he rounded the corner out of his neighborhood, his cell phone rang.

"Yea," he said grouchily into the phone.

"Well hey there, what's wrong with you?" Matt asked laughing.

"Hey Matt, sorry just in a pissy mood what's up?"

"Not much, just checking to see if we were still on for tomorrow, around four o'clock right?"

"Yeah I'll be there. I'll bring the equipment with me so we can go over it, once again sorry I'm tired, didn't sleep enough I guess."

"Yeah, I know it was rude of all of us to stay so long last night bud, I'm sorry." Matt apologized.

"No not that, I had someone cut the lock on my shed sometime last night. Not feeling too good about it, even though nothing was taken."

"What? No shit? Who would do that?" Matt asked surprised.

"No idea, I just put another lock on, and will keep an eye

on it, I guess." John sounded resigned.

"Lots of strange shit going on around here lately. I don't like it!" Matt stated.

"Yeah, me either. Listen on my way to work so gonna get off here. I'll see you tomorrow, okay?" John hated being on a cell phone when he drove.

"Sure, okay. Take it easy, bud, and I'll see ya tomorrow." Matt hung up while going to the window to check his own shed out.

John pulled into the parking lot at work, and decided to call Mark before going in. He hadn't spoken to his friend since that last murder victim had been found. Dialing his number John sat back and looked at the building. It was a great place to work, and his company gave him complimentary rooms, if he traveled in an area where a company hotel was located. He used that benefit, traveling to speak at paranormal conferences often.

"Hi John," Mark chirped into the phone.

"Well you sound better. How's it going?"

"It's going, just trying to get in the right frame of mind before I go into work. How was the investigation?"

"Interesting, I'll fill you in later when we have time. I just pulled up at work, but wanted to check on you since I hadn't heard from you, you doin' okay?"

"Yeah, better, thanks for asking. I just was a tad pissy to my rookie last night, so trying to be in a better mood for tonight."

"Why pissy? He getting on your nerves finally, you know you do that every time you train someone new." John laughed.

"Really, do I? Huh. Well last night I was just tired and short on patience, then Lilly called, said she saw someone in the backyard."

"What? Last night? Could she tell who it was?"

"Yeah last night, and no, said it was a man smoking a cigarette, but couldn't see him clearly. Chad and I came by here, but he was already gone."

"Mark, someone cut the pad lock off my shed sometime last night too." John said sitting up straighter.

"What's missing? Did you file a report?"

"Nothing's missing that I can tell so no, no report. I'm really not liking this and even more now, what do you make of it all?" John asked worriedly.

"Huh, not sure, I suggest keeping your eyes open for a while. You said you're at work? What time you get off?"

"I'll be home a little after midnight. Don't like leaving Chrissy alone knowing this shit."

"Yeah, I know whatcha mean, I feel the same way about Lilly."

"Okay gotta get in there, don't wanna be late. I'll talk to you soon okay?" John was really worried. "Hey it's going to be fine. No worries." He said not sure if he tried to reassure his friend or himself. He wasn't feeling too good about any of this at all.

"Sure thing John, talk to you later." Mark shut his cell phone stuffing it in his shirt pocket.

FIVE

John stood at the kitchen counter making a peanut butter and jelly sandwich. He was deciding on a plan of attack for the day. He had a couple hours before he was due at Matt's, and Chrissy was at work so...what to do?

Gathering his sandwich and drink he went to his office to get what he needed to take over to Matt's house. He really looked forward to going through the video and audio. Of course they wouldn't make it through all of it, probably not even half of it.

Taking the last bite of his sandwich John began carrying the equipment to his truck. He decided he wouldn't stay too long at Matt's house, leaving Chrissy home alone for another evening.

Pouring sweat by the time the equipment was all loaded he went in to shower and got ready to head out.

The town was buzzing about the fourth murder. Chrissy walked quietly through the library listening to people chat about it. She couldn't shake the feeling she was being watched. She'd been sitting behind her desk working on a new card catalog, when the hair on her neck and arms began to rise. She looked around and couldn't see anyone or anything out of the ordinary. She decided to get up and walk around taking a closer look at everyone in the library.

By the time she reached the rear staircase to the second level, she had heard several tidbits on the murders. Knowing the bodies had been mutilated had been the extent of her knowledge, but now she knew the victims had been drained of all blood with their eyes and hearts missing.

Turning back toward the Occult section of books, Chrissy decided it was time for some research on rituals. She wanted to know what the killer was hoping to accomplish and why. Research was her forte, and if she tried maybe she could help provide information on this type of ritual. Hoping it was a documented ritual, and not one the killer was simply winging, she took several books back to her desk.

Matt helped John unload everything when he arrived. They both settled into comfortable chairs at the kitchen table to begin the tedious work ahead of them.

"Thanks for coming over here John, I know it would've been easier to do this at your house, but Jersey and I appreciate it." He looked over at his loyal lab in the corner on her bed. She wagged her tail, but didn't bother to lift her head.

"No prob., how's she doing anyway?" John realized the normally energetic dog, didn't bother to greet him this time.

"I think she's depressed."

"Really, why?"

"Not sure, I mean she's healing fine, but not her chipper self, ya know?"

"I noticed she didn't greet me as she usually does. Maybe she's just sore still, give it a few days." John suggested.

"Yeah I will, but if she doesn't perk up soon then I'll take her back to the Vet. Want a beer?"

"Sure."

Matt got up to grab a couple bottles of beer. He bent down in front of Jersey, and gave her head a pat. "How's my girl?" He spoke sweetly to Jersey. Thumping her tail she acknowledged her favorite human. Matt opened the fridge, and grabbed a couple bottles of beer, taking them back to the table they got to work.

* * *

Mark enjoyed a quiet dinner with Lilly before getting

ready for work. He filled her in on the latest victim of the killer, now being dubbed 'The Surgeon', since he expertly drained blood and removed eyes and hearts, with the skill of a surgeon. He didn't hold back any pertinent information because he wanted to scare the hell out of her. He wanted to make sure she didn't end up like these other four women.

He finished dressing and placed his .45 in the Sam Brown belt. Looking in the mirror he noticed the deep lines around his eyes. He loved his job, but when things like this occurred, and they had no leads he stressed badly.

Making his way to the kitchen he turned Lily around to face him. "You're staying in tonight right? No plans?"

"Yep, I'm here for the night. You be safe my love." She reached up and kissed his lips.

"Call me before you go to bed. I love you." He kissed her again and stepped back.

"I will. You don't worry about me, I'm not going anywhere." She smiled at him.

Mark put his cell phone in his shirt pocket, said goodbye, and left the house. Getting into his patrol unit he checked into service. The radio steadily buzzed, and it was still early, he knew that meant it was going to be a busy night. Backing down the driveway he looked around his house. He and Lily had been happy here for a good many years, yet this was the first time he didn't feel good leaving her at home alone. Was it just his imagination or was it intuition? Cop's depended on their gut instinct. He stopped at the end of the drive and looked at the house. Saying a silent prayer he left.

Lilly looked out the window as Mark backed out of the driveway she had noticed the lines etching their way around his beautiful eyes, the strain of stress and fatigue his face held. She knew he worried about her and she would do everything she could not to add any un-do pressure.

Chrissy grabbed a couple of the books she had chosen to read, and gave her pass-on to the relief librarian before calling John. Once settled in her car, she made a quick call letting him know she'd be on her way home. This is a daily call she made on workdays. John liked to know when she left work, and when she made it home.

After the brief conversation she pulled out of the parking lot. The drive home wouldn't take long, and they agreed she would just send a quick text when she made it. She felt relief that John would make it a short evening away. She didn't like being a lone at home right now, especially after the lock on the shed door had been cut. They were both grateful nothing had been taken, but it was still very odd.

Her thoughts wandered to the victims, and the fear they must've felt, the pain they had to endure. She silently hoped they were dead before he took the eyes and hearts. She couldn't shake these murders. Thoughts were ever present. She vigilantly watched everything around her. John may be right in that, the women could be convenient and not a certain type.

* * *

Mark made it to lineup. The Lieutenant filled the group in on their assignments. When she finished she yelled at Mark, and told him to meet her in her office.

Everyone was busy chattering about the killings. Mark's rookie joined in the fun, and joked about how he had an ex-girlfriend he would be willing to tell 'The Surgeon' about, just to get her off his back. He stopped running his jaws when he noticed the looks Mark gave them. Ducking his head, he quietly left the small boisterous group, and walked over to his FTO (Field Training Officer).

"I know it's all fun and games for you right now Dingler, but you wouldn't be laughing if you had seen that poor girl the other night. Go get the unit filled with fuel, LT wants to see me, then I'll meet you out there." He handed a spare key to Dingler, and when the rookie didn't ask any questions Mark walked away.

Entering the Lieutenants office he waited for her to acknowledge his presence. Standing there he waited silently, and watched as the lieutenant signed some papers and look over a report. Tossing a file to the side, Lieutenant Gina Washington, looked up and smiled. "Mark come on in and have a seat." She gestured at a chair in front of her desk.

Mark took the offered seat quietly. "How's that rookie doing?" Lt. Washington inquired.

"He'll be fine. Just needs to learn when to keep his mouth shut is all." Mark was very straightforward.

"Good, good." She smiled again. "I know you're wondering what you're doing in here, right?" She laughed.

"The question had crossed my mind LT."

"Well, I know you were out the other night when the fourth girl was called in. The Chief's putting together a task force, and asked that you be a part of it. You interested?" She watched his reaction.

46

Chad was one of five new officers recently hired. He felt honored to have Mark Mason train him. He'd heard the other officers talk about Mark, and knew he was in good hands. At twenty-two and recently graduated from the police academy, he was happy to be learning street smarts from none other than Mark Mason. Yeah, he's an asshole to deal with at times, but he knew what he talked about. Typically each rookie had four different FTO's, each one for a month. His time with Mark should be just about over then he would either, be cut loose, or go to another FTO for another month, that is if the higher up's didn't feel he was ready. Being trained by Mark would give him a great start on his own. He hoped he would be on his own soon. He was eager to learn and fit in, knowing he had to work hard to gain respect, and knowledge. Cutting up had been something he witnessed the other officers do, and wanting to be accepted by them, he may have went overboard on the joking, he'd tone it down some. He went to fill the car with gasoline and wait.

Lilly finished the dishes then emptied the trashcan. Pulling the plastic bag free of the silver can she tied the bag closed. Lifting the full bag, she went out the back door and over to the large blue contraption on wheels. Throwing the bag in, she turned to make her way back into the house, when she heard a scraping sound in the rear of the yard. She stopped and turned in the direction of the sound. The yard was dark; she couldn't see that far back. Rubbing her hands up and down her arms she hurried back inside. Locking the door with both locks she peered out the door window. The shadow of a man emerged from the darkness into the yard. Lilly stood riveted, trying to see the man clearly. He stopped just short of being seen in full view. She could make out the jean clad legs and heavy work type boots.

Stepping back from the door she grabbed the phone from the counter and called Chrissy. John would come over and check things out for her. She didn't want to worry Mark. He had enough to worry about with his job. It was probably just a homeless man that wandered into the yard by accident, she told herself. After seeing a man in the backyard the other night and Mark not finding anyone she didn't want to bother him. He had to work, not run home to find an empty yard yet again.

Chrissy explained that John was over at Matt's house listening to the recordings from The Ledge investigation, but she would call him and tell him about the incident. After making sure her friend was all right she hung up and called her husband.

Lilly turned off the kitchen light. It was the only light on in the house. She felt her way to the stairs and climbed them in the dark. She knew where Mark kept the small 9mm on the closet shelf. Going into the closet she shut the door, and pulled the chain for the light. The bright light blinded her for a second then she reached for the gun. Pulling back the slide she sent a bullet into the chamber, and felt better immediately. Turning off the light she stepped out into the master bedroom.

Standing quietly she listened for any sound. The house was dark and silent, so quiet, the silence made her nerve endings jump. Switching on the nightstand lamp, she made her way back down the stairs. Let him think she was upstairs, she thought to herself. Going back into the kitchen she crept up to the door, and standing off to the side she looked out to see if he was still there.

John and Matt headed for Mark Mason's house. John filled Matt in on what Chrissy had told him, and explained they were going to check it out. He understood not bothering

Mark, but knew Mark would be pissed if he weren't informed. John had every intention of calling Mark, as soon as, he checked the place out. Calling Lilly he told her he was parking a ways down the street, and not to shoot him because he was going to be sneaking around the house. He knew if she were frightened the first thing she would do would be to get a gun. Cop's wives were always armed, he thought to himself smiling.

Lilly slid into a kitchen chair and waited.

SIX

He slipped quietly over the back fence and made his way to his car parked two streets over. He had been sly parking so far away, and walking. He liked the idea he was seen by Mason's wife. He knew he frightened her, and it tickled him. He could've grabbed her so easily when she brought the trash out. Laughing out loud he formulated a plan in his mind.

He knew he had a few more women to offer to his god of darkness, before he needed the ultimate sacrifice, and he wouldn't waste Mrs. Mason, indeed not, he would savor the fear he was building in her. He would relish her fear, when the time came.

So glad his mind was finally made up, and it would be Mason's wife, not Bingham's. He liked the idea of using one or the other, and was excited to realize it would be the cop's wife.

He already had the place in mind, all he needed was the others out of the way, and then it would be done. He had a few more to give away first, just 'nothings' really, but they would help in finding favor with his lord.

He drove off in complete satisfaction of his plan.

John and Matt had thoroughly searched the property, and found nothing. No one! John was getting irritated that someone could slip so easily in and out of the area without being seen. He knew this was the second time a man had been in this backyard in less than a week, and it didn't sit well with him. He took his cell phone out and called Lilly.

"Open the back door Lilly." He said and hung up.

Lilly turned the light on in the kitchen, and then the back

porch light. She peered out to make sure John was standing there before unlocking the door. "You didn't find him did you?" she asked with fear dripping from her words.

"No. We searched all over, and nothing. Did you get a look at him this time?" John asked while Matt stood looking out into the dark yard.

"Just his pants and boots he stands back just out of the light so I can't see his face. This is twice John, and I'm getting freaked out here!" Lilly started to panic. "Mark is stressing so bad, I can't have him worrying about me too."

"I know he is, but you're his concern not his job. Don't hide this from him Lilly."

"I won't, I just hate that he's under so much pressure right now. I'm sorry I wasted your time too, and Matt's as well."

"Hey, stop that right now!" Matt stepped up to the door. "You know you're family, and we're here for you." Their group was close, and they thought of each other like family, even though they didn't share a bloodline.

"He's right Lilly, you know that." John hugged her tightly. "I know you're scared, and you should be, but Mark has to be told." He drew back and let her go.

"Yeah, I know guys, come on in while I call him." She stepped back and held the door open.

They both took seats at the small table in the kitchen corner. John texted Chrissy to let her know everything was all right.

Lilly grabbed the cordless phone lying on the counter, and looked back at the guys before dialing Mark's cell phone. She really hated doing this, but knew she had to.

"It's okay Lilly, go ahead." Matt encouraged.

She smiled tentatively and began pushing the buttons. Taking a very deep breath to calm her voice, she waited for Mark to answer.

Mark looked at the caller ID and felt his heart lunge to the pit of his stomach. It was too early he knew Lilly wasn't going to bed yet. "Hey babe everything alright?" he asked quickly.

"Yes honey everything is okay." She looked at John.

He nodded to her that it was going to be fine. He hated that she looked so worried, but Mark had to be told. He was glad it wasn't him having to call Mark after the fact.

"What's up?" Mark asked with a suspicious tone. Lilly never just called to talk.

"Well babe, I hate to bother you while you're working, but thought you should know that, um..." She hesitated.

Mark didn't like the sound of her voice. "What's wrong Lilly?"

"That man was back, Mark, but don't come home," she hurried to say, "John and Matt are both here and they've already checked everything out. He's gone again."

"You called John? Why didn't you call me? I'm on my way right now." He was angry. Didn't she know she could depend on him?

"Mark! Stop and listen. He's gone, I called Chrissy, and she sent John over here. Everything is fine you don't have to come home." She looked pleadingly at John.

He stood up and walked over taking the phone from her. "Hey Mark, everything here is fine, no worries. Lilly really doesn't want you worrying about this." He knew his words were futile, but he said them anyway.

"What the fuck? My wife calls you because she's worried about me? I'm on my way, just stay with her till I get there okay?" He hung up.

John looked at the now dead phone and shook his head at Lilly.

"He's coming home isn't he?" she asked, already knowing the answer.

"Yep and he sounds pissed." John laughed.

Lilly took the phone and put it back into the cradle. "You guys might want to escape while the getting's good." She laughed nervously.

"No way, he told me to stay here until he got here." John sat back down.

Matt sat quietly not willing to say anything to upset Lilly. He didn't know about the other night, but he heard and felt their concern.

Lilly got a couple bottles of beer from the fridge and gave them to the guys. Sitting down at the table she regretted not calling her husband first. She knew it was the same man in her yard both times, but wasn't sure she should tell Mark that. She wanted to protect him, but maybe he needed to know.

John and Matt watched Lilly, and knew she worried. They looked at each other and then both took a drink of beer. They would leave her to her thoughts, and not put her through all the questions twice, since Mark certainly would question the hell out of her once he got home.

Tension hung heavy in the small kitchen, and John decided it was time to break the silence. He looked over at Matt. "Hey, when we leave here I'm gonna just drop you by your house and head home. I know we didn't get through much of the findings, but I don't want Chrissy alone." He wanted Lilly to see this was the way most husbands felt, Mark wasn't trying to be over protective, he was just concerned.

Matt understood perfectly and said so. They all three sat there forcing small talk while waiting for Mark.

The front door open and slammed shut. Mark and his rookie came in together. Chad stayed in the doorway while Mark scooped his wife into his arms. He couldn't stand the thought of something happening to her.

"Babe I'm okay." She said hugging him back.

"He withdrew and looked down at her. What the hell happened?" he asked a little too gruffly.

Lilly went through the entire incident then added "I know you can't run home every time something happens, that's the only reason I didn't call you first."

"Yes I can. Don't you ever feel that you can't call me Lilly." He turned toward John and Matt. "Thanks, guys, I really appreciate you coming over. You didn't see anyone leaving the area as you came in?"

Let the questions begin, John thought. "No we were watching everything as we got to the neighborhood, nothing moved out there." John said and Matt nodded.

"Yeah, we checked the area thoroughly Mark, we didn't want that bastard to get away." Matt said.

"I appreciate both of you, but Lilly, you should've called me. Was it the same man?"

"I believe so, yes." She wouldn't lie to him. He was really upset that she didn't call him. "I'm sorry honey, I just didn't think." She tried to put him at ease.

"I know you, and you didn't want to worry me. Did you think I wouldn't find out?" he asked harshly.

"Mark, take it easy I don't think that was her intention." John said standing up. He knew his friend, and he wasn't usually this upset. He wondered what else had happened, but knew this wasn't the time to talk to him.

"Don't tell me to take it easy John, she's my wife!" He glared at his friend daring him to intervene again. "I want you to go to your mom's until this is over Lilly." He said looking at her.

She didn't want to leave him, not with so much going on. He needed her here with him, not at her mothers. "Mark, we'll talk about that tomorrow. I know you're worried about me I can take care of myself. I got your 9mm out and it's loaded, I know how to use it I'm fine here really." She put a brave front on. She wasn't going anywhere.

"That's just it, if you felt the need to get my gun, you're scared. I can't have you sitting here by yourself. Please, go to your mom's." He implored.

"We'll talk about it tomorrow." She turned away from him and took the two empty beer bottles off the table. Throwing them into the trashcan she said "you all get out of here. I'm going to bed."

"This isn't the end of it Lilly. We will talk tomorrow, and you will be going to your mom's house. I'll explain it to you tomorrow, you'll understand why." He didn't want to get into the task force thing right now. He didn't even know he would accept that position until now. "Lock up tight and you call me if you need me." He gave her a stern look.

"I will." Leaving them standing in the kitchen she went to the living room to get her book off the coffee table. She had planned on reading in there, but now she would read in bed with the gun next to her.

John dropped Matt at home and headed for his own house. It had been a long few days and his back felt tense with stress. He understood exactly where Mark was coming from wanting Lilly to leave. Maybe he should send Chrissy away too.

He wondered what the odds were, that the man in the Mason's backyard, and the person that cut the lock off his shed, could be the killer, heck for that matter what were the odd's they could be the same person?

He cranked his radio up in the truck listening to his favorite rock and roll station. He needed to give his mind a rest.

Lilly called Chrissy as soon as they cleared out of the

house. "Can you believe he wants me to go to my mom's?" she asked angrily.

"That may not be a bad idea Lilly. He does have to work nights, and this is twice that you had that man in your yard." Chrissy tried to reason with her.

"Don't you think I know that? I can't leave Mark right now. You should see him, the stress is getting to him, and I need to be here for him."

Chrissy listened to her friend vent and didn't interrupt her. She hoped to be off the phone by the time John got home. He had texted to tell her he was taking Matt home and then would be on his way. She knew Lilly just needed someone to talk to. She hated being home at night a lone too. She thought about finding the loaded .38, and John's note on the nightstand, and how she had laughed at the idea, now she was thankful.

Lilly was steadily talking and Chrissy realized she missed a lot of what had been said. She concentrated on paying attention.

"I'm going to bed Chrissy, I'll talk to you tomorrow." Lilly said quietly.

Chrissy felt guilty that she hadn't listened to her friend. "I'm here if you need me." She said quietly.

"I know and thank John for me again when he gets there. I'll talk to you soon." She hung up. Looking around the quiet bedroom, she settled back against the pillow propped behind her head and picked up her book.

SEVEN

Mark let Chad drive the rest of the shift. He had a lot of soul searching he needed to do. This task force wouldn't be a piece of cake, it would be long demanding hours away from home, gruesome details that would haunt him, sights and smells that would linger in his mind's eye for days. He really wanted to be a part of stopping the sadistic sonuvabitch, but Lilly…

He was so deep in thought he didn't hear the dispatcher calling his number over the radio. Chad looked over at Mark when he didn't answer.

"Hey they're calling you." He said loud enough to bring Mark out of his reverie.

"What, who?" Mark was confused. His mind had been so wrapped around this task force idea he wasn't paying attention. That wasn't good.

"Dispatch, they just called your number." Chad looked at Mark curiously. What the hell was he over there thinking about?

Mark grabbed the mic. "12-33 go ahead."

The dispatcher informed him they needed to head to a domestic disturbance in progress, and gave all the pertinent information.

"Do you know how to get there?" he asked Chad.

"Ye," Chad answered flipping a U-turn in the middle of the roadway.

"Okay this one's all yours. I'm standing back and letting you handle it."

"I got this. No worries!" Chad wanted to prove he's ready to be on his own, this was his chance.

They arrived at the address given, and Mark walked slowly behind Chad. He would stay in the background, and give the kid a chance to show him he knew what he was doing.

John tried to convince Chrissy it would be wise for her to leave for a while too. They had been talking heatedly for over an hour and a half. "Your job will wait for you Chrissy, you really need to go."

"My job will wait for me?" She glared at him.

"Yeah, you've been there long enough to take an extended leave of absence."

She threw the small blanket off her shoulders onto the sofa and stood up. "I'm done with this conversation, I'm going to bed."

John turned the lights off and followed Chrissy up the stairs. He wasn't about to give up. They both went through the motions of getting ready for bed. Once they were settled he turned to her. "Look I know your job means a lot to you, I'm not belittling that at all. You are my world Chrissy, and I can't take a chance with your life." He reached out to her back as she lay facing the other direction.

She lay there listening to him, her heart understood exactly what he said, but her mind wasn't having any of it. Not bothering to turn over and look into the gaze she knew would be filled with love, she said. "It's not the job John. It's leaving you I'm not willing to do." Squeezing her eyes shut she willed the tears to stay back. "It's not me you need to be worried about Lilly's the one he seems to be stalking."

John lay back against his pillow, how was he going to convince her to leave? Rubbing his hand around her back, needing the physical touch between them, he thought quietly. He would get her out of town if it were the last thing he did.

Chrissy waited for his hand to stop moving and the

arguing to stop. When nothing else was said she turned over and leaned across John to turn off the nightstand lamp. "Goodnight John." She said as she pulled the covers up to her chin.

John sighed and gave her a light kiss goodnight. He would let her think she'd won. He would let it go for tonight, but not for good.

Mark stood at the bottom of the porch steps and watched Chad position himself near the wall next to the front door. Good move, Mark thought to himself. Chad reached over and knocked hard on the wooden front door. He tried to hear movement in the house, but nothing, no yelling, nothing breaking, all in all, very quiet. He knocked again this time a bit harder.

The door swung open and a young man stood facing Mark. Chad stepped out and startled the young man. "Sorry to bother you sir, but we've had a complaint there's a fight going on here." Chad observed the shock on the young man's face.

"What? No there's no fight here. We're just watching some TV." The man turned sideways allowing Chad a view of the living room.

Two other young men sat there with the TV on, nothing looked broken, or out of place. Chad turned to Mark, then back to the young man. "Uh, mind if we come in and take a look?" he asked unsure of himself.

The young man stepped back. "Sure help yourselves." He was confused why someone would report a fight at his house.

The officers stepped in following the young man, looking around. "Is anyone else here besides the three of you?" Chad asked looking back and forth between the men on the couch and the man that answered the door.

"No, just us can I ask who called this in?" The young

man asked.

"We don't know who placed the call. Do you all have identification on you?" Chad asked them.

They scurried to get their IDs from their wallets and handed them over. One of the guys on the sofa grabbed the remote, muting the TV.

Mark walked over and looked into the kitchen, neat, clean, and empty. He strode over to the other doorways, and looked into each room while Chad ran the IDs through dispatch. The small house had a warm, cozy feel to it, and Mark knew nothing had taken place here. This was a prank call, and he didn't like the feel of it. Chad went through all the normal questions and handed the men back their IDs. "Sorry to have bothered you tonight. Any idea who would've call this in? Is someone angry with you maybe?" Chad talked directly to the young man that had answered the door.

"No sir, no idea at all. I don't have a lot of friends, but the one's I do have are not mad at me. I get along fine with my neighbors too." He looked confused.

"Well once again, sorry to have bothered you all tonight." Chad turned and followed Mark out.

Settled back in the patrol unit Chad cleared the call. "What do you make of that?" he asked Mark.

"Not sure, but definitely a bull-shit call." He took out his cell phone and checked for a missed call. No one had called. His gut was telling him something wasn't right. He had no clue what that something might be. "Let's run through my neighborhood." He told Chad.

"You think this was a diversion Mason?" Chad had an uneasy feeling.

Mark hadn't thought of that. "Could be, now drive!" Mark's stomach did a flip at the thought that someone may have tried to keep him busy to get to Lilly. His fingers itched to dial the home number. He wouldn't do it though, he was sure Lilly's fine and sleeping. He said a silent prayer as he watched the scenery fly by.

He felt so proud of himself. It was a stroke of genius to call in the domestic disturbance to keep Mason busy. He made his way in through a basement window. The upstairs light went off over an hour ago. He knew she would be sleeping by now. Dropping the five feet to the floor caused little pain for him.

Standing still in the dark basement he let his eyes adjust. The house was very quiet and he enjoyed the idea of being in the house knowing she was here alone. He made his way to the stairs and took them silently two at a time. Opening the door that lead into the kitchen he listened before moving into the room.

His heart was beating so fast he felt exhilarated at the idea he could take her now if chose to do that. No! He wouldn't ruin his plans he just wanted to see how easy it would be to get in here when the time was right.

He made his way up the stairs to her bedroom. The door left open, an invitation to enter. He wanted to walk slowly toward her. He wanted to see her sleeping form, and know that she was within his reach.

He stood in the doorway and let his eyes roam around the room. He could see her on the bed sound asleep, curled on her side with her arm over her husband's pillow. Her missing husband's pillow, he mused.

Walking ever so quietly, he approached her side of the bed, and looked down at her. He was tempted to touch her. No! He had to control himself. Squatting down he lay his head softly on the bed next to her. She smelled wonderful as her body heat reached out to him.

He moved slightly when she began to stir. Did she sense him? He wondered. He had to leave before she found him there. It would be too late then, he knew if she saw him her fear would excite him beyond his control, and it would ruin everything.

Slowly he backed out of the room and down the stairs, exiting the way he had come in. The window would remain unlocked, he couldn't do anything about that, and if he were lucky they wouldn't notice anyway.

He stood in the backyard out of sight for a bit, reliving the memory of her within reach, and relishing the fact he could have her anytime he wanted.

Chad drove faster than normal to reach the subdivision. All appeared quiet, nothing moving, no sounds. He drove slowly through each street, shining the spotlight into yards and bushes. They both watched and listened with the windows rolled down. "Wanna take a look around back at your place?" he asked Mark.

"Not a bad idea, yeah"

Chad pulled up and stopped. Looking over at Mark he gave a nod, and they both got out. Walking around the house Mark checked windows and doors. The gate still locked from earlier. Nothing seemed out of place. He told Chad to go ahead and wait in the car while he checked inside quickly. He had to see Lilly and know that she was all right. Quietly going up the stairs he peered in their room. She was curled up and sleeping soundly. Going over to her side, he reached down and smoothed hair from her forehead. He shouldn't wake her he told himself. But when she started to stir he couldn't help himself. "Hey there," he whispered.

Coming awake with a start, she almost screamed. "Mark! What are you doing here?" She was frightened, her heart pounded erratically.

"Sorry, honey, I didn't mean to scare you. Stopped in to use the bathroom, and check on you." He sat down next to her.

"Why? You never do that." She wanted the light on. "Mark, turn the lamp on." She demanded.

"Go back to sleep Lilly, I'm going back to work. Chad's waiting for me in the car." He felt like a total ass.

"He can wait." She sat up, and turned the lamp on herself. "Now, what's really going on?"

He laughed at her attempt to glare at him. She was so sweet and tiny that glaring was impossible for her to pull off. "Nothing, really, I had to go to the bathroom and we were in the area so I came home. Really babe, go back to sleep." He stood and gently pushed her down. Kissing her, he turned the light off. "Sweet dreams, my love," he said as he left the room.

His skin crawled with the idea that someone could've hurt her. He needed to protect her. He took an extra minute to walk through the downstairs and recheck the windows and doors. Satisfied that everything was secure, he left.

The small, enclosed room had taken him years to finish, but as he looked around he was pleased with the result. No one knew about this room, not even his mother. He smiled a big toothy grin at the idea he had worked so hard, so quietly, so diligently, completing his room right under her nose. The harsh laughter he expelled filled the little room. He walked over taking a seat in his black wooden, thrown like chair, with the red velvet backing and seat cushion.

Leaning his head back, he closed his eyes. He imagined himself back in Lilly Mason's bedroom. She lay there, so beautiful, waiting for him to take her. She wanted him, he knew she did. Her fragrance enveloped him, pulling him to her.

He pulled the covers back and slid in beside her. Taking her into his arms he pulled her on top of him. She smiled at

63

him and he felt her warmth radiate through him.

"You're mine you know," he told her in his mind.

"Yes, oh, yes I am," she cooed to him.

"Tell me you want me, Lilly." He grabbed a full breast and squeezed hard feeing his erection grow.

"I want you, I want you so badly, my love," she whispered to him.

He opened his eyes and looked down at his erection. He loved fantasizing about her, and what she would say when she knew he wanted her. He undid his zipper and released his straining penis from the confines of his jeans. Looking around his room he was a lone, and could do what he wanted so badly to do. He talked to Lilly as he did it.

The loud moaning and harsh breathing couldn't be heard by anyone, so he let loose with it.

Disgusted with himself when he finished, he looked around. "Shit! Look at the mess you made, Lilly," he shouted.

EIGHT

After a long restless morning with very little sleep, Mark decided it was time to do something about the situation. He had decided the task force was a go, now all he needed to do was get Lilly out of town.

Throwing the thick covers off he headed to the shower to formulate his plan. He would tell her she was leaving, and that was that. He couldn't shake the idea that call last night was a diversion concerning her welfare.

Lilly heard Mark moving upstairs. She quickly went to the kitchen and prepared his breakfast. Pouring a cup of coffee, she thought about the unusual visit he had made home last night. She was going to get answers this morning, and he would tell her the truth.

Mark walked into the kitchen to find a plate of pancakes and a fresh cup of coffee waiting for him on the small corner table. Smiling he pulled Lilly into his arms. "Good morning beautiful."

She inhaled deeply the fresh clean scent of her husband. Felt him hold her much tighter than usual, and knew something was wrong. Stepping out of his embrace she said "good morning yourself, eat your pancakes before they get cold." She slid into the chair next to his.

"You are too good to me Lilly." He drank a big gulp of his coffee. "Listen hun, I think we need to discuss something really important." He watched her facial expressions.

"Good because I think we do too." She smiled brightly at him. "Let's start with your little trip home in the middle of the night."

He had intended to tell her about the task force, and her

leaving for a while. "Fine we can start there. I told you I had to use the bathroom. I shouldn't have awakened you, and I am so sorry I did."

"So you said, now the truth Mark," she watched him closely. They had been married long enough that she knew him better than he knew himself.

"What? You still don't believe me?"

"Nope"

He looked at her good and hard. Should he be upfront about it all? He took his time thinking. Taking a big bite of his pancakes would buy him a few seconds at least. Deciding to go ahead and tell her everything he swallowed and said. "You're right Lilly, you deserve to know everything. I want you to listen and not say anything until you hear me out. Okay?"

Lilly gave a slight nod, sat back in her chair. Drawing her legs up, she rested her chin on her knees. She would hear what he wanted to say, but if he thought she was leaving him, he was going to learn fast and in a hurry how wrong he is.

Mark took a drink of coffee, and thought the words out before speaking. He would try diplomacy first, and then demand if that didn't work. "Lt. Washington has offered me a spot on the task force working on the serial killings. I really think I could help them, and I want the opportunity to do it." He stopped to gather his next thoughts.

"That's wonderful Mark. I…"

He held up his hand. "I said hear me out. I'm nowhere near finished with what I want to say." Taking a deep breath he continued. "On that note you know that I will be working long, long hours every day." He watched her nod that she understood. "I won't be here for you Lilly. I won't be able to protect you."

"Mark, I don't need you to protect me."

"Please just listen." He stood running his hand through

his hair, and walking over to look out the window. "I want to you listen, I mean seriously from my perspective listen to me." He turned around so he could see her face. "I'm not asking Lilly, I'm telling you, you're not safe. I believe he has fixated on you. I really need to you leave for a while." There he'd said it.

Lilly watched her husband closely. He had just verified her fear. She had been thinking the same thing. Ever since she had awakened to him in their room last night, she couldn't shake the feeling of being watched. Wanting to deny it, tell him no way she was leaving, but she kept her mouth shut.

"Look babe, I know you think you need to stay and take care of me. I know I've been stressing badly, and you're worried about me, but it would be less stress for me if you weren't here." He took her hand in his and pulled her up with him. Looking directly into her eyes he finished his plea. "Lilly, I know I can catch this bastard, but I can't concentrate if you don't leave."

She knew he needed this. Thinking through a lot this morning before he woke up she had already decided to leave, and now she realized it.

He watched her and thought she was going to refuse. "Please Lilly, I need you safe." He pleaded with her.

"I understand Mark. I won't fight you on this." She saw the relief wash over his face and knew she'd made the right decision.

"Thank you babe, I promise I will call you every-day, and keep you up to speed on what's going on. I really thought we would fight about this." He laughed and hugged her tightly.

Matt woke up later than most did. He's a late night kinda fella, and has no qualms about sleeping late. Going downstairs he checked on Jersey, and since she appeared to be doing better, he decided to get to the videos and recordings without John. They had barely begun going through the stuff when Chrissy called. He didn't think John would mind if he continued on his own. Getting a cup of coffee he rewound and started the video search first.

There were several hours, worth, of video to weed through, and he wanted to at least get through a good portion of the tape.

Watching the video and listening to what had been recorded, had him laughing at his group members. They were quite a diverse bunch of characters. He watched as Vinny teased Kaliegh unmercifully. He knew Vinny had been doing that before setup, but had no idea it continued after the cameras were rolling. Poor Kaliegh, he thought, she sure took it like a champ. He thought to himself how pretty she was, and wondered why she had not been taken off the market a long time ago.

Jersey walked over for a head pat and to see what he was laughing at. She was the best dog he had ever owned. "What is it girl?" he asked scratching behind her ears. She laid her head on his thigh and encouraged the continued affection.

Matt saw something flash on the computer screen, so he hit the pause button quickly and rewound. Watching intently he saw what appeared to be a misty type substance flash across the screen he rewound again.

After checking it three times, he tagged the spot to show John. Of course he heard the idle chatter about the apparition at John and Chrissy's after the investigation, but wrote it off as something easily explained now he knew how wrong he'd been. Matt had never seen anything like it before. He continued on with the video. After almost an hour, he paused to answer his cell phone.

"Hey Matt, how are you?" Craig Foster's voice sounded a little hoarse today.

"Good and you?"

"Just trying to ward off a cold I feel comin' on."

"Yeah, you sound like it. What's up?"

"Just wanted to see what, if anything, you and John may have found on the videos from the other night."

"We really didn't a chance to get through much. We were kinda called away on something else. Going through some of it now," he didn't bother to say anything about what they were called out for, figured it wasn't his place to do so.

"Oh okay, well I won't keep you, just had a few minutes left on a break, so thought I would check. I hate calling John cause I never know when he worked the night before, and don't want to wake him up," he gave a short laugh.

"Yeah, I hear ya. No problem. I'm sure he'll get with the group once the stuff has been gone through."

"Alright then, talk to you later, pal." He hung up before Matt could say goodbye.

Matt got up and let Jersey outside, then grabbed a fresh cup of coffee. Going to his backdoor he watched Jersey slowly walk around the backyard. He could tell she still felt some pain. He loved to watch her walk the perimeter and check everything out thoroughly. Opening the door he stepped out into the brisk early afternoon weather. The sky was cloudy and it looked like possible rain. They could really use it before the snow began falling.

Jersey finished her area check and business then slowly made her way up the back porch stairs. "Still feeling a little under the weather, aren't ya girl?" Matt said tapping Jersey's head lightly. "Come on, let's go get comfortable." He opened the back door and let her in first.

Walking over to her dishes she looked back at him and sat down. Matt walked over, gathering up the dishes he began to fill one with food and one with water. "When are you going to start feeding me?" he asked her with a laughing tone.

She just sat there looking at him and waiting patiently.

"Glad to see your appetites back, girl," he said setting the dishes back on the floor in front of her. Once she dug in he went back to put the big plastic container of food in the pantry. His stomach growled loudly and he realized he hadn't eaten anything yet, so he went in search of something for himself.

The small, dilapidated building in the Forest, known as, the 'Shack' was a favorite place of his to visit. He stepped inside and walked over to a corner across the small room and plopped down onto the dirt floor.

Sitting there he let his imagination run wild. He thought about the sacrifices he had yet to make. They were trivial to him he just wanted them finished so he could get to his main gift. Lilly!

He licked his thin lips as he thought of her. He needed to think of something else, or he would lose control like he had last night. He hated losing control.

Standing up he walked around the small room. His thoughts went to the next woman he would use. He needed to get one picked out so he could get on with it. Realizing that, he decided there was no time like the present.

Walking the short distance to his vehicle he took deep calming breaths to keep his excitement in check. He loved the euphoria their terror brought him. The more terrified they were, the more excited he became. He often thought of using their bodies for his perverse pleasure, but didn't want to soil them before giving them as a dark gift to his god.

He knew these rituals would bring him the normalcy he craved, especially after Lilly was gifted. He laughed wickedly. "A peace-offering," he said out loud. Piece by piece, made her a peace offering of a different kind. He laughed at his pun. Shook his head and left in search of his next treat.

"Lilly," Mark yelled up the stairs. "Come on, I want to walk you to the car and make sure you're in safe and sound, ready to go, before I have to get ready for work. Get the lead out."

Lilly was doing a slow walk around the room. What was she forgetting? She asked herself for the third time. She was packed, had her cell phone and charger, all her clothing and toiletries, what the heck was she missing? The nagging feeling drove her crazy.

She stopped walking and stood in the doorway looking at her bed. "Okay, think," she told herself. "Dang, that's it." She walked over to her nightstand and grabbed the novel she had been reading. Smiling she ran down the stairs. "I'm ready," she called out.

"It's about time. What were you doing up there?"

"Trying to figure out what I was forgetting, and here it is." She held the book out with a big smile plastered on her face.

Mark shook his head. They walked out to her car together. Mark had his arm around her shoulders and hoped fervently she wouldn't cry. She always cried when she left him for any length of time. "Now you're going to call me, as soon as, you get there right?"

"Yes, sir." Giving a mock salute she giggled trying to hold off the tears. She hated crying and feeling like an idiot.

Mark opened her door, and she turned in his arms for a tight embrace. He held her to him, loving her scent as it floated around him. Inhaling deeply he pulled back to look at her, and then took her mouth with his in a lingering kiss. "Thank you for doing this for me," he said pulling her against him again.

She held on tightly. "Mom is thrilled that I'll be visiting

71

for an indefinite amount of time, are you kidding? For you, ha, she believes it's because I'm angry and we're separating." She laughed.

He pulled back and looked down at her. "What? Why would she think that?"

"Joking honey, take it easy. I'm trying to keep the mood light, you know how I get." She pushed him back and slid behind the steering wheel.

He closed the door and leaned down for another kiss. "Call me. I love you Lilly Mason," he said as he stepped back.

The tears glistened in her eyes as she smiled, shook her head, and backed out of the driveway. Mark lifted his hand, pointing his thumb and pinky like a phone and put it to his head. He smiled at her and watched her drive off.

Thank God she was going to be safe. Far away from here, and safe!

NINE

Chrissy left work and headed to the grocery store. She was trying to decide what to do for dinner when her cell phone rang. Glancing at the caller ID she noticed it was Lilly. "Hey girl, what's up?" she asked, thankful for a reprieve from thinking.

"Chrissy, so glad I caught you. I wanted to let you know that I am on my way to my mom's, for God knows how long." She needed to talk to put things into perspective for her while the hard part would be to keep her tears held back.

"What? You're leaving?" Chrissy couldn't believe it.

"Yeah, Mark and I talked, and after everything that's going on, we decided it was best if I go. I fought at first, but you know Chrissy, I just feel creepy, like I'm being watched, or something. Sounds crazy huh?"

"No sweetie, it doesn't sound crazy. John and I have been worried about you. Actually I'm glad you're going."

"Really, you don't think I'm a terrible wife leaving Mark to deal with everything?" Damn the tears were coming anyway. She sniffled trying to hold them back. No use. The floodgate opened and she wept openly.

Chrissy heard her friend crying. "No, not at all, you stop that. You're doing what he needs you to do. This is the best decision all around. The only thing that bothers me is now John will have fuel to use against me." She laughed trying to lighten the mood for Lilly.

"Use against you? I don't understand Chrissy."

"He wants me to leave town too. I just don't see any reason to. I mean the guy hasn't been stalking me. I don't need to go anywhere."

Lilly took a tissue from her purse and swiped her nose. "Oh I see what you mean."

"Exactly." Chrissy pulled into the parking lot. "Okay Lilly I have to go into the grocery store and my phone signal won't be good. You call me if you need to talk, okay?" She hated her friend being so upset.

"I will, thank you." She sniffled. "Chrissy?"

"Yeah?"

"Maybe you should go ahead and leave too. Just to be safe, ya know?"

"I'll think about it, talk to you soon sweetie." Chrissy disconnected the call. Dropping her cell phone into her purse, she left the car.

The parking lot was pretty full, which meant the store would be a real pain to get through. She hated fighting the crowds and long lines. Maybe she would just reward herself with a nice bottle of wine. Smiling at the thought, she walked through the automatic door and grabbed a shopping cart.

He waited in his car just down a ways from the private high school. Thinking he would find a delectable younger delight. He had been choosing twenty something's and knew this would throw a wrench in the profile they were trying to put together on him. He smiled to himself, feeling smug and smarter than all of them.

He pulled his sunglasses into place as he heard the last school bell ring. His choices would be prancing about any minute. Leaning his head slightly against the headrest he prepared to look as if he were sleeping in his car, while he perused the first group of girls.

Not paying attention to the ones that headed directly for the line of buses, he watched the group of five that stood in front of the school, laughing, flipping their hair, and smiling as a group of boys walked up to them.

He watched as the slight breeze lifted their skirts teasingly. He noticed a small brunette lick her lips and pull her arms in trying to make her small breast appear larger, as she flirted with a boy wearing a letter jacket. She was a tease for sure he thought. Maybe she needed to learn that wasn't very nice…

The young boy walked up to her and threw his arm around her shoulders. She looked up at him and smiled brightly. He watched as the boy leaned down and took possession of the girl's lips. He felt himself grow, as she stepped closer to the boy, rubbing her body against his. Looking down at his erection he became angry. Closing his eyes he sucked in a deep breath and decided if she walked away by herself she was his.

The small group laughed and joked with each other while the other kid's made their way home quickly. This would be the popular group, not caring about homework, or chores, or what anyone expected of them, they only thought about themselves. These were definitely the ones that deserved to learn they weren't any better than the rest.

He looked over each one with interest, and decided the little brunette would be the one. Patiently he waited.

John mowed the yard, inhaling the fresh cut grass smell. He relaxed his mind with his favorite music flowing through his headphones. Not allowing thoughts to process, he took his time. The yard looked good too bad it would be covered in snow soon.

Looking down at his watch he realized it was time for Chrissy to get home. He flew through the last few rows of grass, wanting to be finished before she arrived. He had enjoyed himself immensely being one with nature. He found he relaxed easily when out of doors and alone.

Pushing the lawn mower into the shed he looked around.

Pulling his headset off he checked yet again for anything that could be missing. Still nothing appeared to be gone, or out of place. Stepping out he closed and locked the door. He would weed eat later. He wanted to get Chrissy back into conversation about her leaving.

He hoped Mark would be able to talk Lilly into leaving too. He worried about both of them. He knew many more females in the area of course, however, he only knew about incidents at the homes of these two. Chrissy, of course, was his main concern. He would let Mark handle Lilly, and do his best not to interfere. Chrissy, however, was in for a major fight if he couldn't get her to agree. He still had that damn nagging feeling he knew something, but couldn't figure out what.

Going into the house he got a bottle of beer. Ice-cold beer is the best he thought. Chrissy had always been very good at keeping it on hand for him. Leaning against the counter he crossed his legs and drank his beer. His mind focused on the tactics he would use on his beautiful wife.

So deep in thought, he almost missed the scraping sound coming from the basement. Straightening his legs he shoved off the counter and crossed the kitchen. Standing in front of the basement door he put his ear to the door. The noise stopped abruptly as he pulled the door open. Peering down the darkened stairs he listened again. Still no noise he flipped the switch and made his way downstairs. He loved his basement, so much paranormal activity in this house and a lot focused down here.

Stopping at the bottom of the stairs he looked around, noticing immediately the two bar stools that typically stood against the bar in the corner of the room, were now situated next to the pool table. He had made an entertainment type room down here, with a full bar, pool table, ice hockey table, and basketball machine. They had planned on good times with friends and family down here, but the constant other worldly activity, put a stop to that. Chrissy just about refused to even come down the stairs, let alone party down here.

John walked over to the closest chair. Placing one large hand on the back of it he stood very still and looked around. Scrape marks lightly scarred the concrete flooring. These two chairs had definitely been pulled across the floor. A bottle of his favorite whiskey sat on the bar, with a glass next to it.

He spun the seat of the stool around and sat down. Rubbing his hand around the day's growth of beard he looked at the bar. "Huh! I haven't had a drink down here in over a month, so who is helping them self to my best whiskey?" he asked the now quiet room. Hearing the back door close he stood. "Put these chairs back and stay the hell out of my whiskey," he ordered quietly to no one he could see. He sure didn't want Chrissy to hear him talking down here. At the bottom of the stairs he took one last look around the room before climbing back up.

Chrissy left two bags of groceries on the counter, and was coming through the door with a case of beer in her hands, dropping her purse, and the beer on the counter she felt her husband's arms slip around her. "You smell like sweat," she said smiling.

He rarely just sat around, always had to be up doing something. "Working man baby, was working hard." He pulled her tighter. "See you've been busy too, huh?" He let go and reached for the case of beer.

"Not really, work was pretty light today, and then a quick trip to the grocery store for a few items we were out of." She put the items away while waiting for him to start in on the fact that Mark had successfully gotten Lilly out of town. She knew it was coming.

"Well I knocked out the backyard, hopefully for the last time this year, shouldn't be too long before it snows."

"I don't know it's been pretty mild weather so far." What's up the with weather talk? She thought. Why was he delaying?

"Hmm yeah, maybe." He took a long drink watching her. He felt like she was avoiding something. What was she up to now? He wondered.

She took her time selecting the spices she would use for the baked chicken she planned for dinner, all the while waiting for the hammer to drop. Keeping her back to him, she wished he would just get on with it already. Maybe she would bring it up and get the ball rolling. The sooner it began, the sooner it would be over. Taking her garlic powder and a few more spices out, she set them on the counter next to the stove. Then she turned to John. He was casually leaned against the counter with his legs crossed, watching her intently. "What?" she asked thinking there I gave you an opening, now let's get this over with.

He stood up and set the bottle on the counter, "nothing babe, just watching you. I love watching you move around the kitchen. It's so damn domestic." He laughed.

She narrowed her eyes and glared. "Oh come on already. I know you're dying to throw the fact that Mark got Lilly to leave in my face. Just do it dammit." Was that shock registering on his face? Surely he knew already, didn't he? Oh my God.

"What?" John took a step toward her. "He got her to leave town?" He looked stunned. The way Lilly acted last night, he was sure it wouldn't be easy to get her to go.

Chrissy shrugged her shoulders, and turned back to what she was doing. Dang she gave him information to use against her. Slowly reaching down into a lower cabinet she removed a cookie sheet. Lightly sprayed it with oil and began preparing the chicken breast for the oven.

John watched and waited. He knew she was expecting

him to use this on her, but he wouldn't give her what she expected yet. He could wait her out, knowing she'd be dying to get this conversation over with. Maybe if he's lucky, just letting her stew a bit would make her realize all on her own that she too needed to leave.

The emotions filling the kitchen were intense. Both quiet in their own thoughts on how to get the other to do what they wanted. The fight had truly begun without either being aware. The thick silence was suffocating to both, still neither willing to relent just yet.

John took his beer over to the table and sat down. Chrissy kept her back to him and prepared the chicken. They'd been together so long they didn't even realize they were using the exact same tactic against one another.

"Where were you when I came in?" Chrissy asked trying to get on a different subject.

"In the basement, seems we hardly ever go down there anymore." He would let her think he was letting this go for now.

"We don't, at least I don't." She bent to place the pan in the heated oven. "What were you doing down there?"

He thought for a minute before answering. He didn't lie to her and he wouldn't start now "thought I heard a noise."

She spun around and looked at him "a noise?"

He smiled and shrugged his broad shoulders. "I didn't see anything while I was down there hun. Take it easy."

Chrissy didn't mind paranormal activity, actually she enjoyed researching it very much, but she didn't want to live with it. She set the oven timer and began pulling ingredients out for a garden salad. While she put everything on the counter, she decided they may as well finish the conversation about her leaving. No need to leave it hanging in the air between them. "Why were you so shocked that Lilly left?"

Uncomfortable with the idea of a major fight between

them he decided to beg if necessary. "Last night she was dead set against it. I can't believe she left."

Lilly told me she felt creepy, like someone watched her. I don't think Mark had to do a lot of convincing." She wiped her hands on a small kitchen towel.

"When did you talk to her? Did she feel that way because of the guy in the yard?"

"I'm thinking no, I mean she made it sound as if... I don't know John. I talked to her when I left work on my way to the store."

"Is she going to stay with her mom?"

"Yeah indefinitely, I felt so bad for her, she started to cry." Chrissy shook her head and turned to look at her husband. "Why do you guys think we need to leave?" Her eyes were shinning bright with unshed tears.

John stood and walked over, taking her in his arms he held her tight. "We just know that sick sonuvabitch is out there, and he will strike again babe. We don't want you two in harm's way."

"That's just it. Why do you even think we are?"

"Can't take any chances, we've had the lock cutoff our shed, Mark and Lilly have had a guy in their backyard twice now, and we don't know if it's the same person, if it is, is it the murderer? We just don't know Chrissy, and you can't blame me for wanting you safe!"

Pulling free of his arms she went back to the salad making. He leaned against the counter next to her and watched silently.

TEN

Messages in his box had Mark scrambling to find his rookie, Chad Dingler. He had been assigned to the task force as of today, no longer assigned as Dingler's FTO. A recommendation regarding Officer Dingler's ability to proceed on his own, or if another FTO should be assigned to finish the last couple weeks of the field training process would be needed immediately.

After a brief meeting with his supervisor, Mark took off to inform Dingler he'd be on his own starting today. He hoped he had done the right thing, giving his recommendation that Dingler was ready. Usually a stickler on the, most minute, detail concerning a rookie, he couldn't believe he truly thought this kid was ready. Only time would tell, and he prayed silently he wouldn't live to regret this.

The only problem he had with the kid was his mouth. He didn't pull any punches with Dingler over this either. Matter of fact, he may have been too harsh in stressing his point about a time and place for playing. This job was tough and everyone needed to let off steam, most did it by joking and playing around. Others did it with alcohol, or another not so wise choice. Anyway he told himself he had made the right decision and tried to clear his head for the important activity he still couldn't believe he was taking on.

Mark arrived in time for the first task force meeting. He sat in the back of the room and looked around at his fellow officers. Each and every one of them would pay a price for participating in this search.

Lt. Washington stood at the front of the room. She smiled at Mark when he came in. "Good to see you all here.

The Chief has requested each of you in particular." She made eye contact with a balding man sitting in the front row, his back to the room. Giving a slight nod of her head at the man had him standing and approaching the podium.

"This is FBI Special Agent Marlowe. I want all of you to pay attention to what he has to say." She stepped back.

The man straightened his tie and shuffled some papers. "I would like to say I'm glad to be here, but I'm not. When I have to show up at a department meeting like this that means we have a very sick individual on the loose." He looked down at the papers he had placed on the podium. "Lt. Washington has been very gracious with the information your department has gathered so far. With that, we had a criminal profiler give us an idea of what you are all looking for. I am giving each of you a packet of information I've put together, and would appreciate you each, taking the time to look it over. I haven't come here to step on toes, or push anyone to the side and take over. I'm here to help in any way I can." He stopped talking and began looking at everyone in the room.

Mark silently laughed, thinking this was some kind of intimidation thing. The FBI always tried to push and step on toes. Besides he wondered, why are they even involved at this point? Didn't they usually come in after the killer crossed state lines? He looked directly back at the agent when he felt he was being scrutinized, and didn't flinch at all. Some of the other officers seemed to shrink under the man's direct gaze. Not Mark.

"How many of you have been involved in this type of task force before?" the agent inquired.

Out of the ten or so officers in the room only two hands went up. Mark's was one of them. "I see we really have our work cut out for us here. Those of you that have experience know what I mean." He turned to the table behind him and grabbed a thick stack of paper. Going slowly around the room he handed everyone a packet. Mumbling started amongst the officers as they looked through the material. Mark slowly turned the pages skimming the headlines and photographs.

The Agent walked back to the front of the room, and told everyone to take a pen and pad out. "I'm going to give you my personal cell phone number, and avail myself to you day, or night." He went on to give the information he wanted them to have, and talked for another hour on the workings of such a task force. Disseminating information and techniques the FBI utilized in similar cases he assigned each person to a group. Once the groups were formed everyone gathered their belongings, and went to the room they would use as their home office, for the duration of the investigation.

Pegboards and dry erase boards were set up around the room already. Some took photographs of the crime scenes and began organizing them on the boards, while others scanned the police reports provided. A few were assigned to the profile aspect, and delved into possible suspects from the data system provided by the FBI. Mark was assigned to the profile team.

Mark looked through the profile information provided by the FBI profiler. Reading the limited info, he wondered what the hell they were supposed to be looking for on the database.

Agent Marlowe and Lieutenant Washington stood in the back of the room watching the officers as they began putting their room together. Talking quietly between them, and keeping an eye on each officer as they worked as a team. Agent Marlowe listened while the lieutenant filled him in on each of the people in the room.

"You seem especially pleased that Officer Mason is here, or am I reading you wrong Lt.?" he asked watching the fellow sit quietly by himself and study the packet he had handed out.

"No, you don't read me wrong. You will find that Officer Mark Mason is going to be one of the most productive people in this room. He's the type that works well a lone, or as a team member, he sinks his teeth into something, he doesn't let go! He's a valuable asset to this task force." She turned and looked at Agent Marlowe. "You've been watching him dissect that packet. What are you thinking?" She had worked with Mark for quite a while, and had been on a very difficult team case with him before, that was when he had earned her respect.

Agent Marlowe stood very still, and didn't take his eyes off of Mark. "Out of everyone in here he is the only one to study that packet like I suggested. Look at the rest of them scurrying around setting everything up." Tucking his hands behind his back, he continued to watch Mark.

Mark took out a pad and began writing info in his spiral notebook. Going back and forth between reading and writing, flip a page, go back a page. Mark read and reread the profilers report to get every bit of information on the suspect that he could. So intense in his digging that he forgot he was in a room full of people.

After going through the entire profile more than once, Mark quietly put his pen in his pocket, closed his spiral notebook, and looked around. Spotting the FBI Agent in the back talking to Lt. Washington, he got up and walked toward them. He noticed the pictures and the small huddles of people talking, but he wanted to talk to the Agent. Nodding at them as he approached he watched their conversation end while they waited the last few steps for him to reach them. "I don't think we have formally met Agent Marlowe, I'm Mark, Mark Mason." He reached out his right hand to shake the Agents hand.

"Officer Mason it's a pleasure." Lee Marlowe smiled and took the outstretched hand. "I noticed you studying the information I gave you. What do you think?"

"I think it's too open, too broad. Quite frankly if you don't mind my saying so, it's bullshit." He watched for the Agents reaction.

Lee busted out laughing. Lt. Washington looked incredulous at Mark.

"The name is Lee, please, call me Lee. I love your honesty Mark. May I call you Mark?" Agent Marlowe asked after he stopped laughing.

"Sure Lee." Mark studied the man.

"You're absolutely right. I agree with your astute findings. The profiler said at this point this guy could practically be anyone. The broad age spectrum, the stature of the person, most everything could fit too many people at this point. As a matter of fact, the only things we know for sure, is that your killer is right handed, and completely enjoys torturing his victims."

"So what's the purpose of even having a profile at this point then? I mean its lacking content, it's useless, I don't understand what we're supposed to do with it," Mark was beginning to get a bad feeling here.

"Mason, what Agent Marlowe is expecting you and your area team to do is utilize the data base he brought with him, and list all the suspects that fall into that profile," Lt. Washington stated.

Shaking his head in disbelief, he looked from one to the other of the two people standing before him. What? Were they both fucking crazy? That would be just about everyone in that database he was sure. "Lt. I understand that is what is expected of my group, that's why I'm over here talking to Agent Marlowe, that would be, probably, most every person on that database. We don't have time to waste on that."

"You're once again correct Mark. I was wondering how long it would take for someone to realize that." Marlowe gave a smirky type grin.

Mark couldn't believe the man had just admitted it was a waste of time. He looked from the Agent to the Lt. and back. "What gives?" he asked both of them.

The Agent patted Lt. Washington's arm. "I got this." He looked from her, back to Mark. "At this point Mark, we are getting groups set up with different jobs so everyone has something to do, we want you to each become well-oiled machines, if you will, working with one another."

"So in the mean-time you're going to waste our fucking time on games Lee, really? Is that how the FBI does it?" He glared at the man.

Lee liked this guy, he's quick, he's observant, and he wasn't afraid to speak his mind. "No Mark, that isn't how the FBI does it. Lt. Washington and I got together and set this up. She already knows each of you personally, knows how you work. I don't know anything about any of you. This is an idea I wanted to implement to find out what I wanted to know." He felt pleased that his idea was working, at least where this man was concerned.

"Don't you think you could've accomplished the same thing by sitting down, one on one, and getting to know us? I don't see how wasting our time is getting us anywhere."

"Mason that's enough, you've made your point." Lt. Washington stepped in. "Give us a few minutes to discuss this." She dismissed Mark arrogantly, she knew his temper, and he was heating up quickly.

Mark stood there a few seconds, threw his hands up in the air, and walked away. He looked at everyone else in the room. Were they stupid? There they were, like a bunch of lab rats running around doing busy work. Didn't they realize they weren't being productive? He walked over, shoved his chair into the table hard, and stormed out of the room.

"I like him," Marlowe told Lt. Washington. "He's the

only one that has figured out quickly this exercise is a complete waste of time." He rubbed his balding head.

"I told you he's good." She smiled with pleasure. Mason's at the top of this group of officers, secretly glad he's here she asked "how long are we going to let them go before we stop this?"

"Just a few more minutes let's see if we can get at least one more to figure this out." He stepped back and leaned against the wall, folding his arms over his chest.

Mark went to the men's room, tossing some cold water onto his face, he looked up into the mirror. "Get a grip Mason." He told his reflection. Taking a handful of cheap paper towels he dried his face. Leaning on the sink counter with both arms extended he composed himself.

He followed the young couple to the park, and watched them play what he called, a stupid mating ritual. The little brunette didn't walk away with the group of girls, but she did with the young man in the letter jacket. He watched them make out in the grassy area for a bit then the boy pushed the girl on the swings for a while. Now they were back to the grassy area. He looked at his watch, it's getting late, almost eight-thirty shouldn't they be hungry? He thought to himself. He would give it a few more minutes, knowing already he wouldn't get her tonight he still needed to know where she lived. She was definitely going to be his next dark gift. He laughed at that "dark gift, I like it."

Matt had waited as long as he could, now would be a good time to call John. He had gone back to the video several times throughout the afternoon and early evening to watch the mist appear and disappear. He couldn't way to get John's take on it even though John already knew about it. Settling Jersey back on her bed he called John.

John and Chrissy had just started a movie and were cuddled closely on the sofa. Stomachs still full from dinner they decided no popcorn tonight. Chrissy sipped her wine and John enjoyed his beer.

"I'm glad you took the night off. This is really nice babe." Chrissy leaned into his shoulder.

"Yeah, me too, we don't do this enough." Just as he laid his head on top of Chrissy's his cell phone blurted the Ghost Busters theme song

"Really, you haven't changed that ring tone yet?" She smiled at him.

"No. I love it." He looked at the caller ID, Matt. "It's Matt I'll call him back later." He pushed the silence button and tossed the phone back onto the coffee table.

When Matt heard the voice mail begin he figured John was at work, so he left a quick short call back message and hung up.

John's phone gave the voice mail signal and he looked at the phone again. Chrissy noticed his reaction and said. "Pause the movie hun, and call him back it may be important. I want to check on Lilly anyway."

"You sure?"

"Yes, I'm sure, go ahead." She got up to get her cell phone. Lilly should be just about to her mom's by now, and Chrissy really thought as upset as Lilly sounded earlier it would be a good idea to check on her.

ELEVEN

Sam Tate ran the local watering hole in Freetown, 'Tate's'. He had dreamed of owning a bar ever since he and his high school pals drank at the Assonet Ledge. He remembered their late nights sharing scary things they had heard, or just made up. Realizing, drinking alcohol, as an adolescent lead to his future career choice, made him smile. He enjoyed the times his old pals would come in, and they would reminisce about the nights on The Ledge. As a matter of fact, it was about time for the group to come in. It had been a few months already, he decided he would call one or two and encourage a get together soon.

Standing behind the bar he watched Maggie flirt with a few of the regulars. Maggie Porter had been with him a long time. He depended on her a little too much sometimes. She was a pretty woman with a vivacious personality. He was lucky to find her. She loved to sway her hips as she walked, and wear low cut tops to show her ample bosom. Her natural red hair and pouty lips completed the 'sexy as hell' package.

The front door opened and in walked Eugene Lowery. Eugene was a high school friend. He'd had a tough time in school being bullied by a lot of the kids because of the way he walked. He had some kind of hip problem at birth that went undetected and caused one leg to grow longer than the other. He still kinda walks like a duck, Sam thought as Eugene approached the bar.

"Hey guy, been awhile. Whatcha been doin'?" Sam asked as Eugene claimed a bar stool.

Eugene twisted around to watch Maggie. "Not much Sam, what about you?" he asked not taking his eyes off

Maggie.

"Workin'. What'll it be?" Sam already knew the answer, but waited for Eugene to tell him.

"Beer, really cold beer," Eugene said turning with a smile.

Sam began pouring from the tap. The frosted glass was a must for Eugene, and Sam knew that. "Just what I thought," Sam said placing the glass in front of his old high school pal.

"Business is booming for you I see," Eugene said taking another look around.

"I can't complain. What have you been doing with yourself? Haven't seen many of you guys around lately." Sam dried glasses while he talked.

"Not too much really, my arthritis has been flaring a lot with the coming of winter. You mean none of the guys have been in recently?" He took a drink from the glass.

"Nope, was just thinking about you all when you walked in. Funny how that happens isn't it?"

"Guess so." He looked up at the TV in the corner and saw a news report on the murder victims. "Whatcha think about all that?" He nodded his head toward the TV.

Sam turned to see what Eugene was talking about. He walked over and turned the sound up. "Crazy shit. That sucker is sick from what I hear." Sam turned back to Eugene.

"Wonder why they always give them a nick name?" Eugene said.

"The Surgeon, huh, I bet he doesn't even have a damn education. These media folks like to sensationalize bad stuff way too much. I say we do the same thing to him that he's doing to those poor women," Sam said and turned away to place a few glass bottles on the shelf behind him.

Eugene sat and watched the news anchor report the limited information the police were releasing. "I see the FBI is involved now huh?"

"Who cares, not like they're going to be much help. I say all women should stay inside until this asshole is caught. He's a real sick S.O.B." Sam wasn't interested in talking about the murders. He looked over at Maggie and wondered if she had given all of this much thought. It really hadn't registered until now the danger she could be in. She was a beauty and still pretty young. Sam decided that starting tonight he would see Maggie home safely after work. He would have a talk with her too, and make sure she was aware of the danger lurking in the area. He knew a lot of women didn't consider themselves in danger for one reason or another, but they all were as far as he was concerned.

Eugene noticed Sam watching Maggie. He didn't say anything as he took in the concern in Sam's eyes. He had known Sam since high school, and even though the guys let him hang out with them on occasion, he really wasn't accepted completely. He always figured it's because he's handicapped and they weren't. He hated the fact that he wasn't normal like all the rest of them. Sure they had been decent to him, to the point of kicking some ass when he had been bullied, but they never really took the time to understand his pain.

The small group at the pool tables called out to Maggie for another round of drinks. She laughed and slapped at them as they teased her by playing Rod Stewarts "Maggie May" on the jukebox.

As Maggie approached the bar she saw Eugene sitting there, quietly drinking, and watching her every move. He was a strange sort for sure, but she always secretly enjoyed the fact when a man considered her sexy; Eugene certainly did. "Hey guy." She smiled at him acknowledging him before giving her order to Sam.

"Hi, Maggie." Eugene looked away quickly. He loved

watching Maggie float around the bar. She was always friendly to him, but he thought it was because she felt sorry for him. He didn't want pity.

Maggie and Sam chitchatted while he filled her order and Eugene listened intently while he pretended to watch the TV in the corner.

Cody Stone approached Mark. They had worked together since Cody came back home from Boston a few years ago, and was thrilled with the smaller department's workload. He'd tired of the long hours, and caseload he had dealt with in Boston fairly quickly. He and Mark went to high school together, upon graduating Cody left for the bigger city, while Mark stayed put. They had always gotten along, and Mark had been glad to have him back home.

"Hey Mark." Cody pulled a chair out to sit next to Mark. "I see you're not very busy so wanted to ask something if you don't mind."

Mark looked dazed as he sat watching everyone else in the room. When Cody took a seat next to him, Mark didn't say a word, just lifted his brows in question.

"You look pissed, am I bothering you?"

"No. What did you want to ask me?" Mark controlled his tone to reflect boredom instead of the anger that was building inside him.

"I saw you storm out a little while ago, and I wanted to follow you. This shit they have us doing makes no sense to me. I know departments do things differently, of course, but what I am missing here?" He shifted in his chair to look in the back of the room. "This is a waste of time." He kept his voice low.

Mark, thrilled his friend had picked up on the lack of sense this exercise made. "Took you long enough," he stated simply.

Cody laughed. "I know my group detail is a waste of time so I decided to check out the other groups. Nothing productive at all that I can figure. I thought I must have been missing something until I saw you storm outta here. What gives?"

"This is a waste of time. That FBI Agent is trying to figure us all out, or so he thinks. Go on back, and tell him what you think." Mark continued to keep his eyes on the others in the room, shaking his head at their apparent stupidity. "Look at 'em. They actually think they're doing something productive."

"They're doing what they were told to do. You can't fault anyone for following orders Mark. What'd ya mean, he's figuring us out?"

"Just exactly what I said, he devised this little exercise to see who can think on their own."

"Fuck that." Cody got up and stormed to the back of the room.

"You think Mason filled him in?" Marlowe asked Lt. Washington as he watched the approaching officer.

"Nope, this will be your next best in this group," the Lt. said with a smile. Just as Cody reached them Lt. Washington began introductions. "Agent Marlowe this is Officer Cody Stone. Cody comes to us from Boston."

"Boston huh," Lee said extending his hand yet again. "Lee Marlowe."

Cody looked at the extended hand and thought about ignoring it. Instead he reached out and gave a strong grasp. "Cody Stone, and actually I'm from here just detoured through Boston." He looked at the Agent with determination.

"Why Boston?" Lee asked.

"Experience of course. Speaking of which, what gives?" Cody decided the direct approach would get him farther.

"What do you mean?" Lee asked.

93

Waving his arm around to encompass everyone in the room he said, "This bullshit you got us doing here." He looked over at Lt. Washington "pardon my language L.T."

Mark had turned to watch the exchange in the back of the room. He hoped this would be enough for them to call the exercise off, and let them get to something worth doing.

"Ah, Mason filled you in I see." Lee tested the waters.

Looking at the Agent like he grew a set of horns Cody felt flabbergasted. "What? Hell no he didn't, I have a brain in my head. I don't need anyone to fill me in." Cody didn't like this arrogant FBI man. "We don't need help wasting our time we do that well enough on our own. So what gives?" he asked again.

"Just a little exercise to get your feet wet Cody. May I call you Cody?" He left it as a question.

"I don't care what you call me, let's just do something here." Cody turned and walked away. Heading straight for Marks table he glowered at Mark's smile.

Plopping down in the chair next to his friend he crossed his arms over his chest. "What an arrogant asshole," Cody stately loudly enough that everyone in the room heard.

Mark cracked up and slapped his pal on the back "Yep." He looked back at the pair standing with their heads together. "I think maybe now they'll stop this stupidity and let us get on with our jobs." He pulled his cell phone from his pocket to check for any missed calls. He knew it was about time for Lilly to be calling. Not seeing a missed call he put the phone back in his pocket, deciding in the next few minutes he would check on her.

The room, quiet now, as most had witnessed not just Mark's anger, but now Cody's as well. Some just took seats and sat waiting, while others continued to talk quietly amongst themselves.

Lt. Washington and Agent Marlowe walked to the center

of the room. Nodding her head at a few officers when they looked inquiringly at her, she said, "Have a seat everyone." Glancing over at Mark and Cody she smiled brightly and gave a wink.

Once the room had quieted and everyone took their seat, Agent Marlowe began. "Thank you everyone for getting the room in shape so quickly. As some of you have recognized, this was an exercise in futility." He looked over at the smug pair staring directly at him. "I know some of you think it a complete waste of time, but let me assure you, it gave me valuable insight." He gave a smug look of his own in their direction. "Now, we have ten officers in this room. Two have proven they can think on their feet." He nodded in their direction while looking at the others. "We only need six officers for this task force, which means four of you will be sent back to regular duties." He waited while complaints went up around the room.

Mark elbowed Cody in the side. "You thinking what I'm thinking?" he asked.

"Shit, yeah I think I am." Cody slouched down in his seat.

Lt. Washington stepped over behind Mark and Cody's chairs. Placing her hands on their shoulders she said. "Mason and Stone here will be team leaders. You will get your orders directly from them." She patted them as she turned away.

Mark placed his elbow on the table and leaned his head down into his hand. Looking over at Cody with his hand shielding his eyes, he did an eye roll.

"We're going to break for about fifteen minutes stretch your legs grab a coffee, smoke, or whatever. Be back here in fifteen minutes." She turned back to Mark and Cody. "Except you two, stay please."

Mark wanted to call Lilly. He would just explain to the L.T. that Lilly left town and he needed to make sure she made it to her destination. He stood and pushed his chair in. Cody did the same, wondering what Mark was about to do.

Grumbling sounds were being made by most as they exited the room. Every one of them were wondering who would remain.

Mark walked over to Lee and the Lt. "Ma'am I really need a few minutes to make a quick phone call." He looked down at his watch.

Gina Washington looked over at Lee then back to Mark. "We'll give you a few minutes when everyone gets back from break. We want to talk with you and Stone first." She seemed agitated, and Mark wondered if he and Cody would be going back on patrol since they complained. He felt the sweat pop on his brow. He went back to stand by Cody.

After a brief exchange of looks between her and Lee, she said "we appreciate the two of you waiting for us. Don't look so damn nervous." She laughed at their faces.

"We shoot our mouths off sometimes L.T. doesn't mean anything. We both really want to be a part of this task force." Cody said quickly.

"Take it easy, fellas." Lee put in. "We aren't sending you two back to patrol, didn't you just hear the Lieutenant say you were both going to be team leaders?" He laughed.

Both, Mark and Cody felt like idiots she had just said that. Mark thought to himself he needed to quit worrying about calling Lilly and listen. This is going to be important. He gave a grin to Cody. "Yeah, she sure did, be a little patient man." He tried to play off his own nervousness.

"Listen guys, we have decided the two of you will be the team leaders for the six of you that stay on the task force. With that being said we want recommendations on the other four," Gina told them.

"Before you make your decisions, however, we want you to factor in why you want them to stay. You will not have final say, we're just asking for your input," Lee told them.

"You want us to do this in fifteen minutes?" Mark asked astounded that such an important decision could be expected in such a short amount of time.

"No, of course not we want the two of you to leave when the others come back. Go have some coffee and discuss. We'll give you a couple of hours. Think it through very carefully. This is of the utmost importance," Gina explained. "We will take a break once again when you return, so the four of us can go over your findings." She took a step back.

"Why us?" Cody wanted to know. "We don't even have the most law enforcement experience in this room."

"Maybe not, but the two of you come highly recommended by your Lieutenant here," Lee said. "We want this worked out tonight. We have to get moving on this quickly. Tonight is the only down night, so to speak, that your Chief allowed us to weed through all the bullshit."

"Okay, then. Come on, Cody let's get them what they asked for." Mark was ready to roll.

The door opened and people started to trickle back in from break. Mark and Cody headed out. They were met by some questioning looks, but didn't bother with idle chat.

TWELVE

Deciding to run by and check on Lilly Mason, he made a quick U-turn in the road. Looking around carefully making sure no one spotted him he drove with fervor to get to her.

He drove by very slowly, noticing the house in complete darkness. Looking down at the clock on his dash, he realized it was awful early for her to be in bed. The blinds were all closed, and some of the windows he knew had drapes, as well. Maybe she was watching TV and he just couldn't see the blue tint with everything shut tight.

Reaching the end of the street he decided to drive by once more. If he couldn't detect any light he would sneak in. After all, she could be sick, or hurt, and needing him.

As he drove slowly he saw a man pushing a trash container to the curb, the man looked up to see the vehicle pass, and gave a wave. The driver turned his head to look out the other side just as he passed the neighbor, hoping a shot of the back of his head would be all the man noticed. It also gave a good excuse not to wave back, like the wave went unnoticed.

He watched in the mirror as the neighbor went back inside his house. No issues there, he thought. He probably didn't even notice my vehicle. The hideous laugh that escaped his lips made him proud. He had his evil persona down pat, although, he would have to be careful not to slip up in company, other than his women that is.

Still not able to detect light of any kind he made the block and parked. He would make his way to Lilly just to make sure she was fine. He didn't want to worry about her, and he knew if he didn't check he would.

John and Chrissy settled onto the sofa once again. Both had completed their phone calls and were just about to get back to the movie, when the basement door slammed shut violently. The windows in the living room shook with the ferocity of the slammed door. Chrissy practically jumped on John, grabbing his arm "what the hell?"

"Hey, hey, babe, it's okay, hun." He pried her fingers off and stood up.

"Where the hell are you going?" She screamed.

"To check the kitchen I'm sure everything is fine. You okay?" he asked, knowing she was scared shitless.

"Hell no I'm not okay. Who would be, with ghost running amuck." She felt her face color, the heat rising at an alarming rate.

"I'll be right back. You wait here." He turned to leave.

"I'm not going anywhere," she said through stiff lips. Completely sick of the spirits getting the best of her, she knew to expect the unexpected, but never quite prepared.

John walked into the kitchen and flipped the light switch. The room was empty just as he knew it would be. Walking over to the back door he checked the lock. The deadbolt was thrown and the chain still in place. Turning toward the basement door he saw a crack all the way down the door. It had been shut with such force the wood split. Solid wooden doors don't split or crack easily. Running his fingers along the crack he felt a slight vibration.

Stepping back to allow room to open the door he took a deep breath. Sometimes he could feel the hair on the nape of his neck stand up, and this was one of those times. He hesitantly pulled the door open. The dark stairwell was quiet. He listened for any movement in the darkness below. Nothing moved. Flicking the light switch he took a step down.

"Well?" Chrissy said from right behind him.

John jumped, his foot missing the step he grabbed at the air trying to stop the fall that was inevitable. "Holy Shit," he shouted on his way down the wooden stairs.

Chrissy screamed, but stood still. She wasn't going down there if she could help it. "John, oh my God, John," she yelled when he landed on the concrete floor. "Are you alright?" Her breathing sounded labored and loud.

John lay on the cold concrete, mentally checking for injuries. He felt the sharp stabbing pain in his left ankle before he even moved it. Looking up at Chrissy he said very calmly "give Matt a call; ask him to come over here. I think I may have broken my foot." Forgetting the reason he was down there he laid his head down and closed his eyes.

Chrissy ran for the phone and punched numbers quickly. Explaining to Matt in a hurried, high-pitched voice, she hung up without hearing anything he asked or said in return. Running back to the doorway she called down to her husband. "John?"

"Yeah," he ground out between clenched teeth.

"Do you need me to come down there?"

"No. Is Matt coming?" He knew the last thing she wanted to do was to come down into the basement. She couldn't do anything for him anyway.

Realizing she didn't wait for an answer she lied. "Yes he's on his way." She looked back at the counter where the phone lay and wondered if she should call Matt back. No she was sure he got it all and would be on his way.

Staring down at John she willed her breathing to slow down. "Can you see anything John?" Get his mind off the pain, she thought.

John raised his head and looked at her. "Chrissy, everything down here is fine. It was just a door slamming." He tried to sit up, but the pull on his ankle had him giving that idea up quickly. He lay back and breathed slowly, but deeply, trying to alleviate some of the pain radiating up his leg. Looking toward the bar he saw the bottle of whiskey sitting there. Wishing he could reach it he shut his eyes, he'd have Matt give him a swig when he got here. That would surely help dull some of the pain.

A tinkling sound had him opening his eyes to see the bottle of whiskey now sat next to him. Looking around he noticed Chrissy wasn't standing in the doorway. "Thank you." He said taking the lid off the bottle and drinking deeply.

A chair slid slightly from the bar. John knew he wasn't alone. Looking up the stairs and still not seeing Chrissy he turned toward the bar. Tipped the bottle and took another swig.

"Hey, where'd you get that?" Chrissy yelled down from the top of the stairs.

John almost choked. "Where'd you go?" he asked instead of answering the question.

"I went to unlock the door for Matt. Where did you get the whiskey?" she asked again.

"It was on the floor within reach. I figured it would help with some of this damn pain."

"Uh huh, if you say so." She would leave it alone for right now. She knew he never kept alcohol on the floor it was always behind the bar. "You think I should call an ambulance?"

"No, Matt can help me." He sure didn't want the cost of that ride.

Chrissy sat on the top step feeling inadequate because of a ghost. Crazy the affect they had on her even when she knew they didn't mean any harm. "So you don't see anything out of place down there?" She tried to calm her jumping nerves.

"Nope, not a thing." He knew he needed to slow down on the whiskey, or even with Matt's help he wouldn't make it up the stairs.

The front door slammed shut and Matt came running into the kitchen. Spotting Chrissy sitting there he asked "is he okay?" Then he tried to get past her on the stairs to make his way down to check on John.

Chrissy slid to the side and made room for Matt to get by. "He thinks he broke his foot," she said.

John watched Matt make his way down the stairs to him. He sat the bottle on the floor and smiled. "Sorry pal didn't mean to scare ya."

"It's okay what happened?" he asked leaning down to take a look.

"Fell down the damn stairs. What do you think happened?" John laughed. Yep he was feeling the whiskey now.

"Let's have a look at your foot, which one hurts?" Matt asked.

"The left one, don't move it."

"Just going to have a looksee buddy you try to relax." Gently pulling up John's blue jeans Matt noticed the swelling. "You think I should take that shoe off?"

"Hell no I don't think you should take my shoe off. Just help me get up, and then we'll see what needs to be done." John dreaded moving at all.

The whiskey had helped, but not enough as Matt pushed John into a sitting position by grabbing him under the arms and pushing him forward. John gritted his teeth through the pain of being moved.

When he sucked in a rush of air and his face turned red, Matt wanted to drop him and run. "Hang in there John, I know it hurts like hell, but we gotta move it to move you."

Sitting now he reached for the whiskey bottle again. "Hang on." He hissed out angrily. He didn't want Chrissy to hear him.

Matt knew how bad this hurt. It was the leg, not the foot.

He didn't want to say anything causing more of a problem. He was glad the leg bone hadn't made its way out yet. "You let me know when you're ready." Matt squatted back down behind John. Ready to lift when his friend was ready.

"Chrissy, go pull the car up as close to the door as you can get it." John wanted her out of the house in case he screamed.

"Good thinking." Matt whispered.

"The car, not the truck you'll have more room in the truck?" She wanted to make sure. He always took his truck, complaining the car felt too confining to him.

"Yes the car, I don't think I can get in the truck." Taking one last long pull from the bottle he set it aside. Checked to make sure Chrissy was gone and said. "Let's do this." taking a deep breath he held it while Matt began to lift.

Struggling with the huge man Matt pulled with all his might. He was tall and muscled, but John was very tall and dead weight. Realizing this wasn't going to work he stopped pulling, and slid to the floor.

"We need a better plan. You weigh too much for me." Matt shook from exertion. Looking around he tried to find something that would help.

John looked around too. "Hey get me up a long side the rail there. I will pull up as you push."

"That will require moving your legs around, are you sure about that?"

"Don't have much choice now do we," John stated still convinced it was his foot that was broken.

Matt turned the idea over in his head and decided he better come clean. "Uh, John, it's not your foot you have to worry about, it's the lower part of your leg that I think is broken. Not so sure I can move you the way we need to. Let me call EMS," he suggested.

John sat still for a minute, his leg? Wow that really

wasn't good. He tried to move his legs himself, but pain shot straight through him like an electrical shock. "FUCK!" He shouted. "No we can do this!" He reached for the bottom of the rail to pull himself over.

Matt shot out and grabbed John's injured leg and held it steady. They moved excruciatingly slow. "Take your time, that's it, move slowly…"

Out of breath John grabbed a hold of the wooden rail, three feet high with a wooden slat in the middle. Wrapping his arm around the center slat he said. "You hold my leg while I pull myself up. Keep it off the floor." Looking Matt in the eye to make sure he understood. Satisfied he did, John nodded and began to pull with his upper body strength. He had to release the middle slat and grab for the top rail quickly. Breathing fast and heavy he was standing in minutes.

Both men were spent, and they still had to make it up the stairs. Not to mention with the leg now dangling the blood rushing down made John feel like he was going to throw up. "I gotta sit down Matt," he sputtered.

Matt grabbed a bar stool and pulled it over quickly. "Here you go, nice and easy. That's it." Matt let out a sigh of relief once John was sitting on the stool.

"I need my leg up," John all but yelled.

Looking around desperately Matt couldn't see anything to place John's leg on. "Hey, hang on I have an idea." He raced up the stairs.

John sat there breathing slow and deep, concentrating on the pulsing blood pounding his leg.

Matt raced back down the stairs carrying an ironing board and some duct tape. "Here we go," he said out of breath. "This is going to hurt like hell John, but bear with me okay?"

"What the hell you gonna do with that?" John asked eyeing Matt suspiciously.

"I'm going to steady your leg. We don't have a board and this is the best I could think of. Lucky for you I know where a lot of your shit is kept." He laughed trying to keep John calm.

"Are you crazy?"

"Nope, let me know when you think you're ready." Matt stood there holding the ironing board. The tape sat on the steps within reach.

"Shit, give me that whiskey bottle." John bit out.

Matt laughed and handed the bottle over. A scraping noise sounded near the bar and Matt turned quickly. "What the hell was that?"

John took a good long drink. "My buddy, just ignore him." He said and drank again.

Matt stood there patiently waiting. Chrissy reappeared at the top of the stairs.

"Where is he Matt?" she asked fearfully.

"He's right here on a bar stool. We're going to have to secure his leg before we come up." He said looking up at her.

"His leg?" She took a sharp breath not sure she wanted to know but asked "why?"

"It's broken Chrissy, it's not his foot. He isn't going to be able to come up with out something to hold his leg steady.

"What are you doing with the ironing board? Surely you're not going to use that?"

"Yeah, why?"

"What? That's way too long. Dammit, hold on." She disappeared again.

John looked at Matt and shook his head. "Leave it to a woman to figure it out. She's absolutely right. I may be tall, but think about it. I'm not that damn tall." He laughed and drank some more.

Chrissy ran out to the shed. Throwing things around until she found a couple of nice sturdy shorted boards. Grabbing them she ran back in. Realizing as she entered the kitchen she was going to have to go down into the basement. Stopping just out of sight of the stairway she gulped in air and prepared herself. "You're not keeping me from him," she said through gritted teeth and went down the stairs.

"Here." She handed the boards to Matt. "These will work much better." Taking a look at John she noticed the glassy look in his eyes and the paleness of his skin. "How much of that have you drank?"

"Not enough." He struggled to get her into focus. Yep he had drunk almost the whole bottle. "Okay Matt, let's do this."

"Chrissy, do you think you have the stomach to help me out?" Matt looked at her.

"Yeah." She felt her stomach lurch.

"Okay, we'll put one of these boards on each side of his leg, I'll hold them and you tape them okay?"

"Okay." She leaned down with the tape in her hand.

Matt stepped in front of John and bent down, taking the injured leg he said "deep breath, and hold it John, I have to put your leg up on my knee to hold it straight."

John handed Chrissy the bottle, leaned his head back, closed his eyes, and sucked in a deep breath.

Matt very carefully took Johns leg, placing one hand under his heel and one hand on his thigh, he gently began moving the leg. Once the heel was resting on Matt's knee he grabbed a board and held one on the outside of the leg, and one on the inside of the leg. "Okay Chrissy, tape 'em," he instructed.

Chrissy began pulling the tape and wrapped around the thigh first. Once that was in place she moved just below the kneecap, and did the same thing. Then down around the ankle area. She couldn't believe the wood worked so well, the different lengths played nicely with the longer one on the outside of his leg. That was pure luck.

John kept sucking in air and fighting back a scream. He

106

wanted to scream badly, but refused to scare Chrissy. His, fist were balled tightly, and his nails were cutting into his palms.

When the leg was wrapped completely Chrissy sat down on the bottom step. She felt sick to her stomach. She knew John was in excruciating pain.

"We're done John, take some time then we'll give the stairs a go." Matt didn't move, keeping John's leg steady.

John wasn't ready to open his eyes just yet. He gave a nod of his head, and willed the whiskey to stay put in his stomach. He wondered just how bad the break was. The stairs would be the hardest part, and he knew he needed to get Chrissy out of there before they attempted that.

Matt felt his own leg going to sleep from the added weight of John's leg, not to mention the way he was squatting. "What's the game plan for the stairs John?" He hoped John had that figured out.

"I guess I will hop the best I can. Chrissy go on up and wait in the living room. We'll be there in a bit."

"No, I want to help you babe." She insisted.

"It'll be a bigger help to me if you're not here in case I feel like yelling." He smiled at her.

"You're kidding, right?" she asked looking at him.

"Nope, not even a little."

"John, do you really think I would think less of you if you felt the need to scream?"

"Nah, babe, but I don't want to scare you, and I know how you are about being down here."

She smiled at that. He always thought of her first. It warmed her heart. "No I'm going to help you up those damn stairs."

"Good the more the merrier." Matt said. "Are you ready John?" he asked hopeful.

Giving a nod of his head he prepared for the worst part.

Matt slowly moved John's leg back down. The pulsating

pressure began immediately. John reached forward for the handrail and pulled himself up. Leaning to the right he kept pressure off his injured leg, but the wood length made it very difficult to stand on his own.

"Chrissy, you stand behind us as we go." Matt told her. "John hopping is going to be jarring to say the least, it may be easier to sit down, ease your way up on your butt."

John looked at both of them and gave a short hop toward the steps. He immediately wanted to throw up. He stopped abruptly and felt the sweat begin to pour.

Chrissy watched as he suffered in silence. Feeling like there should be something she could do to help him she'd had enough of his macho attitude and told him "sit down John, I'm calling an ambulance, this is ridiculous."

"No," he shouted. "Just go on up and leave us alone. I got this dammit." He was tired of the pain. He was sick to his stomach and fighting to keep the whiskey from spewing.

Chrissy shrugged her shoulders "fine." She went up the stairs without another word. If he wanted to be the big tough guy, then she'd let him. They weren't so broke that they couldn't afford an ambulance. He was just being stubborn.

John sat on the third step from the bottom. "Matt you guide my leg while I scoot up backwards I think this is the way to go." He didn't want another jolt like the one and only hop caused.

Matt grabbed John's leg and held on. John moved slowly backwards up the steps, stopping every few steps for a breather.

It seemed like forever before they were at the top. John swiped the sweat off his face. Using his shirtsleeve he rubbed his eyes. They stung from the sweat.

"We made it bud how you doing?" Matt asked.

"Just trying to figure out how to get out to the car from here." John felt very nauseated now. "You might want to get me the trash can, I think I'm gonna be sick."

Matt scurried around John and brought the small kitchen container back. "You've done awesome, I was wondering how long it would take." He felt sorry for his friend.

John threw up.

Matt went for a glass of water and a kitchen towel. Handing them to John he turned his back to allow for some privacy.

THIRTEEN

He was furious, the house was empty. Where the hell was she? He had to get out of there he wanted to destroy the place.

She had left, he was sure of it. Where did she go? He knew she was gone from the single toothbrush hanging in the master bath. Mark's was still there at least, he was sure it was Mark's. How many women had blue toothbrushes?

He would go home and think this through. Maybe she just went out of town for a few days, family issues or something. He would bide his time, he knew she was the last one. She had to be.

He got into his car and tried to calm himself. What would he do if she left and didn't return in time? He had to have her.

He started the car and put his seatbelt on. Taking deep calming breaths he turned on the stereo and let the classical music of Wolfgang Amadeus Mozart fill the interior of the car. The music would calm his nerves and allow for clear thought. He enjoyed classical music even when unmercifully his friends had teased him because he loved it.

He drove home feeling his body respond to the beautiful music.

Mark and Cody went through every person in the group, making notes on the pros and cons for each. They both already knew whom they wanted to work with, but went through the formality that had been asked of them.

They had been gone an hour and a half. Mark looked at his watch for the fifth time and tapped it. After talking to

Lilly he felt free, she had made it to her mom's house in record time and even told him she was glad she went.

"We're almost done, stop tapping your damn watch Mason." Cody told him while glaring at him.

"Sorry it helps me think." Mark smiled sheepishly.

Cody finished up writing the list and began picking up the extra sheets they had scribbled on. "Come on let's go see what they think." He took his coffee cup with him and left the small coffee shop.

Briskly walking to catch up to Cody, Mark said. "Damn, boy when you're ready you don't B.S., you just take off." He held his cup between his teeth and slid into his jacket.

"Sorry, it's habit."

The walk back to the station, a short one, the air outside just on the cool side with a nice fall breeze blowing. The leaves that had fallen already scented the air with that rich autumn smell.

The traffic diminished drastically, the night quiet. "I love New England, especially in the fall." Mark said. He couldn't believe the way he felt, as if a weight had been lifted off his shoulders. The FREEDOM it brought completely exhilarating.

"You sure are in a good mood."

"Yeah, got Lilly out of town, now I don't have any worries, except the job of course." He smiled over at Cody. "Feels wonderful, I could work non-stop to catch this maniac now."

"Good, we may have to." Cody laughed.

They reached the police station and greeted other officers they passed. Both felt jovial, this task force would consist of a good group to work with, if their choices were accepted.

They entered the room quietly not sure what the group was up to. They were amazed in the short time they were gone, a lot of work had been accomplished. There were pictures of each victim, with timelines, aerial photos of each murder scene, and routes mapped out from last location alive to the scene of their murder.

"Now this is what I'm talking about." Mark nudged Cody's side.

"Wow, for sure, they've been busy." Cody agreed.

Lt. Washington and Agent Marlowe were standing in front of the seated group. Explanations were being made as to why the group would become smaller and more effective.

"Let's take another break guys, you've all been very busy the last couple of hours and we're happy with the progress. Go ahead and stretch your legs a bit. Don't take too long, let's say fifteen again." Lt. Washington said.

As the group got up to file out they saw Mark and Cody standing in the back of the room. A buzz of comments began with looks of questioning toward the two officers as people left the room.

"That wasn't uncomfortable at all," Cody said laughing.

"Put yourself in their shoes, can't blame them." Mark said. "Come on, let's get this over with." He left Cody's side and headed for the front of the room.

"Were you two able to break down the group?" Lt. asked.

"Yeah, we have the list for you. We did a pros and cons list, as well." Mark told her.

Cody handed the list of names, and a separate sheet of paper with the pros and cons list, over to Lt. Washington. "Hope this helps."

"It's difficult to cull, good from good, but you two did it fairly quick," Marlowe said.

"It was difficult, but we're familiar with each one of these guys, which makes it even harder." Mark told him.

"Well give us a chance to see what you've come up with.

Go take a break with the rest and we'll see you both in ten." Lt. Washington turned to walk away with the list in her hands.

Marlowe slapped them both on the shoulder as they turned to leave. "Good job," he stated simply then turned toward the Lt.

Mark and Cody left the room. Only two of the group, were smokers they went outside to indulge in their habit while the rest headed for the break room.

"Come on Cody, let's bypass the break room, they'll all be asking what we've been doing," Mark pulled Cody toward the patrol room, thinking it would be empty and they could wait out their break in peace.

FOURTEEN

Debbie Milo awoke from a sound sleep. Those times were few and far between for her. Being a medium didn't leave room for much rest, even when one was out like a light.

Deb had worked with John's team for a while now, and she loved the enthusiasm of the members of N.E.P.R.

Sitting up in her bed a little dazed, wondering what woke her up. She glanced at the bedside clock, "Eleven, really, what the heck?' She said out loud. She had been sleeping for less than two hours, but felt like she'd slept most of the night already.

Standing and looking around her room, she couldn't see anything resulting in her being awake.

Filling a teapot with water she tried to remember if she had been dreaming. She knew she hadn't, but it was unsettling to find her-self awake with so little sleep. Something's going on, she could feel it.

Placing the teapot on the stove she felt the hair on her neck rise. Turning slowly she knew she would find someone in the kitchen with her.

Spirits always operated in their own unique way. Not surprised to find she wasn't alone, she was surprised to find more than one spirit standing in her kitchen.

The two young women stood very still, the color of death surrounding them. Deb always took that look in stride, not noticing the grey undertones of their skin, or the haunted look in the eyes of almost every spirit she encountered. Walking over to the cupboard that held her cups she smiled at the pair. "Want a cup of tea?" She joked. Of course, she received no answer. "Guess not then, huh?" She laughed a

114

loud. "What can I do for you two?" Trying to keep it light, she went about preparing her tea. The spirits still had not moved, nor tried to speak to her. "Hmm, is this going to be a guessing game?" She smiled at them.

It wasn't that unusual to have more than one spirit visit together, oft times if they died together, or had something else in common, they would appear together. She was the one that had to put the puzzle pieces in place when they didn't, or couldn't speak to her.

Taking a sip of tea was not the smartest thing she had ever done. The moment the hot liquid touched her lips, a flash went off in her head, causing her to tip the cup, filling her mouth with the scalding liquid. Spitting the tea across the floor, she jumped and ran for the water faucet. Filling her mouth with handfuls of cold water she tried to sooth her burning tongue.

The flash went off inside her head again, showing her a basement. She turned the water off and wiped her mouth with a towel. Deb ignored the flash while she began cleaning the tea off the table. Looking over at the two women watching her intently she went to the small closet in the corner of the kitchen removing a mop. Deb began cleaning the tea off the floor. She was prepared for another flash when it went off. They were insistent she pay attention to them, and not the mess they caused.

"You two will have to hold your horses while I clean this up. I will not leave sticky tea everywhere while you toy with my brain." Deb rarely became irritated with spirits, but sometimes when they were pushy, or uncooperative, she found her patience sorely lacking.

As she rinsed the mop at the sink another flash assaulted her mind, a figure dropping into the basement from a very small window. This time she didn't bother to comment to the two, she knew it would do no good. Continuing with her task

115

of cleaning the mop she simply ignored them.

Satisfied the mess was cleaned, Deb sat down. "Now where were we?" she asked ready to devote her undivided attention to the impatient pair.

For minutes the two remained quiet while flash after flash played through Deb's mind. An empty Forest scene, a basement, a figure coming through a window, in the same basement, a figure standing in a residential hallway, a fleeing vehicle in the dark, but absolutely nothing concrete. "What am I supposed to do with this?" she asked confused.

A tear rolled slowly down the ethereal cheek of one of the women. She lowered her eyes to the floor. Reaching over she took the hand of the second woman and together they faded away. "Wait," Deb shouted. Standing she walked over to where the two spirits had stood the entire time they were there. "Come back, I can help you, but I need more information," she pleaded.

Looking around the now empty kitchen she hunched her shoulders, and lowered her head. She knew they would be back, but when? What were they asking of her? How could she help them if they wouldn't help her? The same questions she had asked a thousand times before.

Larry had refilled the coffee machines, mopped the floors, and emptied the trashcans. He was contemplating locking the front door while he used the restroom. He had hoped if he waited long enough an officer or two would come in for coffee and he could leave them to look after the store. Removing the key from the register he walked around the counter to the door. Taking a large ring of keys he locked the door and taped a paper to the glass that read 'Be back in five minutes'.

Typically he wouldn't have bothered with all of that and just left the door unlocked for the locals that wandered in during the nighttime hours, but with a killer on the loose he didn't feel comfortable.

Freetown had a population of less than ten thousand people, not a lot, however, more than a small town where everyone knew everyone else. Larry knew the regulars that frequented the small convenience store, but you always had a few, just passing through.

Making quick work of his bathroom break he hurried back out to unlock the door. He saw a figure huddled near one of the gas pumps when he turned the lock. He removed the paper sign and waved to the person. Returning to the counter he checked the gas pump and noticed a credit card had been used to start the pump.

Moving quietly behind the counter, Larry kept an eye on the gas pump area. He thought the person seemed familiar to him, but with two of the lights above the pump area burned out he couldn't see well enough to be sure. Making a mental note to have them replaced soon, he heard the pump chime off and gave a brief wave to the person.

The vehicle left the pump and headed for a parking space in front of the store. Larry watched with anticipation.

When the man exited the vehicle Larry recognized Eugene Lowery. Releasing a pent up breath he didn't even know he had held, he smiled as Eugene came in. "Dang, long time no see mister. Where ya been?" he asked feeling the tension leave his body.

Eugene used to spend a lot of time in here chatting away with Larry when he had nowhere else to go. He found the man to be easy going, and although boring, preferable to being a lone sometimes. "Hey Larry, been busy how have you been?" he asked on his way to the cooler to grab a pop.

"Same ole, same ole around here, just working my life away, what're you doing out so late?" Larry knew that Eugene would come in to talk when he was bored, but wondered what kept the man busy lately? He would get around to asking a lot of questions. He wanted the company for some reason tonight.

"Just left Tate's hadn't been there in a while so dropped in to see if any of the old gang was there." He set the pop can on the counter.

Not sure if Eugene would hang around for idle chatter Larry sweetened the pot "why don't you put that back and get a fountain drink on me?" He hoped if nothing else Eugene would feel obligated to hang around a bit if he gave him a free drink.

"You don't have this flavor in fountain drinks. I really want this for some reason." He laughed as he pulled his wallet from his rear pocket.

"Alright just trying to be nice." Larry rang up the sale "so Tate's huh?"

"Yeah Sam's obviously doing good business." Eugene settled back and popped the top on the can. He leaned against a shelf preparing to visit for a while.

"I bet, and it sure doesn't hurt when you have someone like Maggie there to keep 'em comin' back." He laughed.

"You got that right. Maggie sure is a sweetheart. I don't know how she puts up with the men pawing her all the time." He looked out the window, as if picturing Maggie.

Larry watched him something seemed different about Eugene tonight. "I don't think she lets them get away with that much, if you know what I mean."

"I hope not, she's too good a woman for that behavior. Not the cheap type, really not even the bar type." He looked reflective, staring out the window.

Larry watched Eugene's face as he talked about Maggie. Realization hit hard "oh shit. You've got the hots for Maggie." Larry howled.

Eugene straightened his body and glared at the man.

"What? No way I've known her a long time, I like her well enough, it's just I can't figure out what she's doing working in a bar." The heat climbed his neck. "Side's I think Sam has dibs on that one." He tried to laugh it off.

"No way, Sam could've had her a hundred times over." Larry hit a nerve and knew it. He just wanted to joke back and forth, but saw the rush of heat hit Eugene's face, and wasn't sure if he should.

"What do you mean? Maggie isn't that type." Eugene's anger began to rise.

"Take it easy Eugene, not sayin' anything bad about the woman. She and Sam have worked together long enough if he was interested, she would already be his." Larry tried to sound nonchalant.

Eugene took a drink of his pop and calmed himself. He wasn't usually this easily affected by things he didn't care about. Not that he didn't care about Sam and Maggie, he did. He just wouldn't care if they were together. Would he?

Before Larry could engage Eugene in more conversation two Freetown police cruisers pulled into the parking lot. Both men looked out to see who they were. Chad Dingler and another officer exited their patrol units and proceeded into the store.

"Hi, Larry, is the coffee fresh?" Chad asked looking Eugene over as he passed.

"Of course it is, how you boys doin' tonight?" Larry asked strangely relieved.

Eugene held his pop can up in a hello gesture, nodded at Larry and walked out.

FIFTEEN

John lay back on the gurney as he rolled from the x-ray room back to the ER. The shot they gave him finally dulling some of the pain he relaxed a bit. He'd lied about the amount of whiskey he had consumed so the doctor would okay the painkiller.

Once his shoe had been cut off, and his jean sliced up the entire length of the leg he had had enough, and demanded they give him something for the pain.

Chrissy and Matt waited in the little curtained off area in the emergency room. Dozens of makeshift rooms occupied the area giving little privacy to the patients being cared for.

"Don't know what we would've done without your help tonight, Matt. Thanks again." Chrissy leaned over and patted his knee.

"Don't give it another thought Chrissy. Wish I could've been more help. Poor John went through more hell then he should've. I just couldn't pick his big ass up." Matt laughed.

The curtain flung open and John was wheeled back into the open space left by the bed when they wheeled him out. "Big Ass? Did I hear you right?" He glared at Matt.

Chrissy and Matt cracked up laughing. John's face serious looking as he struggled to look mad, but being stoned on the painkillers he started laughing too. "I know I've put on a few pounds, but damn man, that was harsh." He tried to chastise through the laughter.

The x-ray tech set John back up on the machines he'd been hooked to prior. The only one they had taken with him had been his IV and pole. "You're all set John, the doctor will have the results shortly. You take it easy." The guy leaned over touching John's shoulder.

"Thanks man." John said with a burst of laughter. He couldn't control the laughing. He enjoyed himself for the first time since falling down the stairs.

The tech laughed, shook his head, and told Chrissy good luck as he left them.

Chrissy and Matt watched John continue to laugh until tears began rolling down his cheeks. He held his stomach and gasped for air. They started laughing again too.

"Shh, we need to keep it down." Chrissy said. They sounded ridiculously loud to her, and she tried to settle them down before they were thrown out of the ER.

Finally the laughter subsided and John looked heavy lidded. "That doctor better get his ass in here pretty soon, or the big fella's going to be asleep." Matt observed.

John lifted his lids with effort. "There it is again, the reference to my being a fat ass. What gives?" he asked Matt.

"No, no, no." Matt looked over at John. "You're not fat man you're just a big man. Let's face it you're not average in any sense." He hoped that sounded better to John and Chrissy than it did to him.

"Oh so now I'm not only a fat ass, I'm not normal either." John knew what Matt tried to say, but couldn't let the guy off the hook just yet.

"Babe, what Matt is saying…" Chrissy began.

"I know what he's saying Chrissy." John cut her off.

Matt rolled his shoulders preparing for an argument. "John, all I'm saying is you are exceptionally tall, and weight proportioned to your height. You have to admit you're nowhere near average on height." Matt stood. "Damn, I'm considered tall, and you tower over me."

Just then the curtain pulled back, and in stepped Doctor Cahill. She was a pretty woman, her look said she was a no nonsense type. Blunt and to the point she began. "So Mr.

Bingham, it looks like you've cracked your Fibula. The break is pretty small, still intact, you shouldn't need surgery."

"Wow, that's great Doc. You gonna cast me up so I can go on home?" John asked slurring his words slightly.

"I'm afraid it's not quite that simple, you've got a lot of swelling going on here." She pulled the sheet back and gently touched his lower leg. "What's going to happen is we're going to put you in a boot type soft cast. You'll need to follow up with an orthopedic doctor once the swelling goes down. That doctor will be the one to cast you."

"With this boot thingy I'll be able to walk?" John inquired.

Dr. Cahill shook her head "absolutely no weight bearing on that limb at all. You will need a set of crutches, if you have some we won't provide you a pair, if you don't have any, then you will have, when you leave here tonight. You're going to have to stay down with this leg elevated on pillows or something to help get the swelling to go down. I'm going to give you a prescription for some Percocet to help manage the pain. Do you have any questions for me?"

"No I guess not. I've never taken Percocet before, how will they affect me?" He wasn't big on medication at all.

"They'll make you tired, help you sleep through some of this pain. They may make you nauseous so make sure you eat something before taking them. I don't see anything in your paperwork about allergies." She rifled the few pages in her hand. "Are you allergic to any medications that you know of?"

"Nope"

"Good, okay let's get you booted up and out of here." She turned to leave.

Chrissy smiled, "thank you Doctor."

"That doesn't sound too bad bud." Matt said.

"Maybe to you it don't you're not the one laying here,"

John bit out. "I'm going to be out of work for a while Chrissy." He dropped his head back onto the pillow.

Chrissy heard the disappointment in his voice, and she understood he would be a bear to deal with, at least for a while. "Hey babe, think of the bright side." She stood and walked over next to his bed "you'll be home with me. I won't be alone." She gave him that beautiful smile he loved so much.

How could he fault her way of thinking, it's true he wouldn't have to worry about her being home alone every evening. He squeezed her hand.

The nurse strode in with a plastic wrapped Ortho-boot. "Let's get you fixed up and out of here Mr. Bingham," she said with a smile. Pulling the plastic wrap from the package in her hand, she deftly moved about preparing to take care of her patient.

Chrissy stepped back and stood near Matt. Matt stood up so he could watch. The little curtained area was quiet for pretty much the first time since John arrived. Everyone watched the nurse's movements.

"You doing okay on the pain, or should I ask Dr. Cahill if I can give you a little more before we begin." The nurse looked directly at John.

Wiggling his toes he felt a tingling sensation, but no shooting pain. "I think we're good. Let's just get it done."

Pulling back Velcro straps she laid the boot between both of John's legs. "I'll be as gentle as possible, but you will feel some discomfort." She told him reaching under his left heel she lifted very gently. Sliding the boot under his leg she placed his foot down onto the open boot.

John cringed and sucked in breath, but realized it didn't hurt that bad. "Oh you're good." He smiled.

"Thank you." She began pulling the Velcro straps together from the top of the boot down. Not too tightly, but tight enough neither the leg nor foot could move. "Do you have crutches?" she asked finishing the task.

John looked over at his wife "didn't even think about those when I needed to get up those damn steps." He watched Chrissy shrug her shoulders apparently not remembering the crutches either. "Yes, we have several pair between my wife and me."

"A little accident prone, are you?" She smiled at them.

"Yeah, you could say that." Chrissy giggled.

"Okay then, let me get your paperwork, and we'll get you out of here." She patted his good leg and left.

"Crutches would've been a big help, how the hell did you two forget you had crutches?" Matt looked back and forth between the two.

"I know right?" John couldn't believe he didn't think of them.

Chrissy blushed, "I guess through the panic and chaos I forgot too."

John looked over at the pieces of wood laying on the floor and thought of the ironing board, laughter rolled uncontrollably from him as he remembered the desperation he had experienced at the thought of getting up the stairs. Crutches would've helped immensely even though the pain of holding his broken leg up to climb the steps might not have been possible.

Matt and Chrissy watched John as he laughed and pointed toward the now discarded wood. After the laughter subsided he explained to them what he found so funny and ended by admitting the crutches would've been useless with the whiskey he'd consumed.

The emergency room didn't appear too busy tonight, but as usual it seemed to take forever for the nurse to come back with John's release papers. When she did, Matt took the car keys from Chrissy and went to pull the vehicle closer to the door. The nurse took John's IV out and bandaged him, handed him some papers to sign and left yet again, this time to get a wheel chair.

"All in all, babe, not too bad," Chrissy said leaning down as she kissed his forehead.

"Well, not exactly the way I wanted to spend our evening. I didn't take a night off work to break my leg, but you're right. This could've been a lot worse."

"Definitely could've been worse." She pulled her light jacket on.

John watched as she pulled her long hair up and fluffed it over the jacket collar, she's beautiful, he thought to himself as he heard *clackity clack, clackity clack*. "I think my ride's coming." He laughed.

The nurse brought two male orderlies back with her, and the wheel chair. "Thought we could use some muscle to get you into the chair." She smiled at him.

John looked at her, then his wife, and finally at the two orderlies. "What's with all the fat jokes tonight?" he asked sincerely.

"No, Mr. Bingham, that's not what I meant." The nurse blushed.

"He knows that, don't worry," Chrissy told her.

The orderlies helped John from the bed into the awaiting chair. The nurse handed Chrissy their copy of the paperwork as they left the small room.

Clackity clack, clackity clack, the sound of the chair had the small group laughing.

"Guess we need some oil or something on that chair," the nurse said.

"Or something." John laughed.

Matt got out of the vehicle to help get John loaded. After a little pushing, pulling, and adjusting he was in.

"This is awkward," John said shifting his body to

accommodate his leg on the seat.

"Hang in there pal I'll have you home in a jiffy." Matt got behind the wheel.

Lt. Washington and Agent Marlowe were pleased with the recommendations and were pleased, as well as, the reasons given for the decisions made by Mark and Cody.

The small group that remained sat quietly in the room awaiting instructions. The Lt. and FBI Agent had stepped out into the hallway for a minute. Mark pulled his notepad out and read over the few notes he had taken. Not much in way of information, but it helped him begin to put things into perspective.

Cody sat there staring at the photographs of the four victims. The officers that filed the original reports didn't have a lot of details on their personal lives, but he knew that would change soon. They were attractive women, all in their twenties by the looks of them, but nothing stuck out to pinpoint a particular type. His thoughts were interrupted when the Lt. and Agent Marlowe came back in.

"Okay, let's get this show on the road." Lt. Washington said as she walked past everyone on her way to the front of the room. Agent Marlowe remained in the back of the room.

"As I've already stated, Officer Mason and Officer Stone have been appointed team leaders. We are breaking the six of you into groups of three, one team leader and two officers per team. We have absolutely nothing in common with the vics yet, so that's the first, most important aspect you will work on. Team Mason will work on the vics, Team Stone, on the crime scenes themselves. I'm going to let you set your own hours and work when you need. In other words you will not be solely days, nights, week days, or weekends. You will have total freedom to come and go as needed. You will report to your team leaders and they will report to me." She took a sip of her coffee. "Now let's get the teams set up. Ian Patton and Ricky Borland you both are on Team Mason; Kyle Hilliard and Alex Norman you are Team Stone. Any questions before we get started?"

"L.T. when you say we don't have set hours, we come and go as needed, I want to clarify we still need to put in a minimum of forty hours a week right?" Alex Norman asked.

Agent Marlowe walked forward, barely containing the laughter threatening to bubble out uncontrolled. Clearing his throat he said. "Rest assured you will not only get your forty, but probably many more hours a week. What Lt. Washington is saying, is you will find you're needed around the clock. Not just days or nights, but all the time. I hope you understand what you've agreed to, by being on this task force. You can forget time off, family time, vacations, hell, sleeping even. You will live, eat, and breathe this case." He had pounded each item home by slapping his hand on the table in front of him.

He stood up straight and looked around at the faces staring back at him. He knew for some this was just sinking in. "Alright, you all have my number, use it. I look forward to helping in any way I can. With that being said, I'm going to get out of here, and leave you with it." He nodded to Lt. Washington and left.

Mark walked over to the boards with the victims photos already lined out. Ian and Ricky moved to his side.

"Okay guys, we need to start with a physical description of each vic. From there we'll go through personal aspects, jobs, hobbies, vehicles, where they lived, where they went to school, where they shopped. Everything these women did, we're going to know about." Mark laid the original police packets on the table. There were copies of police reports, copies of photos, and copies of autopsy reports. Copies of everything compiled so far on these women.

"Why vehicles, Mason?" Ricky asked.

"We will leave no stone unturned. Think about it, what if they all drove the same make of vehicle, and we didn't bother to check. It could be the damn salesman. We can't take anything for granted." He watched the evidence of Ricky's embarrassment glow. "Don't think any question is stupid and don't get embarrassed by asking anything, that's how we learn. Actually Ricky that was a good question, most officers have no experience with this type of case, we are each here, because we bring different experiences, thought processes, and ideas to the table. None of us know it all, if we work together, we'll succeed in catching this bastard. If we don't speak up because we think someone may think we're stupid, he wins. Plain and simple." He hoped he put them at ease. He didn't want them too afraid to ask anything.

Stone was walking his team through pretty much the same information. Lt. Washington stood back and watched the two, as they took control. Well satisfied that the teams were on track, she quietly left the room.

Deb paced her living room wondering about the flashes the two spirits had given her. We're they victims of the Surgeon? Why did they leave so abruptly? Of course, that was a silly question. She'd had this gift long enough to know the spirits ran the show. Typically she would've gone back to bed, but she felt completely rested. Seeing the TV remote had her heading to her bedroom for the novel she'd been reading. She would choose reading a good book, over TV any day.

Not only did she grab the novel she was reading, but her journal as well. Keeping notes on what happened helped her keep perspective. If she were lucky they would come back tonight. How odd she thought, not so long ago she wouldn't have considered her visits with the dead anything, but disturbing, certainly not lucky.

After jotting a few quick notes in her journal, she decided to see if Mark was busy. He would be the best person to ask about the Surgeon. It was after midnight, but she didn't think that would matter to Mark since he worked nights. Even if he was off tonight she figured he had to stay on schedule, he should be awake. If not, she'd leave a message for him to call her back.

Mark, Ian, and Ricky, each had a different victim's information sitting in front of them. They were dissecting every ounce of information on the first three victims.

The vibrating of his phone, in his shirt pocket, had Mark jumping unexpectedly. Pulling the phone from his pocket he checked the caller ID "Mason." He said into the phone.

"Hey Mark, its Deb, hope I didn't wake you."

"I'm at work, what's up, everything alright?" He stood up and paced away from his team.

"Sure, everything's good, I just wondered if you had a couple minutes to talk." She asked feeling somewhat awkward. "If you're busy we can talk later."

"No, no, we can talk now. What's up?"

"I don't mean to bother you while you're working, but I had a strange visit tonight." She said cautiously.

"What do you mean?" He knew her well enough to know what she meant, but short on time he wanted her to tell him quickly.

"You know the type of visitors I get. This time there were two of them, and for some reason I think it has something to do with this serial killer we've got running around the Forest.

Mark had a sinking feeling. "Why do you think that?"

'Well first off they were two young women, and secondly they showed me flashes of the Forest."

His heartbeat accelerated. "Okay, describe the women to me." He turned to look at the photos of the vics hanging on the board.

"Sure okay, one was I'd say early twenties, blond shoulder length hair, petite little thing. The other probably mid-twenties, short brown hair, medium height, both were very attractive."

Mark was sure Deb described victims one and four. "You could be right Deb, what did they say?" He was hoping for a major break, even though he couldn't share this particular information with the team.

"They didn't say anything, just a few quick flashes floating through my brain. The point is I know they'll be back, I'm hoping you can help me, help them."

"You certainly gave good descriptions of two of the victims, but I can't say for sure. How can I help you?"

"This may sound strange, but they showed me a basement too. Were they dumped in the Forest, or uh..." Before she could formulate what she was trying to ask he cut her off.

"No that's where he killed them. What does a basement have to do with anything?"

"I'm not sure, that's what I'm trying to figure out. They showed me a figure dropping from a window into a basement, a residential basement I think."

"Maybe this has nothing to do with this case then. Let me know if you get anything else from them." He felt disappointment set in.

"Don't write it off just yet Mark, I don't know why, but I'm sure it has to do with this killer. I was sure he must've gained access to one of them through this basement window. Huh."

"No Deb, none of these women were taken from their home. Each was accessible in a public way. I have no idea what the basement could mean."

She hated second-guessing her intuition. "Mark, I hate to

ask this, is there any way you can get me pictures of the two victims you think I described. That's the only way we're going to know for sure."

"I'm a bit busy to break away, but you can see them online. Look up information using 'The Surgeon Serial Killer' on the net. You may need to put Freetown Mass in there too."

Excited she went to get her laptop. "Thanks Mark, I'll do that right now."

"Good let me know if you come up with anything."

"I will, right now I'm interested in finding out if they are victims of this serial killer."

"That's right, one step at a time." He laughed.

Deb snickered "You know it. Will the web-site give me the name of a contact at the police station, if and when I feel I have something?"

"Oddly enough, Deb, that will be me. Let me know."

"Really you're working this?" What luck.

"Yep, one of six on the task force, as of tonight."

"Poor Lilly, does she know yet?"

Laughing he said. "Yeah she knows, sent her to her mom's till this is over."

"Oh good, okay let me see if I can help you out with any of this. Thanks, Mark."

"Sure, I won't hold it against you if ya can't though."

"Gee thanks, later, Mr. Skeptical." She laughed and hung up.

SIXTEEN

Clean up at Tate's had taken longer than usual. Sam chalked it up to all the talking he had to do to convince Maggie to let him see her home every night until the killer was arrested. She had put up quite an argument, but he won.

Waiting at the front door of the bar for her to get out of the restroom, he looked around at the business he had built. Not the actual building, of course, it was an historical building, but he had converted the old antique store space into a thriving bar business. The pride swelled in his chest as he took it all in. He secretly wished the building owners would sell the whole building to him. He wanted to knock most of the ceiling out and use the second floor for more tables and chairs near the walls all the way around, with a decorative railing surrounding the open space. That way there would be more room for the bands to set up on the weekends with plenty of floor space for dancing. He could picture it looking up seeing the tables and chairs all the way around and people leaning over the rail to watch the dancers and bands on the first floor. Oh he had plans to expand, just not the means.

Maggie tugged his arm. "What are you so deep in thought over?"

"Damn woman, I didn't even hear you come out of the bathroom." He jumped.

"I know. So again, I ask, what were you thinking about?" She smiled at him.

They stood there a few minutes longer as he shared his dreams with her. He walked her through each change he had in mind, the space it would provide, business growth possibilities. He talked excitedly, pulling her into his vision.

As he pointed to areas, and described in detail, he painted a picture for her.

Dropping his hands to his side he said. "Well we better get you home. It's late."

Smiling up at him she replied. "Or early, depends on how one looks at it."

He chucked her under the chin. "You're absolutely right. Come on." He pushed the door open and stood to the side to allow her passage.

Tucking her safely into her car he waited for her to lock the doors then turned, climbed into his car and proceeded to follow her home. Once there he watched her unlock the front door. She waved goodbye to him and closed the door.

Sam put his car in gear and drove away.

Maggie looked out the front window to see Sam driving away. He's such a nice man she thought, feeling the crush she still harbored for him. She looked around her small living room. It felt warm and cozy, just as she had intended. She was a simple woman really, not needing a life of luxury, just comfort. She sat down on the sofa, and thought about turning the television on. Reaching for the remote she secretly hoped for an old black and white film.

Leaning back into the sofa she pulled a throw pillow onto her lap, and flipped channels. Her mind wandered to romantic notions as she searched the movie menu, 'The Ghost & Mrs. Muir', ah perfect, she loved the salty sea captain. Deciding this movie is exactly what she hoped for she threw the pillow aside, turned off the TV, and ran for her bedroom.

Changing quickly into her pajama's she settled into her big comfy bed, turning on the small TV. Snuggling down under the comforter she watched, as Rex Harrison and Gene Tierney went head to head over the adorable seaside cottage.

Chrissy watched John snooze in the recliner. She and

Matt thought it the best place to situate him for the night. Two pillows held his broken leg higher than the rest of his sleeping form. She hoped that would help with the swelling.

Matt left after promising to come back tomorrow. John made him agree to bring the equipment with him, and together they would go through the tedious work of checking all the video and audio taken at The Ledge.

Chrissy went upstairs in search of bedding for the sofa, and to get ready for some much needed sleep. Putting on comfy pajama's she grabbed her e-reader, sheets, pillows, and a light blanket. Carrying everything down with her she quietly made her bed. She wanted to be close in case John needed her.

After the couch was made up she walked over to her husband, snoring lightly in his chair. She pushed a tuft of hair from his forehead, and gave it a soft kiss. "I love you, ya big lug." She said turning off the lamp.

Laying quietly reading her newest novel on her beloved e-reader, she thought she heard a noise in the kitchen. Sitting up and listening, she dreaded the idea of investigating, but knew she had little choice. Praying fervently it wasn't the spirits tonight. Her skin crawled as she approached the kitchen doorway. Stopping completely before actually entering the kitchen she hoped there would be nothing there when she gathered the courage to enter the room.

Taking a deep breath she took a few steps into the kitchen. The light shone bright, and nothing appeared out of place, except the basement door stood open. "Maybe we left it open earlier." She told herself. Finding the courage she stepped toward the open door. Just as she reached the door, a scraping sound emanated from the dark space below. Not wanting to follow up on the sound, she quickly grabbed a table chair, threw the door closed, and slid the chair under the knob.

Her heart pounded fast and hard. The hair standing on her arms and neck, she wasn't going to stay in there a minute longer, turning off the light she all but ran for the sofa.

Quietly laughing at herself, she looked over at her husband. He had enough painkillers in his system that assured her he wouldn't be awake, or helping her anytime soon. Picking up her e-reader, and immersing herself in the novel she forgot about unnerving incident.

Reading into the wee hours of morning, Chrissy finally shut the e-reader down. She got up and checked John one last time before going to sleep. She snuck over to his chair, placing her hand on his cheek, and forehead she checked for fever, he felt cool to the touch. She tucked the blanket around him again. Leaning down she touched her lips to his cheek, and whispered. "Sweet dreams, my love."

Deb finished vacuuming the small-carpeted areas throughout her house, since she was wide-awake, she figured she, may as well use the time wisely. Cleaning always invigorated her. She waited for the women to return impatiently. Putting the vacuum back in the closet she retrieved her dusting supplies.

The radio continued blaring some pretty intense eighties rock n roll. Deb found herself singing quite loudly, 'Another One Bites the Dust', by Queen. She danced and frolicked around the living room dusting when a movement caught her eye.

Turning about sharply, she saw them. The same two young women as earlier stood before her. "Well, hey." She smiled and grabbed up the remote control. Turning the stereo down she asked "Where ya been?"

The taller woman closed her eyes, and Deb felt the familiar jolt, as pictures began flooding her mind. She stood still and closed her own eyes, just a formality really since it didn't matter if they were open or closed she couldn't see anything except the display in her mind.

The same pictures as earlier assaulted her. The only difference now was the speed of the show. When Deb opened her eyes the women were still there. "Good for you. That was much nicer than one here and one there. So, let's get to work, shall we?" She went to her laptop and pulled the cover open. There on the screen were the photographs of the four victims. "Penny Ames and Angela Brown," she said and turned to face the women.

The two women glided forward and took in their faces on the screen in front of them.

"Yes, I've been busy." Deb said with a smile. "Now that I know who you are, I want to know how I can help you." She watched their faces intently. Neither seemed to move or talk. "I can't …" In her mind she heard the words. "You must stop him."

"Stop who? The killer? How?" She threw the questions out rapidly and waited. The women just stood there. "Help me here. I can't do this alone ladies."

Just when she thought they weren't going to say anything else, the pictures of the person in the basement went through her mind again. "What's with the basement? You weren't killed there. What's this about?" She listened with her mind. "He's there," is all she heard "He? The killer?" Nothing but silence once again. "He lives in the basement?" She tried again.

The small blond, Angela Brown, stepped toward Deb, reaching her hand out as if to touch her. The small hand went right through Deb's arm. Deb knew it took a lot of energy for the dead to make contact through touch. This poor girl hadn't been dead long enough to understand that.

Angela's face looked horrified at the possibility that she couldn't touch Deb physically. Deb reassured the girl.

136

"Angela, it takes too much energy for your touch to feel real. Let's focus on sound. Can you talk to me?" She knew some spirits communicated freely, while others seemed incapable of speech. There were ways to communicate if the women couldn't talk. When neither woman responded Deb suggested. "Yes and no questions are easy enough. I can see you, so a simple nod will do. Are you willing?" She watched the spirits. Unsure if they would try, she began. "The figure in the basement is that the killer?"

Penny Ames glared at Deb. Okay, Deb thought, not going to be so easy. "Does he live there?" Again no response she continued "it's not his basement?" She watched for any sign they might try to give. Not willing to give up, "is it the basement of one of the victims?" Still nothing "okay, let's try again, Penny is it your basement?" She wanted to laugh hysterically this was absurd. "Is it Angela's basement?" Deb turned back to the computer screen, "Is it Jessica's basement?" She'd asked a lot of questions to no avail. "What about Shannon, is it Shannon's basement?" At a loss, Deb wasn't sure how to get an answer. She had been through all four victims and the killer. Whose basement, is it? "We'll get back to the basement then. Did the same person kill all four of you?" She pointed to the pictures on the computer screen. "Is there more than one killer?" Beginning to feel hopeless now of ever getting a response, Deb still tried. "Is it someone you all knew? Is it a woman? Is it a man?" Deb stopped asking questions, she tried to think of more things to ask. The basement really had her perplexed; she wanted to get to the bottom of that. While trying to formulate a question regarding the basement she noticed the women begin to fade. "Wait! I need answers!" She stepped toward the now empty space. "Dammit!" What was she supposed to do now?

Should she call Mark? She thought. "Why, I got nothing."

* * *

Lilly got up for the second time tonight to use the bathroom. She'd been doing that a lot lately. Even through the sleep-induced fog, her brain registered something was wrong. Too tired to give it much thought she trudged back to bed.

Crawling into the warmth once again, she curled up on her side, hugging the extra pillow close. She missed Mark already, and it hadn't even been a full twenty-four hours.

The pillow she held tightly against her brought the tenderness of her breast to mind. Sitting up suddenly, she realized the possibility of what that might indicate. Could it be? She wouldn't allow herself to believe yet.

She would talk to her mother in the morning. If needed, the pharmacy always had home test. The excitement grew in her, waking her completely. Deciding sleep was now not an option, she tiptoed to the kitchen. A cup of hot tea would help her relax. Taking the teakettle she filled it with water, and placed it on the stove. Moving about quietly, not wanting to wake her mother, she gathered the teabag, cup, and honey.

While she waited for the kettle to heat, she thought about checking on Mark. No, he'd be busy, she thought. The long hours he was going to be working would take enough of a toll on him she didn't want to give him more to worry about.

Removing the kettle just as the whistle started, she poured the hot water into her cup. Dipping the teabag repeatedly, her mind wandered. She could almost picture what a baby of hers and Marks would look like. They had tried for so long both had given up believing it wasn't meant to be.

She laid her right palm against her abdomen rubbing the area gently she smiled, and hope sprung to life. Stopping the hand motion in mid rub as her mom walked into the kitchen.

"What are you doing up?" Patricia asked leaning heavily against the counter.

"Did I wake you?"

"I saw the light on, you didn't answer my question. Did you have a nightmare or something sweetie?"

Lilly smiled at her mother, Patricia Farmer, had been a loving, caring, nurturing soul for as long as Lilly could remember. "No, just got up to use the bathroom, and then couldn't fall back asleep. Do you want to join me in a cup of tea?"

"No, it will keep me awake too much caffeine in tea."

Lilly looked into the dark liquid. Caffeine, dang she didn't think about that. Would that be bad for the baby?

The look of fear that flashed quickly across Lilly's face would've been missed by most, but not her mother. "What's wrong Lilly?" Patricia pulled the chair out next to her daughter and sat quickly.

"I don't think anything is wrong Mom." Her face always registered her thoughts to quickly, making them transparent to anyone watching. "Everything is fine, really." She reached over and patted her mother's hand.

Patricia wanted to believe her, but she felt apprehension pulling at her over the fear she knew she had seen. "Honey, you know you can talk to me about anything, right?"

"Of course Mom, truly, I'm fine." She wanted Mark to be the first to know if she were pregnant, but her mother was sitting right here, and she had planned to run everything by her in the morning. Why not now? "You know Mom actually there is something I would like your thoughts on."

Patricia splayed her hands wide, palms up on the table. "What is it baby?" Concern filling her lined face.

Noticing her mother's drawn brow and crinkled forehead she said "don't look like that, it's nothing to cause concern I promise." Wanting badly to tell her mother what she thought, but not wanting to get her excited until they knew for sure, Lilly thought about changing the subject. Oh who am I trying to kid she told herself. With her face lit up she blurted out "I think I might be pregnant."

"Maybe I will have that tea." Her mother said standing to help herself to a cup.

SEVENTEEN

Mark's team had finally completed a detailed description on each victim. They had outlined questions for the families, friends, neighbors, and coworkers of each. They compiled a list of contacts for each victim, and now they would go home, and try to get some much-needed sleep. The day ahead would be grueling.

Quickly filling Lt. Washington in Mark left the station. He thought about Lilly, and how empty the house would feel. He hated to send her away, but her safety, more important than the feel of an empty house.

His schedule was going to be turned upside down for a while, and acclimating to sleeping different times of the day or night would take some getting used to. He had been on a task force one time before, and he remembered damn near reaching exhaustion from lack of sleep and too many hours on the job. This time he hoped would be different, since he knew what to expect.

The drive home through the sleepy town in the early morning hours proved to be quiet. No traffic on the roads made for a quick trip.

Pulling into the driveway he turned the engine off. Staring at his house for a few seconds before exiting his vehicle, he felt the hair on his neck rise. He wondered what the hell caused that. Standing next to the car he waited. Gut instinct kicked off alarm bells, something he never ignored.

Taking the time to look around outside, he didn't see anything out of the ordinary. Opening the front door he stepped inside the dark living room. Standing very still he listened for any sound. After a minute he pushed the door closed and turned the lock. He walked through the darkened rooms one by one.

After a thorough search revealed nothing, he began to relax. A nice hot shower was in order, he thought. Heading up the stairs he did just that. The shower soothed his aching shoulder muscles. Longing for a nice back rub from Lilly, he wondered why he kept thinking about her. Way too early to call and talk, he set the alarm clock, giving him time to awake and call her before heading back to work.

While he lay there trying to shut his mind down enough to sleep, he thought about the strange call from Deb. She'd described two of the victims almost perfectly. If it were true, the women were trying to contact Deb, this would be a huge break for them. He dared not hope too much. Knowing how much he needed sleep, he decided to try a relaxation technique he'd learned. Closing his eyes, he inhaled deeply, held it, than exhaled slowly. Doing this over and over, he felt his body relax. His mind occupied with each breath, he slowly fell asleep.

Maggie felt the pang of loneliness when the wonderful old movie ended. She lay there in her bed wondering why she didn't have someone next to her. Oh, there had been countless opportunities she knew, but for one reason or another she moved on.

Smiling in the darkened room she thought to herself, it was probably her damned stubborn Irish nature. She would try to be less opinionated, more open minded. Mr. Perfect didn't exist, she thought then laughed at her inability to be less opinionated and more open-minded.

Pushing her pillows behind her head to make them comfortable, she rolled to her side and placed one between her knees. Absolutely comfortable now except the openness behind her back, leaving her feeling vulnerable; she always felt like someone stood behind her. Stopping that thought process quickly she closed her eyes, and thought about Sam.

Working together for years now, she'd often wondered why Sam wasn't married. He was a great looking guy, wonderful personality, and owned his own business. He would be a good catch for any female.

His playful ways, made him appealing, always flirtatious with her he'd never shown any real interest. Maggie had to find out why. They would be good together. "Why not?" she asked aloud in the empty room "why not indeed." Now with her plan of attack against Sam she drifted off to sleep.

Deb couldn't get into her book so she finished cleaning her little house. She loved that even though she suffered some anal-retentive mind thing, she could have her home finished in a couple of hours. Even to her satisfaction which said a lot.

Looking out the window, hoping for sunrise soon, she felt panic rise within her. Dropping the curtain, she stood straight, alert, searching the room. Gulping in air at a rapid rate, she felt her limbs begin to tingle. She was going to hyperventilate if she didn't stop. Having no control over her breathing though had her searching frantically for the reason behind this panic attack.

The room remained eerily quiet. Deb grabbed a hold of the nearest object, a table lamp. The room began spinning from lack of oxygen, the lamp no match for the darkness quickly filling her line of sight crashed to the floor along with her body. Deb lay there unconscious.

An elderly woman sat rocking in the chair, while watching Deb's body, lay unmoving on the floor.

Patiently the woman waited. Rocking slowly back and forth, the chair making a slight creaking sound with each movement the chair made. The lamp lay shattered next to Deb's body.

Eugene heard the teakettle whistle loudly. He turned over and covered his head. His mother would turn the thing off any second now. He hated that she always got up so early. Sometimes when she was in one of her moods she would insist he get up, at a decent hour, as she put it. He lay there feeling his anger rise. "What the hell is she doing?" He uncovered his head and sat up. "Mom, turn that damn thing off," he shouted. He waited, but the noise continued. Throwing the covers off, he got up and stormed into the kitchen.

He knew sometimes she turned the burner on under the kettle and went to the bathroom. That must be where she is he thought. Finally reaching the kitchen with the damn shrilling whistle blaring he went around the table to the stove, stopping dead in his tracks he saw his mother laying on the floor directly in front of the appliance.

Falling to his knees, he forgot about the kettle. Lifting his mother's head into his lap he began to cry. "No, no, no," he shouted.

Mrs. Lowery's lifeless eyes stared up at her son's tear streaked face. He began feeling for a pulse, knowing he wouldn't find one. Gently laying her head back onto the floor, he stood and turned the burner off. Immediately the kettle stopped whistling. Eugene took the phone off the counter and sat back down next to his mother. Dialing the emergency number he explained what he'd found.

Cradling her upper body to him he sat on the floor and waited for the police and ambulance to arrive. He held her rocking back and forth as he sobbed. What would he do now? She was all he had.

Patricia sat down with her cup of tea. "You think you may be pregnant? Why do you think that?" Patricia dared not hope yet. Lilly and Mark had tried for so long to make her a grandmother, she couldn't get excited until she knew for sure.

Lilly put her hand protectively over her abdomen. "Well, to begin with I feel like I'm peeing every ten minutes, then you add in dizziness, tender breast, and well, you get the picture." Lilly smiled.

"Have you said anything to Mark?" Patricia felt the flutter of excitement building, but she needed to keep it under control. She was getting up in years, and didn't want to get too hopeful.

"No, not until I know for sure."

"Are you going to make a doctor's appointment here?"

"I thought I would get one of those over the counter test first."

"Oh, I see. You know Dr. Phillips is still practicing here, and he's familiar with your history." Patricia really wanted a doctor to confirm the answer for her.

"Yeah, I know Mom, I want to take one of those test first. I would feel foolish if it turns out I'm not. Ya know?"

"I understand how you feel. We can get a test in a couple of hours. Why don't you try to get some sleep?" Patricia got up and took both cups off the table, placing them in the sink.

Lilly watched her mom clean up, and knew it wouldn't be possible to sleep. She would go to her room though, and let her mom get more rest. Standing she hugged her mom tightly. "Sweet dreams."

"You too baby girl."

They left the kitchen as the sun arose in a spectacular colorful display right outside the kitchen window.

Deb opened her eyes slowly, trying to remember what had happened. She felt a burning sensation in her lower left arm, and heard the rocking chair squeak. Trying to sit up, she twisted her arm to take a look. There was a small gash, and

145

some blood. Shaking her head she turned toward the rocking chair. An old woman watched her. Deb tried to scoot away from the broken glass left by the lamp. She held her arm to stop the bleeding, and stood up. "What the hell happened here?" she asked the old woman.

"You must stop him," she said.

"Who?" Deb needed to get to the bathroom and wrap her arm.

"He's evil, he will kill again." The old woman stopped rocking.

"Who is he, and who are you for that matter?" Deb gripped her arm tightly.

The old woman didn't answer. Deb shook head and said "look I have to attend to my arm, if we're going to talk in riddles here, let me take care of this first." She turned and headed for her bathroom, unsure if the spirit would follow.

Deb took the items she needed out of her cabinet and set them on the counter. Washing her arm she realized she wouldn't need stitches. She dried her arm and applied medication. Watching in the mirror for the woman to appear, but she didn't. Once she had her arm wrapped she went back to the living room. The old woman was gone, of course. "Hello?" She called out. When nothing happened she decided to clean up the mess on the floor. She had broken glass and blood on her carpet. "Great, I cleaned for nothing," she said aloud. Going to the kitchen closet she grabbed a broom and dustpan. Scooping all the broken glass up, she tossed it in the trash, put the broom and dust pan away. Taking the vacuum back to the living room she removed the small pieces, and scrubbed the blood. Finishing the job she muttered "I clean more messes made by other people in my home where I live alone." After putting everything away she sat down on the sofa. "Okay so maybe not people so much as spirits popping in and out causing me to make messes," laughing, because she now talked to herself out loud more than normal. Deb closed her eyes and tried to remember her panic attack and make sense of it all. Very few spirits caused a reaction like that, and if this one was strong enough to do that, then wait for her to wake back up, why the hell did she leave before making her point? Deb shook her head. "Why do you guys keep disappearing on me?" She shouted to the empty room.

The sun had come up and she decided to get out of the house. She was hungry, and wanting to see living people she made up her mind to go out for breakfast. Sure she could cook something for herself, but she was frustrated and had a desperate need to be around the living.

Trying to roll to his side, John awoke with a shooting pain that shot him to full wakefulness and anger. "Dammit, what the hell?" He tried to sit up, but the recliner did not cooperate.

Chrissy jumped up. "What's wrong?" She ran to him.

"Guess I forgot I was in the recliner." He laid back and pushed up with his hands. His leg throbbed unmercifully.

"Dang, you scared the hell out of me." Chrissy had not slept all that well to begin with, and then to be wrenched awake like that, she felt her own anger rise. "Do you need a pain pill?" she asked.

"Probably should put something in my stomach first, but yeah I need one." John watched his wife look toward the kitchen. "What's wrong?"

She looked back at him and smiled. "Nothing let me get you that pill." She strolled out of the room, gathering courage as she headed for the kitchen. The chair still propped under the doorknob, but everything else looked normal. Getting a cold glass of water, she took one pill out of the small envelope the hospital provided last night. She would need to go to the pharmacy pretty soon. It was too early to go now so she would get some breakfast going and coffee brewing. She needed coffee.

Taking the water and pill to John she handed them to him. "I'll go get something ready for you. Take this now, I don't think fifteen minutes will make a difference to your stomach." She waited for him to hand the glass back.

"Just make some instant oatmeal hun, I need something in my stomach to stop from feeling sick." He handed her the glass.

"You sure, you don't usually eat that stuff." She looked at him.

"Yeah, this is going to be hard enough without you feeling like you have to cook full meals at every turn.

"I have to make sure you eat right though. You're not going to eat a bunch of junk while you're laid up."

He laughed at her. Laying there while she went to the kitchen he willed the throbbing to stop. The pill would kick in, in a few minutes. Closing his eyes against the pain he thought back to last night. He remembered the entity pushing the whiskey bottle over for him. He smiled at the thought. He couldn't wait to get back down there and try to communicate with whatever it was. He decided he would call his boss, as soon as, he had consumed some coffee. He wasn't the worst morning person, but he preferred having caffeine in his system before dealing with anything important.

He knew they would take it well, but he hated making the call. He had to call Matt too. Matt sure came through for them last night, he never would've made it up the stairs without him.

Chrissy brought him a bowl of oatmeal and a fresh cup of steaming hot coffee. "After I do the breakfast dishes I'm going to get your prescription filled. Do you need anything else while I'm out?"

He took the cup and bowl. "Nah, I'm good. Thanks." He

148

took a quick drink of coffee then set it aside to dig into the oatmeal.

Chrissy grabbed her bowl and cup bringing them to the living room to eat with her husband.

John turned the morning news on and they sat eating in silence watching the weather forecast.

EIGHTEEN

Eugene stood in the quiet house looking lost. What would he do now that he was alone? His mother had always been there for him. He felt cold, and frightened. He knew she would die eventually, but had never really thought about it.

There wasn't even anyone he had to call to inform. His sadness enveloped him, and he sobbed yet again.

The police and emergency people had been very kind, and he wished they were still there. He looked forlornly at the phone sitting on the counter and tried to think of someone he could call. The only person that came to mind was Maggie.

Maggie had been sweet to him, but she wasn't what one would call a friend. He hated the feelings he had for her, when he knew they would never be reciprocated. What a pathetic life he had lived, absolutely no one to call a true friend. His mother hadn't faired any better in life. She didn't have any either.

Dragging himself to a standing position, he left the room. Thinking of getting out of the house if for nothing more than a bite to eat, he went to his room and dressed. Leaning over his bed he began pulling the sheet and coverlet up to tidy his room, then remembered his mother would never nag him about that again. He turned and sat down on the bed, giving in to the tears once more.

A few of the neighbors had watched the traffic in and out of the Lowery house and gathered on the sidewalk to chat about it. They wondered what Eugene would do now, and more than one admitted they hoped he would sell and leave their neighborhood. Most thought of Eugene as an odd duck, some even feared him. He had never been neighborly, but his mother had.

Eugene would've misunderstood the gathering as something of pity or sadness had he seen them. He knew he frightened some of the older folks, but always chalked it up to his handicap. He never even knew how rude he was to them. He didn't much think about anyone besides himself.

The little group dispersed just before Eugene came out. He stood on the small front porch and looked around at all the houses where he had grown up. None of these people would give a fig he just lost his mother. Did any of them even know yet? He wondered did they see all the emergency vehicles and people. As he stood there he realized, living here is whole life seemed like such a waste. These people with their families and friends didn't care one iota about him or his mother. Sure he knew his mom had talked to them, but they never talked to him. He walked out and got into his car before he let the tears roll down his cheeks.

Lilly left a note on the table telling her mother where she went. She couldn't wait any longer to find out, and now that the stores were opening, there wasn't a reason, she should. Leaving the house quietly, she took her keys and headed for the car. The morning dew looked a little frosty this morning. She knew it wouldn't be long before snow covered the ground. The new day brought freshness with it. She loved this time of morning. Breathing deeply she slid behind the wheel. The big ole houses stood like sentinels as she drove through her childhood area. Everywhere she looked had a memory attached to the site. She couldn't wait to show her child her old stomping grounds and share stories of her youth.

While her reminiscing continued she had a fearful thought, what if she wasn't pregnant? They had tried so long she just couldn't think that way. "No," she said to herself and pulled into the parking lot of the small corner store.

Going inside she felt almost giddy greeting everyone she saw with a good morning and a beaming smile. Her beautiful face simply glowed, and had she saw her own face the doubt that tried to creep in would've been shut down quickly. Going up and down the isle's she searched for the morning test kit. Finally finding the correct isle she became over whelmed. Who knew there were so many different tests available now? Picking each one up she read the box, making her choice she went to stand in line.

The woman in line in front of Lilly was a real talker, after boring the man in front of her she turned to Lilly.

"Oh I see congratulations may be in order for you, sweetie." The woman smiled.

Lilly looked down at the box in her hands. "I sure hope so."

"Yep, you have that look about you, sweetie no worries." The woman reached out and patted Lilly's hand.

"I do?" asked Lilly surprised. "What look would that be?" She looked down at her almost flat stomach.

The lady laughed heartily and said "oh no sweetie, I don't mean you are showing, I mean you are glowing."

Lilly reached a hand up to her cheek simply saying, "oh," as she blushed.

"I've seen that look a million times, you've got it for sure."

"I hope you're right. My husband will be thrilled. We've tried for years, and finally just gave up." Lilly wondered why she'd told a complete stranger that. It's so unlike her to chat away about her personal life, especially to a complete stranger.

That's the key sweetie, to stop trying. God blesses us in his time, not ours."

Lilly thought about that, it had been almost an entire year since she and Mark talked about having children. Like most couples, when they first married, she took birth control, then after two years they quit the birth control and started trying, with no luck conceiving they decided not to get tested. It wouldn't matter which couldn't produce a child, they were not giving up on each other. Lilly looked up and realized the woman still talked to her. "I'm sorry I didn't hear what you were saying. I guess I let my mind wander."

"Understandable, I was just saying when couples have trouble conceiving they jump into adoption, and then *BLAM!* Before you know it they are having one of their own." She did a *tsk tsk* thing with tongue and teeth.

"Adopting is having one of their own." Lilly said.

"Yes it is, you know what I'm trying to say." The lady smiled as a slight blush climbed her neck and face.

Lilly didn't know what the woman meant, but didn't pursue an explanation.

The lady put her goods on the conveyor belt still rattling on and on, but Lilly's mind had wandered back into never-never land.

Jersey jumped on Matt's head growling. He rolled over and looked at her. "What's up girl? You need to go out?" He threw the covers off and got up. "You must be feeling a lot better. You haven't jumped up like that in a while." He gave her head a rub, and pulled on his jeans. "Come on," he yelled as he left the room.

Taking her outside in the brisk morning air was exhilarating to him. He would pack her and the stuff up to take over to John's house, as soon as, he got something to eat and a shower. He wouldn't call first because that would give John a chance to put it off another day. He knew his friend would be in pain, but what better way to take his mind off of the pain. He watched Jersey make her rounds around the yard, and after relieving herself he called her in.

153

Filling her dishes quickly, he started on his own breakfast and coffee. Inhaling his cereal and coffee he headed for the bathroom. It wouldn't take long to get himself together.

Making his bed he did a mental list of the equipment he needed to pack up. Jersey would be easy, just her traveling dish, a baggie of food, and she was ready to go. He knew John wouldn't care if he brought her along.

Jersey stood back and watched her master work fast. Standing by the doorway, her tail wagging, she waited patiently. Matt finished up and noticed her. "Whatcha looking at?" He patted her head as he passed her. She followed of course.

He gathered everything he needed in his truck, and came back for her. "Let's go girl, we're going to visit John." He locked the door, and they left.

Chrissy gave John a light kiss, and headed to the store. "Call my cell phone if you think of anything you need babe." She yelled back as she opened the door.

The coolness of early morning kept people inside if they didn't have to work. Those that had to work would already be long gone. She marveled at the quietness of her surroundings. Walking to her car she felt a sense of calm wash over her. She'd already called in and let her boss know she would be taking a minimum of a week off to get John taken care of. She really enjoyed her job, and rarely took time off, there was no concern they wouldn't grant her this week. John's going to need her more than they would, and he is her first priority. He had called his boss too, and they were scrambling to get a temporary in to replace him. He would need a lot more time off then she would. His company really cared about their employees, and even went so far as to tell him he could come back, as soon as, he was off the pain pills. They would put

154

him somewhere he could sit down, and save his sick time.

Dropping the prescription off to be filled she was told it would be a thirty minute wait. Chrissy headed for the book isle, she rarely bought books since she worked in a library and owned an e-reader, but she missed perusing the books and decided to look for a couple that John could read while he was laid up.

Browsing the non-fiction paranormal section wouldn't take too long. The store wasn't a big chain store, nor was it a book store, the selections were limited. Finding one that he had not already read would be the challenge. John was an avid reader, and since forming his paranormal investigative team, he kept up on as much information as possible. She stood there lifting one book after another, reading the synopsis on the covers.

"Mrs. Bingham, how are you?" Eugene felt elated to see someone he knew. He'd decided to drive around instead of eat, and couldn't believe his luck when he observed Chrissy pulling into the parking lot.

She dropped the book she held and jumped. She had been so deep in thought while looking at the books, she didn't hear him approach. "Eugene, you startled me." She leaned down to retrieve the book.

He watched her bend over, Chrissy had always been a pretty woman, and he was one to appreciate looks. "I'm sorry I didn't mean to scare you. How's John?"

Standing back up and looking around her, she tried to think of a way to get out of a conversation with him. He had always made her uncomfortable, the way he would stare, or try to find a way to put his hands on her somehow. "I'm afraid not too good at the moment. That's why I'm here, getting a prescription filled for pain pills. John broke his leg yesterday."

He watched her squirm at being near him. He felt it fuel

his anger. Why did everyone react like that towards him? "I'm very sorry to hear that. If you need anything, anything at all, please don't hesitate to call. I can be there to assist you or him at any time." He watched her take a step back as if he'd slapped her.

She felt her skin crawl at the idea of this man in her home. "What a sweet thing to say, Eugene, but we'll be fine. I've taken time off of work to stay home and care for him. How's your mother?" She would do the right thing, courtesy dictated to her even when her mind screamed to leave.

His face became stormy, and he inhaled sharply to control his anger. She didn't care about his mother, she was trying to be polite, and so would he. "I'm afraid I lost my mother, just this morning in fact. Truth be told, I've been wandering around trying to come to terms with it." He looked over her head he couldn't stand to see the shock and sympathy in her face. It disgusted him.

Chrissy reached out and touched his arm, then pulled back her hand as if she'd been burnt. "I, I'm so sorry Eugene." She took another step backwards. "What happened?" Why was she asking questions? She wanted to leave, not talk or comfort him.

"I don't know for sure, we are assuming a heart attack." He knew she looked for an out, so he decided to play on her sympathy and make her engage in conversation. "Please let John know for me. I have to make arrangements for the funeral of course. I will let you both know the details when I've finished." He smiled at her.

"Of course, I will tell John, as soon as, I get home. If you need anything Eugene, you give us a call." There she could leave him now, she had said that as an ending to the conversation, but something pulled at her heart. It was the sadness that surrounded Eugene. She knew he was all alone now. She stood there like an idiot.

"How sweet, thank you." He took her hand before she could stop him, and gave it a quick kiss.

Chrissy jerked her hand away and swiped it down the side of her pant leg. She saw him watch her. Feeling the embarrassment of her actions she nodded and turned to walk away.

Rushing back to the pharmacy counter she enquired if John's prescription was ready. She wanted out of the store. Feeling bad for Eugene had been difficult, and all she could think during the conversation with him, was good for Mrs. Lowery, she's finely free of that parasite she called her son.

Eugene stood back and watched the emotions play across Chrissy's face. He realized he could use the sympathy of these people to get back into the group. Maybe John would even let him join his paranormal team. He snickered to himself. He didn't believe in the paranormal, but he was a good actor.

NINETEEN

John heard the doorbell ring, and frustration at not being able to get up to answer the door had him yelling. "Go away!"

Matt stood outside the door and laughed. John was a hoot. "Hey lazy ass, get up and open the door." He knew John couldn't, and that made him laugh even more.

John could hear Matt laughing. "Funny, real funny, get your ass in here."

Matt push the door open and he and Jersey stepped inside. "Well good morning to you too."

"Why didn't you just come on in, did you have to have a laugh at my expense?" John looked at his friend. "Hi girl," he said to Jersey.

"I thought Chrissy would answer the door. I didn't want to scare her by just walking in."

"She went to get my pain pills."

"That explains your mood, you in a lot of pain?"

"No I gotta piss and can't get out of this damn chair." John slapped his hands down on the arms of his recliner.

Matt howled with laughter.

"Really you're gonna stand there and laugh at me? Help me up dammit!" John shouted.

Jersey helped herself to a spot on the sofa while Matt grabbed the crutches for John. Leaning down he grabbed a hold of John's arm and pulled him up. Placing the crutches in front of John, Matt held on till he knew his friend was stable.

"Thanks now get your dog off my couch." John snarled and headed for the bathroom.

Jersey looked up at her master innocently. "Get down girl you can't help yourself to just anyone's furniture. Come on lay over here." He pointed to a corner near the end of the sofa. Getting her settled on the floor he went to get the equipment from of his truck.

Walking on crutches was like riding a bicycle for most people and John had been on crutches off and on most of his life. His mother always told him he was an accident waiting to happen. He laughed at the memory. Finishing his business he made his way back to his chair. "What are you doing with all that?" he asked Matt, as he took in the equipment sitting in the living room.

"Well bud, I thought since you're laid up anyway, might as well make good use of your time, besides last night you told me to bring it with me."

Chrissy walked through the door before John could respond. "Hi ya, Matt." She walked over to John and handed him the bottle of pills "you doing okay?" she asked as she kissed his cheek.

"Well I was, till he showed up." John nodded in Matt's direction.

Chrissy noticed all the video equipment lying about. "What are you two planning to do?"

"We aren't planning to do anything. He is," John said emphatically. He wasn't in the mood to work.

"Awe, come on, this needs to be done, and you need something to keep your mind occupied," Matt said.

John looked to Chrissy for a little help. When he realized she wasn't going to give him any he glared at her.

"Oh I almost forgot, guess who I ran into at the store?"

They both looked at her questioningly. Then, when she didn't say who, John asked. "Well are you going to tell us?"

"Eugene Lowery, I don't know what it is about him, but he really makes my skin crawl."

"He's all right he just doesn't let anyone get close to him," John said.

159

"He's a weirdo," Matt said.

"I agree Matt. Can you believe he was just out driving around town when his mother died this morning?" she asked incredulous.

"What? Mrs. Lowery died? What happened?" John asked.

"Not sure, Eugene said they think she had a heart attack."

"Man, he must be feeling pretty lost, the old lady's all he had." John felt sorry for Eugene. "Guess I should give him a call, huh?"

"Probably, but not today, I think he's still out driving around. He said he would let us know when the funeral would be."

"Poor guy." John really felt bad for him.

"I know, I feel sorry for him, but honestly I can't stand to be within twenty feet of the guy." Chrissy shuddered at the thought.

"I don't know him very well, only ran into him a few times at Tate's, but I didn't care for him." Matt knew exactly how Chrissy felt.

"I went to school with him, trust me, he's okay. He takes his handicap too seriously, and has always felt people didn't like him because of it. He used to hang out with us at The Ledge and stuff. He's alright, really." John felt badly he hadn't tried harder to become Eugene's friend. He was always nice to him, he tried to include him in their group when he'd run into him at Tate's or wherever. Eugene wouldn't accept John's attempts at friendship or anyone else's for that matter.

"His handicap isn't the reason I'm hesitant to be around him. He's creepy," Chrissy said. "He always wants to touch me, and his hands are cold and clammy feeling. It's just gross."

"Yeah, I've watched the way he watches you and Lilly.

He can't seem to get enough of you two," Matt told her.

"Come on guys, he's just lonely, I mean you're both good looking women. If I had to live with my mom, and didn't have a girlfriend or wife, I'd be checking you out too." John tried to make light of the way Matt described Eugene's behavior.

Lilly went directly to the bathroom upon returning to her mother's. She couldn't wait to take the test. Reading the instructions, she followed them precisely. Now she had to wait a few minutes for the results.

Placing the stick on the sink she got up and paced back and forth. It would only take a few minutes, but her pulse quickened and her heart beat rapidly. She could hear her mom moving about. Would she tell her mom or Mark first? She gave that some thought while she waited.

Patricia could hear Lilly walking around the bathroom. Knowing her daughter must've taken the test she could hardly wait for her to open the door, and give her the news. Of course, there was always the possibility that she wouldn't say anything until Mark knew. Patricia couldn't fault her daughter if she wanted to give the news to her husband first, she would just pay close attention to Lilly when she came out. Her actions might give it away.

Lilly picked the stick up and read the results. Dropping the stick in the trash can she stared hard at her reflection in the mirror. She wished she was home with Mark. She needed him right now. Turning she walked out in a daze.

Patricia was filling her mug with hot water when Lilly came in. She watched her daughter closely. Her cheeks were pale, and as she set her mug down for Patricia to fill it, her hands trembled "everything all right?" Patricia asked.

Lilly looked up at her, nodded yes then looked back down quickly. Her mind was tripping over her thoughts as they rushed around her brain.

Patricia continued to watch her daughter's actions. She wanted to ask what the results were, but if Lilly decided to tell Mark first, she didn't want to push her. She slid the cup over to Lilly, and sat down with her own. She wouldn't ask, she told herself again.

Lilly absently squeezed the honey into her cup. She wanted to talk to her mom about the test, but she was hesitant. Slowly stirring the tea she made her decision. "Mom," she said and laid the spoon down. Looking up she saw the excitement on her mother's face. She laughed and reached out for her mom's hand. "I can't wait." Lilly took a deep breath and watched her mother's face as she said "you're going to be a grandmother."

Patricia squealed with delight "seriously? Are you absolutely sure Lilly?" She grabbed her daughter into a tight hug.

"Yes I'm positive." Lilly laughed at the pun.

They danced around together, hugging and squealing. "You can't let Mark know I told you first. Promise me." She pulled back and looked directly at her mother.

"Of course I promise. I can't wait to tell everyone."

Lilly laughed at her mom's excitement. She knew exactly how she felt because she couldn't wait to tell everyone too.

When can you call Mark?"

"I'll give him a couple of hours I'm not sure what time he got home from work. I don't want to wake him up."

"What do you mean you don't know what time he got in? Does he do that often?" Patricia asked concerned.

"No Mom, he's working a special assignment right now, so he doesn't have set hours. That's why I'm here."

"Oh that's nice dear."

If you only knew, she thought to herself. "He didn't want

me home with so much time alone he thought it a good excuse for me to visit." Lilly wouldn't tell her mom that Mark thought she was the target of a serial killer.

"I see, well I'm glad you cleared that up, I thought the two of you may have been having trouble, or something."

"No Mom, we're not having any trouble. I'm not the type to run from a problem."

"I know that sweetie. It's just wonderful having you here." There's more to this Lilly, she thought to herself. She wouldn't push, as long as, they weren't having marital problems she'd wait until Lilly wanted to tell her everything.

He sat in his car wondering about the young girl from yesterday. Maybe he would skip her. She was young, and he could excuse her actions citing immaturity as the reason. He needed to find out where Lilly Mason went, but more importantly when she would return. He had an awful urge eating at him, but Lilly couldn't satiate that urge. She was his final gift, not someone to fill a need.

He decided to pick someone out, right now. Even though it was early in the day, now that his mother was dead, he could take his choice home, and wait for nightfall.

The thought thrilled him. That would give him time to play with her, really get her fear factor going. He grew very excited, in more ways than one. Looking down he saw the bulge expand in his pants. As he licked his lips he tossed around the idea of sexually assaulting and terrorizing this next victim. Why not? He thought he deserved to fuck just as much as the next man. He had a handicap, so what? She couldn't very well tell him no, now could she? He laughed out loud at that. "No she won't tell me no, she'll welcome me when she sees how good I am," he told the empty car.

He drove around slowly, watching every female that passed his way. He would find one soon, he felt it. He pulled over for a passing police car running lights and siren. Snickering as he thought they had no idea who they just passed. He enjoyed the idea that he was right under their noses. Looking to merge back into traffic he spotted a young woman coming out of the bank. He watched her walk to her car. "Tag, you're it," he shouted to himself.

He waited for her to pull out of the bank lot and followed her. He felt a strong need to touch himself. As he looked around he unzipped his pants. Reaching in, he pulled himself out and slowly slid his hand up and down the length.

She turned left at the light, perfect he thought as he turned with one car between them. His hand began moving rapidly, up and down, up and down. He felt his eyes begin to close as he enjoyed the building tension. An oncoming vehicle blew their horn in short burst, to get his attention back on his driving. He swerved over into his lane in time to avoid a collision. Shoving his penis back into his pants he pulled his zipper up. "That was stupid Eugene," he shouted as he looked at his reflection in the rear-view mirror.

Bringing attention to himself at this point would be detrimental to his plans. He not only had to figure out how to get this woman into his vehicle, but then he needed a plan to get her into his house without his nosy neighbors seeing them. He almost changed his mind to plan things better, but his need wouldn't allow it.

She turned onto a short, dead end residential street. He turned and pulled over at the corner, watching her. She continued almost to the end of the street pulling into a driveway.

The house, a small one, no garage, not much of a front yard, would yield little protection for her. He watched as she began carrying grocery bags in. She came out to get more, no one followed to help. Either she lived alone, or no one else was home right now. He sat and waited for the right moment to grab her. She took the last two bags out and shoved the door closed with her hip. Going back inside, she closed the front door.

He pulled closer, but stayed in the car. Watching the little neighborhood that appeared lower middle class he waited.

The alarm went off and Mark hit the snooze button. He rolled over and drifted back off to sleep. Reaching in his sleep he pulled Lilly's pillow close and hugged it tightly to his chest.

Just as the nightmare was forming in his mind the alarm rang a second time. Mark forced himself into a sitting position. He didn't want to go back to the nightmare. Looking at the clock it was a little after noon. He would make a pot of coffee then check on Lilly.

The phone ringing had Lilly jumping up excitedly. She knew it would be Mark. She had been trying to conceive an unforgettable way to give him the news. "Hello, my love," she said smiling at thought process.

He smiled himself. "Good afternoon love of my life."

"I need you to do something for me okay?" she asked.

"Sure, what do you need?"

"Call me on mom's house phone. I want to send you a picture of something and I will need to hear your reaction when you see it."

"Well okay. Bye." He hung up and dialed his mother in laws number.

Lilly grabbed the phone off the table on her way to the bathroom. She answered on the second ring. Patricia followed Lilly, quiet as a mouse. "Okay babe, give me a second here." She said reaching into the trash can she pulled the stick out. Laying it on the counter she took her cell phone and snapped a quick, up close picture. "Sending it now, you got your cell

165

phone near you?"

"On my way upstairs right now to get it." He climbed the stairs two at a time. He heard his phone chime as he reached the top. "I heard it go off, what the hell's so important you had to send a picture?" he asked laughing.

"You'll see." She winked at her mom. They stood together holding hands waiting for his response.

"Okay, got it, let me see…" He looked again. "Lilly am I seeing what I think I'm seeing?" he asked.

"I don't know, what do you think you're seeing?"

"Are we? Are you for real? This has a plus sign that means…" he couldn't speak another word.

Laughing Lilly listened. "Mark? Are you still there?"

"Uh huh." He sat down on the bed.

"Well, what do you think?" She squeezed her mother's hand hard.

"Babe, is this yours? I mean are you?" He wanted it to be badly.

"Yes Mark, it's mine and yes Mark, I am, we are." She giggled.

"Oh my God." He gasped. "I can't believe it."

"I know I'm in shock too. Are you happy babe?" she asked quietly.

"Are you insane? I'm beyond happy. It's a shame you can't see me, I'm doing my naked dance." He laughed.

TWENTY

John and Matt went to work on the videos from the investigation of The Ledge. Chrissy decided to stay clear of the living room, giving the guys space. She hated pouring over the video and audio segments. Knowing it would take a few hours she went about her daily routine of straightening up the house and figuring out a dinner menu.

Going up the stairs to start in the bedroom she replayed the conversation with Eugene Lowery in her mind. For the life of her she couldn't figure out what it was about the man that bothered her so much. His handicap had nothing to do with it, if anything she felt sorry for him, as far as that went. He had never been rude, or mean to her, but she sometimes she felt he undressed her with his eyes. That was enough to make any woman uncomfortable.

Resigning herself to give him a break, and the benefit of doubt, she made up her mind to call him in a day or so to offer any help he may need with arranging the funeral for his mother.

The orthopedic doctor's office gave John an appointment for tomorrow. She should be able to devote some time to help Eugene after that. She wished Lilly were here, she hated the idea of being in his company by herself.

Making the bed and general dusting didn't take long. She headed back downstairs to see if John and Matt wanted some lunch.

After a brief discussion it was agreed that grilled cheese sandwiches and potato chips would suffice. Going into the kitchen she prepared the bread slices with butter, took out the frying pan, and tossed them with cheese into the pan. Turning she noticed the chair still under the door knob to the basement. If Matt had not been there she would've left the chair where it was, but she knew if he happened to see it she would have to explain why she put it there. John knew her unease with the basement, but she didn't think the team members knew how much she hated the spirits in her home. Most paranormal investigators didn't have to live with spirits, or entities, they helped others to deal with that sort of issue. Knowing John didn't mind them made her feel silly, but they truly scared the hell out of her. She especially hated it when they were active in the kitchen. Sometimes her cupboard doors would fly open, dishes would drop to the floor, or lights would turn off and on. If they would contain themselves to the basement it wouldn't be all that bad, she didn't have to go down there by herself.

Moving the chair back to the table gave her a panicky feeling. What if they decided to act up while she's in here alone? No. She wouldn't think about that. Going back to the stove she flipped the grilled cheese sandwiches, and then set paper plates out.

Sticking her head around the corner she yelled out "okay guys find a stopping point, lunch is almost ready."

Chrissy finished filling each plate, and glass, then carried them to the living room for consumption. She and Matt sat on the sofa to eat, while John stayed in his recliner.

Deb didn't want to go back to the house, and deal with spirits popping in and out, so after breakfast she drove to the Forest for a leisurely walk. Most people would've called her crazy, after all, this is where she's most likely to run into the young women that bother her at home, or even the killer, she shuddered. The need for fresh air won over danger.

The time didn't end up being leisurely by any means, she found herself walking briskly through the over grown foliage winding through the Forest. Taking her mind off the murders she thought about Tate's and giving Maggie a call. It had been too long since they had a girl's night out. She would give Chrissy, Lilly, Sue, Kaliegh and Joellen a call to join them if Maggie could take some time off. The problem with Maggie's job was she worked every weekend. If for some reason she couldn't get a night off maybe she, and the others would just go to Tate's and drive Maggie nuts.

Making a quick turn-around she headed back toward her car. She had walked a couple of miles already. Instead of walking back she would jog. Taking off at a slow sprint felt good to her, she should do this more often. Too much time spent giving readings, or speaking at paranormal conferences. She needed the fresh air, the freedom of the openness that being outside afforded.

Her car would be insight soon, a few more curves before she would be able to see it. Slowing down to a fast paced walk she could cool down and catch her breath. Leaves rustling and a few twigs snapping brought her to a dead stop, she listened. Off to her right she heard the same noises. Peering into the thicket she watched for signs of small animals. Surely it was a squirrel or raccoon.

She bent over with her hands on her knees and kept watch, finally a doe and her baby passed by, staying just inside the thicket. Deb felt her breathing returning to normal, with the noises cleared up, she took off jogging again, ready to get to the car, and her cell phone.

As she rounded the last curve her car came into view. Slowing her pace again she cooled down before stopping completely. Being after two in the afternoon, she assumed Maggie would be awake.

He opened the car door with the intention of getting a closer look, around the small house. As he reached the sidewalk one house down from hers, her front door opened. Stopping abruptly he spun to face the other way as if that was the direction he had been walking. He needed to be able to follow her if she left, he wasn't about to lose this one.

Settling himself behind the wheel he watched her back out of the driveway. Starting his car he drove past her to get turned around. She didn't seem to take notice of him, and that excited him. She made a right turn at the corner. He quickly turned his car around making a right turn. She stayed a couple of cars ahead of him, but he felt that gave him cover.

He had a million things to do, and following her wouldn't be one of them, but he had to get her taken care of before he would be free to work on the rest. His mind couldn't concentrate on anything right now, but supplying a need to fill his urge.

"Where on Earth are you going little girl?" he asked out loud after making yet another turn leading to nowhere. "That's alright I'm right behind you, no worries, you're not alone." He laughed his evil laugh, and took pleasure in the sound of it.

Finally her little car pulled into a driveway in the middle of nowhere. An older woman stepped out the front door to greet her. He drove past watching the two embrace each other. Going further up the road he found a place to turn around and pull over to wait out her visit. Feeling anger rise over the difficulty she was causing him had him thinking he'd made a bad choice. He should've already had her in his house. He would not, however, give her up.

Turning on his classical music he prepared for the wait.

Mark met Ricky and Ian in a small diner to discuss their plan of action. He'd given it lots of thought and decided they would not split up to go talk to the list of contacts they'd compiled, they could accomplished more working together than separated. Besides he didn't want anyone walking into a dangerous situation without backup.

After they ordered their lunches and settled into a normal discussion, Mark told them what he expected. "We have a long list of places and people to hit up today. I thought it would go quicker if we did it together. I say we start with Penny Ames, the first vic, and get all her information first."

Ian watched his team leader spill all the reasons he wanted them to stick together. He much rather preferred to work on his own, but kept his mouth shut and went with the flow saying, "I get it, we do each one completely then compare notes for anything they may have in common."

"That's the idea, what do you two think?" Mark asked.

They sat there for a minute thinking it through, and both agreed that would be the best way to go.

"Sure would've been easier if we'd had groups of four. At least then we could work independently, and cover more ground quicker, but you're right Mark, I don't think we should leave one man out on his own," Ricky said.

"Yeah that's the way I see it too. So after we fill our guts, let's get to it." Mark laughed. He wanted this to be a productive time, but he saw no reason the three of them couldn't enjoy themselves, at least a little.

The waitress brought their meals and each dug in hastily. They were all eager to get moving. This case was the most important thing the department had going, and each considered them self-honored to be a part of it.

Mark knew Stone had his men out earlier today going over the crime scenes. He understood daylight being a huge factor in their part of the investigation. His team, however, had the luxury of investigating whenever they could catch people available. That was much easier then dealing with a light or dark thing; although, his team had the dangerous part, the human factor.

Families especially were hard to deal with when they lost a loved one, not to mention the way these families lost theirs. Usually you could tell the family, 'they went quick. It was painless' and give them a measure of peace, but not these families. Everyone in the area knew how much these poor women suffered. Mark had to quit thinking about the details it was beginning to ruin his appetite.

"Did you guys explain to your wives what's going on? How much time you're going to have to spend away from home?" He just threw this out there to start conversation. They had all been eating quietly, and he needed to occupy his mind.

Both nodded their heads and Ricky said "yeah my wife wasn't too excited about it, but she understands my need to do it."

"My wife practically shoves me out the door," Ian said. "I mean, wait that didn't sound right." He laughed. "She just wants this asshole caught. She has a lot of young friends that are single, and she worries about them."

They all got a good laugh out of his comment about being shoved out the door.

"I sent my wife to her mother's. I don't want her anywhere near this place. I want her as far from here as I can get her till he's off the streets," Mark told them.

Continuing to talk through their meal they all felt better not using the time to think about the poor women they were investigating. By the time they'd finished their meal, Mark felt good about his team. He had known both men, of course, but didn't know them personally. He liked them, they were good men.

"Let's go to the PD and drop some cars, we'll all go together in one," Mark suggested.

The three pulled out of the lot following one another.

* * *

Maggie answered the phone huffing and puffing for air. "Hello."

Deb heard the breathlessness in her friend's voice. "Maggie, everything okay?"

"Yeah, just doing my daily workout, hang on a sec while I shut the TV off."

Deb waited for Maggie to come back to the phone. She turned the car radio off, and put her phone on speaker. Laying it on the passenger seat so she could have her hands free for driving, she knew people would think she was talking to herself, but she didn't care.

"I'm back. Sorry about that. What's up?" Maggie asked still out of breath.

"Must be a heck of a work out you're doing."

"Girl, you have no idea."

"I hear ya, I did a little jogging for my exercise today." Readjusting her mirrors she continued "I wanted to see if you could burn a night off and let's go have us a girls night. I'm in desperate need."

"Hmmm, I don't know, when are you thinking?"

"Soon, I'm not particular what night."

"Okay, I can talk to Sam tonight and let you know something tomorrow."

"Cool, if you don't get a night off, me and the girls will come there. We'll drive Sam crazy, just tell him that."

"He'll just say 'whatever, you know you all will come here anyway'." She giggled. "That's where we go, and you know it."

"Yeah, but we're nice about it, tell him we won't be."

"I will, right after I floor him with, I want us to date and see where it takes us." Maggie laughed nervously.

Deb knew this was a wonderful idea, and had pushed Maggie in this direction for quite a while. "It's about time. I've told you over and over the two of you are meant to be."

"I know, it's just working together could really get awkward if it doesn't work out. I love my job, and I don't want to quit."

"Listen to me Maggie, you're not going to have to quit. You and Sam are destined to be together. This won't be a mistake, just follow through."

Dare she hope? Maggie took a deep breath. "Girl, you better be right."

"I am, trust me." She smiled to herself. "Okay, get back to your workout and holler at me when you know about the night off thing."

"Will do." Maggie hung up and went back to the routine she'd been working on.

Next step Deb needed to call Mark. She still had not told him the spirits were the murder victims. After locating his cell phone number in her contact list she decided to hold off and call John first. For the life of her she didn't know why.

Chrissy, cleaning the lunch mess when the phone rang reached across the food she'd left out to grab the phone. "Hello."

"Hey girl, whatcha doin'?"

"Hi ya, Deb, just cleaning up the mess I made preparing lunch. What are you up to?" Chrissy liked Deb, she was easy to talk to, funny as all get out, and what better way to keep her from thinking about being in her kitchen, then idle chit chat with a good friend.

"Not much of anything if I can help it. You know that."

"Nothing wrong with that, I wish I was more like you."

"Well it's not too late, come on over to the dark side." Deb tried to sound mystical.

They both got a good laugh out of that. "Where's your hubby?" Deb asked.

"He's in the living room with Matt, their going over some evidence from the last investigation."

"Anything good so far, wait is that the investigation on The Ledge?"

"I have no idea, and yes it is."

"Joellen told me John and Matt went over that stuff like a week ago."

"Uh, yeah, they were, but we've had some excitement around here, so it kinda took a back burner if ya know what I mean."

"What kind of excitement?"

"Shoot girl, I'm not sure where to begin. Let's see, we've had our shed broken into, Mark sent Lilly to her mother's because the killer was stalking her, and John broke his leg so he's off work." She stopped to let it all sink in.

"What? Oh no, how did he do that?"

"He fell down the damn basement steps. Thank God Matt came over and helped him up so we could get him to the hospital. He wouldn't let me call an ambulance."

"Why not?"

"Mr. Cheapskate strikes again. I swear he thinks we're poverty level or something."

Deb busted out laughing. "He is a frugal man, I always just thought he was the conservative type, unless it came to tattoos of course.

"He spares no expense on his tat's that's for sure."

"Well damn, with him stuck at the house with a broken leg you're not gonna want to do a girls night out, if I can arrange one."

"Depends, when you planning it?"

"Not sure yet, Maggie has to check with Sam about a night off. I'm hoping soon."

"I can't promise anything, but if it's doable I'll go. Maybe I could get some of the guys over here to spend the evening with John. That would free me up."

"Great, do you need anything? I mean I have all this free

time right now, and I know you're stuck there, so?"

"Nah, we got it covered. If you're bored though, you know you're welcome to come over anytime."

"Thanks I just might do that. Give John my love and I'll let you know when, after Maggie calls me tomorrow."

"Sounds like a plan. I have to take John to the orthopedic doctor tomorrow, but other than that I should be around."

"Cool, well holler if you need anything." Deb hung up. Now to call Mark, she thought.

Looking down at his vibrating phone Mark excused himself from the conversation taking place in the Ames kitchen. Walking out the back door he answered Deb's call. "Hey there," he said in a quiet voice.

"Hey yourself, you busy?"

"I'm in the middle of something, but I always have time for you."

"Glad to hear it, I won't keep you long, just wanted you to know that it is the girls from your serial killer, at least two of them."

"How do you know?"

"I took your advice and looked up their pictures on the internet."

"All of them? Did they tell you anything you can share?" He felt his heart beat faster.

"No just Penny Ames and Angela Brown. Unfortunately, no they didn't tell me anything, just kept showing me pictures of stuff that made no sense. What about the basement, anything new?" That's the part frustrating her the most. That damn figure in the basement.

"Basement?"

"Yeah, we discussed this. They keep showing me a figure in a basement. Is it possible any of them were abducted from a basement? I know you said they weren't taken from their homes, but they keep showing me this guy in a

176

basement."

That confused him, as far as they knew the women were all taken from public places. "No, nothing concerning a basement, can you identify the guy if you saw him again?"

"Uhn uhn, he's just a dark figure, the basement is pretty generic, but I'm sure it's a residence."

"Okay, well keep me informed you never know if you're going to get something I can make sense out of even if you can't."

"I had another visitor too Mark. This one an older woman that told me to stop him, he's going to kill again."

"That one talked to you, but the other two didn't?" He knew Deb was extremely gifted, and her gift was dependent upon the spirit's strengths, but surely if one could talk the others could.

"Yeah, I know it doesn't make sense, I'll keep at it. They've been to see me more than once, they'll be back."

"I hope so. This guy's really sick, and I'm not ashamed to say he scares the hell out of me."

"Nothing wrong with admitting that, heck Chrissy told me you sent Lilly away because he was stalking her?"

"We're thinking it's him, we don't know for sure, but yeah I don't want her here until we get him."

"I can certainly understand that, no sense in taking a chance that it is him. I promise Mark, I'll let you know if I get anything tangible. By the way did you hear John broke his leg?"

"What? Hell no I hadn't heard. When did he do that?"

"I think yesterday, Chrissy said he took a tumble down their basement stairs. There we go again, basement. Huh." She wondered why basements kept popping up. In her experience this basement held significance, she didn't know in what way, but it did.

"Thanks for letting me know, I'll check on him in a bit,

but right now I better get back to my investigation. Keep me informed, and Deb?"

"I will, yeah?"

"Stay safe." He hung up.

TWENTY-ONE

Finally she was back in her car and heading out. He followed her closely, resigned to the fact he was beyond controlling his urges. Hell he wanted to just ram her vehicle right off the road.

She watched him in her review mirror. Had she seen the same car earlier? Of course, she like most of the young women in Freetown we're being more cautious right now with the killer in the nightly news. She'd just keep an eye on the car and see if it followed her.

He saw her watching him, and that just fueled his excitement. He knew he should back off, and make it easier on himself, but the thrill of her fear had him barely controlling himself. He would follow her as far as he needed to assure himself she was going back to the small house where he assumed she lived. Once he knew that's where she was going he would head home, and take care of a few things concerning his mother. He would come back for her as soon as darkness fell. He'd reasoned it was the only way to hide her from the nosey neighbors.

They both stopped at a traffic light, he was directly behind her, when she noticed the handicap plaque hanging from the mirror in his car. Feeling pretty stupid at this point she let her guard down. Surely the killer wasn't disabled, she told herself. Not bothering to watch the vehicle anymore she headed home.

He made sure she turned down the same street before veering off to go take care of business. How strange it was to think of mother's home as his house. It had always been mothers, even when dad resided there. Not anymore, now it belonged to him, he was sure she left everything to him. After all, she had no one else.

Arriving home he saw Clara, the busy-body from next door. She would of course inquire about all the activity this morning. Still trying to get a grip on the fact that his mother's death had been a mere few hours earlier, he got out of the car and waved at Clara.

"Eugene, oh Eugene, I just wanted to tell you how sorry I am about your mother, dear. She's going to be sorely missed around here. You poor, poor thing," she said walking into his yard.

"Yes, thank you." He tried to side step her and go into the house, but she wouldn't let that happen easily.

"What in heaven's name happened to her?" She eyed him suspiciously.

"I'm not quite sure, the coroner is assuming she had a heart attack." He felt the tears sting. He would not allow this biddy to see him cry. No way in hell.

"Oh goodness, a heart attack, I just find that so hard to believe your mother was in good shape for her age Eugene. Did you tell them that?" She knew he wanted to go into the house, but until she felt satisfied he had nothing to do with it she would keep him there talking.

"No, I didn't say much this morning. You know the shock of finding her is still hard for me to cope with. Now if you'll excuse me, I have a ton of things I must do." He turned to walk away.

"Eugene, I'm sure it was shocking for you. Where did you find her?"

Glaring at the house and inhaling a deep breath he turned back to Clara "on the kitchen floor," he stated simply.

"On the kitchen floor, so she got up this morning like normal?"

"Apparently yes, the tea kettle whistling is what awoke

me."

"Well gracious, she must've been feeling herself to go in the kitchen and start the kettle."

"I guess we'll never really know. Now as I said, I really must attend to some things." He walked away knowing he behaved badly, but not really caring one way or the other. He knew if he stood there talking he could be stuck for an hour. It amazed him, how no one in the neighborhood usually took the time to wave let alone talk, and now he'd have a hard time keeping them away.

Clara watched his retreating form. She didn't like him not one bit. She believed he was guilty of something he didn't seem to give a fig about his poor mother. Putting her hands on her hips she stood right there in the front yard and watched him all the way into the house. She hoped he looked out the window at her. She wanted him to see the distain on her face. What kind of a son was he that he could behave so coldly about his own mother?

Mark and his team finished up at Mrs. Ames house. She wasn't very helpful, but they already knew she wouldn't have much if anything to add. On to the next place, Penny's apartment building, it wasn't an up to date type either. Old red brick building with walk up floors. She had lived on the third floor, but they would start on the first floor with the manager.

"Ian you take the manager's interview," Mark advised.

With a nod of his head Ian approached the door, and knocked loudly. A middle aged man opened the door with a chain still attached and peered out.

"Yeah?"

"Excuse me sir, we're with the Freetown police department, we'd like to talk to you."

The man looked at all of them then shut the door to remove the chain. "What can I do for you?" he asked blocking their view inside.

"I'm sure you've heard about the young woman upstairs that was murdered?"

"Yeah, what's it got to do with me?"

"We just have a few questions sir, if you don't mind." Ian was nervous, he didn't like this guy.

"Well I don't really have anything to tell ya." The man didn't budge from the doorway.

"Why don't you let us be the judge of that it will only take a few minutes," Ian pushed. "You'd be surprised what people know that could be helpful."

The manager finally stepped back allowing them entrance into his apartment. The place was a mess, newspapers dropped on the floor, food containers from last night's dinner sat on the coffee table, and empty beer bottles were everywhere. "Sorry I wasn't expectin' company," he said sitting in a chair near the window.

"It's alright, we understand." Ian kicked some shoes away from the sofa to sit down. Mark and Ricky remained standing near the door.

"As I said we're here about Penny Ames. How long did she live here?" Ian began.

"Uh, let's see, I'd say about four years or so. She was quiet, and paid her rent on time. Didn't cause any trouble so, no one took much notice of her, other than her looks of course." He snickered at his answer.

"Uh huh, you found her attractive did you?"

"Hell yeah, any man with eyes in his head woulda."

"Did she have much company?"

"Not that I noticed."

Ian continued with the questions, and then asked for a key to the Ames apartment. After taking the key he told the man he would bring it back when they were finished in the building. He explained they would question some of Penny's neighbors, and asked if there were any in particular they should make contact with. After leaving the manager's apartment, they conversed in the hallway for a few minutes before continuing.

It was agreed they would split up in the building and talk to as many residents as possible.

John and Matt were making quite a few findings in their evidence. They had at least three EVP's, the apparition's appearance, and the K2 meter incident documented, but not on film.

Matt could see John feeling the effects of the pain killers, but since they'd made such progress he pushed him a little further. "I know your beat, probably ready to crash, but we're almost done. Can you hang a little longer?"

John looked over smiling at his friend "I'm good, you might have to poke me if I nod off, but yeah I can hang. Let's finish this."

Two hours later they'd finally made their way through all the video and audio evidence. The only thing left were the notes made by team members.

"I'll take the notes home with me, you get some rest," Matt told him.

"Sounds like a plan, I'm really ready to nap." John laughed feeling old. "Look at me, it's the middle of the afternoon, and I need a nap."

"It's the best thing for you don't make a big deal out of it." Matt laughed at his friend.

John laid his head back, the pain pills made him extremely sleepy. He knew the medication helped to ease the pain mostly by putting him to sleep, taking reality away for hours at a time. "You're right, rest is important, it's just you know, we always think of old people needing naps in the middle of the day." He laughed and continued "all this sleeping makes me feel really old."

"Old people and sick, or injured people." He cut his eyes down to John's leg. "Besides I think Chrissy mentioned you were going to get your cast tomorrow is that right?"

"Yeah, I guess."

"What do you say then, we call the team and meet at Tate's tomorrow night, have a few drinks, get you out of the this house, and share our findings with everyone?

John wiggled his toes in the Ortho-boot, testing for pain. If the cast is half as good as this boot he would be fine to go out tomorrow night. "Let me run it by Chrissy." John shifted his body in the chair and hollered for his wife. She had given them time to weed through the audio / video stuff without much interruption.

Chrissy came in expecting to hear they were hungry again. "What do you guys need? Are you getting hungry?"

"No hun, we're about done here. We've found some amazing stuff, and we're talking about maybe getting together with the team at Tate's tomorrow to discuss our findings."

"Do you think you'll be up to that after the doctor's visit tomorrow? That's a lot of moving around." She would leave it up to him.

"I think I'll be alright, it doesn't hurt too much, besides it'll be nice to get out and have some fun."

"It doesn't hurt too much because you're not moving around a lot." She laughed at him.

Matt watched the two of them, and decided to put in his two cents "how about we plan it around seven tomorrow evening, and if after John's appointment he doesn't feel up to it I'll fill everyone in on what we found?"

"There's a plan, you call everyone Matt, set it up we'll be there if I'm not in too much pain." He turned to look at Chrissy "that work for you?"

"Yep sounds good, now are you two getting hungry?"

"You know me babe, I can always eat. It's about time for another pill and I'll need something in my stomach." He couldn't remember when he'd taken the pill earlier, but knew Chrissy would know.

She looked at her watch. "Uhn uh not yet, are you in pain?"

"Nothing I can't handle just seemed like it would be time. Never mind then, I think I'll nap for a bit." He looked at Matt "we're pretty much done here, so if you don't mind making all the calls, I'm going to get some rest, didn't sleep that great in my chair last night."

"Sure no problem, I'll take care of the team calls, and give Sam a call to let him know we're coming in. You get some rest. I'll let you know what everyone says." Matt stood up and began putting the equipment away.

John snuggled down into his chair as Chrissy covered him, and kissed his cheek.

Deb didn't feel like going home. Spirits flitting in and out without good communication skills frustrated the hell out of her. Wanting her help wasn't the problem, it's when they became insistent, but refused to help her through the process, she took issue with. Of course, the most frustrating is when people expected her to be a go between the dead and the living like right now with the young women and the police. She hated not being able to help either side.

Not one to just drop in on someone unexpected, she felt guilty she hadn't called first, but pulled up to the curb outside Chrissy's house. She would visit a while if Chrissy wasn't busy and felt up to company. Hopefully John and Matt would still be going over the evidence, and Chrissy would be free to chit chat.

Putting her keys in her purse she climbed out of the car. Taking a look around the neighborhood as she walked up to the front door she felt an uneasy feeling, not like someone was watching her, but like a residual heaviness in the air. She raised her hand to knock as the door opened, and there stood the handsome Matt.

"Well hey good looking, I was about to knock." She winked at him.

"Dang what a surprise, didn't expect to see you standing there when I opened the door." He reached down and hugged her tightly. "It's been awhile cutie, where ya been hiding?"

"Not hiding, just busy. I heard you were here, did ya'all get much from the investigation?"

"Oh yeah, here let me get out of your way." He stepped to the side.

"Good can't wait to hear all about it. Is Chrissy around?" She walked past him.

"Yeah in the kitchen, John's going to take a nap so Jersey and I were just leaving."

Deb looked back and saw Jersey waiting behind Matt, funny she hadn't even noticed the dog. "You're finished going through the stuff already?"

"Most of it, very little left. The big guy got sleepy, the pain pills and all." He shrugged his shoulders, "I'm giving all the team members a call to meet up at Tate's tomorrow to go over what we have, you interested?"

"Heck yeah. What time?"

"Around seven, we'll see you there. Go on in and visit with Chrissy, we're gonna get outta here."

"It's good seeing you Matt, you too girl," she said as she patted Jersey's head. With a wave over her shoulder she passed through the living room noticing John in the chair. He looked to be sleeping already. Tip toeing on she made her way to the kitchen. Chrissy was putting a chair under the basement door knob as she walked in.

Chrissy turned as Deb spoke and a scream escaped

Chrissy's lips before she could stop it. "Dammit you just scared the piss out of me Deb." She went past her friend to make sure John hadn't heard the scream. He was sound asleep. "Sorry about that," she said giving Deb a quick hug. "Just don't sneak up on me. What brings you by on a week day?"

"I'm so sorry girl, didn't mean to frighten you, I was in the neighborhood, besides do I need a reason to stop in to see my friend?

"No, of course you don't need a reason, it's just you've been so busy lately with all the conferences we've not seen you much. When we talked earlier I told to stop by anytime, you could've said you were going to." She laughed to ease the fear still fluttering inside.

"I didn't know then."

Chrissy looked at Deb, she could tell something bothered her, but she wouldn't ask, she knew when Deb wanted to talk she would. Deb wasn't one you could push easily.

What's with the chair?" Deb asked pointing to the door.

"Oh that, uh, it's the unwelcomed guest I have a problem with." She tried to laugh it off pointing down to the floor.

"Are you worried about them? You know that chair won't stop them right?"

"Actually, yes I know that, but for some reason it gives me a small measure of peace. I wish they would leave for greener pastures."

"I know you do. You want me to try to talk to them again? See if I can get them to understand?"

"Sure if you want, that'd be great." She walked over and removed the chair. "Just be careful, John broke his leg on those damn steps."

"I know, and I will." Deb went past Chrissy down the basement stairs. Standing at the bottom of the steps she looked around. She could feel the presence of more than one spirit. This wasn't the first time she talked with spirits in the Bingham house. They could be an entertaining bunch, but the unusual thing about this house and the other world guest was she rarely encountered the same spirits. "I'm not here to scare any of you, I want to help you." She walked over to the bar area and took a seat. "If any of you want to cross over I can help." Deb looked around the large room. "You know you make the lady of the house very uncomfortable, and that's not nice. If you want to stay then you must behave, and not do things to frighten her. She's really very nice, and more than willing to share her home with you."

She got up and walked around the room while talking in quiet comforting tones. "Who are you?" she asked as she pushed a pool ball across the green felt top. "Do you want help crossing over?" She listened to the whispers coming in all directions. Trying to distinguish one from another, she said. "One at a time, I can't understand you when you all speak at once. I have all the time you need so let's do this one at a time."

A man in uniform began forming behind the bar. He was tall and broad shouldered, wearing an ancient military uniform, he stood straight and proud. Deb waited for him to speak. He stared hard, the mustache dropping at each corner of his mouth made him look like he was frowning. He watched her push another ball across the table.

"You going to just stare at me?" she asked looking directly at him.

He leaned against the bar. "The young man, he's not hurt too badly I hope," he said very formally, and his accent, very thick.

She tried to figure out where the accent came from. "Young man?" Deb didn't understand. She stayed near the pool table not wanting to spook the spirit, with that thought

188

she almost busted out laughing. A picture of John lying on the basement floor flitted through her mind's eye. "Oh, yes, no, I mean he's not hurt badly, a broken leg is all."

"That is serious," The spirit stated standing straight and rigid.

"No, no, not at all, at least not like it would've been back in your day. Today with medical technology it's not a big deal. Are you the one that's been scaring the Mrs.?"

"I don't bother anyone. I try to get the hooligans to understand that's not our purpose here." He moved his arms wide, as if to encompass the whole room.

"I see. What is your purpose here?" She inquired since he was being so forthright.

"To be," he said.

"To be?" Her brow furrowed "I'm sorry I don't understand."

"It is not for you to understand, madam." He faded away.

"Wait, I still have questions. Please don't leave yet." Deb stepped closer to the bar.

TWENTY-TWO

Eugene contacted the funeral home making arrangements for a memorial service, and cremation to take place the day after tomorrow. The coroner's office assured him his mother's remains would be ready tomorrow. He then called the newspaper to place an obituary as a form to notify the neighbors.

"Hopefully that will take care of all you nosey-bodies," he said out loud. Walking into his mother's bedroom he sat down on the bed. Everything was meticulous in here, as it always is, he thought. He knew how she hated anything left lying about. There's a place for everything, and everything has a place he remembered her telling him. She'd go into his room nagging about his untidiness.

The tears began to gather again this time he let them flow unchecked. He already missed his mother very much, the loneliness he'd felt up to this point would be nothing compared to what he knew he'd feel soon. Lying down on his side, curled into the fetal position and cried like a baby.

Mark's team finished the interviews in the apartment building. The sun set low in the sky. "We got a lot done today guys, I know it doesn't seem like much, but trust me we did."

"Feels like we should've had more of the Ames side of this case finished today, all we've done is her apartment building," Ricky complained.

"This is tedious work Ricky, it takes time. If you're looking for excitement then a task force isn't for you," Mark explained.

"No that's not what I mean I just think we should've

190

covered more ground today."

"I know it feels like we haven't accomplished much, but trust me we have. This is one of the most important aspects of the task force, gathering pertinent information for comparison." Mark understood exactly what Ricky meant. He was pleased with their work so far, but this type of work could make it feel like time stood still.

"I don't know about the two of you, but I'm frickin' starving here. Whatcha say we go grab something to eat?" Ian suggested.

"Sounds good to me, Ricky, you going?" Mark's head began to pound from hunger.

"Yeah, sure, I'm ready." Ricky turned to walk to the vehicle.

Mark hated to see Ricky so down, but this task force business has a way of giving you the highest high to the lowest low. He knew given time Ricky would adjust. They all climbed into the vehicle and decided on pizza and beer, with their work day over, why not?

When they got to the small pizza joint Mark told them to order a pitcher of beer and get whatever they wanted on the pizza, he had to make a quick phone call. After they acknowledged and went inside he called Lilly.

"Hey babe, how are you feeling?"

"I'm wonderful my love, how's it going for you?"

"Been a long day, we just stopped for something to eat, and I wanted to check on you."

"I'm good babe, don't worry about me. Mom is good company, and spoiling me rotten. You're going to have your hands full when I get back." She laughed.

"Give her a hug for me, and tell her thank you for taking such good care of my babies." He loved the sound of that.

She giggled "I will. Have you told anyone yet?"

"No, you know I wouldn't do that without talking to you

first."

"Mark, it's fine, you tell whomever you want to. Trust me I'm going to when I talk to my friends."

"Yeah? It's okay to tell everyone?" He sounded excited.

"Of course, I made an appointment today with the doctor I grew up with, going in for a complete checkup, day after tomorrow."

"Good for you Lil, I wish I could go with you, but I better get in there and eat before they eat all the pizza up. I love you babe."

"Love you too. Call later if you feel up to it." She hung up the phone and rubbed her hand across her belly.

The smell of good food permeated the entire building as Mark entered. Taking in a deep breath he looked for Ricky and Ian spotting them in the far corner he made his way through the tables. "Did you order already?" he asked sitting down.

"Yeah we ordered a large supreme. The waitress poured your glass of beer for you, so drink up." Ricky took a drink from his glass.

Mark picked up his glass and tipped it saying "a toast." Once Ian and Ricky tipped their glasses in clinking them all together, Mark continued "to a great team that will accomplish a lot in a short time." They all took a drink.

The restaurant had red and white checkered vinyl table clothes with hanging lights that matched over each table. Country music flowed from a juke box on the far wall making conversation difficult.

Deb turned from the bar with intentions of going back upstairs. As she pushed another ball movement caught her attention. There stood Penny and Angela. Rolling her eyes, and dropping her head she said "really? Now you're gonna follow me?" At once she felt fear spread through her body, the picture show began in her mind, her body experiencing the assault. Angela lay on the ground, hands bound to wooden stakes. A man hovered nearby grabbing clear plastic tubing, a scalpel, and whistling. She shut her eyes when the man turned around, trying to force them open, but couldn't. Her breath labored as she fell to the basement floor. This time they were going to take her through the murder with them. They may not be able to talk, but they would certainly get their point a crossed.

Deb felt the first stab of pain as he sliced a small incision and inserted the tube. He drained their blood with tubes, her mind screamed. The pain unbearable as he placed each tube in a different artery, the night air frigid her naked body unprotected from the bitter cold. She could feel his hands caress her as he moved slowly around her whistling. Each puncture held a tube sucking the blood from her body.

"Stop this," she cried out to them. "Please, stop this!"

Chrissy came to the door way, she could hear Deb screaming for someone to stop. Her knees shook with fear, but she had to go down there. Quickly running down the stairs she saw Deb lying on the floor wreathing in pain. "Deb, Deb," she yelled as she ran to her friend. "What is it? What can I do?" she asked lifting Deb into her arms.

Immediately Debbie opened her eyes sucking air into her lungs. The images and pain ceased. Looking up into Chrissy's fear filled eyes she licked her dried lips, and tried to form coherent words. "I'm okay, let me sit up." She pulled herself from Chrissy's embrace.

"What the hell's going on?" Chrissy visibly trembled.

"I'm sorry Chrissy it's not your spirits that caused this. Give me a minute, and I'll explain."

Chrissy looked around the room, she felt a chill sweep over her. "I'll meet you upstairs," she said shakily. "If you're sure you're alright."

Deb understood Chrissy didn't like the basement. "Sure come on we'll both go up. I'm done down here anyway."

The two women walked upstairs together. Chrissy went to check on John, while Deb pulled a chair out to sit at the table. Her breathing returning to normal, she hated it when a spirit took her through the motions of all they endured at the end of their life. She felt their pain, their fear, the sadness that over whelmed them, and the knowledge that death was imminent. Laying her head on her arms she relaxed her body, she felt exhausted.

Chrissy came back into the kitchen "he's still asleep thank God now tell me what happened down there?"

Deb slowly lifted her head to look at Chrissy. "I was talking to a very nice military type man about your spirits. He understands your fear. I think he'll try to keep the others under control."

"Good, but you were in pain, screaming out for it to stop. What's that all about?" She pulled a chair out and sat down.

"This may freak you out a bit, but sometimes spirits follow me. They can be like children, persistent, once they get your attention they don't give up."

"So you're telling me you brought more ghosts with you? What, you think we don't have enough already?" She looked around the room like she could see them.

Deb laughed. "Don't worry their not here anymore, and when I leave they won't come back." She reached out to pat Chrissy hand. "I'm sorry I didn't expect them to show up like they did."

"What the hell were they doing to you?"

"Walking me through one of their murders, they've been visiting me since yesterday, and apparently we're having trouble communicating with each other. They tried something different this time." She rolled her shoulders like it's no big deal.

Chrissy shook her head in disbelief. "I sure wish I could be as nonchalant about them as you are, fact is they scare the shit out of me."

Deb looked at her friend with a smile lighting her face to make her comment as soft as possible sounding "you give them that power over you, if you would act as if they are nothing special, may be they'd get bored and leave."

"I can't, every time I hear them I freak out."

"I know, but at least you can't see them. Thank your lucky stars."

"I don't know how you deal with it, not only do you see them, and talk to them, but you feel their pain. How did you ever get so comfortable with it?" She really wanted to know. Hating the fact she only lived in part of her own house. Hated giving them power to dictate where she could go.

"I guess since I've always pretty much had them around me, it's never bothered me. All I can tell you is you're in control of how you feel, you cannot give them the power to make you miserable."

Chrissy just shook her head. She wasn't able to deal with them.

"Okay look at it this way consider them uninvited guest that come to stay, but you can't turn them away, so you just put up with them. You still go through your life living it the way you normally would, and side step them when they get under your feet."

"Chrissy," John yelled scaring the hell out of them both.

Laughing Chrissy jumped up, "be right back."

John listened, but only heard Chrissy's voice, "who you talking to?"

"Deb came by we're sitting in the kitchen. We didn't bother you did we?"

"I need a pill," he grumbled.

"Be right back." Going to the kitchen, she got a glass of

195

water, a pill, and a yogurt. "He's in pain give me another minute." She hurried back to him. "Here babe, eat this yogurt before you take the pill "

"I hate that shit." He handed it back to her "I'll be fine without it," he said taking the pill and water.

"You want a sandwich then? You really should put something in your stomach, John."

He swallowed the pill "no, I'm going back to sleep."

She took the glass of water and left him alone. "He's a grump when he's in pain," she said pouring the rest of the water out in the sink. "You want something to drink?" She offered.

"No I'm good. I guess I should get out of your hair. I know you have a lot to deal with right now."

"Are you kidding me? I love visiting with you, besides we really haven't had a chance to visit yet." She came back over and sat down "tell me what's new."

TWENTY-THREE

Maggie ran from table to table taking orders. The bar filled up quickly, as she barely kept up. She'd hoped to talk with Sam about a night off, but now hesitant to even ask.

Sam stood behind the bar filling orders and watching Maggie to make sure she didn't have any trouble. Seeing her run around had him making a quick phone call. He would surprise her with some help shortly. He'd been doing a few interviews earlier in the week before the bar opened. He knew Maggie couldn't keep the pace she'd been working for much longer.

Sam decided on a young woman earlier today, but wanted to talk to Maggie before committing to the woman. Now he decided he'd surprise her instead.

Cindy Schmidt ran around like a chicken with her head cutoff. She couldn't believe Sam Tate offered her a job if she could come in tonight. She had to arrange for her mother to come watch Bryan, making sure everything needed for him was taken care of. Bryan was her four year old son, the absolute joy of her existence. Her mother would, of course come stay with him. She had already told Cindy when she found a job no matter the hours Bryan would not stay with a stranger.

Bryan had been with her mother all day today, in fact she hadn't had him home more than a few hours when Mr. Tate called.

Maggie stumbled into the bar, grabbing it to stop from falling, "What the hell?" She looked down at a drink that had been spilled. "Dammit someone spilled a drink. Here's my order Sam, I'm going to get the mop." She handed him a slip of paper.

"No Maggie, I'll get it, you've been running around here non-stop. Stand there and catch your breath while I get these drinks up, then I'll get the floor." He turned to fill her order.

Maggie leaned against the end of the bar watching Sam as he made the drinks, opened the bottles of beer, and completed her order. "Thanks, boss," she said as she took the tray of drinks winking at him.

He went into the small janitor's closet taking the mop out of the water bucket, giving it a good twist in the ringer, than cleaned the floor while giving that wink from Maggie some thought. Two guys at the other end of the bar were yelling for refills. "Hold your horse's fella's I'll get to ya," he yelled at them, deciding to think what that wink meant later.

"This place is a madhouse," someone said from the center of the room.

"Tell me about it." Maggie laughed. She loved her job, and when it was like this she doubly loved it. The exhilaration of nonstop activity kept her young.

Cindy came through the front door stopping to let her eyes adjust. Maggie yelled "take a seat sweetie, be right with ya."

Sam looked up, saw Cindy looking around and waved her over. "Glad you could make it. Here's an apron, and there's the crowd." He gave her a shove.

Laughing she made her way into the crowd and began taking orders.

Eugene drove slowly up the street to the small house. More than ready to get his hands on the young woman he'd spotted earlier, he drove past slowly taking a good look at the little house. The lights were shining in the front of the house which is usually a good sign. He parked just past the house on the same side of the street. Sitting there a minute or two he simply watched.

Feeling good about his decision he decided it's time. He'd go to the back of the house, and look for a way in undetected. Slipping around the side of the house he looked over the fence for any sign she had a dog. He hated dogs. Not seeing anything he stood there a minute longer just to be sure.

The postage stamp sized yard backed up to a thicket. What luck, he thought, sliding down the back of the house he looked in windows to see inside. He finally made it to the back door and took a peek. His blood began to boil as he took in the scene, an old lady and a small boy? Stepping back he looked at the house. He looked inside again. They were sitting on the couch apparently watching TV.

"Fuck, fuck, fuck," he said quietly. "Where are you?" He went back to his car. He'd waited all fucking day for this. Where was she? Who was the old lady, and whose brat is that? He thought to himself. If he didn't get a woman soon he'd go mad.

Getting back into his car he punched the steering wheel. Even his classical music wouldn't take this rage away. He peeled away from the curb, spinning his tires beyond caring if anyone noticed him. Driving in a blind rage he tore out of the quiet neighborhood.

This had been the day from hell for him first he lost his mother, than he lost his prize. What to do? What to do…

Larry stood behind the counter of the Stop and Go. His shift had started really busy, but finally the store was empty except for him. He looked around at some merchandise that had been randomly knocked over, and the coffee / drink area that had been left a complete mess.

Leaving the counter behind he went to put the store back

in order. He would make fresh coffee, fill the soda tanks, pick the packages up, and wash everything down. He really didn't mind this part of the job. The bathrooms were the part he detested. People were such pigs.

Lost in thought and work he didn't hear the little bell above the door ring. Eugene watched Larry's back as he moved about cleaning the drink area. The over whelming feeling to plunge a knife into Larry's back became an urgent need. He stood rooted to the spot just inside the door, his blood pounding feverishly sweat beginning to pop on his upper lip. As he took the first step reaching into his pocket for the knife he always carried, Larry turned around.

"Oh hey there Eugene, I didn't hear you come in." He stepped to the trash can dropping the wet paper towels into the receptacle.

Eugene didn't answer, his mind busily trying to think through a way to pull this off. Larry unaware of the danger continued to clean with a cloth this time, he liked to make the stainless steel gleam.

Eugene walked over to the back Larry had turned in his direction, the approach quick, quiet, and deadly. Placing his left hand on Larry's left shoulder he plunged the knife into Larry's back. Eugene felt pure pleasure pulse through his body as he repeatedly thrust the knife into Larry. His blind rage at losing the young woman earlier took over. The knife entered and retreated poor Larry's body more times than Eugene was even aware.

The metal counter no longer held Larry up, his knees buckled as he collapsed onto the floor. Eugene stood there looking down at the bloody mess he'd made. Coming to his senses he panicked, looking around for witnesses, or cameras. Had he touched anything he wondered. What would that matter, he's a regular customer here, easily explained away. He went to the camera behind the counter and putting one foot on the shelf below he pushed up to pull the wires loose. Hopping down he noticed a bloody smear he'd left on the cash register. Quickly wiping his hands on a dirty white towel he found lying below the counter he spotted the video machine resting on the same shelf he'd stood on to reach the camera wires. Removing the antiquated video tape he laughed at the old system. Standing up straight he looked around double checking for any other cameras.

Steadily moving around the store checking everywhere for anything he may have missed had him thinking about what he just did. Larry could not be considered a good friend. He'd been someone to talk to on the occasion that Eugene stopped in the small store. He didn't feel badly about his actions, but questioned his lack of control. He needed to think this through when he had time, and now was not the time. Eugene took one last look around and left the store.

Driving home he noticed the blood covering his clothing, speckled about his face and the lingering smears dried on his hands. The loss of control brought his anger back to the surface. He never allowed such foolish behavior, what the hell happened to him back there?

"I must not lose control like this again," he chastised himself, knowing if this had happened during the daytime he'd never make it home covered in blood such as he was.

Looking around at the trickling traffic he felt thankful for the cover of darkness surrounding him, the dim interior light from the dashboard not bright enough to bring attention to the blood spatter he wore.

He couldn't wait so long in the future to satisfy his needs, no more loss of control, no more risk like this would be tolerated. He must remain in control from this moment on.

Patricia prepared the taco ingredients, setting everything on the table. Hoping Lilly would enjoy the meal, she stepped back from the table and prayed Lilly wouldn't get sick from the spicy smells. Remembering all too well the way smells made her sick when she had been pregnant.

She loved making Lilly's favorites, having Lilly home, and the idea of being a grandmother. That last thought made her heart flutter, a baby. The idea of the shopping she'd be doing soon brought her joy.

Lilly entered the kitchen smiling, "Mark says to thank you for taking such good care of his babies." She stopped short upon entering the room, "ooh something smells wonderful."

"Does it? It isn't making you nauseated is it?"

"What? No it's making me hungry." She laughed, hugging her mom. "Taco's?"

"I hope that's okay with you."

"Okay with me? Are you kidding? You know tacos are one of my favorite things to eat." She pulled away from the hug, and took her seat "let's dig in."

Laughing Patricia sat down. "Yes I know they are, now eat up sweetie, you're eating for two," she said.

"I know doesn't that sound wonderful?"

"More than you know trust me. I've waited a long time."

"So have we, Mom. I didn't think it would ever happen."

Patricia reached over and squeezed her daughter's hand. "Let's give thanks, why don't you say the blessing tonight."

With bowed heads Lilly thanked God for more than the food, and she asked that he keep Mark safe. When the prayer ended they both filled two taco shells each, and ate with conversation centering on the baby.

"Are you going to find out the sex when you can?" Patricia asked not sure if she wanted to know herself.

"I really haven't given it much thought."

"There are benefits to knowing, but I never wanted to know."

"You didn't, why not?" Lilly asked surprised they had that technology when her mother conceived her.

"I don't know, may be your dad and I wanted to be surprised." She shrugged her shoulders "I remember hearing somewhere, not sure who said it, but that it's worth waiting to find out at. You know something to look forward to, and take your mind off the pain."

Lilly took a bite of her taco. While chewing she thought about that.

"Of course, you must count the babies toes and fingers as soon as it's born too. Don't ask me why, just do it." Patricia laughed.

"Yeah, I've always heard women do that, never really understood it."

"It's the first protective thing you will do as a new mother. Checking to make sure everything is alright."

"Well it's not as if the baby only had nine fingers or toes, it would be loved any less." Lilly shook her head.

"No honey, it's meant to put your mind at ease, and know your baby is perfect."

"Oh Mom I just know this baby is perfect, I wish Mark could be here to share it all with me."

"Lilly, you two have many, many, years to share it all. Don't fret my darling."

"I hope you're right." Lilly put her hand once again across her abdomen.

Patricia watched the emotions place on her daughters face. "What are you not telling me Lilly?" she asked concerned, and thought it's time to get the whole story.

Not looking up right away she thought of the best way to tell her Mom why she'd left Freetown. "There isn't an easy way to say this so I'll just say it." Lilly took a deep breath.

"That's usually the best way."

Lilly dove right in. "We have a serial killer in Freetown

203

that's already killed four women. Mark thought it best if I came here until the killer is caught."

"What?" Patricia looked horrified. "Why did Mark want you to leave? Do you fit a pattern or type? I mean why send you away? What aren't you telling me Lilly?"

"No Mom, it's not anything like that, it' just that Mark has been put on the task force and will be gone so much he didn't want me there alone."

"Uh huh, what are you leaving out?" She knew her daughter well enough to know there's more to the story.

"I'm not leaving anything out. The killer doesn't have a particular type of woman he goes after. Mark feels that all women are potential victims. He's over protective."

Digesting this information, Patricia still felt Lilly left information out. There had to be more for Mark to send her away. It didn't matter, what mattered most is Lilly's safe, she told herself. When she's ready she'll tell me the rest. Patricia let it drop.

TWENTY-FOUR

Cindy took her third order to the bar for Sam to fill it. "Is it always this busy?" she asked smiling.

"Not always, it happens in spurts," he said taking her order. "We never know when it will be like this. You'd think it happens only on the weekends, but not so." He turned to get the drinks.

Maggie walked up with her order. "Hey there, thanks for helping me out." She stuck her hand out for Cindy to shake "the names Maggie."

Cindy reached out and shook hands "hi I'm Cindy, and you're thanking the wrong person." She nodded her head in Sam's direction.

Sam turned around to watch the two women. When he noticed Cindy tossing her head in his direction he smiled. "Thought we could use the help, can't have you exhausted now can I?" He smiled at Maggie "you work way too hard around here, it's about time I got you some help."

"Yes it is." Maggie smiled at both of them. "Well welcome Cindy it's a great place to work." She threw her order slip onto the bar.

Sam filled Cindy's order and sent her on her way. "Hey Mag's I want you to know, I wasn't going to hire anyone till we talked about it, but I've been interviewing for the last few days. I didn't want to surprise you, but when this crowd started in tonight I made the call." He watched for her reaction. He hoped she understood the meaning behind wanting her input. He wanted her input on a lot of things from here on out, and he would make sure she knew that.

"You don't have to ask my permission to hire anyone

Sam, it's your bar." She was touched he wanted to ask her.

"Yeah I know that, never mind we'll talk later."

Maggie thought she saw hurt flash through his eyes. "Sam it means a lot that you wanted to let me in on the decision, I look forward to talking later." She beamed her beautiful smile at him.

He put both hands on the bar and leaned in "that's my girl, now get back to work." He snapped the towel he'd had on his shoulder and smiled back at her.

The sirens wailing gave comfort to Stanley Willis as he waited outside the Stop & Go. He still couldn't believe what he found when he stopped for cigarettes. That poor man he thought again.

The police cars pulled into the parking lot, lighting up the night sky with their bright lights. Two policemen converged on Stanley with guns drawn as one yelled at him to raise his hands in the air.

"What? No, no I'm the one that called you guys," he yelled back raising his hands like he'd been told.

One of the officers put his gun away and approached Stanley. "You're the one that reported this?"

"Yes, I just came in for cigarettes, and well, go see for yourself," he said stepping to the side of the doors to allow the policemen access.

The officer told Stanley to stay right there. The two policemen entered the store. Larry lay in a pool of blood near the coffee counter. An officer bent down and checked for a pulse he knew he wouldn't find. Shaking his head to the other officer they methodically checked the store for the assailant, knowing he wouldn't be there.

The scene inside the small store was quickly sealed off for crime scene techs. The officers that had entered the store cleared it quickly and called for detectives and the coroner.

Stanley didn't move except to light a cigarette. He listened as the officers called for whom ever else they would need. He sucked hard on the cigarette hoping it would calm his nerves. Thankful he had nowhere else he needed to be.

Eugene paced the floor of his small secret room. He really didn't need to come in here now that he had the whole house to himself. His mind going over the entire day's events had him mentally rechecking his steps in the store. He'd never killed like that before. His murders were always well thought out, and planned precisely down to the smallest detail. This was how most killers were caught. They didn't plan every step. What the hell had gotten into him? Since when couldn't he control his own damn actions?

He took a deep breath. "You better get a grip, Eugene," he yelled at himself still pacing about the small room like a mad man.

Stopping abruptly he sat in his thrown like chair. "I didn't leave the knife, I got the video tape, no one came in while I was there, and I didn't touch anything." He went over every step. Satisfied he'd been careful he felt the tension begin to ease. He would wash the knife off in the kitchen sink where he had left it.

He wondered if anyone had found Larry yet. Surely they have, that little store does pretty good business. He leaned back in the chair and thought about going to the store to see for himself. That idea gave him a laugh. "Maybe I could call it in." He laughed yet again. "Yeah I gotta go see what's going on." He left the room dropping the tapestry that covered the door back into place.

Pulling into the parking lot of the Stop & Go his excitement grew. There were police vehicles, unmarked cars, a couple normal looking cars, and a flurry of activity. They had found him. Wonder what they think happened here, he laughed to himself. Probably a robbery, dang should've taken the money from the cash register he thought. "Oh well it's too late now," he said getting out of his car.

A police officer stood guarding entrance to the store. "You can't go in there," he said to Eugene.

"Why not, what's going on?" He looked surprised to be stopped.

"We have an investigation going on. Don't you see all this?" The officer said waving his arm around to encompass all the vehicles.

"What do you mean an investigation? The store is closed?" He thought he was a great actor.

"Yes it's closed." The officer looked at Eugene like he was ignorant or something.

"So what's going on?" Eugene tried again.

"Nothing I can talk about, find someplace else to shop tonight." The officer crossed his arms over his chest and dared Eugene to question him further.

"Well that's some shit right there." Eugene stared back at the man. "Won't let me in to get what I need and won't even tell me why. What's your name Officer?" He thought sounding outraged would look good even though he cracked up laughing on the inside.

The police officer pointed to his badge. "My number is on the badge."

"I didn't ask for your number, I asked for your name."

The officer pointedly ignored Eugene.

"You fucking pigs think you're better n everyone else. It makes me sick," he said and spit on the ground. When the officer didn't come down to the level of bait thrown at him, Eugene stormed back to his car.

Matt called everyone on the team that attended the investigation on The Ledge. Told them about the meeting planned for the next night at Tate's. Everyone was excited to meet up and go over their findings.

Matt filled each of them in on John's broken leg too. He told them how he broke it and how they struggled to get him upstairs. He felt good after returning home. He had taken Jersey out for a jog, straightened up his house, and even cooked himself some dinner.

Now with everything finished he felt restless. Too late to call and talk with any one and he didn't have anything else to do around the house. Trying to think of something to do when Jersey wandered back in from the kitchen caught his attention, he decided to put her leash on and go for a walk.

The night air felt very crisp. The neighborhood, darker that usual with a few street lights out, had him looking around. He wasn't worried about being attacked or anything, but something felt off kilter to him. He slowed down taking everything in. Most of the houses were dark, people were asleep.

He completed the block and crossed the street to come back up the other side. Jersey wanted to investigate a particular area so he stopped, giving her the opportunity to check it out thoroughly. While standing there watching his dog he heard footsteps behind him. Jersey's head snapped up and Matt turned quickly to see 'Old Man Duncan' carry a trash bag over to the trash can.

"Hey there Mr. Duncan," Matt called out.

Mr. Duncan looked up and squinted. "Who's there?"

Laughing Matt tugged Jersey over to Mr. Duncan's driveway. "It's me Mr. Duncan, Matt Downing," he smiled at the man.

"Matt?" Mr. Duncan stepped closer. "Oh so it is, how's ole Jersey doing?" he asked congenially.

"She getting better every day sir thanks for asking."

"What're you doin' out so late young man?"

"Just taking Jersey for her last walk of the day, kind of late to be taking the trash out isn't it?" He thought it rather funny old man Duncan would question him being out in his own neighborhood. Maybe the old man was a tad lonely and wanted to converse with someone too. Matt stood there for a few more minutes talking to his neighbor then they bid each other goodnight, and Matt and Jersey moved on.

The rest of the way was quiet and unsettling. Matt wondered what could've caused the feelings he had stirring inside. Shaking his head, he and Jersey sat down on the front porch stoop. Matt continued to watch the quiet street.

The quietness is not what bothered him, after all its always quite here he thought. "What is it?" he asked himself.

Jersey sidled up close to him, and lay down. Placing her large head on her outstretched front paws she watched in silence.

The sky looked very clear with a bright moon, and a zillion stars. Matt wanted to share a night like this with someone, other than Jersey. Yawning loudly he got up and went inside locking everything up tightly for the night.

Tossing his t-shirt and jeans onto the floor he crawled between the sheets in his boxers. Jersey crawled onto the bed with him as he reached for his novel.

Cindy had worked every bit as hard as Maggie had tonight. Both Sam and Maggie hoped she would come back tomorrow night. They talked for a while after the cleanup process had been completed, by all three of them. Of course Cindy said she would be back, but Maggie remembering her first days on the job had her doubts. Not that it was a bad job, just a very demanding one.

After Cindy left the discussion turned personal. Apparently Maggie and Sam had been having very similar thoughts about one another, and they agreed to see each other on a personal level, as well as, a professional one.

Sam followed Maggie home again tonight. This time he did not wait in his car for her to get in safely he followed her in and stayed the night.

TWENTY-FIVE

Tate's over-flowed with excitement. Everyone seemed to find their way to the bar tonight. The place completely packed, and with N.E.P.R. in the house, the noise level seemed almost deafening. Not that they were a loud group, but with everyone talking over each other and the juke box, conversation became difficult.

Every member of N.E.P.R. present, with the exception of Mark Mason. Sitting in the back near the pool tables John and his team tried to talk about the investigation evidence. His leg propped up on an extra chair throbbed horribly with each beat of music the juke-box sent out.

Chrissy watched her husband endure the pain just to be here with his group. The orthopedic doctor left John's leg in the boot rather than cast it, the crack in his bone, not bad enough to warrant surgery, but still extremely painful. Also a constant reminder to Chrissy of the spirits that inhabited their home and the question she planned to pose to N.E.P.R.

This team helped people to get rid of spirits, and entities that caused problems, why couldn't they help her? She made a mental note to ask them, before this night ended.

John had refused any pain medication, knowing he would have a few drinks, now wishing he had foregone the alcohol for a pain pill.

Sue James talked with Dave Dawson about the investigation. She had missed this one because of a competition she'd entered to represent her gym. Well it wasn't her gym per se, but the gym she worked for.

Dave filled her in on the K2 smashing into his head. Sue expressed sympathy, but laughed just the same. Unwittingly

Dave reached up to the spot just behind his left ear, the knot long gone.

Sue noticed his actions. "Is that where it hit you?"

Realizing what he'd done he smiled shyly, "yeah, crazy huh?"

"Not at all, I've seen some pretty wicked things during investigations. I'm just sorry I missed this one. Did you see the apparition everyone talked about?"

"No totally missed it, but I understand no one saw it except those behind the monitoring system."

"Oh yeah, they did say that." She giggled like a young school girl.

Matt and Kaliegh talked quietly at the end of the table. John watched the pair with their heads together to hear better and he elbowed Chrissy, "take a look at those two." He smiled.

Chrissy turned to see who he referred to. "Well I'll be damned, it's about time."

This had Debbie looking at the couple too. "Don't be so amazed Chrissy, those two are written in the stars."

"Oh we all knew it, we just couldn't figure out why they couldn't see it." She picked up her drink.

"Kaliegh has known for a while, it's Matt that stuck to his stubbornness, refusing to accept it." Debbie picked up her drink and clinked glasses with Chrissy.

Joellen cackled loudly at something Vinny said just as Maggie walked up to the table.

"How's everyone doing back here?"

"Good, now that you're here to get us more drinks," Vinny said sliding his arm around Maggie's waist.

Reaching back she gently removed his arm. "Uh huh, what can I get ya?"

"Don't be like that, sweetheart," he said looking offended.

"I'm here to get your drink order, not to be fondled in the process. As for sweetheart, the names Maggie." She liked Vinny well enough, but always drew the line when it came to touching.

Sam quietly approached the group behind Maggie. When he heard her telling Vinny her name and removing Vinny's arm from her waist, he busted out laughing, "that's my girl." He slid both arms around her waist and pulled her into him.

Maggie laid her head back against Sam's chest and smiled widely. "Gotta keep this one under control." She nodded in Vinny's direction.

"You know I'm not that bad Maggie." Vinny noticed the way Sam marked his territory, "since when are the two of you a couple?"

"Since we made the decision to be." Maggie spoke before Sam could.

"Yeah that answers my question. Okay, I see you're off limits point taken, now can we be friends again?"

Everyone laughed sending Vinny looks and thumbs up.

"Okay people I gotta get back to the bar." Sam released Maggie kissing her neck possessively.

Eugene Lowery walked through the bar door, taking the large crowd in. It had been a while since Tate's had a crowd like this. He stood just inside the door looking around to see who he knew.

Deb closed her eyes gasping to breathe. She felt like all the air had been sucked out of the bar. Chrissy noticed her panic stricken face.

"What's wrong Deb?" she asked leaning in closer.

Deb shook her head trying to clear it. "I don't know, I couldn't breathe for a second."

"How strange, does this happen often?" Chrissy asked concerned.

"Not really, I don't know what happened. It's bizarre."

Deb began breathing normal again shaking it off.

John noticed Eugene and waved him over, Chrissy noticed Eugene then.

"Geez, why'd you wave him over here?" She whispered in John's ear.

"I want to tell him how sorry I am to hear about Mrs. Lowery. What's wrong with you?" He looked at his wife. She didn't like Eugene he knew, but surely she expected him to give his condolences.

"Fine, just don't invite him to sit down." She quickly turned her eyes toward Debbie.

Eugene waved back and began making his way through the crowd of people. Finally reaching the group he bee lined for John. "Hey buddy, I heard about your leg, you doing all right?" He reached out and shook hands firmly.

"Yeah, a minor break, more importantly, I heard about your mother. I'm sorry man."

"Thank you my friend, it truly came as a shock." He hung his head.

"I'm sure, do you know anything yet?" John felt bad keeping the man standing, but knew if he told him to pull up a chair, Chrissy would have a cow.

"Yeah, apparently, per the coroner, she had a massive heart attack."

"I heard that's what they were thinking sorry man, really sorry." John kept eye contact with Eugene. He noticed how Eugene kept looking at Chrissy. Probably wondered why she didn't acknowledge him. John wanted to get her attention, but he couldn't without Eugene seeing him.

Debbie watched Eugene, not caring for him at first sight. Never having met the man, but listening to her instincts which told her something's off about him, she paid close attention to his conversation with John.

"I see the gang's all here, except the Mason's, where are

they?" Eugene thought he was slick, he had been wondering about Lilly.

"Mark's at work, you know how cops are, never around when you need one." John laughed.

Chrissy listened to the conversation, but kept her eyes on Debbie. She watched Deb's reaction to Eugene and thought it peculiar. "What do you make of him?" she asked quietly.

"I don't like him. Who is he?"

"An old high school friend of John's, he's weird, really weird."

"There's something familiar about him. I just can't put my finger on it." Deb glared at Eugene.

He felt the woman staring at him, dare he acknowledge her? While talking to John he turned slightly to get a better look at her. When their gaze met he felt a cool breeze blow through him. Squaring his shoulders he stood straighter and stared directly at her. There's something about this woman, he didn't know what. Yet.

"Mind if I pull up a chair?" Eugene asked John, curious to know more about this woman.

John looked over at Chrissy who still pointedly ignored them. "Sure, go ahead," he said loudly.

Chrissy's heart plunged to her stomach. Damn, now she would have to speak to him. John certainly would get a piece of her mind when they got home. As she turned to greet Eugene, Cindy, the new waitress came out of the bathroom. Chrissy didn't miss the intake of air Eugene sucked in. Interesting, Chrissy thought, he would probably try to pick the poor girl up.

He watched her walk to the center of the bar. He couldn't believe it. This is where she went yesterday huh? He thought to himself, small world for sure. He heard talking near him, and turned to see who disturbed his moment. Chrissy had apparently been speaking to him. "I'm sorry

Chrissy, I didn't hear you. It's so loud in here." He tried to play it off.

"Loud, or interesting sights?" she asked her gaze following Cindy's movements.

"I'm sorry, what?" He got her meaning, but didn't much like that she noticed.

"Nothing, I was just saying I'd be happy to help you with anything you may need. I know losing someone can be not just painful, but a lot of work." She truly hated making eye contact with him. "You know for the wake or service?"

"Oh, oh yes, thank you. I do want to tell everyone about the memorial service." He cleared his throat and continued, "I've made the arrangements for tomorrow. A short service, no burial of course, I'm cremating mother."

"Tomorrow, that's pretty quick isn't it?" Chrissy asked.

"No point in putting it off. Mother likes things done in a timely fashion you know." He smiled at her.

Chrissy's skin crawled at that smile. She could do this, she told herself. "Well then I guess you better tell me what I can do to help out." Pasting a fake smile of her own, in place.

"I could certainly use help setting up at the house after the service, if you're sure you can leave John. I mean with his injury and all." He didn't like the way she seemed tuned into him where the cute waitress was concerned.

"I'm sure one of the fella's can bring John along. Of course, I can help you out." She watched him as he pointedly ignored Debbie, very intriguing she thought.

"That's thoughtful of you." He smiled again, should he ask about Lilly he wondered.

John didn't miss a thing. What the hell was Chrissy up to? She hated being near Eugene. He decided this must be pay back for allowing Eugene to sit down. He shook his head, his leg hurt, and he wasn't engaging in childish play.

Debbie would not be ignored for long. Listening to the

exchange between the two she decided to jump in with both feet. "I'm sorry I don't believe we've met, I'm Debbie Milo." She stretched her hand out, hoping for a bit of direct contact with him. Maybe she could get some kind of read on him.

Eugene looked at her hand with distain. He would not touch this woman for anything at least not until he knew more about her. Ignoring the outstretched hand he gave her what he thought of as his charming smile "delighted to meet you, I'm Eugene Lowery."

Debbie realized he would not shake hands with her, and wondered about that. "Did I hear you've just lost someone special?" She knew about his mother, she'd been listening.

"Yes, my mother passed recently."

"I'm very sorry for your loss Mr. Lowery." Deb stared directly at him. What are you hiding? She asked herself.

"Thank you." He turned from her back to John. "I'm surprised to see you out so soon after your accident." He hoped the woman could take a hint.

John engaged in conversation again with Eugene. Debbie and Chrissy looked at one another amazed at the man's behavior.

TWENTY-SIX

The task force met up at the station. Mark and Cody wanted to compare notes, and decide where to go next. They were both surprised to find Lt. Washington and Lee Marlowe waiting for them when they arrived.

"We need to discuss some things after you all get settled," L.T., told them.

Mark and Cody both acknowledged this with a nod of the heads. They both dreaded what they were about to hear. Must've been another murder they thought. Neither of them had heard about it yet, so they wanted details quickly. They ushered their teams in as fast as they could.

Mark knew by the look on the Lt.'s face whatever she was about to tell them had her upset. Lee took the lead going to the front of the room.

"I'm sure you've probably all heard already about the murder at the Stop & Go. So let me tell you what the Lt. and I are thinking about it." He stopped abruptly when he saw the faces of the men seated in front of him. Had they not heard? He didn't even consider that possibility.

"The Stop & Go?" Mark asked. "I'm sorry we don't have a clue what you're talking about Agent Marlowe." He looked at the other faces and knew none of them knew what the Agent referred to.

Agent Marlowe looked at Lt. Washington, "For a small department word doesn't circulate too well."

"We strongly discourage gossip." She grinned.

"Yeah okay, well guys, this is the deal, a clerk at the Stop & Go was brutally murdered. Now some would say since this murder happened to be a man it's not our serial killer." He let that sink in for a second. "However, the Lt. and I are inclined to believe it could be."

"What are you talking about? What clerk from the Stop & Go?" Cody asked confused.

Mark hoped like hell they wouldn't say it had been Larry. Larry always had a smile for you when you came in. He knew that cops dealt with negativity so often that when they had some down time it needed to stay light and upbeat. He'd made a point of keeping things that way for as long as Mark could remember.

Lt. Washington stepped to the front of the room. "I take it none of you have heard about this." She looked at each of them. "Okay, I guess we'll fill all of you in on the details." She took a deep breath and began "last night the clerk, Larry Anderson, over at the Stop & Go on Main Street either really pissed someone off, or had been in the wrong place at the wrong time. He received about fourteen stab wounds to the back." She watched as they all looked at her in horror.

"Larry, are you sure it's Larry?" Mark asked hoping he'd heard wrong.

"Yes, Mason, we know it's Larry Anderson. I know a lot of you knew him, and I'm sorry to have to tell you this, but we need to stay on track here." She gave them a minute to digest everything.

Mark didn't understand how anyone could kill Larry. He'd always gone out of his way, to be helpful, and nice. Not seeing a connection between the stabbing death of Larry and the murders of the four women, he tried to wrap his mind around what he was missing. Pushing his hand through his hair and rubbing his five o'clock shadow he felt at a loss for any possible connection.

Cody had the same problem. He threw his head back and looked up at the ceiling, as if the answer could be found up there.

The last two days had been extremely long. The men were feeling a bit unhinged with the fact a brutal murder could take place practically right under their noses and they had not even heard about it. Some task force they were, Mark thought. Hell when someone can be killed within the last twenty four hours and not one of them knew it, what chance did they stand to solve these murders?

Agent Lee Marlowe watched the emotions play across their faces. These poor saps were actually kicking themselves in the ass for not knowing. "Hey guys, let me make something perfectly clear for you. I can see what's going on in your heads without you even opening your mouths. You're wondering how you hadn't heard about this. Quite frankly I thought the same thing at first, but I forgot how all-consuming something can be, namely a task force. There's no way you can keep up with the day to day shit along with the intense investigating you're having to do, think about it, you're all out there beating the bushes for answers, not standing around the water cooler chatting. No one is going to call you and fill you in when they have no clue if you're working or sleeping. Besides this murder is so very different than what you're working on, most people wouldn't put them together." He hoped that help them off the hook they were hanging themselves on. "Why don't you all take a few minutes, go smoke or grab a cup of coffee, then we'll continue with what we've been thinking that ties this all together."

The group made their way out of the room, all except Mark. He sat there dazed at the fact Larry had been murdered and he knew absolutely nothing about it. How could that happen in a town this size? They had all been working the entire day, out and about in public, and not one word of the store clerk's murder reached any of them. Completely stunned by this he realized how focused they all were on the four

221

victims. It seemed an impossibility something so significant could get past all of them.

He stood and paced over to the windows. Knowing they were working so diligently to catch this sicko, and yet he managed to kill again less than twenty four hours ago, and they didn't even know it. Totally baffled by this newest revelation had him wondering how they could walk, talk, eat, in public places, see other officers coming and going from the station, yet not one fucking person on the task force new of this murder.

So deep in thought, Mark didn't hear the group coming back in. Cody walked over to stand next to him. "Hey, you okay?" he asked Mark.

Looking directly at Cody, Mark shook his head. "No I'm not okay, how's this even possible?"

Cody understood perfectly what the man meant. "I don't know, been trying to figure that out myself."

Mark turned around as everyone took a seat. Feeling like a complete imbecile, he couldn't reason any of it. Shaking his head, slumping his shoulders he gave up. Let them try to explain it he thought. Nothing made sense any more.

After Mark and Cody took their seats, Agent Marlowe started again. "We're going to give each of you a copy of the report taken from the Stop & Go murder. Look it over carefully, look at each photo carefully." He walked around handing each man a packet. "We're going to give you time to assess this crime, and then we're all going to talk particulars. While you go over these photos and this report, keep in the back of your minds the four murders you're working on. Tell us what, if anything connects these cases."

Mark read the report first, the photos would be difficult for him to view, but as a professional he would remain indifferent. He'd been a cop long enough to turn his emotions off until he could deal with it in private.

The report reflected just the facts, as he knew it would. The clerk, as Larry had been reduced to throughout the report, had been attacked from behind. He still held the cleaning rag tightly gripped in his right hand. The body had been found by an unsuspecting customer a very short time after the murder took place. The customer, Stanley Willis, felt for a pulse, after not finding one he called 911. First officers on the scene secured the building for investigators, and crime scene technicians.

The autopsy showed fourteen definite wounds with a possibility of several wounds having multiple impacts. The blade had a serrated edge with a possible four inch blade, one inch width. Most of the wounds showed bruising where the hilt of the knife hit the victims back stopping further penetration. A frenzy, urgency, or something of that nature hit Mark in the face. This person had been beyond angry, he thought. What could Larry have done to make this person so mad? He leaned back in his chair, and began shuffling through the photographs.

Larry lay face down on the floor with one arm tucked underneath his body, and the other hand out to the side holding a golden colored cloth. The cloth had soaked up some of Larry's blood. The back of his smock had been sliced to shreds, and drenched in blood.

Mark closed his eyes and squeezed the bridge of his nose. His head throbbed, and he felt his blood pressure rise. This poor man didn't deserve a death so horrendously painful. He thought about the photographs, and the report. The gruesome details crawled through his mind, he needed air. Never would he have believed how much a casual acquaintance such as Larry's meant to him. He stood to leave the room knowing, no one would stop him.

Once again he found himself in the bathroom splashing cold water onto his face "you getting soft, Old Man?" he asked his own reflection.

The door opened and in walked Lee Marlowe. He casually acknowledged Mark, but turned toward a urinal. He'd noticed Mason leave the room after looking through the photos and wondered about his reaction.

Mark took paper towels and wiped his face and hands quickly. He didn't want to get into a conversation right now.

Lee sauntered over to the sink zipping his trousers. Mark nodded at him, and turned to leave.

"Hold up a second Mason."

Dropping his head clearly not happy being waylaid, he stood there, and watched as Lee washed and dried his hands.

Lee watched Mason's reaction to his request. "It's no big deal Mason, chill out, just thought I would walk back with you."

The two men walked back to the task force room at a leisurely pace. Mark waited for Lee to start in on him. He knew his face didn't hide his emotions well, and his anger was quite apparent. He could understand Lee questioning this since Larry had just been a store clerk. How could he explain Larry's disposition when officers came into the store? How he had always made sure there would be fresh coffee waiting on them, or how he'd throw in a bag of chips, or candy bar, at no cost along with the coffee.

"You seem to be taking this clerks death pretty hard. Did you know him that well?" Lee watched Mason's face.

His anger contorted his features. "He has a name, it's Larry. Yeah you could say I knew him."

"Okay, sorry didn't mean anything by referring to Larry as a clerk. How did you know him?"

"Just casually, you know stopping in for coffee that sort of thing."

"Why so personal for you then?"

Mark stopped walking. "Listen Agent Marlowe, I don't

know how you FBI boys are, but we work the same area all the time. The people we get to know while doing our job become important to us. We spend time getting to know them, talking to them. Larry has been at that store a long time. He always smiled and joked with us. Kept fresh coffee made for us, he went out of his way for those of us on the night shift." He spoke with passion, he wanted to make his point without getting angry, and that took some doing.

"I understand, Mason, he became a friend to a lot of you. I'm sorry you found out the way you did, but it's important you keep your head right now. I don't mean to sound like a callous asshole, but your team is watching you, your reactions, everything must remain professional. If you need to take a few minutes to get yourself in the right frame of mind for this investigation then do it. Just watch the way you handle this." He wouldn't put on kitty gloves for a grown man in Mason's position.

"I hear you loud and clear, I assure you I can, and am, handling this in a professional manner. The part I'm having issues with, is we hadn't heard a damn thing about it. How the hell is that possible?" He looked directly at Lee. "I mean every one of the officers that work here, especially the night shift officers know this man, yet no one is talking about it?"

"Yeah it's a little strange to me too, I don't have an answer for that, let's get back to work, and find this killer." He left Mark standing there.

TWENTY-SEVEN

Debbie decided to wait to pursue the conversation with Chrissy over this bizarre man. She watched Maggie approach the group. She'd hoped Maggie had a chance to ask for the night off, and what better time to discuss it since everyone except Lilly is here.

"Hey, Maggie." Debbie pulled her over to stand next to her. "Did you get a chance to talk to Sam about a night off?"

"Sure did, since he's hired Cindy he said just to let him know which night I needed." She smiled brightly.

"Great, we'll all discuss it and let you know before we leave here tonight. This is going to be wonderful. I can't wait." Deb felt better.

"Sounds good to me too, I think it will be beneficial to all of us." She glanced around the group "does anyone need anything from the bar?" she asked loud enough to get their attention.

Taking the orders pretty quickly since she knew what most drank anyway, Maggie headed back to the bar. She'd noticed Eugene sitting back there and thought that a little odd. She didn't know he'd joined N.E.P.R.

Kaliegh, a tad reluctant to leave off conversation with Matt to meet up with the girls at the other end of the table, still sat talking to him. She figured they could fill her in on what everyone decided. They knew she had been after this man for a while, and she'd be damned if she would let anyone get in the way. He actually appeared to be enjoying her company.

Craig, Vinny, and Dave joined John, and Eugene's conversation. Eugene had been trying to get information on their investigation, but they all wanted to discuss his mother's passing. He wanted to know about Lilly, and wondered why she and Mark weren't here. He couldn't devise a suitable reason for asking, which made him work over-time controlling his anger.

He found himself explaining several times about the coroner's findings, and the memorial service information. Quite frankly he was tired of talking about his mother.

The group had shifted seats with the women going to one end of the table while the men went to the other. Except Kaliegh and Matt who stayed exactly where they'd been, oblivious to the rest of the group.

"I guess we all agree then, tomorrow we'll attend the service for Eugene's mother together as a team," John said while watching Eugene struggle to stay in the conversation. He wondered what had the man so preoccupied.

"Good, good, I'm so glad you will all be there. I know I don't know some of you as well as others, but it's comforting to know you care." Eugene put his fake smile in place. "Now if I may ask, where is Mark and Lilly tonight?"

"Mark had to work. You know he can't take off whenever he wants to join us for a drink," Craig Foster said.

"True, poor Mark hardly ever gets to join us." Dave Dawson tossed in his two cents.

"I understand, police work is demanding, and they work the whole shift, weekends, and holiday thing." Eugene tried to sound nonchalant. His mind screamed 'I don't really care about him, where the hell is Lilly?'

Vinny Muso the group cutup stayed unusually quiet. He didn't know this man too well, but wondered why he asked about the Mason's. He knew Eugene went to school with John and Mark, however, John had made it pretty clear in the past they'd never been friends really. Yet he couldn't shake Eugene's apparent interest in the Mason's. It didn't seem right.

He asked about them twice already, seemed preoccupied after getting the same answer, yet tried to make it appear as casual interest. This guy's definitely interested, the question is why, Vinny wondered.

Maggie began serving a round of drinks to everyone. Observing the seriousness surrounding the men's end of the table she wondered what they talked about. Some of them were uncharacteristically quiet, for some strange reason this bothered her. She dropped their drinks quickly, and went to the women's end. "What's going on down there?" she asked Chrissy.

"What'd ya mean?"

"I don't know they seem to be pretty serious. Is everything okay?" She nodded toward the other end of the table.

Chrissy looked at John, she knew they were discussing Eugene's mother's memorial. "Oh yeah, they're all talking about Eugene's mother dying." She shrugged her shoulders.

"Ah that makes sense okay, now give on Kaliegh and Matt? Aren't they adorable?" She giggled.

"Yeah we invited her down here to talk about our girl's night out, but I think she's refusing to leave his side." Joellen laughed "which, by the way, is going to be a blast."

"I know, what did you all come up with?" Maggie wanted to be part of the planning, but the bar being so crowded she simply couldn't.

"We're thinking night after tomorrow, now we're talking about where," Deb informed her.

"Yeah that works for me. Um why don't we just go to one of our houses, that way if we get too snockered we can just crash," Maggie suggested.

Chattering began going through the women's end of the table. Everyone thought this a great idea and began tossing ideas on whose house to invade, when Maggie left them to figure it out.

Lilly wondered what Mark thought about the whole baby thing. She sat there day-dreaming. Mentally putting their nursery together, and thinking about baby names had her preoccupied when Patricia realized Lilly wasn't hearing a word she said.

Her daughter sat looking out the front room window, her head apparently in a faraway place. Patricia didn't mind Lilly's day-dreaming. She remembered what it felt like when she first found out she and her husband were with child. The decisions and planning took precedence over everything else. Nothing could compare with that feeling.

Taking a drink of her ice water, Lilly absently rubbed her belly. She wanted to be home more than anything right now. This experience should be shared with Mark from the beginning. Making up her mind that very instant, she would follow through with the doctor visit tomorrow, then pack up and head home to her husband.

Turning from the window to face her mom she said, "Just so you know, I plan to see the doctor tomorrow then I'm going home."

"Is that wise? I mean with that killer still loose, and Mark working long hours?" Patricia didn't like the idea at all.

"I don't know what's wise. I just know I want to be with Mark right now, I need to be with him." She continued to rub her belly totally unaware.

"Lilly, I understand exactly where you're coming from. I just don't think you're making a good decision."

"Probably not, but I don't want to argue about it. It's something I need to do."

"Will you call Mark before you leave?" She hoped he would be able to talk some sense into her.

Lilly thought about that. If she called Mark he would

talk her out of it. "I may just surprise him."

"You mean you may just make him angry." She would make sure Lilly called Mark somehow.

Lilly smiled she knew exactly what her mother tried to do. She knew he would talk her into staying. She'd get around calling him. "What do you say we watch one of those wonderful old black and white movies?"

"Nice change of subject missy, you're not getting off the hook easy. You must realize the danger of going home, Lilly. We can't have you or the baby in harm's way."

"I know Mom, I'll think it through I promise." Picking up the remote control she began searching for a good old movie to take their minds off her plans. She wouldn't call Mark, and she would go home tomorrow.

"Now that you've all had an opportunity to look at the reports and photo's let's discuss why we think it's our killer." Lee Marlowe pulled everyone's attention to the front of the room. "Can any of you tell me why this might be the same killer?"

Cody Stone stood up and cleared his throat. "The killing M O is nowhere near the same. The victim isn't close, in any way to the other victims, but these guys have a need to kill. May be he couldn't get his hands on a female. May be he just lost it." He picked up the photo of Larry lying in a pool of blood. "This wasn't a robbery it's a vicious attack plain and simple." He threw the photo back onto the table.

"You're absolutely correct in your assumptions, Stone. This was a vicious attack from behind. Clearly not well thought out, a loss of control." Lee, very pleased with Cody asked "anyone else have anything to add?"

Kyle Hilliard took the floor. "He's still gripping the cleaning rag. That tells me he felt completely comfortable with whoever walked through the door. He knew him, didn't mind keeping his back to this person, continued to clean up."

"Good reasoning Hilliard. These are all the things Lt. Washington and I have been discussing. We think because of the brutality of the attack it is indeed the same killer. He needed to kill again and couldn't find a female, for whatever reason. He strolled into the store, not with the intent to kill, but the opportunity arose, being too great to ignore. He lost control."

The idea the killer can't control himself chilled Mark to the bone. "He's losing it, that's definitely not a good sign," he said to the group. "Once they get to the point of frenzy, or urgent need such as this, the only good thing is, he will start making mistakes."

"Right, but also he's much more dangerous now. Let's think about this, he had a pattern, he didn't particularly have a type except females. Now he's filling the urge with the most convenient person. This can happen anywhere, at any time. A loose cannon, completely unpredictable." Lee wanted to make sure they understood the full impact of this recent murder.

Lt. Washington stepped to the center of the room. "I've already pulled this case from CID, it's ours now. We aren't alerting the media to our opinion on this, and we don't want to frighten the public. We do need, however, to ask for a curfew, or push the buddy system. Make it as difficult as possible for him to get his hands on another unsuspecting victim."

"That's right, so Lt. Washington and I have already set up a press conference for both of you to press this issue home." He pointed at Mason and Stone. "Handle this carefully fella's we don't want to start a lynching out there."

"The media will meet you two here in front of the station at eight tomorrow morning. Have your statements prepared, and be ready for a lot of questions," Lt. Washington said.

"L.T. don't you think you are a better person to handle this? I think it would serve us well to soften the blow so to speak, and not saying because you're a female that would help, but because you are a ranking officer. People respond better to higher ranks." Mark hoped he said that right.

"Mark I appreciate what you're saying, we've thought about it, and believe this needs to come from the Task Force. We'll be standing by if you need us." She understood what he meant, and didn't take offense at all.

"L.T.'s right, the public will be told about the task force, as well as, any pertinent information you two give them. Make it clear, as of now, there isn't a curfew in place, but it could be forth coming soon." Lee pushed for the curfew, but Lt. Washington shot him down. This small town wouldn't take it well, and rather than arrest unnecessarily, which is what would happen, she elected to try scaring the hell out of the public first.

Mark and Cody nodded their understanding. Lt. Washington made certain they understood clearly what would be expected. She wanted to make sure they put the fear of God into these people. Push enough to get their attention, but not enough to cause panic. Let the killer know, they knew he was losing it.

TWENTY-EIGHT

The sun hid behind snow clouds. The temperature dropped over night, winter set in over the little town. Pretty soon a blanket of white would cover everything. The world white with purity would seem out of place in this terrified town. Thoughts of snow plows busily cleaning streets, people shoveling walk ways, children having snow fights, and building snowmen, had Cindy looking tiredly at her little boy.

Bryan always got up early, and just because she had a job that kept her up until three in the morning didn't mean he would change his ways. Tearing up a bowl of cereal, his little cheeks puffed out like a chipmunk made her heart melt. She laughed as she tweaked his nose. "Do you know how much I love you?"

He smiled through his mouth full and shook his head.

"Good because I love you all the way to the moon and stars and back," she told him.

"Mommy can we do somethin'?"

"We are going to do something, as soon as, you finish your breakfast we're going to the living room to watch cartoons." She hoped to rest on the sofa while he watched TV. Cindy despised mothers that used the TV as a babysitter, but today she would join their ranks. She needed rest, four hours of sleep wasn't sufficient for her.

"No I mean outside," he complained.

"I know what you meant, but I'm tired Bryan. Just let me rest a little while, then I promise I will take you out to play." She left him sitting there to finish his cereal and went to turn on the television set. A news alert caught her attention, and she sat down to watch.

"Freetown residents must take this seriously, this killer is randomly choosing his victims, any one of you, could be next," the detective stressed. "You must not go anywhere alone, use the buddy system at all times." He looked solemn, grave, standing there with a stern demeanor, he took on the media.

"Detective Mason, is it true this killer chooses young, attractive women only?" A report fired the first question.

"This killer doesn't seem to have a certain type he prefers. So let me stress again, any one of you, could be his next victim."

"Detective Mason, is that really being realistic? I mean serial killers usually focus on a certain type, are you saying this killer will just randomly pick up the most available person?"

"Let me make this perfectly clear, this murderer does not have a particular preference to any type, as far as, we can tell. He takes the easiest way out. He will take whatever or whoever he can get his hands on. He is a weak individual, with limited intelligence. No one is safe at this time."

"So far all of the women he has killed were taken from public places, is it safe to say it's enough to just stay in our homes?"

"So far that has been the case. However, I strongly suggest you keep everything locked up tightly, even when you're in your own home. He has not shown a particular pattern in any sense at this point. To second guess him, would be a mistake. We ask that you take everything we've said as if your life depends on it, because it does."

Cindy shivered at the detectives words. Looking around the room she decided to check her windows and doors, double checking they were locked.

"Have there been any new developments the public should be aware of concerning this killer?"

"Nothing that I can share with you at this time, just please we ask you to use the buddy system, stay home with everything locked tight if you're able, and don't take safety for granted. None of us are safe. If you see anything out of the ordinary, a car slowly driving in your neighborhood, a vehicle following you, stranger asking for help, anything at all, don't take it at face value call us, let us determine if it's important."

"Detective it's been a couple of weeks since the last killing, and this killer had been killing every two weeks or so, is it time for another murder? Do you feel he's on the prowl right now?"

"It's interesting you point out every couple of weeks, he hasn't shown a significant time period, we feel he's always on the prowl as you put it. We're going to put our contact information on the screen now. Please don't call us for any reason other than this killer on these numbers. These numbers are for the Task Force only. All other complaints or questions should be directed to the local police department numbers. Thank you." Mark and Cody stepped away from the podium even though the reporters continued firing questions at them.

Cindy found a station with cartoons then went to check every window and door in her house. She remembered the car that followed her yesterday, the handicap placard had given her a sense of relief, but this detective just said not to take anything for granted. She shuddered at the thought.

Bryan strolled into the living room "yay Spiderman is on." He plopped down onto the floor to watch the cartoon.

Cindy ruffled his hair as she walked past him. "I'm going to lay right here on the sofa, if I fall asleep you know not to open the door for any reason right?"

"Yes ma'am."

"If you need anything Bryan you tell me. Don't get into anything, and do not go outside for any reason." She kept her voice stern.

"Yes ma'am."

His manners had her smiling as she fell into a deeper sleep than she'd wanted.

The task force members gathered again in the designated room. Lt. Washington and Agent Marlowe were very pleased with the press interview.

"You did a great job out there," Lt. Washington said.

"Yeah, you got your point across very well." Agent Marlowe echoed the L.T.'s opinion.

"Thanks, let's just hope the public tuned in, and they pay attention. I'm feeling uneasy about this whole situation," Mark said.

A serial killer in their mist kept everyone on edge, the uncertainty of when he'd strike again and where was the hardest for them to accept. Law enforcement types are very controlling types, having no control in situations like these were the toughest for them to deal with.

"Well let's get to work." Cody Stone told his guys. "We got a killer to catch."

Both groups huddled to plan out their day. They each had the last two victims to deal with. The scenes had pretty much been the same, except the last one involving the pentagram. The victims were different as night and day in most ways, the only commonality being they had all been women, until Larry.

Eugene caught the press conference while he drank his morning coffee. He delighted in their confusion. "No particular type." He laughed out loud. The limited intelligence comment miffed him a bit, but what could he expect from keystone cops he thought to himself. Today would be difficult for him. His mother finally put to rest.

He found himself in his secret room. Picking up one of the many occult books he collected. He became cognizant of the fact he would need to complete these rituals quicker than anticipated.

Knowing he couldn't rush the gifts to his dark master in order to gain his healing quicker, he flipped through one of the books on rituals to formulate a new plan, speeding up the process. With his mother gone, he experienced a sense of panic in the timing he'd allowed in the original plan.

He groped for a way to use Larry's death as a gift, but finding no conceivable path he threw the book against the wall, breaking the spine. No hope for a swift resolution, he had no choice, still two must die.

His thoughts rushed to Lilly. High hopes of her being his ultimate sacrifice surfaced yet again. He had to have her. Chrissy lingered in his mind as well. They were both delectable in their own way. He licked his thin lips, his heartbeat accelerated, and the pull in his loins began.

He pictured them both laying side by side, tied to stakes, and naked, waiting for him to have his way with them. Lilly would show more fear, however, Chrissy would be a better challenge. Where Lilly is feminine, soft, and graceful, Chrissy is spirited, passionate, and feisty. Together they would be the ultimate gift. Making up his mind right then and there, he would have them both.

Today, using his grief he planned to find out Lilly's whereabouts. Then he'd figure out the best way to get both women. Laughing his wickedly evil laugh he walked out of his secret room. He suddenly gave thought to Cindy. She just might have to die still, he wanted her too. Rubbing his hands together he heard his stomach rumble, he needed some breakfast, coffee not enough to keep him going had him missing his mother yet again. She always made his breakfast.

Rifling through the fridge he turned his nose up at most

every item one would eat for breakfast. Closing the door he went to the pantry. Nothing, absolutely nothing, looked nor sounded appetizing. Finally deciding to ingest something to stop the noises his stomach made he settled on simple toast.

John and Mark talked for over an hour catching up this morning. Mark had been surprised to hear about Eugene's mother. He vowed to make time for the memorial service.

Almost giddy after sharing the news of the baby with John, Mark couldn't wait to talk to Lilly. He sure missed her bright smile in the morning and her warm welcome when he'd return from work.

The cold and empty feel of their house, upon his daily return from work, already getting old had him wishing he could just bring her home now. He didn't want to miss one minute of their experience with their baby. Shaking himself from the wishful thinking he made arrangements with his team for time off to attend the memorial service.

Eugene had never been a close friend, but he felt a need to be there, maybe out of respect for Mrs. Lowery. She had always been a sweet and kind woman. He'd felt sorry for her having to deal with Eugene and his whiney demands over being handicapped.

Mark had never really considered the limp a handicap, but Eugene milked it for everything he could. He remembered how he and John used to protect Eugene from some of the other boys. They were ruthless in their teasing sometimes, and he tried on several occasions to get Eugene to stand up for himself. Finally giving up on that idea he and John handled the bad situations on Eugene's behalf. Mrs. Lowery always thanked them with cookies or some other home baked treat.

He knew he had time to call Lilly before her doctor's appointment. He wanted to tell her about Mrs. Lowery anyway, so he picked up the phone and called her.

Their conversation had been a brief one since Lilly need to get out the door to her appointment. They talked about the baby, about missing each other, and the fact he'd told John. Lilly, of course, had been slightly disappointed as she wanted to be the one to tell Chrissy, but knew how important it was to Mark to tell his friend. She realized she may not get to tell anyone by the time she got back home, surely everyone would already know.

Chrissy and John went through the morning meal making plans for their day. He wanted to tell her about the baby, but knew she had a lot to do in a short amount of time. She wouldn't have time to sit on the phone with Lilly like she'd want to. He decided to wait. After a brief telephone call with Eugene about the food for the wake, she agreed to bring most of the dishes before the service to his home. She'd called Debbie, Joellen and Kaliegh, giving them a couple dishes each, to prepare. Sue had a competition and couldn't commit to helping out, which didn't impede Chrissy's momentum. Once she set her mind to something nothing stood in her way. She knew the only reason Debbie had jumped in with the rest of them on this idea of taking over the wake, and handling everything was because Eugene bothered her. She needed an excuse to get close to him.

Chrissy wanted this business with Eugene over and done as quickly as possible. The only reason she even agreed to help the man at all, had been for her husband. The team would take care of everything for the wake. Eugene had been absolutely thrilled by the time he and Chrissy's conversation ended, and why shouldn't he be. He had to do nothing, but show up for the service.

Running around the kitchen like a chicken with her head cut off Chrissy had already whipped up potato salad, coleslaw, had two different pies cooling, and a brisket baking. Looking around at all the progress she'd made in a few short hours had her plopping down onto a chair at the table, swiping the sweat from her forehead.

Now she had to iron her dress, steam a few wrinkles from John's suit, and get them out the door. Well at least, get herself, out the door, the guys would be by to pick John up.

TWENTY-NINE

The beautiful picture of his mother sat on an easel in front of the room, surrounded by flowers. The beautiful urn he'd picked out sat squarely in the center of a decorative table. The picture looked nothing like his mother it had to be forty years old. He'd chosen this particular photo because his mother looked young and beautiful, not old and miserable like she had at the end of her life.

Eugene, seated in a chair in the front row listened as the minister talked about how wonderful his mother had been. He droned on and on about all the people she'd helped in the church, and her endless hours of volunteer work.

Eugene noticed Mark Mason entered alone. Still no word on Lilly, but now he'd have an excuse to ask about her. Absently wiping nonexistent tears, he wished this boring imbecile would stop his preaching, and wrap the service up.

He stared at the Urn which held his mother's remains, and pictured how happy she'd have been to see the turnout in her honor. She truly had been a wonderful mother, and he wondered about his lack of tears today. He'd cried so much in the last couple of days, why couldn't he cry today?

Ducking his head in hopes of faking a moving show for everyone, he let small sounds escape, as if he just could not control the pain and anguish, he should've been feeling.

Guessing the lack of tears, and bereavement pain, must've been because his anticipation of getting a hold of Chrissy and Lilly stimulated pleasure, far exceeding the mournfulness today should've brought to him.

He felt the tenderness of a rub on his back here and there. He knew he gained attention of those closely seated to

241

him. Keeping a tissue tightly against his eyes he pushed in trying to make them water. He knew the masquerade would gain him a lot of attention. Eugene always enjoyed the way people felt sorry for you when someone close to you died. He remembered when his father passed a way it had been a delightful time for him, with all the well-wishers showering him with compassion. His mother had a hard time dealing with the loss, but he learned to appreciate the kindness he could get from people at times like these, when in reality they'd typically snub him, or ignore him altogether.

"We must avail ourselves to poor Eugene. He feels broken and alone, but we shall all be there for you son," The minister said looking at the hunched over young man falling apart, sitting by himself. He felt such sympathy for the young man, now left with no family at all. "We ask that you join us for a celebration of Lorene's life and memory following this service at the home of Eugene. For any of you that may need directions please see me immediately following this beautiful music Eugene has chosen to play for Lorene." The minister nodded toward the back of the room, and music began to flow softly.

Eugene knew that everyone would pass by now and give him their condolences. He snorted loudly pretending to compose himself, and gave his eyes one more poke each, successfully reddening his eyes and making them water. He certainly looked like a man in pain.

As everyone formed a line, Eugene readied himself for the impersonation, or pretense of the grief stricken son they all expected. He should get an Emmy for this performance he thought.

Excepting their whispered words of support, comfort, understanding, and sympathy, he actually felt the tears drop. Finally, he thought with relief. Thanking them, and even hugging a few, gave him immense pleasure at his acting ability.

Debbie Milo approached Eugene, wanting to touch him badly, but not sure how he would respond. She felt her skin crawl as she came closer to him. What on Earth is this man hiding? She wondered. Leaning down low she reached to slip her arm around his neck and say something sweet. Eugene reared back from her, as if he'd been burnt.

She stood abruptly, awkwardly, and said "I'm so sorry for your loss." Seeing his face fill with relief that she hadn't touched him, gave her a clear indication he knew somehow, to avoid physical contact with her. She moved on with the rest of the line of people, but kept looking back at him.

Not knowing how, or why, he knew not to touch that woman. What is it about her? He stared directly at her as she told him how sorry she was. Ha! She didn't even know him or his mother, why would she feel sorry? Resolving to get information on her today as well, he watched her follow the line of people.

Patricia went with Lilly to her first doctor appointment. Old Dr. Hill had been pleasantly surprised by Lilly's choice to see him.

"You have grown into a beautiful woman, Lilly, just as I knew you would. My, my, I believe you exceeded the beauty I thought you'd become." He stood back in the small room, not wanting to exclude Patricia from conversation.

"Oh stop it Doc. You'll make me blush." Lilly smiled.

"My little girl is expecting, Doctor Hill, can you believe that?" Patricia beamed.

"Wonderful news, I understand you took an OTC test, is that right?"

"Yes and the box said the test would be 95% accurate, I need you to confirm the results, and tell me everything is fine." Lilly blushed profusely.

"Well we should have an answer in a few minutes, I know they are already working on the urine sample you provided, so let's have a look. Patricia will you be staying for the exam?" He looked at her.

Patricia stood to step out of the room and Lilly called her back "Mom its fine, stay."

"Alright then let me just get my nurse in here and we can get this done." Dr. Hill opened the door slightly and waved the young nurse in.

The exam didn't take a full five minutes. The nurse began putting the instruments into a small sink in the corner, as Doctor Hill dried his hands from the rigorous washing he'd given them.

"I'm going to check on the test results, why don't the two of you meet me in my office once you're dressed Lilly." Doc walked out of the small room.

The nurse handed Lilly a couple paper towels then left the two of them alone. Patricia turned away giving her daughter privacy to get up, and dressed.

"Thank you Lilly, for allowing me to be part of this joyous time. You have no idea what it means to me."

"Mom, I should be thanking you for not having to do this by myself. If Mark couldn't be with me, there's no one else I would rather have here." Lilly finished dressing quickly. "All done, shall we?" She waited for her mom to follow her to Dr. Hill's office. Patricia smiled widely, and followed closely.

Dr. Hill sat behind his desk as the two women entered his office, "have a seat ladies," he gestured to the two chairs directly in front of his desk.

Lilly felt her nerves stretch tightly, what if she wasn't pregnant? How could she face Mark's disappointment? She reached over and took her mother's hand. Patricia patted her daughter's hand softly while they waited for the doctor to give them the news.

Doctor Hill looked over a single sheet of paper he held. A stern expression on his face he looked up at the two women waiting. He set the paper down and began. "Lilly, you are indeed pregnant." He smiled tentatively, "However, you have extensive scar tissue that concerns me." He stopped talking to watch Lilly. Observing the fear in her eyes he continued. "Lilly, don't look at me like that. The hard part, which is conceiving is already done, you will have to take it easy during your pregnancy, and then we can remove the scarred tissue. All I am saying is we need to watch you closer than others to make sure this tissue doesn't stop the placenta from attaching in a good spot. I'm sure everything is fine, but I want to do an Ultrasound to see where everything is."

"I won't lose this baby, will I?" Her eyes began to water.

"Now young lady, let's not get carried away. We are not going to consider that possibility at all. You've already made great strides in simply conceiving. I'd say the hard part is already over." He smiled at her.

"I won't be here for this entire pregnancy Doc I'll be going back to Freetown soon." Lilly squeezed Patricia's hand.

"That's fine, no problem, let's get you back into a room, do the Ultrasound and see what we're dealing with." He stood and walked over to Lilly. Taking her free hand he patted it kindly. "I'm sure everything is fine Lilly. You two wait here and let me get this set up."

"I'm not worried at all darling, you just put your faith in God, he'll take care of you both." Patricia tried to comfort her daughter.

Lilly silently prayed. The joy she should've been feeling held back by fear. Absently she rubbed her belly. No way would she let anything happen to this baby. She would stay in bed the entire time if she had to.

The young nurse poked her head in the office, "we're all set up if you'll follow me." She led them down a long hallway to the last room on the right. "There's a gown on the bed, Doctor Hill will be right with you." She closed the door quietly, leaving Lilly and Patricia alone again.

Patricia fumbled through her purse while Lilly put the gown on. Pulling a stick of gum out, she offered one to Lilly. After seeing the negative shake of her daughters head, she removed the wrapping slipping it into her mouth. "Smile honey, everything is fine, you'll see."

Doctor Hill came in smiling. "Are you ready?"

Lilly nodded her head, not trusting her voice to be steady.

"This is going to be cold." He laughed as he squirted the gel onto her stomach. Placing the probe onto her abdomen he began moving it around.

Patricia and Lilly watched the monitor for their first look at the baby. Watching the screen definitely showed the womb, but not much else.

Lilly turned to face Dr. Hill. "Do you see anything that concerns you?"

"Nope, everything looks good." He pulled the probe from her belly and smiled. "I don't think you're going to have anything to worry about." He wiped the gel from her skin.

"Really, everything looks normal? Did you see the baby?" she fired the questions one after another.

"Yes really, yes everything looks normal. No, it's way too early to see the baby. I would say you are about five weeks along. Do you have a physician in mind in Freetown, or do you need a recommendation?" He pulled her into a sitting position.

"I have my regular medical doctor, should I do a specialist?"

"I would certainly say an OB. Let me put a packet together for you to take back with you. This will save you from going through some procedures new doctors like to put patients through." He had printed two pictures from the machine. "I will include this with all the blood work and lab results. You get dressed it'll be waiting for you at the front desk." He squeezed her shoulder. "It sure is great seeing you again Lilly."

"You too Doc, and thank you so much for putting my mind at ease. I sure wish I would have you through this pregnancy." She'd meant that wholeheartedly.

"I'm sure you will be in good hands. I'll get a couple of names for you to contact. Good OB's." He smiled and left the room.

"See sweetie, all is well." Patricia stood and presented her back to Lilly so she could get dressed.

"He said five weeks along." Lilly laughed "we have a long way to go." She hurriedly straightened her clothing. "Thank you Mom."

"I don't know why you're thanking me, but you're welcome." Patricia opened the door.

THIRTY

The house filled to capacity, had Chrissy running around making sure the food, and drinks stayed plentiful. She hoped everyone would keep Eugene occupied and out of her way.

Eugene seemed happy to be the center of attention, Deb noticed. Standing just out of his range of sight, she watched his every move. He appeared to enjoy being surrounded and doted upon. Anytime someone mentioned his mother, he changed the subject quickly.

Chrissy came into the dining room, arms filled with dishes. Struggling to set them down she turned to Debbie "a little help here," she said exasperated.

Debbie rushed to her aid taking the dishes one at a time and setting them on the table. "I'm so sorry Chrissy, I should be in the kitchen helping you."

"No, no that's fine, Joellen's in there I just tried to carry too many things at once."

"Still, all I'm doing is watching that man enjoy all the attention he's getting." She thumbed over her shoulder toward the living room. "I don't know what to make of him."

Chrissy arranged the new dishes and removed the empty ones "who?" she asked totally unaware.

"Mr. Lowery, of course."

"Attention? What the hell are you talking about Deb?"

"Well the way I see it, he should be in mourning, right? Yet he's in there laughing, talking about anything, and everything, except his mother. I mean, he acts like this is a party, not a wake."

Chrissy stood with the empty dishes tucked in her arms. "He's a strange one for sure, but may be he's just trying to get through all of this."

Debbie looked at her friend, "I don't think so, I have a feeling he's putting on a great act of grieving, and every time I try to touch him, he pulls away from me. It's as if he knows if I touch him I may see the truth."

"Can you do that?" Chrissy asked in awe.

"Sometimes, yeah, but he refuses to make contact with me at all." They walked back into the kitchen together.

Joellen stood near the sink making a fresh pot of coffee, "you guys ready for tomorrow night?"

"Yeah, I just have a few things to pick up at the market before you all get to my house," Debbie said excitedly.

"Glad we chose your house? Most of us would've tried to get out of the extra work." Chrissy laughed.

"Nah, I love having you all over, we're going to have so much fun, I can't wait." Debbie smiled reassuringly.

"We are for sure, no men around pissing on our parade," Joellen said finishing the fresh coffee.

Chrissy handed Debbie a couple more dishes and took two herself "back to work ladies," she ordered. They still had so much food left Eugene will be eating it for days she thought.

"So you had complete success at The Ledge?" Eugene asked Craig Foster.

"Well I don't know I would say complete success, but we did have an interesting time up there."

"I've always been fascinated with the paranormal. Maybe I should go with you all sometime, you know, see for myself." Eugene turned to Mark. "Mark where is your lovely wife?"

Mark chewed the brisket he had in his mouth, holding up a finger to Eugene.

"Sorry, I didn't realize you were eating. Take your time." Eugene apologized to him.

Shaking his head he swallowed hard. "She's at her mother's for a while. I know she's very sorry she couldn't be here."

"Oh I understand. She's just visiting then?" He felt his pulse race.

"Yes."

Dare he enquire more? Yes he would, he needed to know when she'd be back. "So will she be gone long?" He sounded casually interested.

"Uh, no time line really. She may stay for quite some time."

Eugene didn't like the sound of that. "Surely not, you know her place is here, with you, not traipsing off visiting family." Damn, that definitely sounded harsh. "I'm not suggesting anything by my remarks of course, just a personal opinion." He back crawled.

Mark looked at him, he knew he'd always been a tad odd, but he seemed pissed. "No of course you weren't." He watched as Eugene turned back toward Craig.

"So do you think it would be possible to join you sometime, on an investigation?" Damn, he didn't want to end his conversation with Mason, but he'd blew that, might as well pick up where he left off with this idiot.

Craig jumped right back into the conversation, not even aware Eugene paid no attention to what he'd said as he continued to excitedly share experiences, and knowledge on paranormal events.

Eugene tried to appear interested in Craig's information, while he struggled for a way to engage Mason back into conversation about Lilly.

"…medium she helps us immensely," Craig finished.

Medium, what the hell had he missed? "I'm sorry, Craig." He swallowed hard, appearing to struggle with emotion. "What did you say about a medium? My mind keeps wandering on me, you know with the loss of mother and all."

"Quite understandable Eugene, I was just speaking of Debbie Milo, our group medium, and how she helps us in so many ways."

"Oh interesting, I've never met a medium before." He smiled, so that's what her deal is. His heart beat accelerated, did she know about him? Of course not, she would've already told someone, still it interested him. He needed to find out about her, and her gift. Gift, he almost laughed out loud at the idea. Those people are all fakes. Aren't they? He did feel strange when they stared at each other. Eugene decided to do a little research on the matter. He tuned into the conversation.

"She's very helpful, personable, always there for the team," Craig said.

"I'm sure she's an invaluable person to your team. Does she actually see dead people?" Eugene panicked for a mere second at the idea this woman could communicate with the dead. He knew deep down its all imaginary, for entertainment mostly, of course a way to make a living off the ignorant too. Pretty pleased with his acting ability to make this man believe he truly thought that possible.

"Yes, she not only sees them, she talks to them."

"Has she ever provided any of you proof that she has this ability?"

Mark watched Eugene while Craig talked of Debbie's ability. He found it extremely amusing that Eugene almost seemed frightened a minute ago when he found out Debbie talked to the dead. Maybe he'd had a moment of fear thinking his mother would chastise him in front of all these people for something or other. It had him smiling brightly until the thought occurred if someone not paying attention to this conversation noticed his amusement Mark probably appeared cold hearted, laughing at poor grieving Eugene. He almost busted out laughing just at that thought alone. Really Mason, get a grip he told himself. He really needed to get back to work anyway. Standing up he stretched his form exaggeratedly and said, "I'm going to have to get a move on, duty calls. Once again Eugene, I'm sorry for your loss."

"Yes, thank you. I'm thankful you made it to the service today. I understand you're very busy these days with the duties of that dreadful task force." Eugene stood to escort Mark to the door. He still wanted to ask about Lilly's return, but knew he wouldn't glean anymore information from this man.

"You know I thought the world of your mother, I wouldn't miss paying respect to her memory, Eugene."

"Of course, I wish Lilly could've made it as well."

"I'm sure she would have, had she been home."

The two men reached the door as John yelled out, "hey Mark, did you share your news with everyone?"

Mark's hand froze on the door knob. He hadn't wanted to say anything about their wonderful news at a time of sadness. How could he get out of it now? He turned to look at the room of expectant faces. "I didn't think this gathering in honor of Mrs. Lowery would be the proper place or time to say anything." Mark glared at John. He didn't know why it upset him so much to share the information here.

"News?" Eugene wouldn't let this slide.

"Perhaps we can all get together soon and discuss it." Mark smiled and pulled the door open.

"Nonsense, please tell us now. I'm sure we could all use some wonderful news, assuming its good news of course," Eugene pressed.

Mark shut the door and stepped back into the living room. The women had come in from the kitchen and everyone waited for Mark to tell them.

Clearing his throat he looked around the room. These were some of his and Lilly's closest friends, why did his gut scream at him to walk away? John nodded his head in encouragement. He stood there knowing he always followed his instinct and decided today would be no different.

"Thank you John, for reminding me, however, I know my wife wants to be around when we share our news. Unfortunately, today is not the day, but know when you do hear it, you'll understand why I regrettably have to wait."

Complaints from some of the more curious individuals started, and Mark shook his head emphatically. "No, I'm sorry, can't do it." He turned abruptly before he gave in. Quickly leaving the house he prayed John would keep his mouth shut and more importantly he wondered why he felt he shouldn't say anything.

Eugene turned his back to the room of guest and counted to ten silently, trying hard to control his anger. Why on Earth did he allow Mark to leave without finding out more about Lilly? Pulling on his trouser legs to smooth nonexistent wrinkles, he took a deep breath, and went back to his guests. He hated wearing this damn monkey suit and actually wanted everyone to leave.

John couldn't understand why Mark didn't tell everyone about the baby. Sure he knew Lilly would've loved to be here when the news came out, but she wouldn't be home for quite some time. Did Mark really plan to wait until her return?

People stood quietly in the room, waiting for someone to say something, but not wanting to be the one to break the silence. Eugene walked back over to the chair he'd occupied moments before. Sitting, he took a drink of his cocktail. He would have to be the one to get these idiots back on track, and conversation flowing again. He wondered what he should say after that awkward behavior by Mark. Setting his glass down he looked around the room at the people just standing or sitting around, John, he noticed looked bewildered.

"Well, I'm not sure we should stay on the subject, but it

is quite apparent John, that you know what's going on." Eugene watched the struggle in John's face. He wanted to tell the news Eugene could see it written all over the man's face.

John cleared his throat, "yes I do know, however, if Mark thinks it's important for Lilly to be there when this news breaks, then who am I to question that?"

Once again a few complained about being left out of the loop, but John shrugged his shoulders. He wouldn't be the one to tell.

Chrissy noticed her husband's determined look, these people would get nowhere with him, she, however, would once they were home.

THIRTY-ONE

Deb walked into the kitchen behind Chrissy. Her plan being to get her friend alone and pump her for information about the Mason's, but the plan went right out the window when she saw the elderly woman standing near the stove.

"Don't freak out on me, Chrissy, but you should know there's an older woman standing over there." She pointed at the stove.

Slowly nodding her head in acknowledgement to Deb, she backed out of the kitchen staring at the stove. Chrissy wanted no part of ghost. Not home, not here, not anywhere. "Let me know when she's gone."

Deb snickered and approached the woman. "So what do I owe your appearance here to?" The same woman that had talked to her earlier about 'stopping him,' stood before her.

The woman looked around the kitchen longingly, reaching for the tea kettle, her hand moved right through it. She pulled her hand back as if burnt and turned to Debbie. "You must stop him, he can't help himself."

"Yeah, I get that. What I don't get is who he is."

"Stop him!" The woman faded to nothingness.

"I will if you tell me who he is." Deb stood alone in the kitchen. Dropping her head she felt angry and frustrated. How the hell is she supposed to stop someone from doing something when she didn't know who it was? "Chrissy it's all clear, you can come back in here."

Joellen popped her head around the corner, "I'm sorry dear who were you calling?"

"Chrissy."

"Oh I'll let her know, I believe she's talking to John at

255

the moment. Did you need help with something?"

"No, thank you. I thought… oh never mind." Debbie went in search of her friend. She had to figure out who this woman wanted her to stop, but first she wanted to know about the Mason's.

Joellen stepped back allowing Debbie to whiz by. Shaking her head she looked around the kitchen, who had she been talking to, she wondered, the kitchen void of anyone else. She decided to begin the cleanup process. Surely everyone had reminisced enough already.

Lilly paced her bedroom, the itch to pack her belongings and head home intensified sharply after her short conversation with Mark. When he'd told her how much he wanted her there when they told they're friends about the baby. She had stopped short of blurting out her intentions.

She knew he would have a fit about her coming home, but if she were already home when he found out maybe he would be so happy to have her back, he'd just accept the fact and not fight over it. "Yeah right and pigs can fly."

With her mind made up, she threw her suitcase onto the bed and began filling it. Excitement grew rapidly at the idea she would be there when he got home from work. Of course, the argument with her mother would be unpleasant, but she knew her mom understood her need to be with Mark.

Patricia could hear Lilly moving around upstairs and thought she's pacing again. Lilly always paced when on the phone, it had been a nervous habit since her teen years. Patricia remembered the wall phone that used to hang on the kitchen wall and laughed out loud. Lilly had insisted they buy a one hundred foot cord so she could walk around while talking to her friends. Ducking and diving many times to get around their daughter in the kitchen had both of Lilly's parents annoyed and amused on several occasions.

She hoped the conversation between her daughter and son in law would result in Lilly accepting the fact she had to stay here, until it was safe to return to Freetown. Patricia knew Mark could keep Lilly safe, but he obviously had good reason to send her here to begin with.

Her tea grew cold as she sat there in thought. Reaching out for the cup and sipping had her grimacing. The tea now cold, simply couldn't be consumed. She took the cup back to the kitchen where she prepared a cup for both her and Lilly. Hopefully Lilly would be down in a few minutes and they could sip tea while they conversed about her expectations and questions concerning the new baby. She smiled to herself remembering how much she had needed her own mother's guidance when she became pregnant.

Lilly practically flew down the steps with her suitcase in hand. Not seeing her mother anywhere in site she snuck out to tuck the luggage into her trunk.

With the job done she turned to face her mother's interrogation that was sure to come. Hoping they wouldn't argue too much, she sailed into the living room just as her mom set a tray onto the cocktail table. "Oh how nice, you made tea," she said smiling.

"Yes, I thought we could talk a bit. You know, about the baby. I'm so excited Lilly, that you're here with me and I get to share my experience and wisdom with you." Patricia set the cups on saucers and patted the seat cushion next to her on the sofa.

Lilly sat down next to her mom, she would explain her need to go home soon, but right now she would enjoy her mother's company and advice. After all she thought, if she gave her mom the time to tell her all about what being a mom meant, she'd feel like she did her duty as Lilly's mother. She would get it off her chest and be a bit more understanding about Lilly's leaving.

"There goes those flying pigs again," Lilly muttered.

"What, dear?"

Picking up her cup of tea she asked "what did you want to tell me?"

Cindy opened her eyes slowly, the sunshine filtering through the curtains told her, she'd slept longer than she had expected. Springing herself to an upright position she saw Bryan still sitting quietly in front of the television watching a cartoon he typically didn't pay attention to. What a sweet little boy he is, she thought. Obviously he knew she needed to sleep. He had not bothered her at all.

"Come here munchkin," she said quietly.

He looked over his shoulder and smiled. "You're awake." He ran to her jumping into her lap. "Now can we go outside and play?"

Rubbing his head she smiled back, "don't you want some lunch first?"

As if on cue his stomach rumbled. "Okay, but I was good so we get to go outside, right Mommy?"

"Yes, Bry, right after we eat." She set him down and stretched. Getting up she looked outside half expecting snow to cover everything. No snow yet, definitely a good thing she thought. "What do you want for lunch, lil' man?"

"Ravioli's," he shouted.

"Ravioli's it is."

Halfway through opening the can of Ravioli's with the electric can opener it stopped. She readjusted the can and push again, but the thing just hummed. After several more tries she finished the rest by hand with her handheld opener. Tossing the electric opener into the trash she chalked it up as another waste of money.

Bryan stood to the side of his mother and watched as she prepared his lunch. "Is Grandma coming to watch me again tonight?"

"I sure hope so. Did you have fun with your Grandma last night?"

"She's okay I just wish you could stay home."

"I know baby, but we've talked about this, right?"

"Uh huh." He walked over to the table and crawled up onto a chair.

Cindy turned the stove off and pulled two bowls out to fill. As she finished filling the bowls she made up her mind to surprise Bryan with a glass of soda, for being so good while she slept. Very rare occasions did she allow him to drink soda pop.

Sitting his bowl in front of him she warned of the meals hotness and turned to pour their drinks. She could hear Bryan blowing loudly on his bowl and quietly enjoyed the moment.

Eugene knew the women were cleaning up, which meant soon, all of his company would depart. He still hadn't had a chance to corner John on the news Mark refused to share earlier. No way would he let that go, he wanted to know what's going on, and intended to find out.

The conversation finally wound down about the apparition they had on video from The Ledge. At first it had intrigued him, but the more he listened the more he believed it to be a bunch of bull. After all, if an apparition had truly been there, why couldn't one see it with their own eyes? Only on video my ass he thought. John had assured him he would be happy to show him the video anytime he wanted to see it. He would make it a point to view that video and have the last laugh.

"So John, why don't you share Mark's news with all of us? I'm sure he wouldn't mind." He gave it one last shot.

John stirred uncomfortably, his leg throbbing, and his patience with Eugene all but gone. "No can do buddy, if

Mark wanted all of you to hear it, he would've told you himself."

"You could tell he wanted to John, but he owes his wife the opportunity to be with him, you don't. Come on, tell us," Eugene pushed.

Craig, Matt and Dave sat quietly, while Vinny gave John some support. Seeing John rub his knee and appear to be thinking of a way to say whatever he was going to say Vinny put his hand up. "John, I wouldn't want Mark Mason on my bad side. He wants to wait for Lilly to be here to share whatever it is they have to say, I would wait." He looked over at Eugene, "just sayin'."

Trying to think of a polite way to tell Eugene he wasn't about to tell them anything had him silently thanking Vinny. Out of all the team members, he would've been the last John would've expected this to come from. Vinny usually cutting up and joking about everything had an edge to his voice today. John picked up on the meaning behind his friend's words. He didn't like Eugene. "Oh I'm not about to get Mark on my bad side Vinny, but Thank You for understanding. I think it's time to see if my lovely wife is ready to hit the road." He reached down for his crutches.

"Here let me." Matt picked the crutches up and helped John to his feet. "Better yet wait right here." He hurried out of the room to find Chrissy.

The women were just about finished up. A few more dishes needed washing and a couple counters to wipe and they could call it a day.

"Hey Chrissy, John's ready to go. You about finished in here?" Matt startled them.

Chrissy turned to the young man and shook her head. "Not just yet, I have a little more to do."

"He looks like he's in some pain. Maybe I should just take him home, that way you can finish up whatever you need to do."

"Would you mind?"

"Nope not at all, I'll go tell him."

"Why don't the rest of you go ahead and take off, I got this little bit. Thanks for all of your help today." She shooed them out. It had been a long day and she knew it would go quicker without conversation.

Eugene saw the last of them out the door, thanking each for coming and helping him. He closed the door and looked toward the kitchen. He could hear Chrissy in there moving about. His hip hurt him badly from all the up and down activity of the day. Absently rubbing his hip area he went to the bathroom for medication. Looking in the mirror at his own image he suddenly felt like he'd been hit by lightning. She was here, all by herself!

Quickly swallowing the pills he entertained ideas on how to keep her without anyone knowing. Damn what an opportunity this had become. He had his secret room to hide her in all he needed was a way to get rid of her car. That should be easy enough.

Chrissy dried the last dish and wiped the counters down, the immaculate kitchen peaceful, after all the bustling activity today. Laying the dish towel over the sink she picked up her purse and left the room.

Eugene almost collided with her coming out of the hall as she came out of the kitchen. "All finished?"

She jumped back, "oh my, I didn't see you there. Yes, there's plenty of food left over in the fridge. I'm going to get out of your hair."

"What? You have been a blessing today Chrissy, please come sit for a minute. You've worked yourself silly today." He tried to guide her toward the living room.

"No thank you, I really have to get home. I'm sure John's going to need something or other with his leg, you understand."

He felt his anger rise, he couldn't let her just walk out. "Nonsense, I'm sure he wouldn't mind if you had a drink with me after all you've done today."

"No really Eugene, I have to go. I didn't mind helping you out at all. That's what friends do for each other." She pushed past him towards the front door.

Panic filled him he couldn't let her walk out that door. Her hand reached for the door knob and he grabbed her from behind, "I'm afraid I can't let you leave." He began pulling her backwards toward the hallway. "I insist you stay." He huffed hard and fast. The medication not quite kicking in yet shot pain from his hip to his foot. He struggled to hold on tightly, knowing he could make her pass out from lack of air, but he'd have to be careful he didn't break her neck in the process.

Chrissy tried to pull free, she couldn't scream. Fighting him with all her strength she couldn't get out of his grip. "What are you doing?" The question coming out almost guttural, he had such a tight hold against her neck she had to fight for air.

No time for talking he struggled to get her to his secret hideaway. He would answer her questions later. The most important thing right now needed to be securing her in the room and taking care of her car. Pulling and tugging winded him terribly. Almost there he thought. The idea he had her, exhilarated him, giving him the strength he needed to finish the job. Finding the lever to open the hidden door proved to be an obstacle, as he held his query tightly "dammit hold still a minute," he shouted at her.

Chrissy didn't let up, she continued to fight, she had no idea where he tried to take her, but she wouldn't make it easy for him. Scratching and digging her nails into his arms didn't seem to have any effect on him at all. Kicking her legs behind her, she barely got momentum to make contact with him. Her mind frantically trying to come up with idea's to escape even as she felt the blackness rushing in.

Her limp body, too heavy for him, dead weight, he slowly lowered her to the floor. Finding the lever he opened the passage to his secret room. Dragging her body into the room he left her lying on the floor. The room would be pitch black when she awakened, her fear would be delicious, if only he could stay for that. Stepping out he closed the door. "Now to get rid of your car," he said gasping for air and bending over with his hands on his knees trying to pull oxygen into his lungs. She had almost overpowered him twice.

Her purse contents had scattered across the floor as she fought with him. He gathered the stuff up shoving it back inside the purse keeping only her keys. Taking a look outside, he noticed her car on the street near the house next door. Formulating the plan in his head as to, how to get rid of the car, he went to his room and quickly changed into jeans and a thick hooded sweatshirt. He knew he'd have to drive it away from here. The only question he had to answer was how he'd get back home. His leg didn't allow for long walks, he certainly couldn't ask anyone for a ride back. He would just have to take his time and figure it out. Nothing, absolutely nothing, could lead them back to him.

He put his gloves on and wiped her purse down completely. Throwing the hood of his shirt over his head he headed for her car.

Matt got John settled and gave him two pain pills. After waiting almost an hour for Chrissy to get home he decided to leave. John snored in the recliner and he knew it wouldn't be long till Chrissy made it home, there's no reason he couldn't go ahead and leave. Pulling the door behind him he realized he couldn't lock it, but didn't worry too much since John slept

263

inside. No one in their right mind would take on John Bingham to burglarize a house. Even with a broken leg he laughed at the thought, and left.

Mark caught up with Ian and Ricky at the residence of Shannon Snydecki, the third victim. Shannon had been a twenty seven year old woman with dark brown, almost black, hair, and bad acne scarring on her face. She had been a plumb girl and by all accounts pretty much a loner. Ian and Ricky had questioned her friends, family, and coworkers, while Mark attended the memorial. They quickly filled him in on the information they'd gathered, which wasn't much.

The house she had lived in lacked style in more ways than one. The small postage stamp front yard held little grass and no shrubbery at all. Ian put the key in the lock and the tumbler turned. The three men entered the frigid entry hall. Someone had turned the heat off inside and they could see their breath coming out in puffs of white.

They split up taking different rooms to search, knowing they would follow behind one another in case someone missed something. Mark took the bedroom. Shannon must've been an organizer, everything in its place. The full size bed had been made her last morning here, the dresser and small night stand held a few photos, he assumed were family. Closet and dresser held clothes neatly hung or folded. A few shoe boxes hid old checks and receipts, but no letters or personal correspondence.

Ian rummaged through the kitchen, not finding anything of use except a small writing tablet next to the telephone. He reached for a pencil and gently scraped back and forth trying to see the last message wrote. It had been nothing more than a shopping list.

Ricky sat on the living room floor going through all the CD's and videos in the TV stand. Checking the DVD player he found a movie disc and replaced it in the plastic box it had come in. Wading through the little information he came to, he hoped the other two made better progress. All he could tell from what he'd been through, simply put, had him feeling sorry for the young woman. She must've been very lonely. The ton of movie's she had collected provided her only entertainment, as far as he could tell.

After all three finished up they decided not to bother with a follow through on any of the rooms. It had been quite apparent Shannon had no life. She seemed to merely exist for the short time she'd been granted to live. Not that it made her death any easier for any of them. It seemed to make it more pathetic and sad.

They left and met up with Stone's team for dinner.

THIRTY-TWO

Debbie read the same paragraph at least three times before setting the book aside. She needed to figure out why Eugene refused to touch her or allow her to touch him. Her skin crawled with anticipation of touching him not knowing what to expect. She'd tried several different times to make this happen, yet he always found a way around her feeble attempts.

This book had been a last ditch effort to quiet her mind. She would think of something, somehow, she had to touch him. Pacing the floor of her small living room she kept going over the attempts she'd made today, and the way he recoiled at the very idea of her touch. How could he know that if he allowed her to simply put her hand on him she may be able to see what others could not?

Briefly glancing at the clock on her mantle she thought about calling Chrissy. Perhaps Chrissy could assist her with this somehow. Of course, she knew her friend had to be beat after the long day they'd had. All the running around she'd done to make Mrs. Lowery's wake a success had taken its toll on her friend. She could still see the weariness in Chrissy's body language while she shooed them all out of the Lowery residence earlier this evening. Debbie felt guilty leaving her friend there to finish up on her own.

No tomorrow would be soon enough, she'd let Chrissy relax tonight. Besides she needed to come up with a plan before asking Chrissy to help. Not that her friend would do much relaxing, with her husband nursing a broken leg.

Sitting back down she lifted her book vowing to shut her mind off. Reading her favorite paranormal author whisked her away to exotic locals, with hunky hero's involving interesting circumstances. She wished this particular author could zing her books out quicker.

As she settled into the same chapter again, her mind refused to focus on the book, and she thought back to the woman in the kitchen. The same woman that had been here warning her about him whoever the hell, him might be. Over the years of dealing with her gift she never took it for granted. This woman bothered her and not in a little fashion. There's something important about her message, and Deb knew this as sure as she knew she could see the dead. "Who is he?" she asked aloud to the empty room hoping the woman would visit again. Closing her eyes she concentrated on the woman. Breathing deeply, in through the nose, out through the mouth, over and over, picturing the woman in her mind's eye.

The hair on her neck began to rise and she could feel goose bumps lining her arms and legs. Slowly opening her eyes she looked around the still empty room. "Are you here?" she asked quietly, knowing she wasn't alone.

The spine-chilling quiet pressed heavy against Debbie. She knew someone, or something waited in the room with her. "It's all right," she whispered. "Show yourself to me."

The television came on, the stereo started blaring, the lights flicked off and on. Debbie sat back against the sofa. Pulled her legs up to her chest and let the spirit have the tantrum it so desperately wanted to throw. She would let it go for a minute or two, but then her neighbors would start to complain about the noise. Leaning her head back she laughed hysterically, this is one pissed off spirit she thought. Finally gaining control of herself she picked up the remote and turned the TV off, walking casually she did the same for the stereo. "If we're done having fun here, I'm ready to listen."

She sat down on the sofa and waited.

* * *

Chrissy woke up to total blackness, not a crack of light appeared anywhere. Her head throbbed unmercifully. Sitting up she realized the hardness below her must be a floor, but where is she? Feeling terror grip her heart, she tried to concentrate and remember what had happened. She remembered finishing the kitchen at Eugene's, but nothing after that. Her head swam in the darkness, knocking her equilibrium off. Shutting her eyes she scooted forward reaching for anything tangible. Heart thudding loudly in her ears as her hand hit something solid. Feeling the surface her fingers splayed open and wide against the wall, she stood on shaky legs. Keeping her eyes tightly shut she moved down the wall feeling her way around the black space.

Chrissy knew she had to be in a house somewhere, the temperature felt comfortable. She felt a lever of sorts, pulling and twisting she prayed it was a door. When nothing happened with all the tugging, the horror filled thought slammed into her, she was being held captive. She began pounding and screaming at the top of her lungs.

When no one came, she knew something terrible had happened. The door felt solid and tightly fit, not budging under the beating it took. Exhausted she continued feeling further down the wall, she found shelves full of books, books everywhere she could touch. Getting down onto all fours she crawled across the floor. It wasn't a very big space she made it across to the opposite wall in no time. A huge wooden and velvet chair the only furniture she found. No windows, no carpeting, nothing but books and a chair. How odd she thought. Sitting in the chair she willed her mind to remember.

Eugene's hip ached badly. He dropped Chrissy's car off a mere mile and a half from his home. The cold weather seeped into his bones making the pain in his hip almost unbearable. His limp, severe due to the pain he waddled duck like, almost home he told himself pushing hard to make the last block.

He wondered if Chrissy enjoyed the warmth of her room, he sure would have. One more block then he could take his pain pills and settle down in the warmth of his house. He wouldn't bother Chrissy tonight he knew how hard she'd worked all day. Picturing her limp body on the floor of his secret room gave him slight relief from the grinding pain. She looked so beautiful lying there on the floor. This whole thing had been so damn easy, he'd thank her for that. If she behaved he would keep her until he had Lilly.

That should make her happy, to have her friend there with her. They could comfort each other and try to outsmart him. He laughed out loud.

Ditching the car had been easier than he'd thought. He made sure to wipe everything down even though he wore gloves, one couldn't be too careful. He had left the keys in the ignition and Chrissy's purse on the seat, wallet, money, credit cards, all there. They'd know it wasn't a robbery.

Poor John he thought, a broken leg isn't the worst of your problems my friend. He snickered and tipped his hood back as he saw a neighbor sitting on his porch. "Good evening Mr. Samuels how are you tonight?"

"Enjoying the quiet, how about you young man?"

Eugene stopped for a minute giving his hip a rest. "A little silly I'd have to say."

"Oh, how's that?"

"I thought a good brisk walk would help loosen my joints, but the cold is a bit too much I think."

Shaking his head the old neighbor acknowledged Eugene, "yeah exercise isn't all it's cracked up to be."

Eugene laughed "you got that right. Well I better get inside and see about getting off my feet for a while. You have a good night sir."

"Thank you Eugene, and by the way, the Mrs. and I were

real sorry to hear about your momma. She was a good woman."

"Yes she was thank you." Eugene limped on home snorting through his sudden anger. Why did these people insist on acting like they give a shit about my mother?

Cindy played outside with Bryan for most of the afternoon. They had a nice dinner and most of a movie before her mom showed up. Now she stood in Tate's and looked around. The place filled up again quickly, Sam did good business and her tips were nothing to sneeze at. Slapping the tray against her leg she smiled at a group of older gentlemen. These guys would be good tippers she thought as she slipped over to get their order before Maggie could beat her to it.

"What'll ya have?" she asked beaming her brightest smile at them.

They were sliding their jackets off and placing them over the backs of their chairs. Nodding a head here, or holding up a finger there, she waited. Once they had settled themselves the competition to order first began.

"Whoa, fella's I'm good, but I'm not that good. Now, one at a time." She winked and joked.

When they couldn't decide who should go first Cindy placed her hand on the shoulder of the man to her right. "How about you sugar?"

He beamed up at her it had been some time since a pretty young thing called him sugar. He gave his order and then around the table they went, each one of them vying for her undivided attention. She giggled and laughed, played the game of sweetness to ensure her tip, but never allowing anyone to lay a hand on her body. Which they found out quickly, as she turned to take their order to the bar when ole' Mr. Grabby reached out to take a handful of butt-cheek, while smiling at his buddies. Cindy turned and slapped him so hard across the face everyone in the bar stopped what they were doing to watch, including Sam and Maggie.

"Don't you ever touch me again," Cindy said through gritted teeth.

The old guy sat there rubbing his cheek and blushing from embarrassment. "I'm sorry miss, you're absolutely right. I had no reason to do that and I apologize."

His friends all sat there staring between the two. Cindy looked directly at each of them and walked away.

"What the hell got into you Richard?" Sam asked as he approached the table.

"Man I didn't mean anything by it. You know me Sam," Richard said.

"Yeah, I do and you know no one touches my waitresses. That's not what they're here for." He put both hands on the table and leaned down.

"I know, I'm sorry, guess I just got carried away, it won't happen again." Richard stood and held his hand out to Sam. After the two men shook hands, Sam went back behind the bar.

"Hey sorry about that, they're usually good guys. You won't have any more problems out of them, I promise." Sam patted her hand, you okay?"

"Yeah, thank you," she gave the drink order.

Maggie put her arm around Cindy's shoulders, "we don't usually deal with that type of behavior mostly the guys that come in here are respectful. I don't know what the hell got into Richard he's never acted like that before. You okay hun?"

Cindy shook her head, "yeah, I'm okay. Guess I just didn't expect that."

"Don't you worry hun, Sam takes good care of his staff, if it happens again they'll find themselves tossed outta here," Maggie assured the woman as picked up her drink order and headed toward the room with the pool tables.

Sam busied himself filling Cindy's order. He hated it when men treated women like pieces of meat. Not one to ever allow that kind of behavior in his business, hiring people of high moral fiber and refusing to let scum surface.

Cindy picked the tray of drinks up and went back to the table. Laying each drink in front of her customer she remained quiet. Truly at this point she didn't give a fig about a tip. No joking or smiling, just plain and simple service. When she finished she asked if they needed anything else. Her tone implied no nonsense would be tolerated.

Richard felt terrible, he'd never treated women in that manner and had no idea what had gotten into him. He wanted to apologize again, but knew it not only wasn't needed, but would do no good. He gave a tentative smile at the young woman and slid a twenty dollar bill toward her "this is not for the drinks ma'am, it's for you."

She looked at the money, knowing he gave it to her because he felt bad and not because she'd given good service, she slid it back to him, "thank you, but you don't have to do that. We understand each other now, right?"

He pushed it back again, "yes we do, and yes I do. Please take it, you've been a wonderful waitress so far and I'm sure there will be plenty more for you before tonight is over."

Looking around the table at the smiling faces Cindy picked the twenty up and stuffed it in her apron pocket. "Thank you. If you all need more drinks give a holler," she said as she strolled away.

Lilly hit the road after a slight argument with her mother. Not allowing it to become a heated argument she had headed it off with an invitation for her mother to come stay with them. Patricia knew how much it meant for her daughter to be home right now, and she promised to take the invitation into consideration. Now all Lilly had to do is devise a plan to deal with Marks anger over her return.

She planned to head that argument off too, she just wasn't too sure how yet. Driving in the dark with no traffic is a much better time to travel the interstate. She hated rush hour traffic with a passion. Her gas tank had been full when she left, there would be no reason to stop during her trip, if her bladder cooperated that is.

Recently it seemed she spent more time in the bathroom for one end or the other. These first few months are the most difficult she told herself. The morning sickness and constant urinating had her smiling, knowing in the end they would have a beautiful baby. Turning up her radio she sang loudly and danced in her seat. This trip would be over soon, she might as well enjoy it while she can.

Her mother had promised not the tell Mark Lilly left, she only hoped he wouldn't call. Her mother wasn't a good liar and she knew her husband would see right through it. Finishing up the song she lowered the volume and called her mom.

"Hello Lilly, no Mark hasn't called," Patricia answered both phone and question before Lilly even said hello.

Laughing she asked "now Mom what if this had been Mark calling instead of me?"

"Don't be silly I have caller ID I know who is calling, Lilly. How are the roads so far? Are you making good progress?"

"Oh true sorry didn't think about caller ID. The roads are good for most of the way, very little road construction going on right now. Yes I'm making great progress, a little over two hours to go."

"You're going to text me when you arrive right?"

"Yes Mom, I will text you. I love you."

"Love you too."

The conversation ended quickly, and Lilly wondered if Mark would be home when she got there. She had no idea of the hours he worked right now. Turning the radio off completely she began thinking about what she wanted to say to him. He would make a big issue of it, but she anticipated that, she had to prepare exactly what she'd say to whatever argument he threw at her.

Of course, knowing him as well as she did, she would have it down pat before arriving home. Every little angle considered and answered.

Being married as long as they have she knew how he would react, she needed to be ready for battle. Mark didn't like it when things didn't go his way, and this time they were not going to. She wouldn't be going back to her mother's no matter how much he demanded. Nope, Lilly would stand her ground she wanted to be home with her man.

Eugene's pain killers kicked in rapidly. He found himself sitting in the quiet living room pondering the psychic woman. His energy levels hitting a new high, he determined the problems she could cause if he allowed her to touch him. Especially now that he had Chrissy locked up in his home.

He'd wanted to check on Chrissy, but didn't feel up to all the questions she surely wanted answered. No, he needed to drop everything, go get the psychic lady and hold her here too. This is all getting out of hand he thought. Chrissy, Lilly, the psychic lady, he had to have them all. Dammit, he didn't have much choice now, gathering his coat and gloves he left the warmth of his home under the cover of darkness.

He didn't relish the idea of killing the psychic. Psychic? Did he really believe in such stuff? He needed to look into the paranormal realm of things a bit more and see what if anything in psychic awareness has been proven. Eugene believed in dark power without a doubt, but to what extent?

Debbie tossed her book aside. "Look if you want my help you have to help me," she said to the still empty room. "Who are you?"

Getting up she pulled a chilled bottle of wine out of the fridge and helped herself to a glass while she waited. "I can help you," she tried again. The wine glided smoothly down her throat, she hoped it would help to relax her some. This had been a long cumbersome day in more ways than she cared to count. "Hello?"

Sipping more wine and settling back into the comfort of her sofa, her mind wandered again to the older woman. Did she refer to the killer running loose in Freetown or someone else? Why couldn't he stop himself? For that matter what couldn't he stop himself from doing?

"Nothing but questions, you have the answers. Are you going to help me here?"

The front door blew open and the wind pushed Debbie's hair back. Standing she went to close the door. "Nice parlor trick, now can we get serious here?"

Latching the deadbolt she leaned heavily against the wooden door. "I'll tell you what, I'm going to sit back down and enjoy my wine, but if you don't make an appearance soon, I'm going to bed. Tomorrow is going to be another long day and even though I would love to help you out, I just don't have time for this"

Eugene crept along the front of the small frame house. The windows cast an eerie shadow of light on the lawn. The blinds lifted, left no barrier to keep him from seeing inside the house.

Keeping low to the ground he snuck up to the large picture window for a peek inside.

Deb pushed off the door and walked to the sofa. Hoping the spirit stopped these shenanigans being played so they could get down to business. Lifting her wine glass she drank deeply, closing her eyes and relaxing, at least outwardly.

The creaking sound of the rocking chair had her alert once again. There she sat, the old woman. Debbie set her glass down and stared back at the hollow gaze taking her in. After a few seconds the old woman stopped rocking and sat forward. "Why can't I touch things? I go right through them." Her bewildered expression caught Debbie off guard.

"You're no longer of this world, surely you know that."

"Yes I have come to that conclusion. However, I am still here. I know I shouldn't be, but you're the only one I can talk to, the only one that sees me. How is this possible?"

"I have a gift."

The old woman stood, "a gift? I spent my life a Godly woman, why would an advocate of Satan be the only link to this world for me?"

An advocate of Satan, what the hell is she babbling about? Debbie stood too, "I'm sorry, did you just call me an advocate of Satan?"

The woman looked at Deb, confusion written across her face. "Are you denying this?"

"You're damn right I'm denying it. I have a gift, a God given gift. If you can't see that then I don't know what to tell you. Why are you bothering me if you think I'm no good?"

"It seems I have no other choice."

"Oh you have other choices, move on go into the light. Get out of my house." Debbie stood with hands on hips glaring defiantly at the audacity this spirit had. How dare she assume such stupidity?

Eugene watched the woman talk to herself. She appeared pissed off and yelling. He didn't have time for crazy people, which he thought she may be now, but he couldn't take a chance. He walked around the house looking for the easiest method in.

"I won't apologize for my beliefs, I will go now, but you must stop him soon." The old woman sat back down in the rocker.

"I don't know who he is, unless you give me more, I can't do anything to stop anyone." Deb wasn't so keen to help this lady after all.

The old lady appeared to not hear Deb any longer. Her gaze distant she didn't move.

"Did you hear me?"

Eugene checked the back door, it opened quietly. Surprised to find it unlocked he stuck his head inside and listened.

"Great, just fucking great, go ahead and disappear again. Don't come back you silly old bat." Debbie finished off the glass of wine. She was tired of spirits coming and going, wanting her to do all the work. Picking up the empty glass and half empty wine bottle she decided to go to bed.

Eugene slipped into the small, warm kitchen. Closing the door quietly he turned the lock. Crossing the room he wanted to find out who the psychic's talking to. He couldn't risk another person being here, and just because he had not seen someone else didn't mean she's a lone.

The light flicked on as Deb entered the kitchen. Setting her glass in the sink and the bottle in the fridge she felt another presence. Hanging her head she decided to ignore it, she wasn't about to deal with any more unproductive bullshit tonight.

Eugene stepped up behind her putting his gloved hand over her mouth he whispered in her ear, "who else is here?"

Debbie panicked as she struggled against the arms holding her tightly. Shaking her head side to side trying to pry the hand from her nose and mouth, her air intake became minimal and she felt light headed.

Eugene pressed his gloved hand tighter to her face. He

knew she couldn't breathe, but quite frankly he didn't care if she died all the sudden. Struggling to keep a hold of her as she fought hard, he toyed with the idea of just snapping her neck. "Stop fighting me, you bitch," he demanded.

Her lungs burning from lack of air, Debbie desperately tried to remove the hand from her face. His breathing labored from the fight she put up. Finally she could no longer struggle, her body dead weight became too much for him. He dropped her hard onto the tile flooring. Looking around he knew now they were alone. No one had come to help her and surely if anyone were here they would have.

"Who the hell were you talking to?" he asked her limp form. Going into the living room he looked around. Halfway closing the blinds he took a minute before continuing to check the rest of the little house. He had to hurry she wouldn't be out for long.

Thirty-Three

John woke up to darkness. He didn't even hear Chrissy come in. Wondering what time it was he pushed his reclined closed and reached for his crutches. Finding them on the floor next to his chair he got up switched on the light and noticed Chrissy didn't sleep on the couch tonight. He went to the bathroom, grabbed a couple more pain pills and made his way to the stairs.

Dauntingly looking up the staircase he decided not to try it, he'd see her in the morning. Going back to his chair he took his pills and went back to sleep, totally forgetting to look at the time.

Chrissy sat in the only chair she could find in the dark room. She finally remembered Eugene attacking her and knew she had to be in his house somewhere. The question is why? For the life of her she could not figure out why he attacked her. It seemed like forever since she woke up, but surely it had only been a short while. How long before John came to get her, she wondered. Eugene is an idiot to think he can get away with this. Just what the hell was he thinking she asked herself for the hundredth time?

Maybe he lost his mind, had a moment of insanity over the loss of his mother and being left alone. Yes that had to be it. She could persuade him to forget this ever happened if he would just open the damn door. She couldn't even hear him moving around. Where the hell is he?

This behavior's odd even for someone as strange as Eugene. She thought back trying to remember anything she may have said or did to give him the idea she didn't want to leave, but all she'd done was help the man.

It wouldn't be her problem when he had to face her husband. She shuddered at the very idea. John would kill Eugene. Chrissy closed her eyes and felt her way back to the door. Placing her ear to the door she listened, no sounds at all. Banging on the door again made her hand hurt, she opened her fist and slapped at the door repeatedly. "Eugene," she screamed, "open this damn door."

Her palm itched from slapping the wood so hard, she turned and slid down the door to the floor where she sat and cried.

Eugene had managed to get Debbie into his back seat. She wasn't as hard to maneuver as he'd feared. Her hands tied behind her back and tape across her mouth would insure his safety to drive. He arranged the rearview mirror allowing him means to keep watch, knowing she'd gain consciousness before reaching his home. He certainly didn't put anything past her, including kicking him in the back of his head. He should've tied her legs together too he realized frowning at her through the mirror.

Eugene patted himself on the back in his mind for remembering to take her cell phone, purse and keys. The only thing he couldn't dispose of was the car, but the police would surmise someone picked her up. Everything in her home had been left tidy, nothing amiss to make them think foul play could be involved. The living room lamp left burning, the doors locked up nice and tight. Yes he'd done a good job.

Deb began to stir in the back seat. Moaning lightly as her head pounded unmercifully. She couldn't move her arms they felt numb, her legs lifted and moved. Turning her head she found herself gazing into the face of Eugene Lowery. Trying to talk gave way to awareness of the tape covering her mouth.

"Ah, I see you've joined the living." He laughed at his

pun. "Don't struggle now you may cause injury to yourself. Just be a good girl and enjoy the ride."

She struggled even more, tearing at the ropes burning into her wrist, wreathing around the seat trying to get her arms in front of her body.

When he saw what she tried to do he knew a moment of fear. "Stop that," he shouted at her. "You're going to hurt yourself."

She lay still for a minute then continue trying to bring her legs up and her arms down. It seemed an impossible feat since all she could feel of her arms were a throbbing heaviness. The blood flood must've stop circulating due to the pressure of her weight on them and the unnatural angle of being held behind her back. Grumbling through the tape pissed her off even more. When she got her hands on this little handicapped prick she would beat him black and blue.

Lilly arrived home to find Mark's vehicle in the drive way. This could be a problem she thought, what if he shot her? She would make a lot of noise and let him know she'd come home, the element of surprise not preferable to being shot. "Okay here goes nothing," she said out loud. Pushing the button to open the garage door she waited. Once the door fully opened she drove into the garage and pushed the remote again. Turning the engine off immediately not wanting to suffocate on fumes she laughed at the thought. "Not funny Lilly Mason," she said to herself.

Leaving her suitcase in the trunk she unlocked the kitchen door and stepped in slamming the door loudly. Mark, always a light sleeper surely heard that. Not wanting him to come down the stairs with gun in hand she yelled up the stairway, "Mark? I'm home honey."

"I better be dreaming," Mark said to himself as he sat up in bed. Quietly he listened for sound of any kind.

Keys hitting the counter as she tossed them onto the granite caused little noise, dang she thought looking around. Opening and closing a few cabinet doors caught his attention. He swiftly jumped out of bed and took the steps two at a time.

"Lilly?"

"Well hello handsome." She smiled and hugged him tight.

"What the hell are you doing here?"

"Gee nice to see you too, my love," she pouted.

"Stop that you know damn well what I mean. Is everything alright? The baby." He stepped out of her arms and looked at her abdomen.

"Yes Mark, we're fine, just missed you. I don't want to fight about it so I didn't call to tell you."

"You think because you didn't call to tell me we aren't going to argue about this? Are you crazy Lilly? What the hell is wrong with your mother that she'd let you come home right now?"

Looking hurt she picked the keys up off the counter top. "I'm going to get my suitcase."

Mark watched as she walked out then quickly followed her into the garage, "here let me get that. Although you'll just be putting it back in here in the morning."

"No I won't. I'm staying Mark."

"It's not safe here Lilly, you're going back to your mothers."

She followed him into the kitchen. He set the luggage on the floor just inside the door "anything you need in here for tonight?"

Exasperated she wrench the suitcase up from the floor and tried to carry it up the stairs, but he snatched it back, "oh no you don't, it stays down here. You are leaving Lilly, I won't argue about this."

"Neither will I." She tossed over her shoulder and went up the stairs. She'd unpack once he left for work.

Turning the lights off Mark followed her up. Secretly glad she's back, but knowing he couldn't allow her to stay his emotions warred within.

Lilly came out of the bathroom in her nightie, going directly to the bed she pulled the covers down. Settling herself on her the side of the bed she rubbed lotion into her hands and arms.

Mark lay down, rolling to his side to watch her. She felt his gaze on her and knew he wouldn't get into a discussion tonight over her coming home, but she preferred it done and over with.

Laying down she turned to face him, "I'm sorry you're upset with me."

He looked at her face, a face he loved and missed with all his heart. "Babe, I just want you and the baby safe. I can't keep you safe, my hours have been insane. We are all over the map on this one."

"I understand that, really I do, but I don't need you to keep us safe. I won't do anything that will put us in jeopardy, I promise. You don't have to worry about us we will stay right here inside the house."

He laid his head on her chest and fought a losing battle with his intuition, which screamed she should stay away. "I love having you here babe, I really do, I can't deal with the idea something could happen to you." He squeezed her tightly.

"You're not going to have to deal with that we aren't going anywhere, nothing is going to happen to us."

"I'm holding you to that." He pulled her down to him kissing her till her toes curled. "I've missed you."

"Me too," she told him snuggling up close to him. "You feel so good."

He placed his palm on her still flat belly, "how are you doin' lil man?" He whispered into her navel.

She giggled at him, "what makes you think it's a 'lil man', she could be a princess."

"You have a point, okay, hey there little one Daddy loves you." He looked up into her face, "I love you too."

The garage opened slowly as Eugene waited. He had physically struggled too much already today, and knew his hip couldn't take much more. Looking at Debbie in the mirror he tried finesse, "I need you to listen to me very carefully I hate repeating myself."

Debbie stared at him she could sense something terrible coming and needed to keep her wits about her. Nodding her head she waited.

"I am going to pull into my garage, you're going to walk quietly into the house without struggling or trying to cause a scene." He pulled into the garage and pushed the control to close the door. "I already have Chrissy Bingham, if you make one sound, or struggle in any, way she dies. Do you understand?"

Deb's heart fell to her stomach, could it be true? Did he really have Chrissy, or is this a tactic he'd use to get her inside? Her mind battled over possibilities and settled on risk. Debbie couldn't risk him killing Chrissy, if in fact he had her already. She couldn't live with saving herself at the cost of her dear friend. She would just do what he said and find out. Once again she nodded her head wishing she had called Chrissy earlier.

Eugene got out of the car, unlocked the kitchen entrance, and flipped the light switch. His house seemed happy, quiet, and comforting, he thought looking around the room quickly. Walking back to the car and opening the rear door he said, "let me help you."

Deb's legs were free and she fought hard not to kick out and retaliate against him. Badly wanting to protect herself, but not knowing for sure about Chrissy, she couldn't take a chance. Instead she meekly scooted to the edge of the seat and allowed Eugene to help her. As they walked to the doorway he gripped her upper arm fiercely.

The numbness took most of the pain out of his grip, but his display of superiority irritated her greatly. She didn't pull away as she walked quietly inside the house. Striving to keep her patience intact until she could ascertain if he did have Chrissy, simply delaying an inevitable fight, she knew was coming.

"Smart woman, "he said as he walked her to the hall. Once near the secret door he turned her slightly not wanting her to see how he opened it. "Stand just like this, don't move," he instructed. With her back facing him he let go of her arm and reached under the beautiful tapestry for the lever. Tugging hard he heard the slight scraping the door always made on the flooring of his little room.

Chrissy scrambled away from the door as it began to move. Standing against the wall she took in as much of the room as she could in the light that spilled from the doorway.

Eugene violently shoved Debbie into the room and hurried to close the door, he couldn't handle any physical altercations tonight.

Debbie didn't get a look around before the minimal light disappeared putting her in total darkness.

Chrissy knew she's no longer alone, but didn't see what fell onto the floor before the heavy door slammed shut.

Tate's finally emptied out leaving the trio to clean up. Cindy's feet ached so much she slipped her shoes off and cleaned in her stocking feet. She disliked the idea of walking around the filthy floor that way, but her swollen toes couldn't take the shoes another minute.

Lifting the chairs onto the tables they worked quickly, all three pitched in to finished faster. Maggie had cleaned each table top while Cindy knocked out the restrooms. Sam took care of the bar area and now they had to deal with the floors. Once all the chairs were stacked on tables Maggie swept the floors, which left the mopping to Cindy. Sam carried several bags of trash outside to the dumpster.

The night air felt cool and fresh so Sam left the door open wide to air out the musty beer smell and stale cigarette smoke lingering in the bar. A non-smoker himself he marveled at his ability to deal with the stench left behind by cigarettes.

Cindy mopped right behind Maggie as she swept. Both women were ready to get home and relax. Maggie grew excited knowing she had tomorrow night off to spend with her friends. She felt bad for Cindy and told her so.

"You're kidding, you won't be here tomorrow? I have to do all of this myself?" Cindy asked incredulous.

"Well Sam will be here to lend a hand, but yeah don't worry much I've done this for years without help you can do it. It's not a big deal hun."

Exhaustion seeped from her pores she couldn't imagine doing all of this by herself. She needed this job though and would do whatever she had to. She needed to make sure she got plenty of rest before coming in tomorrow night. Bryan and her mother both were not going to be happy about it.

Sam stood in the doorway and watched the women work their way across the floor. He never left until his employee's finished, and left for the night. Hiring Cindy had been a stroke of genius he thought, she worked hard so far, both she and Maggie seemed to hit it off, and he'd been pleased with the way she handled herself and the situation earlier with Richard.

"Almost done, Sam," Maggie called out to him as she swept the last section. Every now and again she heard a little whimper or moan from Cindy, and knew the cause were painful feet. After she put the broom and dust pan in the janitor's closet she waited for Cindy to bring the empty bucket and wet mop in.

Swiping the sweat from her brow Cindy said "I'm so flipping tired who would've thought doling out drinks could be so dang exhausting?"

"Oh hun, we do much more than dole out drinks." Maggie laughed.

"True, I just need to get home and off these feet. They're so swelled I don't think I can get my shoes back on."

"Leave 'em off, go home and soak 'em good in warm water, then put cold towels around them before going to bed. You'll get used to this I promise."

As they came out of the closet Maggie tugged the chain turning the single bulb light fixture off. "Don't worry about tomorrow, Cin, you'll do just fine." She patted the girls back as they walked toward Sam.

Cindy stopped and grabbed her shoes before stepping out into the brisk air. "See you tomorrow Sam, Maggie you have a great time I'll see ya when ya get back."

"I'm going to see you to your car Cindy, I worry about that killer we got running around," Sam said walking with Cindy to the car.

"Thanks Sam, I appreciate you. I hope they catch him soon, he has everyone in an uproar around here." Cindy slid into her car grabbing her seatbelt.

"I know and it's a damn shame. We'll see you tomorrow. You did good tonight," Sam said shutting the door and waving goodbye to her. When he turned around Maggie stood right behind him, "and you," he said grabbing her into a hug, "you want some company tonight?"

Maggie laughed and leaned in for a kiss, "sure do."

* * *

Debbie scuffled across the floor quickly. Her head throbbed where it had bounced off the hard surface. Did she hear a gasping sound as she hit her head? The blackness of the room gave her a feeling of disorientation. Her arms ached something fierce.

Chrissy stood flat against the wall wondering what the hell he'd thrown into the room. She listened intently in the vast darkness. Something big moved across the room. Fearful of what it could be she didn't move an inch.

Debbie felt something hard and solid against her back, getting up on her knees she moved her hands painfully along the edge. Exertion muffled sound through her taped mouth.

Chrissy gasped. "Who's there?" More muffling, a little louder this time, Chrissy knew it was another female. "Hang on I'm coming over there." getting down on her hands and knees she crawled to where she thought the woman might be. Bumping into someone she drew herself back a bit.

The muffling really going now, Chrissy figured whoever she is had tape over her mouth. Feeling around she found the woman's head and felt the tape. "This may sting," she said ripping the tape off.

"Ouch! What the fuck?" Debbie yelled.

"Debbie? Oh my God, Debbie, is that you?"

"Shit, yeah it's me. Damn that really hurt."

Chrissy flung her arms around her friend. "How?"

"Whoa, hey glad to know it's you, but I need some help here."

"Help? What's the matter?"

"Uh, my hands are tied behind my back and I can't feel a damn thing through all the numbness. Here help me." She turned around to give Chrissy access to the ropes.

"How the hell did he get you here?" Chrissy asked

288

untying the knotted rope.

"He somehow got into my house, and before I knew it he choked me out. When I came to I had rope around my hands and tape over my mouth."

"It's Eugene isn't it?"

"Yeah, he threatened to kill you if I fought back, so here I am."

"You knew he kidnapped me?"

"No, I wasn't even sure he had you, but I couldn't take a chance. Damn girl how did this happen to you?"

"I finished cleaning the kitchen after everyone left, and when I told him I was leaving he told me he couldn't let me. Next thing I knew I woke up in here."

"Speaking of here, what the hell kind of room is this?"

"I have no idea, I woke up to total darkness, and except the little light that came in with you, I haven't seen any light at all. I have made my way around the room, it's not very big and I can only feel bookshelves with books and one chair."

"It's some kind of secret room the door is hidden behind a tapestry hanging on the wall. He wouldn't let me see how he opened the door." Debbie felt intense pain as her arms were released from their binding. Intense heat rushed through her limbs as blood flowed freely. "That sonuvabitch is going to pay for hurting me," She said angrily moving her arms encouraging the blood to flow quicker. Shrugging her shoulders up and down helped a little. The two women huddled together comforting one another. Debbie rubbed her arms continuously, moving them in circles trying to get the circulation moving. The pins and needle feeling hurt almost as much as the numbing pain.

"What do you think he wants with us?" Chrissy asked worriedly.

"If I had to guess hun, I'd say he's our serial killer." Debbie hated to admit this thought out loud.

"What?"

Realizing her friend had not put two and two together yet she put her arms around her, "don't freak on me here. There are two of us and only one handicapped fucker, out there."

They both laughed at that, then Chrissy said, "yeah and you know John will find us. Eugene doesn't stand a chance with us, what the hell could he be thinking?"

"I don't know girl, but we need to remember he has already successfully killed four times. We can't under estimate him."

Eugene lay in bed while his hip throbbed through the medication. Even enduring the pain he suffered, the excitement of knowing he had two women concealed in his home and ready to give their lives for him, was almost more than he could believe. He still wanted Lilly Mason, but he didn't need her now. The psychic would be the icing on the cake. Bringing her as a gift to his dark lord would surely count more than the mere women he already gave.

Absently rubbing his hip, he licked his thin lips, and laughed to himself as he remembered thinking how terrible the day would be for him. He'd had no idea how successfully the day would end. When he realized that woman had psychic ability he almost pissed himself, then drumming up the idea to get her too, well that had been pure genius. Of course, psychic ability still remained to be proven, he hadn't had time to research it yet.

The pain from his hip radiated down his leg and up his back, he would never get any rest with this. He gave up and went to the bathroom to get his heating pad. Once he'd settled back in bed with the pad tucked close against his hip he began sifting through ideas on the two upcoming sacrifices.

THIRTY-FOUR

Craig and Dave met early for coffee to talk about a possible paranormal investigation of a local residence. A longtime friend of Dave Dawson's had called him late last evening with the information, and since John had a broken leg, Dave decided to discuss it with Craig. He called Craig right after the conversation with his friend ended and set up an early morning meeting over coffee. The small café didn't seem to draw too many early morning customers. The interior decoration left a lot to be desired with dingy, orange, faded, vinyl covering the booth seating, yellowed Formica table tops that had seen better days, and grease covered copper wall art.

Dave selected a booth in the back corner while he waited for Craig to show up. The waitress brought his cup of coffee just as Craig arrived. Dave took his paper napkin and wiped the spoon down thoroughly before stirring his coffee.

"Smells great, how about one more of those," Craig told the waitress as he slid into the booth.

"You got it, are you two going to order breakfast or will it just be coffee?"

They looked at each other and shrugged. "Nah, just coffee this morning," Dave told her looking around the dirty restaurant. After she walked away he put cream and artificial sweetener in his cup. "We'll talk about the investigation after you get your coffee," he said to Craig as he stirred his cup.

"Sounds good, coffee's exactly what I need to take the chill off." He sat back and looked around the near empty café. "Not a very hoppin' place is it?"

"Apparently not," Dave said taking a cautious sip. "Good and strong."

The waitress set another cup on the table and left the check too, she would be back to refill their cups, but since the refills were free and they weren't ordering food the check didn't matter a lot.

"So what're we looking at here?" Craig asked as he fixed his cup up.

"My friend Billy that called last night said he's been to this house on several occasions, and he finally talked the owner into a paranormal investigation. He said the house is close to one hundred and ten years old, it's been in the same family almost the entire time. The owner lives there a lone these days, his wife has passed and his children are all grown and moved on."

"What kind of activity is he experiencing?" Craig leaned in closer.

"Billy said you can hear knocking on walls and furniture moves across rooms, knick knacks relocate, small items come up missing for days at a time. He said on one visit he and his buddy were sitting in the kitchen and a frying pan on the stove moved from one burner to another and they both watched it happen. He's pretty freaked out about the place, but told his friend he knew someone that could find out what's going on and his friend finally agreed." Dave thrived in places like these, he was pretty good at getting to the bottom of things, de-bunking paranormal claims seemed to be a talent he possessed.

"Sounds right up your alley." Craig laughed "You going to give John a call and run this past him?"

"Of course, you know we don't do anything as a team, or even on our own, with talking to him. I just wanted to run it by you this morning and get your take on a time line for the investigation."

"I'm open any evening, as long as we don't run past midnight, if it's going to be a long one make it a weekend."

"Great sounds good, now don't say anything to anyone else until I get a chance to talk with John. I'll probably give him a call when we leave here and see if he's up for company."

"I'm sure he is, poor guy's bored out of his mind, stuck in a chair right now."

"Yeah, I could see he's still in a lot of pain yesterday. Sure hate that."

"Speaking of yesterday, that Eugene guy's an odd one, huh?" Craig didn't care for Eugene at all. The man just struck him as a weirdo, plain and simple.

"He's is an odd duck, but John and Mark both went to school with him, and they say he's okay, just had a hard time with that handicap of his. Some people can't seem to deal with the little curves life throws at them sometimes." Dave shook his head.

They finished up their coffee and turned down second cups. Neither man impressed with their surroundings. The location of the resident had been discussed and agreed it showed promise from the information Dave received.

Residential haunting's could be very interesting if performed correctly. N.E.P.R. had certainly had their share and on several found significant evidence in various forms.

John's cell phone vibrated on the table next to him, he reached over rubbing his eyes open, "yeah?"

"John, its Dave did I wake you?"

"That's okay, what time is it?"

"A little after eight, sorry man didn't mean to wake you."

"After eight, damn I'm surprised Chrissy isn't down already." John leaned forward in his chair trying to hear Chrissy moving around. "What's up Dave?"

"Just had coffee with Craig, we talked about a possible investigation and I want to run it by you. You up to company later today?"

"Yeah, sure what time you thinking?"

"How about, twoish?"

"Sure see ya then."

They hung up and John reached for his crutches, once he got up and moved around he could tell Chrissy wasn't up yet. After getting a pot of coffee started he hobbled into the bathroom. Splashing some cold water on his face jolted his brain awake. He sure hated to go up the steps, but since it wasn't like her to sleep in, he felt he needed to check on her.

The doorbell rang as John came out of the bathroom. He went to answer the door before trying the stairs. Two uniformed police officers stood on his porch, "what can I do for you?" John asked them opening the door wide.

"Mr. Bingham?" A short pudgy officer inquired.

"Yes, I'm John Bingham." He looked at them and waited.

"Sir, do you still own a two thousand ten Toyota Camry?"

"My wife drives that, oh my God has she been in an accident?" He knew she wouldn't still be in bed.

"No sir, uh the vehicle's been called in as suspicious. We checked it out and found a purse and the keys had been left in the ignition. Where is your wife now, sir?"

"What? Where's the car? I just woke up, here come on in." He stepped back to allow them entrance. "I was just thinking about trying to make it up the stairs to check on her, she never sleeps this late, but when I woke up I could tell she hadn't been down yet. I mean no coffee brewing or anything."

They all sat in the living room. John completely confused about Chrissy and her car.

"I see," the same officer said. "When did you see your wife last sir?"

John thought for a minute, "yesterday, uh, we had been

over at a friend's house for a wake, and she stayed to help clean up. I had a friend bring me home." He pointed down at his leg, "to get my pain medication."

"What time did your wife get in from cleaning up?"

"That's a good question, I guess the pain pills knocked me out cause when I woke up last night it was dark, I figured Chrissy went up to bed." Reality kick started his heart rate it beat so hard in his chest, as he realized she probably didn't make it home last night. Jumping up without assistance from his crutches wasn't the smartest thing he could've done. Falling back into the chair, pain shooting up and down his leg he hollered "Shit!"

"Sir, are you alright?" Both officers sprang off the sofa quickly, ready to assist.

"Yeah, just stupid, look guys my wife has been sleeping on that couch every night since I broke my leg, last night she wasn't there when I woke up. I'm really worried about her. This isn't like Chrissy at all. Where is the car did you say?"

The officers explained to the best of their knowledge about the call received and the vehicle location.

"Something's wrong, no way in hell Chrissy would leave her purse and keys in the car. No reason she should've even been parked there. Hang on let me call my friend, Eugene, see what time she left there." John picked up his cell phone and dialed Eugene.

Eugene stood outside the secret room trying to listen even though he knew it would be impossible to hear anything. His elation this morning when he woke up still lingered. He knew better than to open the door, those two women were going to be a handful and he needed to take precautions before approaching them.

When the phone rang he danced his way to it, clearing his throat he made his voice solemn as he answered, "hello."

"Eugene, it's John." leaving pleasantries out of the

greeting he hurried on "what time did Chrissy leave there yesterday?"

"What? John? I'm sorry I didn't catch what you asked?" he smiled and thought let my acting ability impress me.

"Eugene, listen to me Chrissy never made it home. What time did she leave your place yesterday?"

"What? Oh no John, uh she left here about thirty or forty minutes after you did. Where is she?" His smile beamed brightly as his heart beat accelerated.

"We don't know, the police are here right now. Did she say anything about stopping anywhere?"

"No she came out of the kitchen said she had finished and I believe she told me again how sorry she is for my loss, and left. I don't know what else I can tell you John." Holding back his laughter proved to be difficult, but he managed. He did a little jig standing there, and instantly regretted the pain that shot down his leg from his hip.

"Did she leave with anyone?"

"No she finished up in there by herself, she sent everyone else home when you left."

"Dammit." John hung his head, "Okay Eugene, thanks."

"I'm sure she's fine, but keep me informed. Let me know if I can do anything, anything at all."

"I will thanks." He hung up and relayed the information to the officers adding, "my wife never goes anywhere without telling me, this isn't like her. Something is wrong, bad wrong."

"We understand Mr. Bingham. Do you have a recent photo of Mrs. Bingham?"

John shook his head and crutched his way out of the room. When he returned he handed over a photo of Chrissy, and gave the officers all the requested information. Once satisfied, they had everything they needed, they told John to stay by the phone. Someone would call him soon. When they left he called Mark.

Mark and his team were just finishing up their last report on the fourth victim when John's call came through. He assured John he would be on his way as soon as he talked with his Lieutenant. Mark called Stone on his way to Lt. Washington's office. He had a bad feeling and prayed Chrissy was still alive.

The entire task force including Agent Marlowe converged on the Bingham house. John held it together barely as his worst fears were being discussed right in front of him.

"Let me get this straight, you guys think it's a good possibility that Chrissy's been abducted by this killer." John's heart lurched in fear, "Mark, you have to do something."

"John, I promise I'll keep you informed, I'm not going to tell you not to worry, but know we're doing everything humanly possible at this point." He hated the fear etched in his friends face. "I'll be in touch, call me if you hear anything." Mark walked toward the door, "you need to call someone to come help you out, you can't do this on your own, not with a broken leg."

"I'm not worried about my leg Mark, I need to go look for Chrissy." John picked up his phone. "I'm calling Matt he can drive me around."

"You do that, keep your cell phone on you, I'll be in touch."

Mark had called Lilly and told her about Chrissy. He further instructed her to stay home, since no one knew she'd come back, he didn't want to take a chance on her or the baby getting hurt. She reluctantly agreed, but said she at least had to call John, and offer to help in any way she could from a distance. Maybe she could make phone calls, schedule a search party or something. She couldn't sit and do absolutely nothing when her friend could be in danger. Mark told her he thought that was a good idea, but not to let anyone know she's back in Freetown. At this point he didn't know who he could trust.

John's house now crawling with family and friends held chaos within its walls. People clamored over each other, disorder and confusion evident. Joellen stepped into the living room carrying a tray of drinks. She noticed the level of noise had risen with the anger permeating throughout the room. This is pitiful she thought, someone needs to take charge and get this group in line. Setting the tray on the cocktail table she put two fingers in her mouth blowing out a very loud whistle.

"Now that I have your attention, I want every one of you to sit down somewhere and listen up." She placed her hands on hips, a no-nonsense look on her face and dared them to defy her. Once everyone found a seat, some on the floor, others crowded together she said, "All this yelling over one another is getting us nowhere fast. We need to calm down and put our heads together here. The last thing we need is pandemonium and havoc. Dave, you're a great organizer. I suggest you organize. The rest of you sit quietly until he works out, whatever it is he works out."

THIRTY-FIVE

"You awake?" Deb asked Chrissy, figuring her friend was having nightmares the way she moved next to her. They had spent what they hoped had been night time on the floor, very close to one another.

Chrissy thrashed more trying to get out of the nightmare. She heard Deb talking to her, and subconsciously reached toward the sound. Moaning and squirming, Chrissy fought her way through the horrors in her dream.

Debbie shook Chrissy, "hey girl, come on, whatever you're dreaming let it go. It can't hurt you sweetie."

Chrissy sat up, "Deb." Flinging her hand out, she searched for her friend in the darkness. Finding Debbie right next to her, she gave a sigh of relief. "Damn I hate nightmares." She pushed her hair off her neck and asked "how did you sleep?"

"All things considered, I think pretty good, not so sure how long we've slept, hell not even sure it's morning yet. You seemed to be having one hell of a dream. Wanna talk about it?"

"Wouldn't do any good, but thanks," she readjusted her derriere on the hard floor. "We need to plan something, figure out how the hell to get out of here." Chrissy felt her panic spring to life.

"Yeah, I've been thinking about that. I'm sure the next time he opens that door he'll have a weapon of some sort, and not knowing what this room looks like, or what we have available to use against him, I'm at a loss."

"I know, like I told you, I've felt all over this damn room, nothing but books. What do you think he's planning?"

"You don't want to know what I think." Deb pulled Chrissy close in a one armed hug. "Besides won't do us any good to make assumptions, we need to focus on escaping."

They sat close together for a while not talking, each thinking about getting out of there alive. Chrissy wondered if John knew she's missing yet. How long had they been here? She wondered. "Do you think anyone knows yet that we're missing?"

"Oh I'm sure of it, you certainly, and then when they try to get a hold of me to tell me you're missing, they'll know I am too. If Eugene is the serial killer, and I'm sure he is, then he's covered his tracks well, but taking us is a big mistake. Your husband and our friends will not rest until they find us."

Chrissy didn't acknowledge the fact Debbie thought the same thing she did about Eugene being the killer. Denial went a long way in her book, especially since she wasn't prone to panic attacks, and knew secretly she'd already experienced a few. "I know, but I banged on that damn door a lot, and let me tell you, it's as solid as they come. You said yourself this is some type of secret room, how on Earth do you think anyone will find us? While we're still alive I mean."

"We have to keep faith Chrissy, at least we're together. We can fight him together. Even with a weapon he can only get one of us at a time, we need to keep our heads about us, and take care of each other."

"I know, I just keep thinking you wouldn't be in this mess if it weren't for me. I'm so sorry Debbie."

"Are you kidding me? You are most certainly not the reason I am here. He knows I'm a threat to him because of my gift, he couldn't take any chances. I'm putting the pieces together finally, not that it's doing us much good."

"Pieces together? What do you mean?"

"Oh girl, you have no idea." Debbie cracked up laughing, her nerves stretched to the limits.

"I know, so fill me in. What do you know that I don't?"

"Okay this is what I'm thinking anyway, I'm pretty sure I'm right, but you tell me what you think." Calming her jittery nerves with a few deep breaths she said "I've seen two of the four murdered women, they didn't talk to me, just gave me flashes of pictures right?"

"Okay…"

"Also an old woman that keeps showing up telling me to stop him, he's evil, he can't stop himself, blah, blah, blah. Anyway she would never tell me or give me a hint who he might be, but I believe he's Eugene. I think the old lady is his mother."

"What? Are you serious? Why do you think it's her? Didn't you see her photo at the memorial?"

"Well yeah, but the picture of her at the service had been how old? I mean she was younger and prettier, nothing like the woman that comes to see me."

Chrissy thought about that, Eugene had used an old photograph of his mother, one that depicted her youthful, happy, and healthy. Why didn't she realize that? Looking back in hind sight she could see so many flags flying. Damn how will anyone figure this out, he's very cunning. "I see your point he's a lot more dangerous than I thought. We need to move around in here, try to find something to use against him. I'll be damned if he's the last person I see." Chrissy felt a surge of anger, she wouldn't go down without a fight.

"Now you're talking. You go to the right, I'll go left. Take your time and feel everything, high and low."

"When we reach each other we'll go past each other and check what the other checked. We can't afford to miss anything. Ready?"

"Yep, let's do this before he comes to feed us, at least I hope he plans to feed us I'm starving."

"I am too, but did you have to mention food right now?"

Chrissy laughed.

They both took off in different directions, feeling their way around. If there's something to be found in here we'll find it, Deb thought to herself. She opened her mind to her spirit guide. Help me see without my eyes she asked silently, I know you're there.

Mark had Chrissy's car towed to the station. He had crime scene guys combing it carefully for any signs someone besides Chrissy had been in it. He and Cody pooled their teams to work on Chrissy's abduction. They had hope of finding her alive, and wasted no time, using all available resources on their investigation.

While leaving the guys behind to work on the residential neighborhood where the car had been parked, Mark and Cody went to talk with Eugene.

"He has no idea we're coming to see him, right?" Cody asked Mark once they left their guys and drove to Eugene's house.

"Nope, none, the element of surprise will work in our favor, besides when he is face to face with us we can read his body language, his reactions to our questions."

"You suspect this guy? I thought he's a friend of yours?"

"Not a friend, an acquaintance, and yes I suspect everyone, no one is ruled out yet." Mark had known Eugene a long time, he had a hard time believing the guy could be capable of doing any of this, but at this point he wouldn't rule him out.

"Sounds very professional of you, you want me to take the lead since you know him personally?"

"Yeah, not because I worry about offending him, but because I know him and I want the opportunity to watch his reactions. Gauge his reactions you know what I mean." Mark thought he knew Eugene well enough to know if he lied to them. He hoped fervently he did any way.

"Exactly, sounds good to me. I may get a little rough on him, but I don't want to bother with 'good cop/bad cop', so don't step in okay?"

Mark smiled, "you got it. I'm just along for visual observations."

Eugene paced the floor in the living room trying to gain courage to face his captives. He had purchased a stun gun quite a while ago and relished the idea of seeing the effects it would have on them. He needed to keep them alive and this would be the safest way to insure his ability to meet with them without being hurt. The problem being, he could only stun one at a time and unsure if he used it, it would have enough *umph* to take care of the other if needed.

Looking at the stun gun as it lay on the table he wished he'd used it already to know what the weapon's capable of. One use, two, more? He had absolutely no idea. He feared it may take too long to affect one, giving the other time to intervene. No he couldn't risk it just yet he needed to know more about it first.

The doorbell ringing made him jump, he had been so deep in thought he didn't hear anyone walking on the wooden porch. "Get with it, Eugene, pull your head out of your ass, mister," he reprimanded quietly as he went to the door.

He didn't check to see who was out there. Pulling the door open he was surprised to see the two detectives standing there. "Mark, what a pleasant surprise, I didn't expect to see you again so soon." He tried to pull himself together. Dammit why didn't I look first? He berated himself.

"Good morning Mr. Lowery, I'm Detective Stone, and of course, you already know Detective Mason. May we come in?" Cody took in the man before him, not much to look at, he thought.

"Of course, come in, come in." He limped ahead of them

to the living room. Seeing the stun gun laying on the table he almost had a heart attack, too late now he couldn't hide it.

Cody and Mark followed Eugene, they both noticed the exaggerated limp he displayed and looked at one another.

"Please, make yourselves comfortable, I'll just put this up." Eugene picked up the stun gun and carried it to a corner table, placing it in a drawer. He inhaled deeply trying to get his heartbeat to slow down.

"Rather unusual to have a stun gun lying around isn't it?" Cody observed.

"Is it? I wouldn't think so Detective Stone. Heck in this day and age you never know when you may need protection. I find a stun gun preferable to a real gun if you know what I mean."

"I can't say that I do, care to explain?"

"I'm sure it's not the reason for your visit, but sure I don't mind. I would rather stun someone than kill them. I hope that clears it up for you Detective. Mark, how is John doing? Ever since he called me this morning I haven't been able to get him or poor Chrissy off my mind."

Before Mark could reply Cody said, "Actually Mr. Lowery that's why we're here. We'd like to ask you a few questions if you have time."

"I figured as much, certainly I have all the time you need. I don't know how much help I'll be, I've already told John everything I know." Eugene stared at Mark, why wasn't he talking to me? He wondered. Why use someone who doesn't even know me to ask the questions? His suspicious mind tried to figure out the tactical reason for this.

"Yes, I'm sure you did, but you must've expected us, knew you would be formally questioned since you are the last one to have contact or see Chrissy Bingham." Cody coolly kept direct eye contact with Eugene.

"The last one? I hardly think so detective, who ever took

her is the last one to have contact with her." Eugene settled back in his chair, he would play this game, he obviously is much better at it then this idiot, he thought.

"Took her? I'm sorry do you know something we don't?"

This surprised Eugene, don't they think she had been taken? He cleared his throat and continued, "Why it's the obvious conclusion isn't it? I mean if someone didn't take her, then she'd be home right?"

Cody looked over at Mark. Did Mark see how this guy struggled to control this interrogation? Did he notice how hard the man tried to act nonchalant? "Mr. Lowery, at this point we're not sure what's happened to Mrs. Bingham, or where she is. When did you see her last?"

"Yesterday, she had been here for my mother's wake."

"What time did she leave?"

He seemed to give it thought before he said, "About six, maybe six thirty."

"You don't seem sure about that." Cody didn't like the smugness nor the complacency presented by Eugene, was it for their benefit?

"I'm sure Detective, she finished cleaning the kitchen and left. I haven't seen or talked to her since."

"Did she leave with anyone?"

"No, she left alone, and before you ask she was the last to leave."

"So it had been just the two of you here? Where did everyone else go?"

"They went home I assume. Chrissy told the other women to go ahead she'd finish up without them. I stayed in here out of her way. When she got ready to leave she poked her head in here and told me again how sorry she was about my loss and left."

"I see you didn't get up to walk her out? You stayed in here and she saw herself out?"

"Yes, I thanked her and she saw herself out. It had been a very long day Detective, my hip hurt badly and I may be a bad host, but I let her see her-self out."

"I see. What did you do last night Mr. Lowery?"

"Do? Nothing, I relaxed after a long day."

"You never left the house then?"

"No."

"Can anyone verify that?"

"No, unless of course, one of my nosy neighbors kept watch." then it hit him that Mr. Samuels saw him walking home last night, they'd even talked to each other.

Mark saw the expression that quickly passed over Eugene's face. If he had not been paying attention he'd have missed it, it happened that fast.

Cody caught it too, "Did you remember something Mr. Lowery? I noticed the expression you just made it seemed as if you remembered something." Cody normally would've kept that to himself, but he wanted to see this man squirm. He's hiding something, but what?

"Actually you're very attentive Detective. Yes I did just remember I took a walk last night. A short walk, but I did leave the house."

Cody and Mark looked at each other again. Eugene didn't like the looks they kept exchanging.

"Where did you walk to?"

"Just a short walk down the street and back."

"It's getting pretty cold out at night now, even for a short walk. If your hip hurt as you've mentioned why would you want to go out in the cold?"

Eugene, readjusted himself in his chair, he didn't like this man, and hated having to answer his questions even more. "I don't like your tone sir, are you insinuating something here? Am I missing something?"

We have lift off! Cody thought proudly. "I'm not

insinuating anything, simply asking questions to gain a better understanding Mr. Lowery."

Eugene liked the detective calling him Mr. Lowery, but he still felt uneasy. "I thought a short brisk walk would help to loosen my hip some, as I said it hurt badly, unfortunately all I did taking that walk is made it hurt more. I came in, took a couple pain pills, got my heating pad and went to bed. Now I think I have told you everything I can. Are we done here?"

"Almost, I appreciate your cooperation Mr. Lowery. You didn't happen to run into anyone while you were out did you?"

Eugene rolled his eyes and sighed loudly, "yes I did, Mr. Samuels, a neighbor of mine. We shared a few words then I came home." He tried to look bored, but he knew something didn't sit well with the officer.

"I see. I'm sure you will avail yourself should we have more questions right, Mr. Lowery?"

Finally, they're leaving. He didn't know how much longer he could stand the ridicule this insufferable man put him through, "of course."

"Good then I believe we're finished for now. Thank you for your time." Cody and Mark stood up, Eugene remained seated.

"You're welcome. I hate to say this, but would you mind showing yourselves out? My hip is hurting me again."

"Of course, don't get up." Cody took a business card from his shirt pocket, "If you think of anything else, please call me." He handed the card to Eugene.

"Yes of course. Good to see you Mark." Mark nodded his head. Not one word spoken during this interview by Mark. He had remained quiet the entire time, Eugene wondered about that. Weren't they supposed to be friends? Yet Mark had hung him out to dry. He slumped forward in his chair and put his head in his hands.

Cody stepped back into the room, "Oh and thanks for clearing that up for me," he said taking note of Eugene's posture. "About the stun gun I mean."

Eugene jumped, but Cody was already going out the door. He heard the door close and wanted to scream, letting the detective see him that way.

THIRTY-SIX

Sam Tate called John's house and told Vinny Muso, who happened to be the one to answer the phone, to send everyone over to his bar. He'd provide drinks for everyone while they organized the search party. Maggie filled Sam in on everything she knew about Chrissy's disappearance. Sam couldn't believe one of their little group, could be in the killer's hands. He called Cindy in early and Maggie agreed to come in since girl's night was off.

Dave, John, and Matt, agreed the group would go to Tate's while John and Matt got a head start looking. John couldn't sit around anymore. He needed to be out there looking. He put Dave in charge of organizing and getting the groups sent out. He gave Lilly the task of calling Chrissy's employer and informing them, then asking if they would print up some flyers and get them posted around town. John told Lilly to call everyone she could think of and get them over to Tate's to assist in the search. She couldn't stand the thought of John thinking she didn't care enough to come out and help, she explained to him the promise she'd made to Mark. John told her he completely agreed with Mark, especially since the possibility remained the killer may have originally set his sights on her. He appreciated the fact she trusted him enough to tell him she was home, and further reminded her she had a baby to consider as well.

Matt and John headed for the Forest, the killer, made this area his killing grounds and so help him, if John caught up to him, and he had Chrissy. John couldn't fight the terror that gripped him, he felt completely at a loss as to what to do. The possibility of him walking through the Forest searching for

Chrissy not even remotely doable, Matt assured him they could drive most of it and where they couldn't drive he would hop out and look.

Tate's filled up quickly, the tables were packed. Dave had a list of names for people that volunteered to help. Joellen told Dave she would be there as soon as she ran by Debbie's house. No one had been able to reach Deb by phone all day. Kaliegh had suggested that maybe Chrissy and Debbie were together somewhere, getting things ready for the girl's night out, but John shot that idea down quick, fast and in a hurry. He reminded them Chrissy would've left a note or something, and she sure as hell wouldn't have let her purse and keys in her car.

Joellen walked around Debbie's house, everything locked up tight, even the car in the driveway. She banged on the front door, looked in windows, banged on the back door, Debbie wasn't home.

Joellen talk to the neighbors on both sides and neither remembered seeing Debbie since yesterday evening. Joellen decided to give Mark a call.

"Mason," he answered his phone gruffly.

"Mark, hi this is Joellen."

"Hi, Jo, anything new?"

"May be, we can't find Debbie Milo. I'm out front of her house now and her car is here, but no sign of her."

"I wouldn't worry about Deb, Jo. She's probably at a paranormal conference or something. You know how she takes off on a whim."

"Uh, no way Mark, we all had a girls night planned for tonight at Debs. She wouldn't just take off, besides her car's here. I'm more than a little worried I can tell ya that."

Mark didn't like the sound of this conversation at all. "Can you see inside? Is it possible she's in there asleep?"

"Yeah, I can see most rooms, and no, it's not possible. She's not here."

He scratched his head thinking, "Okay Jo, you go back to John's I'll check this out."

"The meeting party moved to Tate's Mark, I'm going there right now, should I include Debbie in this search do you think?"

"No, not yet, let me look in to it further, I'll get back to you."

They hung up and Joellen went to Tate's, while Mark informed the team.

Cody and Mark had been filling the L.T. and Agent Marlowe, along with task force members, in on their interview with Eugene. Now they had to put that discussion on hold and discuss possibilities where Debbie Milo's concerned.

Eugene knew the women would be hungry, but before he could go into the room with the two women, he needed to find out about the damn stun gun. After thinking it through the idea of calling the manufacturer presented itself, however, the call had been answered by an automated system that couldn't help him. Flustered and more than a little angry he decided to find a human being or two and try the gun out.

After checking to make sure the stun gun was fully charged he drove around town looking for homeless people. They'd be perfect subjects to test the weapon. No one worried about them, they usually didn't have family or if they did they didn't keep in touch with them, an ideal solution for trying out the stun gun. Finding two homeless people shouldn't be this hard he thought. Already at it for over an hour he just about gave up when he spotted one. Turning into the alley slowly, not wanting to scare the filthy, ragged, looking man. Eugene bit his tongue to keep from laughing out loud. He felt his excitement growing rapidly at the idea of zapping this guy. The closer he came to the man Eugene could tell he was an older gentleman. The guy leaned against a shopping cart filled to capacity with what Eugene considered junk.

Rolling down his window he held the stun gun in his left hand, down beside the door. "Excuse me sir, I'm lost. I'll gladly give you a few dollars if you can help me."

The old man looked over at the shiny car and the young man sitting in it alone. "A few dollars you say? Sure, how can I hep ya?" The old man approached Eugene's car.

"I need to find out…" zap! Eugene struck the bum in the neck the old man fell to the ground with a surprised look on his face. Eugene tossed a couple ones out the window and drove off. Laughing so hard he had tears running down his cheeks. His stomach hurt and he eventually had to stop to wipe the water away that blurred his vision.

Finally under control once again he needed one more test dummy. "Damn if that wasn't fun," he said through his laughter yet again.

He'd struck pay dirt, seemed everywhere he looked now he could see them standing or lying around, he needed another loaner. "The alley ways are where I should've been looking all along." He drove down another. Two alleys later he found her. The middle aged dried up, weathered looking woman sat on a cardboard box petting a scruffy pooch. He used the same tactic with her. Once he zapped her he tossed a couple ones at her and headed for home.

Eugene thoroughly enjoyed his ride home. He cranked his classical music up and directed an imaginary orchestra as he drove. He would feed the women left-over's they'd provided themselves, ah the injustice of it all, he thought laughing.

The pain in his hip almost forgotten because of the fun

he'd had. Soon this hip pain would be gone for good. He would be able to run and play, just like all the other boys, he snickered.

Chrissy and Deb had no luck at all finding a weapon to use. Their stomachs rumbled with hunger, and they began to think Eugene would leave them there to starve.

"How long do you think you've been here?" Chrissy whispered to Debbie. She knew her friends head pounded from lack of nourishment. Debbie had complained about it the last couple of hours.

"I don't know, if I had to guess, I'd say about a day maybe." She laid her head back against the chair cushion. "Has he come in here to see you at all?"

"No, I don't understand any of this. How long did he wait after you left here before he came to get you?" Chrissy tried to determine how long she had been missing, her hope of being found soon dwindled by the minute.

"I guess a couple hours maybe, I don't know I didn't pay attention to the time. His mother showed up causing problems and I argued with her, next thing I know he's in my kitchen choking me out."

"Alright at least we know I've been here a couple of hours longer than you have, and even though it's hard to gauge time in here, I'd have to say we've been here at least twenty four hours. So we know they're looking for us."

"I sure as hell hope they know I'm missing too."

"Oh I have no doubt about that, John would've called you about me and when they can't reach you by phone someone would go to your house."

"Yeah, I know that, but what's to make them think I'm missing, just because they don't find me at home doesn't mean I'm missing. Someone needs to go a step farther and actually go into my house."

"Why?"

"My purse, cell phone, keys, car, everything is there." She giggled and said, "you know he had been so careful with the other girls, not to leave a trace, but with me, he leaves a trail a mile long, of course, not anything particularly pointing towards him, but still."

"I wonder what he did with my stuff. You know my car is out front of his neighbor's house." the hope that sprang to life crashed quickly, "no he had to move it he couldn't leave it there and not draw suspicion to himself."

"Oh yeah, if not they'd have found us already."

The door began scraping the floor. The girls couldn't even get over there before he came in. The plan had been to be on each side of the door and attack when he entered. Too late now!

Eugene flipped a switch somewhere they couldn't see, but dim light lit the small room. He pushed a tray in with his foot, "stay where you are," he told them holding the stun gun up for them to see. "I thought you might be hungry."

Chrissy was pissed. She stood up and glared at him, "what the fuck is wrong with you Eugene?"

"Now, now is that any way for a lady to talk?"

Debbie grabbed Chrissy and held her back. Chrissy had every intention of charging him. "Let me go," she shouted at Deb.

"Don't be silly, you don't want him to hit you with that. Calm down, think about what you're doing," Debbie held onto her friend.

"Listen to your friend Chrissy, I'd hate to hurt you. At least not yet." He laughed backing out of the room.

Debbie let go as the door began to close, the tray of food looked better than it did yesterday. Kneeling down next to the tray Debbie hesitated, "what if he laced it with something?"

"Why would he do that, he already has us locked up. No

he plans to kill us the same way he did those other girls." Chrissy sat down and began to cry. "Go ahead and eat," she told Debbie through her tears.

"You need to eat too, stop that, we have to hold it together." Debbie scooped a handful of potato salad into her mouth with her hand since the ass couldn't see fit to bring them utensils.

"I could've taken him down why did you stop me?"

"No you couldn't that stun gun would've hurt you, then he would walk out of here no worse for wear. Eat, keep your strength up, we're going to get through this. At least this time he left a light on for us." Debbie continued to eat and prayed Eugene didn't put anything in the food.

Eugene sunk into his chair, that went better then he thought it would. He wasn't sure the stun gun would even be useful since he'd zapped the two homeless people. Chrissy sure is feisty he thought, she definitely would bring him the utmost pleasure when the time came. He got up and put the stun gun on the charger, he'd make sure it worked if he needed it.

Eugene watched the news as he ate his dinner. He waited patiently for his story to be reported, but nothing had been said. Filled with disappointment he wondered why the news cast didn't air information about the missing women. Maybe he should've gone to see John today. Now he feared it looked bad that he didn't. That Stone fella already suspected him of something, but he'd played it cool, acting like he didn't care what the man thought. Still he needed to go see John tomorrow. He'd use his hip as an excuse for not making it today. For all the trouble this hip caused him, it sure came in handy sometimes.

He went to the kitchen and washed up the few dishes he'd used. He thought about getting the dishes the girls had, but decided not to chance it.

Agent Marlowe and Lt. Washington listened as Mark filled them in regarding the information he just received about Debbie Milo.

"I know this woman, she takes off on a dime to give readings, or speak at paranormal conferences, however, the problem is, Jo told me the girls were planning a girl's night out tonight and Debbie was hosting it at her house. She wouldn't leave with that planned. Her car's in the driveway and the house is locked up, but Jo said she could see in and Debbie's not there.

"You say you know this woman. Is she a friend of the one we already have missing?" Lee Marlowe asked.

"Yes, I need to tell you all something else." He struggled with this, he had always kept his personal life to himself, but he needed to tell them about the group.

Lt. Washington watched the struggle Mark apparently fought, "Mason, just spit it out. What's the problem?"

"The two women we're talking about, belong to a group of people who investigate paranormal activity, and that's not all. This woman, Debbie Milo, is a psychic medium."

The group stood there looking at him disbelievingly. "I know this sounds funny to you, but I believe in these people, I'm a group member." He waited for them to start laughing at him or poking fun, when they didn't he continued, "Debbie called a couple days ago," he took a deep breath, "two of our victims paid her a visit."

Marlowe jumped on board now. He'd seen psychics at work. The FBI used them on occasion to solve crimes, of course, this fact always keep secret to preserve the integrity of the FBI. "Mark, I can see you're concerned what your coworkers will think of you, but let me assure you I've worked with psychics before, and I see nothing wrong with what you and your friends do. Let's focus on what Ms. Milo shared with you."

Feeling a little better with the Agent's open mindedness Mark continued. "Not much, they just gave her glimpses of places and a dark figure in a basement, which made no sense, but Debbie knew these women to be victims because she looked them up on the internet."

"What are you saying Mason?" Lt. Washington asked totally confused at this point.

"He's telling us he's been hard at work, just in an unconventional way. So Mark, do you think these two women were both taken by our serial killer?" Agent Marlowe wanted to keep him talking, get his take on everything this medium told him.

"I don't know, I say we need to go to Debbie's place and check it out."

THIRTY-SEVEN

Matt and John drove around the Forest looking everywhere they could think to look. The coldness that settled in the area kept most people inside. No one walked through the Forest today. John's leg throbbed intensely from dangling down. He needed his pain pills, but hated to leave the Forest without thoroughly checking it out.

Matt could see John's irritation and knew they weren't going to find Chrissy out here. He wanted to tell John that, but didn't want to take his friends hope away.

"Let's try the Shack, I know it's not in Freetown, but it's in the Forest," John suggested. "If she's not there we'll run by my place for my pain pills then go to Tate's."

"Sounds like a plan." Matt wondered what the group was doing. Had they formed a plan yet? Why weren't they out here combing the woods already? If John weren't sitting next to him he'd call Dave, find out what's going on, but John's peace of mind with the group of volunteers out looking too, seemed important, and Matt wouldn't get him thinking they had not started yet.

"Alright, so everyone knows which group they are assigned to?" Dave finally had them ready to go. When he felt comfortable with their acknowledgments he said, "Let's roll, we'll keep in contact by cell phone, each group leader has exchanged numbers. It's important your group stays together. We will meet back here in a few hours, be careful and good luck."

Dave approached Joellen, "Where's Debbie, I didn't see her come in with you?"

Joellen bit her lip, "I couldn't find her Dave. I'm really worried she may be missing too."

Surprise showed on his face. "Why do you think she's missing, did you call Mark?"

"Yes I did call Mark, but he said not to say anything until he had a chance to check it out for himself. I'm waiting to hear from him."

"If she's missing too that could be a good thing, don't look so worried, I mean think about it, they may be together, off doing something."

"Yeah, right they went shopping like women always do, right?"

"Sure, that's a good possibility." Dave felt hope begin to build.

"Dammit Dave come on, Chrissy's purse was in her car, Debbie's car is in her driveway. What'd they do hop in a taxi?" Joellen shook her head in a negative manner. "No they aren't shopping they've been abducted and we need to find them before he kills them." She grabbed her gloves and walked to the door.

Dave couldn't believe he'd forgotten about Chrissy's purse, and since he didn't know about Debbie's car that didn't factor in to his way of thinking. Now his hope dashed and fear set in. "Joellen hold up," he caught up to her just outside the front door. "Look I didn't know about Debbie's car, you're right something's off, but we're going to find them." He slipped his arm around her shoulders and walked to his car with her. They were a team of two, some groups had four.

Cody Stone left Alex Norman to draw up a search warrant while the rest of them headed to the Milo residence. Alex would get the warrant signed and meet them there.

Agent Marlowe insisted he come along. Lt. Washington stayed behind. The group left taking two different vehicles.

319

Alex's vehicle would give them three in case someone had to branch off to check something else out. Marlowe felt if the same person abducted both women he must be confident in his ability to handle two at the same time. All four of the other women had been taken one at a time, and never kept more than a day. Chrissy Bingham had already been missing for one whole day.

Mark, Ian, and Ricky were in one vehicle, Cody, Kyle and Lee in the other. Cody followed behind Mark. Mark's stomach churned with nerves. He had made Lilly leave because he thought the killer wanted her. The guilt concerning his two friends over whelmed him. He couldn't imagine what John must be going through.

Pulling into the driveway behind Debbie's car Mark turned the ignition off. Not totally sure he wanted to confirm Debbie was missing he took his time getting out of the car. The others jumped out ready to go.

Stone gave orders to the guys and watched as they took off in different directions. He turned to look at Mark sitting in the car and then at the man standing next to him. "Agent Marlowe, what do you make of this? I mean psychics and stuff?"

Marlowe scratched his head and looked directly at Cody, "I believe in them, some of them anyway. I've seen gifted psychics at work. The problem lies in people being closed minded. We've used several during investigations that if it hadn't been for them we probably wouldn't have solved the cases." He watched the detective try to accept what he'd said, but knew it fell on deaf ears.

Cody looked away he couldn't buy into the psychic thing. Too many frauds out there took hard earned money from desperate people. Nodding his head in answer he stepped over to Mark's driver side door, "you getting out or what?"

Mark looked at him, pulled the keys from the ignition and opened the door. "Don't think we'll find too much till Alex gets here with the warrant."

"Probably not, but no sense sitting in the car, be sociable." He slapped Mark on the back.

"She's my friend Cody, I already have one friend missing that we know about, I'm not too eager to find another one missing."

Agent Marlowe stood close enough he could hear them talking. Anyone with eyes could see Mason was having a tough time. He walked over, "you know, I've been thinking, it strikes me that if your friend, Debbie, is missing she might've found something out and told the wrong person." Using this line of thinking he hoped to put the man in a working frame of mind and getting him out of the personal thinking mode.

Mark looked at the man, "that would have to mean she knew him. If she knew him then I more than likely know him too."

Eugene went by John's house, but found he wasn't home. Snickering wickedly he thought his friend had to be out searching for his wife. He should feel bad about the pain he caused his friend, but he didn't.

Standing on John's porch Eugene watched Matt's truck pull into the driveway. Let the show begin he thought.

John stayed in the passenger seat while Matt hopped out walking toward Eugene. "He isn't getting out if you wanna talk to him you better go over there." Taking the key John had given him he let himself into the house.

Eugene limped more than he needed to over to his friend. "Sorry I didn't make it by earlier John, I've been worried sick about you and Chrissy, but my hip is bothering me something terrible."

John looked at the much smaller man, who didn't look

like he's experiencing much pain. He didn't look like he even wanted to be there. Chrissy wouldn't want Eugene here anyway. For some reason John wanted to take all his frustrations and anger out on this little man. If Chrissy hadn't stayed behind to help him, she would be here now. "I understand, go on home and take care of yourself." John turned his face forward, away from Eugene. He couldn't stand to look at him right now.

Eugene felt a rush of anger. John practically snubbed him just now. How dare he treat me with such disdain? "Are you angry with me John?"

John didn't bother to look at him, "nope just have a lot on my mind."

Eugene stood there looking at John's profile he knew the man could feel him staring. He wanted to snatch him from that truck and beat the hell out of him. Unbelievable, he thought.

Matt came back to the truck and slid into the driver seat. "Here ya go, I brought the whole bottle." He handed the prescription over to John.

"Thanks."

Eugene still stood there completely ignored. Taking a step back from the truck he didn't say another word. Matt started the truck up, "you finished talking?"

John nodded his head and didn't look at either one of them as Matt backed out. Opening the pill bottle he removed two pills and swallowed them without water.

Eugene stormed over to his car, forgetting he should be limping. He would go home and find a way to get Chrissy and Debbie separated. Chrissy would pay for the way her husband just treated him.

Matt and John headed to Tate's. Matt felt uneasy at John's quiet demeanor. He knew his friend, and his attitude had changed from the time he left him to get the pills, and

322

now. "What happened back there?"

"Not much."

Matt wouldn't let it go, "did he say something to piss you off?"

"Nope"

"He did something, you might as well tell me. I ain't letting it go."

John drew in a deep breath, "he didn't do or say anything. I feel if Chrissy hadn't stayed at his house to help him she'd still be here." He shook his head "I know that's pretty little of me, but that's how I feel."

Matt could understand that, he also knew it wasn't fair to hold the man responsible. "You do realize those feeling are natural, but not feasible, right?"

"Yeah I know."

Matt would let him stew he deserved to be angry, as long as, he could keep it in perspective.

Chrissy and Debbie finished the tray of food. Both had plenty to eat, and felt much better with their stomachs full. The corner they had chosen to use for their restroom really began stinking the small space up. At first Debbie panicked when she had to relieve herself, but the two discussed it and decided they would do what they had to do, and he could clean it up. This actually made them laugh, until now when the stench began to get to both of them

"Wonder how pissed he would be if we tore up a couple of his books to soak up that urine?" Debbie said laughing.

"What a great idea, we could put the wet pages on the tray." Chrissy giggled. "Teach him not to provide us a bathroom won't it?" Going immediately over to the shelves she found a couple smaller books and began ripping pages out to lay over the wet area. The sooner they soaked the pee up the better it would smell in here, she thought.

They had checked out the little room, finding a ton of books on the occult. Debbie started reading one to pass time when she came across a particular ritual that called for human blood and actual sacrifices, to gain one's health back. As she read, a picture began to unfold right before her eyes. Debbie gasped "oh my God, I totally get what he's doing," she said excitedly.

Chrissy turned from her undesirable chore to look at her friend. "What's he doing?"

"Listen to this…" She read the ritual out loud to Chrissy. "The only thing left is two more sacrifices. That's us!"

Chrissy looked on in horror "he thinks this is going to give him good health? Are you fucking kidding me?"

"Nope, the thing is and he isn't smart enough to figure it out," she laughed "it's for health not a deformity. This isn't going to help the stupid ass one bit."

"That could be good then, we need to point that out to him. He won't gain anything by killing us." Scooping up the wet pages with dry ones to keep from touching them, she tossed the stinking mess onto the dinner tray.

"Oh no hun, he'll still kill us. He can't very well just let us go."

"You sure know how to burst someone's bubble girl. So what do we do?"

Debbie folded the page down in the book, "we try to talk to him, reason with him. Hell flat out lie to him. He knows I'm gifted right?"

"I suppose, yeah."

"We make him believe I can heal him. We make him think I have the power to do that." Her eyes lit up as the wheels turned. They could do this, they had to, it was their only chance.

THIRTY-EIGHT

Eugene pulled into his driveway as his cell phone started to ring. He looked at the caller ID, John Bingham, "ha now you want to talk to me, huh?"

John waited impatiently for Eugene to answer. He had the thought occur to him, that Chrissy wouldn't want him to mistreat Eugene. She didn't like Eugene, but she never liked seeing anyone treated unfairly. John had to apologize to Eugene. His conscience was killing him.

"Hello," Eugene said in a cool manner.

"Eugene, I want to apologize for the way I treated you, I had no reason to do that, and I'm sorry."

Eugene felt the tension leaving his body, "thank you, I accept your apology."

"Good, I'll talk with you later then. I gotta get into Tate's and see what the search parties come up with."

"Tate's is where everyone's meeting?"

"Yeah, my house wasn't big enough for the turn out we had."

"Mind if I come over there?"

John really didn't want him to come over, but since he just apologized it would be rude to tell him no. "You can if you want to, but don't feel obligated I know your hip is giving you problems."

"I can't help the search by walking, but there has to be something I can do. I want to be there for you, my friend."

"Okay, see you, if you decide to come." He hung up thinking he gave him an out and hoped he'd take it.

Eugene backed out of his driveway and headed for Tate's.

* * *

Alex brought the signed search warrant. The inside of Debbie Milo's house showed no sign of struggle. Mark felt like banging his head against the wall he leaned on. He knew in his gut she was in trouble.

Lee watched the emotions play on Mark's face the man was being torn apart by guilt. The problem being he'd done absolutely nothing to feel guilty about.

The single wine glass in the sink, her purse, cell phone and keys missing, all made to look like someone picked her up. She'd been here alone, but Lee agreed with Mark, something definitely, not right about the situation. He tossed an idea around in his head about calling a friend of his, a psychic friend.

Cody stood in the living room ready to leave, "we about ready to get out of here?"

Alex, Ian, Ricky, and Kyle walked out the door, "I'm smoking," Kyle told Cody as they walked out.

Cody walked into the kitchen, Lee and Mark both stood there, not holding a conversation, not investigating the room, just standing quietly. "You guys coming? We're ready to go whenever you are."

"Give us a minute, we'll be right out," Lee answered. He wanted a minute alone with Mark.

Cody looked at both men, shrugged his shoulders and left.

Mark pushed himself off the wall "I'm good, let's go." He went to walk out of the room when Lee grabbed his arm.

"Hold up a sec, I know this is really hard on you," when Mark started to say something Lee held his hand up. "Hear me out. I have a friend that may be able to help us find out if Ms. Milo has been abducted too. She's a psychic, a very talented psychic, but I don't want the guys to know if we use her."

"Why not, you afraid what they'll think of you when they find out you believe in paranormal shit?"

"Not at all, it's just this isn't my investigation. I don't want anyone to think I'm stepping on toes. If you want I'll give her a call, but you will have to be here with her and me if she agrees."

Mark didn't hesitate, "call her set it up."

Lee nodded and left by way of the front door, while Mark secured the back door with a hasp and lock. They had to force entry and the back door had been a better choice than the front. He stuck the key in his pocket and met the group out front.

"I think it's a good time for a dinner break," Cody suggested when Mark showed up. "Why don't we call Lt. Washington and discuss over food?"

"Sounds great to me, I'm starving," Mark said getting in his car.

Lee called Lt. Washington and told her they were all going for a bite at the local steak house, she agreed to meet them there.

Mark called to check on Lilly, he felt better just hearing her voice. She told him about her conversation with John and filled him in on her daily activities, by phone only. He'd been pleased to hear she kept her promise, except telling John she's home. He couldn't fault her for that. With a couple more people in the car he didn't want to get into too much detail over the phone. He explained they were on their way to dinner and it would be a late night. He held back the information on Debbie since he had no proof yet. She would be devastated to hear another of her friends may be missing.

The riding arrangements shifted slightly since Alex had his own car. Kyle rode with Cody, Alex and Ricky rode in Alex's car and Lee and Ian rode with Mark. Mark thought Lee set it up so they could talk about his friend's possible help, until he realized Ian was in the back seat. Lee sat quietly in the front passenger seat texting. Mark assumed he was setting up the appointment with his psychic friend. He wondered what her ability or gift was. He liked Lee, the man proved himself to be a team player and definitely not interested in pushing his way to the top of this investigation like most FBI agents were apt to do.

Lee read a text, smiled at Mark, and gave a slight nod. They were on for later that evening. He would fill Mark in, as soon as, they were alone. Maria text 'I'll be happy to C 4 U. 2nite is good, give me a time', he text 9 and the address.

THIRTY-NINE

Eugene arrived at Tate's. He couldn't believe the number of vehicles outside the bar. Parking had been hell. He had to park almost two blocks away. The parking lot and side streets, as well as, the street in front of the bar were filled. Laughing to himself, he wondered if John or Chrissy could be this well known, or if the community folk began to pull together to stop him. Fat chance, he thought, he's so much smarter than all of them he prided himself.

After the two block walk, his hip really hurt. He entered the bar with a painful limp and looked around at the empty space. What the hell, he thought, where is everyone? He noticed Sam and Maggie standing near the bar talking to John and Matt, who were seated at the bar. Making his way over to them he continued to look around.

"With all the vehicles outside I thought this place would be over flowing." He smiled.

"You just missed the crowd. They piled into each other's vehicles and hit the street to search," Sam told him.

"Must've been some turnout." He slapped John on the back.

"Unbelievable turnout actually, everyone and their brother showed up to help out. You want something to drink Eugene?" Sam walked behind the bar.

"Sure I'll have a beer."

Cindy came out of the cooler pushing a dolly filled with cases of beer. "Sam this should hold us a while."

"Thanks Cindy, I'll take it from here." Sam set Eugene's beer mug on the bar and took the dolly from Cindy.

"You sure, I don't mind loading the coolers." She isn't

329

one to stand around if work's to be done. Besides, she felt strange with all these people talking about the missing woman, and her not knowing what to do or say to any of them. After all, she didn't know Chrissy Bingham.

"Yeah, I'm sure. Why don't you get off your feet for a few, we're going to be busy again when the volunteer's come back thirsty."

"It's okay I like to keep busy." She smiled at him.

"Me too girl, but trust me, Sam's right by the time we go home tonight our feet will be killing us." Maggie climbed up on a bar stool.

John had been sitting quietly, he hated that his friends were working so hard to help him out. He thought about telling them so when Eugene came in, and he changed his mind. For the life of him he couldn't figure out why the man suddenly irritated him so badly.

"So what's the word, any new information on Chrissy?" Eugene asked once Cindy found a bar stool to sit on.

"Nothing yet, but then the search actually just began in the last half hour or so," Sam told him.

"How you holding up, John?" Maggie asked him quietly, lightly touching his shoulder.

John didn't say anything, simply nodded his head. Fear held his heart in a tight grasp, and he found it hard to catch his breath. What would he do if Chrissy didn't come back? The thought had tears pooling in his eyes. He blinked rapidly trying to hold them back.

Matt and Maggie noticed, looking away to give him time to gather himself. None of them, except Eugene, of course, could imagine what he's going through. Eugene ate the fear up that radiated off his friend. He couldn't help that the agony on his friends face, delighted him. It made him almost as giddy as the actual killing.

John gulped down his mug of beer, he needed to be

doing something. Sitting here killed him. He looked around the room thinking, strategizing his next move. Sam refilled the mug and set it back in front of his friend. John watched the tiny bubbles make their way to the surface, he kept watching them thinking, 'where are you my love', over and over in his mind.

The girls planned their idea completely. Each had a role to play, and knew their lives depended on it working.

"Have you ever performed Reiki for real?" Chrissy hoped her friend had.

"Nope, but I've watched it being done many times. I know how it works, I know the moves. I just never harnessed the power to perform it on anyone. At least I should say I've never tried to perform Reiki on anyone."

"What if he won't let you try? I mean we need to have a plan B."

"We do, plan B is to kick his stupid ass around this little fucking room. I tell ya Chrissy, I'm ready to chew through a wall. I can't stand being closed in." Debbie paced the small room, she felt disconnected to the outside world, which didn't sit well with her.

Chrissy got up walking over to Debbie, she stopped her friends pacing and said "listen to me, you are one of the strongest people I know, we're getting out of here one way or another. Don't fall apart on me, I need you."

Scooping Chrissy into a tight hug she laughed, "yeah one way or another, it's the, 'another' that worries me." Both women had a good laugh.

"At least we're together imagine, what the others went through all alone. No way are we giving up. Letting him get the best of us, we're both better than that." Chrissy looked down at her hands after letting go of her friend, and laughed. "Uh, guess I should apologize for hugging you with my pissy hands," holding her hands palms up, tears rolled down her cheeks from laughing so hard.

"Euww, you're right, that's gross." Debbie looked down at her sleeves and began laughing pretty hard herself. "Guess you needed something to wipe them on, but did it have to be me?"

The laughter finally subsided and they collapsed onto the floor. Keeping each other calm, important to both of them, when one started to lose it the other held strong.

"You think he'll make an appearance anytime soon?" Chrissy asked.

"I sure hope so, the sooner the better."

"Why can't you get some help from your little friends?"

"My little friends?"

"Yeah, you know your ghost pals?"

Debbie smiled warmly. It always tickled her the way people perceived her gift. "It doesn't happen that way sadly, they appear and disappear when they want. Some don't even talk to me they just show me pictures in my mind. Trust me if it were possible to use them to get us out of this fix I would've already done it."

"That sucks, all for them and nothing for you. Why do you do it?"

"I don't do it for me, besides I get pleasure when I know I've helped someone to cross over."

"Yeah, I don't get that whole cross over thing. I mean if they don't want to be here then why not go into the light?"

Debbie enjoyed this conversation, finally something to take her mind off where they were. "It's more complicated than that. Sometimes they don't see a light, other times they don't want to leave what they know for the unknown. All I know is sometimes they have to take care of something or someone before the light even appears to them."

Chrissy thought about it for a minute then asked "So

what you're telling me is even though we die, we may be stuck here, like in limbo?"

"Yeah, I guess that's a good way to put it. The funny thing is sometimes they don't even know their dead. "

"Well it sucks they're stuck here, but it would really suck to not know you're dead. How do you deal with them? "

"Not really, I find that when spirits have unfinished business, they want to see it through. The ones that chose not to go are comfortable here, so you see it works for them. The ones that can't remember I get them to think, about the last thing they remember, which can be pretty tricky if they don't want to remember."

"You mean some chose not to remember? How the hell does that work?"

"Well yeah, I mean if you experienced something really tragic, would you want to remember if you had a choice? Hell no, neither do they."

"So how do you push a ghost?"

"I don't push, I just keep bringing them back to the point where their confusion seems to begin, eventually they remember, but I forgot to ask you something. What's going on with Mark and Lilly?"

"Mark and Lilly?"

"Yeah, the secret John knows that Mark wouldn't share with us. What's up?"

"Oh that, hell I don't know. I planned to ask him when I got home, but never had the chance."

"Hmmm well I think I know, at least it may be her."

"May be her? What do you mean?"

"I happen to know someone is pregnant, I just don't know who yet?"

"How do you know that?"

"Simple, when someone I know becomes pregnant, I dream of fish going upstream. I had a dream a few weeks ago and have been waiting to find out who it is."

"You're a strange one, Debbie Milo." Chrissy laughed, "but I hope it is Lilly. They want a baby so badly, and have tried forever."

"Me too, they would be great parents."

Chrissy thought about her friend and wondered if Mark told her she was missing yet. If Lilly knew, she hoped her friend wouldn't stress and loose the baby. She didn't think she could handle that.

"What are you thinking? You have little frown lines between your brows?"

"About Lilly, and the possibility she could be pregnant."

"That shouldn't cause you to frown. Come on girl give."

"No really, I thought if she is pregnant then the stress of us missing could cause her problems, you know?"

"Yeah, I see what you're thinking and don't worry, this baby will make its way into the world no matter what."

"How do you know that?"

"I just do, can't explain everything to you."

Everyone gathered around Dave back at Tate's. It had been a long day and with night falling quickly, they decided to plan for tomorrow's search. As promised Maggie and Cindy were running around making sure everyone had a drink. John couldn't believe Sam didn't charge the volunteers. He thanked him profusely. Sam explained he could only do that today, but he was happy to help in any way he could and that included the use of his bar for meet ups.

Eugene had talked with Dave about helping, but was told if he couldn't get out and beat the bushes there really wasn't anything for him to do.

"I understand completely. I really wanted to help John out, but I know he understands I'm no good at walking for any length of time." Eugene stepped away from Dave and headed toward John. He dreaded talking one on one with the man right now. It seemed eerie to Eugene, almost as if John knew he had Chrissy locked up at home. John never treated him like he did earlier.

John saw Eugene heading straight for him, he turned to Matt, "I don't know if I can be civil to him, help me out here."

Matt noticed Eugene's approach and understood what John meant. He thought quickly then jumped up and stood between John and Eugene, "hey there."

Eugene looked at Matt confused, then nodded his head and tried to step around him.

"Sorry Eugene, but John's not feeling well, I'm sure you understand." He wouldn't let the man get around him.

"Of course I understand. I wanted to tell him I'm leaving." Eugene felt his anger rise. It sure didn't take much to piss him off he thought.

"He can hear you, I'm sure he appreciates you coming by."

Exasperated Eugene stood there looking the Native American directly in his face "step aside Matt, John is my friend and I want to tell him goodbye."

"No can do little man, you have a good night."

Eugene felt as if the man had slapped him. Little man! He inhaled sharply to control himself, and notice John squirm on the stool he'd been sitting on. Surely he would turn around and say something.

Matt stood his ground, "You have a good night, Eugene."

"Fine, I see what's going on here. You guys are all having a good laugh at the handicap. Let me assure you this is not the first time and I'm sure it won't be the last time either. You have a good night Matt." Eugene turned to leave.

John felt the sweat pop on his upper lip, he couldn't believe the way he's treating Eugene. He knew Matt just did what he asked him to do, but he couldn't stand the guilt. "Hold up Eugene," John yelled after him.

Eugene stood rigid, his back still toward John. Matt looked over at John and when he saw his face he completely understood. "Eugene," John said again.

When Eugene stood there still not turning, but also not walking out, John picked up his crutches and hobbled over to him. "Listen I asked Matt to keep people away from me. I have a splitting headache, and I'm sick to my stomach, but I can't treat people that way. I know you're all here to help me and it's just not right."

Eugene had kept his back to John while he spoke. He understood his friend's pain. He turned and nodded at John "I understand, I won't keep you, but you tell that man if he ever refers to me as a little man again, we're going to have problems." Eugene glared at John, he understood, however, no one would be little him like that, certainly not in front of all these people.

"I don't think Matt meant it the way you took it." John looked over his shoulder at Matt, his hulking size kept Eugene from seeing him. Matt shrugged his shoulders and turned back to the bar. John wanted to laugh, but caught himself in time.

"Have a good night, John. At least as good as you can under the circumstances." Eugene left. He had been close to the boiling point and quite glad John stopped him. He probably would've gone home and done something stupid. Something he couldn't take back tomorrow.

Lilly had called everyone she could think of. She had the library staff posting pictures of Chrissy. The posters had been printed with a picture and all the information they could think of, giving her age, description and contact number of the task force.

336

Patricia called earlier in the evening to check on her and find out how Mark had taken the homecoming. After Lilly explained everything, and broke down into tears her mother informed her she was on her way. She begged Lilly to take it easy and not stress too badly.

Lilly promised her mom the stress of Chrissy missing, would not endanger her baby. She loved Chrissy Bingham and worried for her safety, but her baby had to come first.

Taking a look at the clock she noted the time, her mother should be there soon.

FORTY

Mark and Lee waited out front of Debbie's house for Maria Erickson to arrive. Lee had explained the FBI used her on several cases, and she was always a big help. He further explained one of the cases had involved his younger brother, and not going into detail he told Mark he and Maria had become good friends.

Hell he even entertained the idea of dating her, but decided that relationship would be doomed before it started. Between his job and her gifts, not to mention, he lived in Virginia and she lived in Pennsylvania. Of course, he didn't tell Mark any of that.

"I can't believe she dropped everything to drive four and a half hours here on such short notice," Mark said impressed.

"She's used to short notices, sometimes we fly her, but when it's personal like this, she drives."

"I can't thank you enough Lee. I hope we find out Debbie just took off on some tangent. Somewhere with someone and not what we fear."

"I know, I hope the same thing, but I have a feeling we're not going to like what we hear."

Mark shook his head he knew in his gut Debbie was missing too. He refused not to hope for better news.

Lee changed the subject, "what do you make of the two homeless people being stun gunned earlier?"

"I don't know, this towns usually so quiet. All this crime is good for business, but bad for the community." Mark looked mildly amused.

"You got a point. I want to take a look at the reports though, can't tell you why, just a feeling." Lee stretched his long form. They'd been standing there for almost half an hour. "Maria must've hit some traffic."

"You're not going to hear me complain about waiting, I'm just happy she's coming."

"Me too, maybe I should give her a call and check on her." Lee pulled his cell phone out and hit a button.

Mark heard Lee laughing and turned to look at him. He hadn't heard Lee say a word. His quizzical expression gave his thoughts away.

"Okay," Lee said and hung up. "She answered the phone 'be there in two shakes' not even hello," he said laughing again.

"I wondered what had been so funny." Mark smirked.

"Yeah, she's got the best sense of humor. You're going to love her."

"Funny, I think I might love her already, just for agreeing to come all this way."

"She's quite a gal," he said turning to watch her car pull up next to them.

"Hey, beautiful," Lee greeted her. "Park right over there, we're going in here." He pointed behind him.

Maria flipped a U-turn and parked her red Mazda Miata on the other side of the street. When she stepped out Mark stared. He'd never seen such a beautiful woman. Maria Erickson was absolutely stunning. A tall African American woman, with curves in all the right places, squared her shoulders and walked towards them. Long light brown hair fell below her shoulders. Her unusual grey eyes sparkled like glitter. The pale bronze of her skin enhanced her beauty, and she knew it. This woman had everything in the looks department and Mark found himself hoping her gift offered as much. If it did they couldn't lose.

Lee pulled her tightly to him, "I hope the drive wasn't too bad."

"For you my friend, never, I would drive to the ends of the Earth for you, Lee."

Lee turned her around, "Maria, this is Mark Mason. Mark, meet my girl wonder."

Mark stuck his hand out, "Thank you so much for coming Ms. Erickson."

Maria looked at him and started laughing "come here Mark, it's my pleasure to help if I can." She pulled Mark into a hug "I don't shake hands with my friends." Stepping back she looked at Lee, "don't tell me much, but tell me something. I hate walking in and finding bloody scenes or shit without warning."

"Nah shouldn't be anything like that sweetheart. Just tell us what you see."

"Good then let's go." Maria followed Mark holding Lee's hand. She smiled up at him, 'he always gives me the warm fuzzies' she thought.

Mark told them to wait while he ran around back. He wanted Maria to enter the house from the front door for some odd reason. Quickly removing the key from his pocket he unlocked the door. Stuffing both the key and lock into his jacket pocket, he went through the small house and opened the front door.

Mark turned one small lamp on in the front room as he stepped back for them to enter. No one said anything. Lee and Mark kept their gaze on Maria as she wandered the small living room. She didn't touch anything, simply looked around. As she entered the short hallway leading to Debbie's bedroom she turned and asked "may I?" When Lee nodded she headed down the hall. Poking her head in what appeared to be a guest bedroom she backed out and continued to the next room. Walking in, she looked around, still not touching anything. Lee and Mark stood in the doorway watching her.

Sitting down on the bed she closed her eyes, breathing in

through her nose and out through her mouth. Not even a full minute later she looked at them, "naughty boys," she said wagging her index finger in their direction.

They looked at each other, then back at Maria. Lee asked "what?"

"You didn't tell me she's a gifted person."

Mark looked at Lee amazed. Shaking his head yes at Lee showed how impressed he was with her already.

Maria closed her eyes again and went back to the same breathing pattern as before. She lifted her hands up in the air, palms up and continued to breathe deeply.

The men stood there quietly watching her. Lee noticed her perfectly shaped breast, moving up and down with each breath she took. He knew he should look away, but found it an impossible task.

Maria opened her eyes and nodded her head in assent, stood and left the room.

She passed the bathroom and went directly to the kitchen. Stepping into the dark room she moved to the sink.

Mark flipped the light switch as he and Lee entered the kitchen. Maria placed her hands on the sink and her head dropped forward. She stood that way for a long time. Mark had given up hope when Maria turned toward them gasping for air and clawing at her nose and mouth. Her eyes were wide open and she had a wild look covering her face. Mark stepped towards her, but Lee pulled him back shaking his head no.

The two men stood there watching her fight for air until she slumped to the floor filling her lungs with much needed oxygen. Once she regained her composure she looked at Lee.

Lee stepped forward and helped her up, "what happened?"

"I need to sit down then I'll explain what I can."

All three of them walked to the living room. Maria sat

down on the sofa and Lee sat next to her. Mark remained standing.

"Your friend was attacked from behind as she stood at the sink. Someone came up behind her placing their hand over her mouth and nose. She fought them hard, but eventually passed out. I can't tell you much else, if anything."

Mark hated hearing what Maria said, but knew it all along. "Can you tell us if she's still alive?"

Maria smiled, "yes, she's still alive. She has a very strong gift. I hope I get to meet her soon."

"Yes, she is very talented. She helps me in many ways with her gifts. Thank you so much, Maria."

"I wish I could tell you more. She didn't see who attacked her, I do know that much."

"Can you tell if it was a man or a woman?" Lee looked at her waiting.

She thought about it for only a second "a man definitely, the hand that covered her mouth had a leather glove over it and he had such a strength about him." She shivered, "he asked her, who else is here?"

Mark and Lee looked at each other then Mark asked, "someone else was here when he attacked her?"

"No, I don't think so, he just asked her that."

"Okay then. We know Debbie has been abducted just like we know Chrissy has. We know it's a man, and we know Debbie is still alive." Mark covered all the points ticking them off on his fingers.

"Who is Chrissy?" Maria asked.

"Another friend of mine, she came up missing yesterday. We found her car with her purse and keys in it, on a side street," Mark told her.

"We have a serial killer here in Freetown Maria, that's why I'm here," Lee informed her.

"Oh no, you think that is who has these two women?"

Maria paled.

"Yes, unfortunately that's exactly what we think," Lee told her.

"What can I do to help? Can I take a look at the car maybe?"

Mark couldn't believe after what this woman just went through, she still wanted to help. "Sure you can, are you certain you want to put yourself through that?"

"Absolutely, if I can help I'm here already. Let me help you."

Lee looked at his watch "it's almost ten, why don't we get you set up at my hotel and start fresh in the morning?"

"Sounds good to me, lead the way," Maria told him.

"Uh Lee, if Maria stays, how do we keep her a secret?" Mark asked concern lacing the question.

"We don't," he stated plainly. "Go home and get some rest. Tomorrow should be a busy day. I'll ride back to the station with Maria and grab my car."

Mark waited for the two to leave before he locked up. He was more than ready to go home, but hated wasting time looking for his friends.

FORTY-ONE

Eugene warmed more food for the women, but had left the tray in the room earlier. He struggled with three dishes and one bottle of water. He wanted to take it all at the same time. Stuffing the stun gun into his back pants pocket, he slowly made his way to the hallway. Sitting everything down on the floor, he lifted the tapestry and pulled the lever to open the door.

Chrissy and Debbie sat across the room waiting, hoping for the chance to put their plan into action.

Eugene yelled into the room as he shoved first one dish then another in, with his foot, "don't move."

The two women barely breathing let alone moving sat together and waited. They saw the three dishes before they saw him. He stepped into the room with a single bottle of water in one hand and the stun gun in his other hand.

"Hello, my lovelies," he crooned, holding the stun gun up for them to see. "Sorry I've been such a bad host...my God what is that stench in here?" Appalled he tossed the bottle of water onto the floor and pinched his nose closed with his hand.

"Yeah, um that would be piss since you didn't see fit to provide us a toilet. What did you expect?" Chrissy yelled at him.

"Chrissy, you know there was no way for Mr. Lowery to do that, behave," Debbie placated him.

"You may not be pissed at him Debbie, but I sure as hell am. Fuck you Eugene." Chrissy glared at him.

"Chrissy, stop that this instant, you know he's doing the best he can." Debbie pointed her index finger at her friend.

"Shut up both of you and listen to me. I'm not stupid enough to think for one minute Ms. Milo, that you're on my side so give it up. As for you Chrissy, you're right I should have been better equipped to accommodate you. I apologize for that. Here's some food and water. I hope it's enough for both of you." Eugene began backing out of the room when Debbie hurried to say, "Mr. Lowery, wait, please."

Eugene stopped and looked at her.

"I, uh," she held up the book with the ritual inside. "This is all wrong."

"What's all wrong, Ms. Milo?"

"The ritual you're killing for. It's not going to help you, but I can." She tried for a smile and failed. This man literally made her skin crawl.

"I don't have time for nonsense Ms. Milo. I know what I'm doing." Taking another step back out of the door he stopped when she continued.

"No you don't. If you would give me a minute of your time I can explain." Debbie found the page she had ear-marked earlier.

"Alright go ahead." He watched Chrissy more than he did Debbie. He knew Chrissy would be the one to jump given the slightest opportunity.

"You can't explain it him Debbie, he isn't capable of understanding. He's too fucking stupid to grasp what you say." Chrissy stood with hands on her hips glaring angrily at him.

Eugene snickered at her display of bravado. Debbie began to read the ritual out loud slowly, when she finished she punctuated the word 'Health' with quotation marks using her two index fingers.

"Exactly good health, so what am I missing, Ms. Milo?" Eugene looked bored.

"Mr. Lowery, you already have good health. You're

searching for a cure to a handicapped deformity, not a health issue. This ritual, these killings, they won't help you, but I can if you'll let me." She looked at him directly, assuredly, letting him know she's completely serious and capable.

Eugene stood there thinking what she'd said through. "You may be right Ms. Milo, I'll be dammed. All this work for nothing." He shook his head as if confused.

"Mr. Lowery, let me help you," Debbie pleaded.

"Why would you help me?"

"Why? Are you insane? To save our lives, Mr. Lowery." Debbie looked dumbfounded.

"What?" Eugene looked surprised "even if you were capable of such a feat as to heal me, I sure as hell couldn't let the two of you walk out of here." He laughed at her.

"You could if we all agree to a plan of action. Trust me I am capable of such a feat, as you put it."

"How could I possibly let you two go? You would run right to the police and then handicapped or not, I would be sitting in prison. Where do I gain anything by doing that?"

"Mr. Lowery, if you could have your deformity healed, no police action what so ever involved, would you be willing to let me heal you?"

He stood there watching the two women, he noticed when Chrissy's face softened and the other women's face became more determined. Is it possible he wondered? The woman does have psychic ability he knew for a fact, but…

Debbie could see him thinking it through she wouldn't give up yet. "Mr. Lowery, take some time and think about it. We're not going anywhere in the meantime, that's for sure." She tried her hand at levity.

Eugene shook his head and backed all the way out closing the door. He had a lot to think about.

"You did great, girl," Chrissy told her excitedly.

"So did you, remind me never to make you mad. I really

thought you were going to try something." Debbie laughed. "Now let's hope he comes back soon. If not we probably don't stand a chance.

The crowd at Tate's began clearing out. John couldn't stand the idea of going home to an empty house. He had accomplished drinking most of the men under the table and still didn't feel drunk. Matt left hours ago to go home and take care of Jersey, but only after Vinny promised to get John home safely.

Mostly the only people left in the bar were members of N.E.P.R. and John knew they wouldn't leave until he did. He struggled to stand with his crutches. Taking the pain pills had not been wise with alcohol, he thought as he swayed. Sam and Vinny both grabbed hold of his arms.

"Steady there man," Sam said.

"I got this, let go of me," John told them coldly.

Neither man let go until they knew he had a good footing with his crutches.

"I'm sorry, guys." John shook his head, "My fuse is pretty short today," he explained.

"No worries bud, we all understand." Vinny slapped him on the back "you ready to go home?"

"Not really, but I figure if I don't then the rest of you will feel obligated to stay."

"We're here for you, John. We stay as long as you need us to stay. If you want to be alone you're out of luck, because we don't plan to leave you alone at all. You're stuck with one of us around the clock." Vinny smiled trying to lighten the mood a little. He knew John wouldn't take too kindly to being coddled, but that's just too bad he thought.

When Vinny's words sunk into John's foggy brain he looked around at his closest friends, "I don't need you to babysit me guys, I'm a big boy."

Joellen came through the front door she'd stepped outside to talk with Mark on her cell phone. The noise in the bar too loud for her to hear what he called to tell her.

Kaliegh noticed Joellen's colorless face the second she stepped back inside. Kaliegh had been talking to Sue and Craig. She jumped up and ran to Joellen. "Are you sick?" she asked worriedly. "Somebody, get Jo some water." She walked Joellen over to a chair.

Joellen patted the hand on her shoulder "No, no I'm alright." She tried to gather her thoughts before she blurted the bad news out.

"You don't look alright, what's the matter, Jo?" Craig leaned down to get a better look.

Cindy rushed a glass of water over to them and handed it to Kaliegh.

Joellen took a drink and looked at all the face's surrounding her. The tears began to pool in the corner of her eyes and she didn't bother to hold them back. "I just got off the phone with Mark." She felt the tears begin to fall. "He told me Debbie Milo is officially missing too."

The murmurs began amongst the few remaining people. A buzzing sound grew louder in Joellen' head as she tried to compose herself and explain what she knew.

John sat down at the table with Jo and several others pulled seats up. They gave her time to pull herself together. Joellen wasn't young, but she wasn't old either, she just had a shock to her system and needed a minute.

Sucking in air she continued, "I went to get Debbie earlier and bring her here, but when I got to her house she wasn't home. A few of us had been trying for hours to get her by phone, unsuccessfully. After finding her car in the driveway, but not Debbie, I called Mark Mason. Mark told me not to say anything until he had time to investigate and make sure she hadn't went shopping or something. Anyway

Mark just called me and confirmed Debbie is now considered a missing person."

"Do they think she's with Chrissy?" John hoped.

"Yes, they believe both women have been abducted by the same person." Joellen shuddered.

John was silently thankful Chrissy wasn't alone with the wacko. He vowed to rip the man apart, limb by limb, when they found out who he is. John reached over and took Jo's hand. "At least their together," he said quietly.

"There's more." Joellen took another calming breath and continued "the police believe Debbie knew her abductor and if she did, we probably know him too."

The noise level reached an all-time high with everyone talking at the same time, looking at each other with suspicion.

Sam jumped up on a chair and put his fingers in his mouth blowing out a loud whistle.

"Hold it down folks we aren't going to get anywhere pointing fingers at each other. Let's talk about this rationally."

Everyone stopped talking and waited for Sam to give further instructions. He stood there looking down at the small crowd. "Let's try to be reasonable here, we know it's only a possibility we may know the killer, let's not jump to conclusions and form a lynch mob." He gave them a few minutes to think about what he'd said.

John felt some sort of relief knowing Chrissy wasn't alone. He knew if she had Debbie with her the two of them could help each other. He held up his hand to let everyone know he wanted to say something. "I want to say we have cause for hope now. If those two are together, they are two of the strongest women we know." He began to choke up.

"John's right, they'll take care of each other. The sorry sonuvabitch that is stupid enough to take both of them deserves what he gets," Vinny said bringing hoots of laughter from the group.

Maggie swiped the tears from her cheeks as she tried to laugh along with the group. These were two of her best friends. She couldn't believe they were in the hands of the merciless killer portrayed on the news as 'The Surgeon'. The things he'd already done to the poor women he killed haunted her. What were her friends going through right now?

Sam noticed Maggie crying and stepped down off the chair going to her side "they'll be fine Maggie, keep the faith," he encouraged.

"What did Mark say they were doing to get our friends back?" Dave asked bringing the laughter to an end. "I mean I'm all about pooling our resources and getting Chrissy and Debbie home. Are they sending out search parties? What are they doing?" His angry outburst started the group up again.

Sam shook his head, he looked at John who looked back at him and shrugged his shoulders. Sam squeezed Maggie's arm and let go. Walking back to his chair he got up again and whistled loudly. This time it took a few extra minutes for everyone to quiet down, but when they did he motioned for John to take the floor.

John stood up "let's not get carried away friends we all want the same thing here. You all know Mark as well as I do, and you know he isn't allowing anyone to drop the ball on this. Let's go home and get some rest. Tomorrow's going to be another long day." He looked over at Dave, "you my friend did a great job today getting the groups together and leading the search party. I can't thank you enough. I hope you will all be back here tomorrow morning to do it all again."

Joellen decided she didn't want to go home alone, not tonight. She nudged her way over to Vinny "you're taking John home right?"

"Yep"

"Well if he can walk on his own, I mean I know he's had a lot to drink, but anyway, I think I will stay at Chrissy's tonight, take care of him in her absence."

"Let me get him home and in the house, he might need some help." Vinny smiled at her. "I think it's a great idea, you staying and looking after him."

She smiled back at Vinny and agreed to follow them to the Bingham house. She wouldn't bother going home to get anything first. Frankly, she didn't care if she had fresh clothes tomorrow or now, they would just be crawling through the woods again.

FORTY-TWO

Mark arrived home to find his mother in law came for a visit. Glad he saw the car in the driveway before he made an ass out of himself by saying something stupid about her being there. He always seemed to make a comment, or face, or something that Patricia could use against him, in a joking manner, throughout her entire visit.

The two of them loved to banter back and forth. He had to admit his mother in law could be quick witted when she wanted to be.

They had always gotten along, but sometimes Patricia gave unwanted advice. Like the time she tried to tell the couple inventive ways to have sexual intercourse that could help them conceive. Mark stood in the driveway remembering Patricia telling him to stand Lilly on her head immediately after sex so the 'little swimmers' could hit their target easier. He hoped she was finally satisfied enough to keep her ideas to herself. He laughed and went inside.

He had called Lt. Washington and filled her in on Debbie Milo, as well as, Maria Erickson. He would give her credit she seemed to take the whole psychic thing pretty well. He also called Joellen and filled her in on Debbie. That had been the hard call to make. Joellen didn't take it very well and he hated to be the one to give her the news.

Now he had to tell Lilly, and considering the long hours he's working and their two friends missing, Patricia's visit became a blessing in disguise he thought to himself.

Lilly and Patricia were sitting in the kitchen when Mark came in. "Hi, babe," he said going to Lilly and kissing her soundly on the mouth.

"You must've had a good day," Lilly said smiling up at her husband.

"Not really." He turned to Patricia "and how's the best Mother in Law in the world?" he asked giving her a big hug.

"I can't complain since I get to spend some time with my kids," she said smiling "and you better not either."

"What? Me complain that you're here? Heck no glad to have you." He tossed his jacket on the back of a chair and sat down. "What brings you here?"

"Well since I couldn't keep Lilly at home, I thought you would worry less if she's not alone. So here I am."

"Wonderful thinking, you're the best." He got up to get a cup of coffee "is this still fresh?"

"Of course it is. Mom and I have been sitting here over our first cup talking about the baby."

"The baby." He turned to look at Lilly "everything's alright isn't it?"

"Yes Mark, would you please stop worrying about me. You have enough to deal with without stressing over us."

He laughed as he poured his coffee, "it's my job Lil, you can't fault me for that."

"I don't really. I know you can't help yourself. What made your day so bad?"

"We'll get into that, right now I want to sit, drink my cup of coffee, and have a normal conversation." He brought his cup to the table. "How was the drive in Patricia?"

"Actually not bad at all, the traffic cooperated with me most of the way."

"How long you planning to stay?" He tried to keep the flow of conversation light.

"I didn't set a time limit, why you have one in mind?" She joked with him.

"Now you know better than that, you're welcome as long as you care to stay. I'll be less worried knowing you're here."

"Mom wanted to do some shopping tomorrow. What do you think?" Lilly wasn't supposed to leave the house or let anyone know she's back. She'd play it however her husband wanted her to.

Mark thought about it and realized if the killer already has two women, he probably wouldn't be too interested in another one anytime soon. "If you feel up to it, I say go shop 'til you drop, and I don't mean literally." He laughed.

"You mean it's alright for me to leave the house?"

"Sure, you're not alone. I don't see a problem with it."

This gave Lilly cause to worry. Mark had been emphatic she not go anywhere, or tell anyone she was back in Freetown. "What's going on? You obviously know something I don't." She worried her lip watching the emotions play across her husband's face.

Patricia sat quietly wondering herself. Mark tried too hard to make this light hearted. She knew he had something terrible to tell her daughter.

He felt his hand shake slightly as he raised the cup to take a drink. He might as well get it over with. Drinking slowly he thought out how to tell her. Sitting the cup back on the table he scratched his day's growth of stubble. "I don't want to scare you Lilly, but I have more bad news."

Before he could say another word, Lilly's hand went to her heart and she asked "is Chrissy dead?" Tears trickled down her cheeks.

"What? No, Lilly, no. Honey you have to give me time to say this right." He reached over and took her hand with one of his, while wiping her tears with his other hand. "What I have to say is bad, but nowhere near that bad okay?"

She nodded her head and choking on a sob said "just say it, Mark."

"Debbie's missing too." He watched her reaction.

"Debbie? What do you mean missing?"

"We think whoever took Chrissy has Debbie too. We brought in a psychic tonight to help us. There isn't any physical evidence Debbie is missing. I mean her cars in the driveway at her house. There hasn't been any kind of struggle that we can see. I mean nothing out of the ordinary at all. So the FBI guy has a friend and he called her for me. She drove over four hours to come check Debbie's house for us tonight."

"What did she tell you?" Lilly bit into her lower lip.

"She said Debbie was attacked from behind in her kitchen."

"Oh my God," Lilly cried.

"I know, babe, but hear me out. This woman said Debbie is still alive, she said that Debbie didn't see who attacked her." He squeezed her hand. "She's still alive babe."

Lilly listened as she cried softly wondering how could this be happening, two of her closest friends missing, and more than likely in the hands of a serial killer, a brutal serial killer.

Patricia remained quiet as her son in law comforted Lilly. She had met Chrissy before, but not Debbie. She knew Lilly thought the world of both friends, talking endlessly about them at times.

Vinny got John settled in his chair while Joellen brought a glass of water for him to take more pills.

John pulled the pill bottle out of his pocket and removed the lid. Looking into the bottle he counted enough pills for one more day, putting the lid back on he handed the bottle to Joellen "will you put these in the bathroom? I don't think I need them anymore." He pushed his chair back and closed his eyes.

Joellen took the bottle from John and looked over at Vinny questioningly. He shrugged his shoulders like. Joellen walked quietly out of the room, pill bottle in hand. Standing there looking down at his friend, Vinny wondered if he should stay for a while. John had been exceptionally quiet on the ride home and now he refused to take his pain meds.

Vinny sat down on the couch. He would wait for a little while to make sure John didn't need him. John didn't bother to open his eyes or engage in conversation. He lay in his chair with his legs propped up.

Joellen put the pills in the medicine cabinet and went to the kitchen to start a pot of coffee. She didn't know if John would want to sit and talk, but in case he did she wanted coffee ready. He wouldn't be getting any more alcohol tonight. The few hours the volunteers spent at Tate's had been all about the search and drinking. Jo had seen John drink a lot tonight, she cringed at the idea he may have taken pain medication too. Men could be damn fools when there wasn't a woman around to watch over them. Chrissy would have no reason to be upset about John being taken care of in her absence. Jo would make sure of that.

Vinny sat back relaxing on the couch listening to John snore softly. He'd been amazed that a man that size could snore so quietly. He sure hated the hell his friend was going through. He knew how hard it was on John since there pretty much had been virtually nothing he could do to help his wife. A leader from birth, John didn't take well anything dictating in his life. He controlled every aspect, every detail, always telling others what to do.

Joellen came back to the living room carrying a tray with her. She noticed John's snoring as she set the tray on the table. Looking over at Vinny she smiled and pointed to the coffee, he shook his head yes and she poured out two cups.

They sat quietly for the longest time sharing a snicker here or there when John would snort a little louder. After they finished their coffee, Vinny whispered he was going home. Joellen walked him to the door where they quietly hugged each other and agreed to meet at Tate's tomorrow morning. Jo assured Vinny she could get John there without help.

After Vinny left Jo took the tray to the kitchen and cleaned up. Checking on John one more time she quietly turned off the lamp and headed up to the spare bedroom.

FORTY-THREE

Eugene awoke bright and early to the sun streaming in through a split in the curtains. He rolled over and tried to block the bright light out. When he found it impossible, he got up to adjust the curtain.

A blanket of white covered the ground giving everything a beautiful glittery sparkle in the morning light. He looked out at the scenery and grunted. Not one to pay much attention to the beauty surrounding him, he climbed back under the covers, throwing the blankets over his head.

Digging around with his hands he located the pillow he kept between his knees during the night. It helped to keep his hip and leg level, preventing some of the pain he'd experience if he slept without it. Stuffing the pillow back between his knees he yawned loudly. He knew sleep wouldn't come again, but he refused to get up this early.

Debbie huddled closer to Chrissy as they slept on the floor. The little room had grown chilly and they only had each other to keep warm. She wondered what time it was, not knowing drove her crazy. Finally giving up the idea of more sleep she sat up and looked around her. This room alone is enough to drive me crazy she thought. Standing she stretched out her cramping limbs.

Chrissy rolled to her back and watched her friend stretch and yawn. "Why bother to get up? It's not like you have anything to do."

Debbie laughed "I know, but I have to move around, I'm freezing. The cheap asshole could use some heat. What the fuck is he doing?"

Chrissy could see the irritation radiate from Debbie. She didn't know how much longer either of them could maintain their sanity. Holding back her comment she hoped to keep her friend from flipping out totally. She leaned up against the chair quietly.

"Wonder if the dickhead will feed us anytime soon. You know for all he's done to us and those other women, I'm thinking maybe screw our plan, we just beat the shit out of him." She started dancing like a boxer and throwing air punches.

Chrissy couldn't help herself she busted out laughing. "That's been my plan all along, now you're seeing him like you should've the whole time. I'm game, I say we stay near the door, wait for him to open it, then before he can think we charge him."

Debbie quit dancing and glared at Chrissy, "are you fucking nuts? He always has that stun gun in his hand. Even if we took him by surprise he's going to get one of us. It will completely incapacitate you or me and the one left standing is fucked."

"I don't think so Debbie, he doesn't react quickly. I think we can take him.

The dancing around helped warm Debbie some, she felt a little better after her blood began moving. "Okay look, I hear what you're saying, but if we're going to take a risk like that then we need to be at our best. So I say we wait until the second time he comes in. You know that way we have energy from the food he'll bring on his first visit. Then you and I will practice take downs with each other while we wait for his second visit."

Chrissy didn't like the idea. She didn't want to be stuck in here any longer than absolutely necessary. "No we do it the first time. I'm tired of being here, it fucking reeks of piss and we're freezing." She stood up and walked over near the door.

"I'm taking him down as soon as this door opens."

Debbie sat down in the chair, this wasn't a good idea and she knew it, but how could she get Chrissy to hold off? Leaning her head back she closed her eyes to give it thought.

Chrissy leaned against the wall next to the door, if Debbie didn't help her she knew she couldn't over power Eugene by herself. Was she being irrational?

Eugene had thought a lot last night about what that psychic woman told him. He knew now that his murders had all been a waste of time, except the pulsating thrills he experienced. He needed to feed them, but wondered at the same time, why he should bother. Last night, before he went to sleep he'd made his mind up to take them both to the Shack today and be done with this whole fuck up.

A thought occurred to him giving him the needed push to get out of his warm bed. He would put a crushed Rohypnol pill in their food this morning. He needed them unconscious to get them to the Shack. Once he had them staked and secure he'd want them awake to enjoy their fear. He used the Rohypnol on two of the other women and had a hard time awaking them for the fun. He would only use one pill on each this time. With two it would be a little trickier. He had to put it in food instead of drink and wasn't sure if they would consume enough.

Throwing the covers back he got up, "shit its cold in here." Quickly getting his robe he went to the thermostat turning it up. His hip hurt unmercifully this morning and he knew the cold caused some of the pain. Once he heard the heater kick on he went to the kitchen to prepare something to eat.

Eugene prepared scrambled eggs, toast, and coffee. He decided to let them think he would play along with that psychic healing him. After methodically planning their meal

360

to insure they each got the drug in their system, he began crushing one pill into a fine powder and lightly sprinkled it over the eggs on one plate, then did the same thing for the second plate of food. He would feed them separately this time even provide silverware so they could eat all of it without problems. He'd tell them he gave them the utensils because now they were going to work together they had to trust each other. He laughed at his cleverness.

Realizing he'd forgotten the damn tray again, he scraped the eggs into a Tupperware, tossed in some toast and put the lid on. He would need the tray for coffee so elected not to give them any. One bottle of water to share would have to be enough. Quite frankly, he didn't care if they drank anything, but the food had to be eaten for his plan to work.

With two Tupperware lidded bowls and one bottle of water he made his way to the room. Once again setting it on the floor he removed the stun gun turning it on. Pushing the lever had the door opening and he shoved the Tupperware inside. "Chrissy, get over there next to Ms. Milo."

How stupid did she think he was? He wouldn't enter the room until he could see both of them.

Chrissy stood flat against the wall next to the open door, still considering an attack. Debbie looked at her and shook her head no, holding her breath she hoped Chrissy wouldn't do it. He was ready with that fucking stun gun.

"Chrissy, I know you can hear me. I know your standing next to the door. You're friend isn't helping you out by watching you. Come on be a good girl. I don't want to hurt you. I think we should talk about your friend's idea." He waited patiently.

Chrissy couldn't believe he'd even entertain that idea. She stood still not sure what to do.

"Chrissy, you're pissing me off, get over by your friend now," Eugene ordered.

Dropping her head from lack of courage to follow through with her plan, Chrissy did as she was told. Stepping over to Debbie, she turned to face Eugene, hate written all over her face. Her defiant stance told him he had made the right decision after all.

"I thought you two were going to work with me? Why are you still trying to attack me, Chrissy?"

Debbie couldn't allow Chrissy to answer. She couldn't hold her anger in check well enough. "She had a bad night, it got pretty cold in here."

"Yeah sorry about that, I didn't know it was supposed to snow last night. Look I included silverware this morning. Thought if we're going to work together we needed to be able to trust each other." He leaned back against the door still holding the bottle of water. "So how does this healing thing work? You can explain while you eat." Eugene wanted to make sure they both ate and this way he could actually see for himself.

Debbie crawled forward and grabbed both bowls, handing one to Chrissy. "It's called Reiki Healing. It will take a few sessions before you notice it working." She dug into the eggs.

"What do you need to do this Reiki?" he asked watching her eat. Chrissy held hers, but didn't eat any. Not sure if he should encourage her to eat and come across too eager, he stood there quietly.

Debbie bit into the toast and looked up at Chrissy still standing there holding the food. "You going to eat that before it gets cold?"

Chrissy looked down at her and shrugged her shoulders. Her stomach rumbled loudly, but she still didn't dig in. Eugene stood there watching them.

Debbie finished her eggs and toast looking at Eugene. "May I have the water please?"

He tossed her the bottle of water as Chrissy began to eat her food. Eugene hoped she'd eat quickly, he didn't think it would be too long before Debbie knew the food had a little something special added.

After taking a good long drink of the water Debbie handed the bottle to Chrissy. She didn't need anything to perform the Reiki and thought about explaining the process to Eugene. They didn't say anything at the moment, everyone seemed tense and Debbie fought the urge to hurry Chrissy's breakfast.

Eugene watched Chrissy poke at the food, eating a little here and there. He felt his heartbeat pick up knowing soon he would be enjoying their torment.

Debbie jerked him back to reality "I don't need anything to answer your question. Reiki is a healing energy that comes from me. I just need you to lay on your good side exposing your bad hip to me."

"I can't lay down with you two running freely," he said surprised. "How the hell do you expect me to do that?"

"Listen, I told you we will work with you. Chrissy and I have talked extensively and she agrees if you're willing to let us go she'll behave."

"No way! I'm not trusting either one of you that much. It wouldn't take anything for either of you to outrun me. No we need a better plan."

Chrissy tossed the empty bowl onto the floor "Look you fucking asshole, I don't care if you ever walk normal. I would just as soon beat the shit out of you then have to wait the couple of days this will take, but Debbie here, thinks she can help you. So you either trust us or fuck you."

Eugene laughed loudly he loved her anger and frustration. He delighted in the knowledge that soon, very soon, her attitude would send him over the edge, thrilling him beyond belief.

Debbie began feeling disoriented, her head and stomach hurt. Bending over she clutched her stomach and groaned.

Chrissy knelt down next to her "What's wrong?" she asked fearfully.

Eugene straightened and watched the two, it wouldn't be long now and they would be down for the count. He knew he had about eight hours give or take, before they would start to come to, once they were completely out.

"What did you do?" Chrissy shouted at him helping a struggling Debbie to her feet.

"I don't feel so good." Debbie's knees buckled and she fell to the floor.

Chrissy started to panic, "what did you put in the food, Eugene?"

"Take it easy Chrissy, it's not going to hurt you. Just relax and let it take you away." He snickered backing out the door and closing it.

FORTY-FOUR

Lee paced the floor while the two homeless people looked through photographs trying to pick out their attacker. Maria sat quietly across the room waiting for them to finish so Lee could take her to the victim's car.

They had been at this for over two hours already and Lee didn't enjoy being stuck in the small room with their body odor.

Looking over at Maria he decided to get her out of there. Why should she have to suffer too? "I'm going to send you over to Mason, Maria," he opened the door and pointed down the hall "second door on the left "he said giving her a shove out the door "tell him I sent you down."

She knew why he'd sent her out and felt grateful. Finding Mark Mason didn't take much effort. He sat behind a desk with two other guys looking over his shoulder. She cleared her throat as she walked over to them. "Sorry to bother you, but Lee sent me in here, said to tell you that."

Mark introduced her to Ian and Ricky. Ricky had never worked with a psychic before and felt it a corny idea, but kept his opinion to himself. Ian rushed to pull a chair out for her and talked excitedly to her about her gift.

Mark sat back controlling his laughter at the two very different reactions his men had. He couldn't read Ricky's mind to be sure, but his reaction said it all.

The crime techs had not cleared the vehicle yet, so they waited patiently for the go ahead. He wondered if Maria would get anything from the car. He knew if they didn't find Chrissy and Debbie soon, it wouldn't be good. Calming Lilly down last night had been difficult, but between him and

Patricia they managed.

Maria enjoyed the reaction she received from men over her looks, but the reaction to her gift sometimes irritated her. She understood few believed in her ability, but to be so blatantly cold towards her pissed her off. Ian tried to hold her attention with questions, but Ricky was the one she wanted to talk to. Why couldn't people keep an open mind and at least give her the opportunity to show them she wasn't a fake?

Law enforcement officers were pretty black and white. Either they believed or they didn't, not bothering to sugar coat anything. She found it funny it didn't matter how educated they were, rather they were FBI or locals, county or municipality, the mentality remained the same.

The group of volunteers trickled into Tate's. The frigid cold, snowy, morning didn't keep too many from their promise to return. John worried a lot of them wouldn't show up since it turned so cold, and snow covered the ground. He sat at a table with Joellen, Dave, Vinny, Matt and Kaliegh, drinking coffee. Many of these people had taken a day off work to help search. Refusing, to allow this killer, to claim even one more soul, John looked around at the faces eager to get started. He didn't know more than half of them, yet here they were.

Sam and Maggie, were on their own this morning. Since Cindy had Bryan to think of, Sam didn't ask her to come in. Usually the bar didn't open for a couple more hours, but Sam told everyone it would be open and serving coffee for the early birds.

"How's the leg this morning?" Dave asked John.

"Better, I'm ready to get back out there." John finished his cup of coffee. "You planning to keep the same groups today?"

"Yeah I figure it'll be easier than trying to confuse

everyone. We'll give them a little while to consume some coffee and warm up before I get them moving. Have you talked with Mark?"

"Mark calls me and updates me regularly. He told me that FBI guy brought in a psychic. She's going to go through Chrissy's car this morning."

"Nice, if she's half as gifted as Debbie, this will be over in no time," Joellen said.

The group of members at the table talked excitedly back and forth over this new tidbit of information. John sat quietly and listened to what they had to say. He knew everyone stayed upbeat trying to keep him positive, little did they know he would never give up hope of finding Chrissy alive.

Dave pulled his map of the Freetown Forest out and began making a list of areas they needed to hit today. He made notes on which groups were going where, and in some cases depending on the size of the area or the terrain he assigned more than one group.

Craig and Sue came through the door letting cold air in with them. People closest to the door shivered in response. They stomped their feet to knock the snow loose and proceeded to John's table, greeting people as they passed.

"Good morning guys," Craig said pulling a chair out. He plopped down removing his gloves. "The snow caught me by surprise this morning." He laughed as he tugged his stocking cap off.

"I don't think any of us were expecting to wake up to the beautiful cloud of white." Joellen smiled. She felt good this morning. Something positive would come out of today's effort she just knew. Everyone seemed eager today, unlike yesterday, where confusion reigned.

Maggie, brought Craig and Sue both coffee as the front door opened yet again letting the frosty air inside.

Eugene stepped inside and stomped first his good leg

then his other less vigorously. He looked around at the people willing to go search in this cold weather. Nodding to a few as he passed them he made his way to John's table. Slapping the big man on the back he asked "how is everyone this morning?"

Craig smiled at him "we're all gearing up to hike through the snow, you gonna joined us out there?"

"Wish I could, but." He rubbed his hip with his gloved hand "my hip don't cooperate much especially in this weather. I just stopped in to see how my buddy John's holding up."

John needed to keep his mood jovial. He had every intention of bringing his wife home today. He looked over at Eugene and said "I'm doing great Eugene. All these good people here, giving up another day to help me out keeps me going. Besides, today is the day my friend." He watched Eugene's reaction.

Eugene didn't disappoint him, he looked stunned. How the hell did these people being here make such a difference in him today? Hell, yesterday the man was depressed beyond measure and today it's like he's a new man. "Today's the day?"

"Yep, bringing my bride home today." John stood up placing his crutches under his arm "you ready Matt?"

Matt swallowed his last little bit of coffee and pulled his coat on "ready John."

"I wish you the best of luck today John." Eugene stepped to the side.

"Thank you, but I don't need luck." John looked around the room at all the people volunteering. "I just want to thank each and every one of you for being here to help me out today. Please be careful out there and all of you come back safely, my wife is going to want to thank you personally."

Cheers, whoops, and hollering, along with clapping followed John out the front door. He felt good this morning, charged and ready to go.

"Where do you want to look first?" Matt asked him.

"It doesn't matter to me I'll leave that up to you."

Maggie brought Eugene a cup of coffee. "Oh thank you Maggie, but I'm not staying, just came by to check on John this morning." He smiled and limped toward the front door.

Maggie looked stunned, "I thought he's a friend of John and Chrissy's?" she asked the group at the table John just vacated.

"He is. Kind of an odd little fellow isn't he?" Joellen asked.

"You can say that again," Vinny said.

Dave stood up and blew a loud whistle to get everyone's attention. As soon as he had the place quieted down he began giving assignments to the group leaders.

Lee came out of the room gulping in large quantities of fresh air. The room stunk badly, and he couldn't take it another minute. He called for a sketch artist to meet with the two homeless individuals who apparently were not in any hurry to leave the warmth of the building or the hot coffee provided.

Lee warned the artist before she stepped into the room, but she assured him she had smelled worse while working homicide for years. He wasn't too sure about that.

He found Mark and Cody talking to Maria in the break room. Maria had been enjoying the sparring between the officers that believed and the ones that did not believe. She kept her mouth shut letting them fight it out.

"How are they treating you Maria?" Lee asked as he approached the small group.

"Wonderfully, we've just escaped a slight argument to come in here and refresh our coffee. How goes it with the stinky people?" Pinching her nose to emphasize her meaning she beamed her gorgeous smile and stuck her tongue out at him.

"They're in there with a sketch artist right now. Didn't get anywhere with the mug shots." He laughed at the face she'd made. He turned toward Mark and Cody "any word on the car?"

"Nope, called down a little while ago they said give 'em an hour," Mark told him.

"Wonder what the heck is taking them so long? They've had it a couple of days." Lee looked at his watch "let me get the Lieutenant to put a fire under their ass," he said pulling out his cell phone.

Cody looked at Mark and laughed, they wouldn't tell him she already did that. Maria stared down into her Styrofoam cup and smiled, she knew what the detectives were doing and thought, let them have their fun she surely wouldn't ruin it for them.

Lee did a lot of head shaking and one word responses to whatever the Lieutenant told him all the while staring at the two detectives. He knew he had played right into their hands and the joke was on him. When the pair knew he figured them out they busted out laughing and high fived each other. He thought about it for a minute and decided he would have the last laugh, he waited for the Lieutenant to say goodbye and he acknowledged with "sounds good." They didn't know she had hung up. He kept right on pretending to talk to her.

Mark refilled his cup and turned with the pot in hand to Cody "you ready?"

Before Cody could reply, however, Lee said "what? You're kidding right? Oh my God. Uh huh, uh huh, okay then we'll be right out." His gaze full of wonder he didn't utter another word.

Mark set the pot back on the burner and waited. Cody

stood staring at the Agent expectantly. Maria once again looked down into her cup with a smile. When Lee didn't offer any explanation Mark couldn't stand it any longer.

"What, you going to tell us or make us beg?" He hoped it would be good news whatever it was.

Lee walked over and poured himself a cup of coffee. He'd keep them hanging in suspense as long as he could. After all he had absolutely nothing to tell them. He picked up the sugar container and poured it generously keeping his back to them the entire time.

Cody looked at Mark and shrugged his shoulders "What gives Agent Marlowe?"

"I'm sorry what?" Lee looked over his shoulder then added creamer to the cup.

"The Lieutenant, what did she say that had you so amazed?" Cody asked as Mark began to smell a rat.

"Oh that? She said you guys already called her about the car." He turned with a gleaming smile in place and stirred the little wooden stick around and around in his cup.

"Yeah, but what..." Cody saw Marks face and knew they'd been had. He hung his head and laughed.

FORTY-FIVE

Eugene pulled into the garage and closed the door. He had plenty of time to get the women to the Shack. He gathered rope, and tape from the garage before going inside. He knew he didn't have to bother with all the ritual stuff this time. He planned to clean the room, getting rid of the urine smell, the dirty dishes, and of course the women. He had to get them into the car, which would be the hard part since they couldn't walk. He looked around and remembered the wheelbarrow, "where is that damn thing?" He thought out loud.

The garage remained a very tidy area. Eugene's mother, never one for clutter always kept it spic and span. Looking around he didn't see the wheelbarrow. He dropped the rope and tape off on the kitchen counter and went to the back yard. He knew the yard man used it on occasion and he hoped he'd find it out there.

Yep, there it sat full of snow, near one of his mother's flower beds. Eugene grumbled on his way to get the thing, making a mental note to have a talk with yard guy. He knew his mother would have a fit if she had known the man left it out in the weather to rust.

Dumping it on its side he used his gloved hand to push the snow out. It's not like there had been a ton of snow dumped over night, but the wheelbarrow looked like it had held its share, may be the wind blew most of it he thought.

Pushing it inside left a wet trail on the tile that he ignored for right now. He would clean that when he finished with everything else. Tossing the rope and tape into the wheelbarrow he included Pine-Sol, a couple towels, a small trash bag, and a wet cloth.

He set the wheelbarrow close to the tapestry, then threw the wall hanging over him and opened the door. "Ah my lovelies," he said to the two women laying side by side on the floor. Pushing the wheelbarrow inside the small room he got to work on their corner.

Gagging and holding his nose as he scrubbed the area clean. He tossed the tray of dirty book pages into the trash can, vowing to buy another tray. The Pine-Sol helped immensely with the urine odor as he finished, tossing the wet cloth into the same trash bag. One of the women moaned slightly when he went to straighten the books on the shelves. He turned quickly worried one might wake up enough to cause him problems.

They both lay there quiet as church mice now that he looked at them. He finished the books and went to the women tying both their hands and feet. Placing tape across their mouths he said, "This should keep your big mouth shut Chrissy."

Satisfied the room didn't stink any longer he gathered the trash bag tying it closed. Struggling first with Debbie, forcing her sleeping form into the wheelbarrow he tossed the garbage bag on top of her. Wheeling both to the garage where he then threw the bag into the trash receptacle in the corner and Debbie into the trunk of his car. Slamming the lid he went back for Chrissy. Going through the same motions to get Chrissy into the wheelbarrow he pushed her to the car trunk.

Debbie lay just inside, not leaving room for Chrissy too. Eugene struggled with Debbie's body to push her back out of the way. Once he accomplished that he finagled Chrissy inside too. Slamming the trunk lid once again, he brushed his hands off and went back inside.

Patricia finally talked Lilly into going shopping with her.

373

Calling Mark while her daughter showered she explained in detail the arguing she had endured over getting Lilly to understand it did neither of her friends any good for her to sit in the house and stress.

Mark congratulated his mother in law on her victory. Lilly could be extremely stubborn when she wanted to be.

While they conversed about Lilly, Lee strode in with the composite drawing the sketch artist had completed. He held it up for the Task Force guys and Maria to see. Mark almost swallowed his tongue as Cody took a closer look.

"I gotta go, Patricia," Mark said and hung up his cell phone. Walking up next to Cody, he wanted a better look.

"Do you see who I see?" Cody asked Mark.

"Yes and no." I mean it kinda looks like him, but not.

The two detectives bantered back and forth until Lee asked "who does it resemble?"

Cody deferred to Mark with a sweep of his hand. Mark looked at the drawing again and said "It looks a little like Eugene Lowery, but he wouldn't do a thing like stun homeless people."

"Fuck," Cody said quickly grabbing his coat.

"What? Where are you going?" Mark grabbed his coat.

"Don't you remember when we went to talk to him he had a fucking stun gun sitting right there, in plain view!" Cody reminded Mark.

As they rushed for the door Lee called them back "you guys want to fill us in before you bolt?"

Mark's mind going over the idea Eugene could be their killer made him sick to his stomach. "Cody why don't you go fill the L.T. in while I fill these guys in? I'll have a warrant drawn up by one of them and we'll head over there as soon as we get everything lined out."

"You got it." Cody virtually flew out of the room.

Mark explained to all of them about his and Cody's

interview with Eugene, and how he had a handicap, and how even though Eugene had been the last one to see Chrissy Bingham, Mark thought he wasn't capable of carrying something like this out.

Lee could see Mark's confusion and doubt as the man struggled to get all the information out to them. Lee looked at Kyle and told him to prepare the search warrant, he told Ian to go release the two homeless people who still waited in the room for Lee to come back. Orders flew left and right as they prepared to investigate the Lowery home.

Eugene made a quick sandwich and headed out the door. He would eat on his way to the Shack in Fall River Massachusetts. This is where he had planned his big finale ritual and even though he wouldn't be having that, he wanted to finish his killings there.

He turned up his classical music and drove while he ate. He planned the killings in his mind during the short drive. He would be there in less than half an hour. First he would get the girls out of the trunk and tie them to the stakes. Then he would work on waking them up, hopefully that wouldn't be too difficult in the snow he laughed out loud.

He noticed a lot of cars at Tate's as he drove by. He really didn't expect any of the volunteers to go to Fall River since he'd committed all his murders to this point here in Freetown.

Eugene had no idea why the Shack seemed important, the place was falling down. Some of the walls were literally crumbling, not to mention the huge gaping holes in the roof would be remiss, but still it had to be there.

The task force guys along with Agent Marlowe, Lt. Washington, Maria Erickson, and five patrol cars converged on the Lowery residence. Mark Mason had the search warrant in hand as he banged on the door. When no one answered the door, Lt. Washington gave the order to kick the door down.

"If those women are in there we're going to find them," she said to everyone within earshot.

Two uniformed officers approached and proceeded to kick the door in. Pandemonium set in as all the officers ran through the door with guns drawn yelling "Police Department," but no one responded. Once the residence had been secured the house was thoroughly searched. The wheelbarrow that sat in the garage had left marks on the floor leading to the wall tapestry. One of the uniformed guys stood there looking at the floor where the marks abruptly stopped. Cody Stone walked up to him and asked what he was doing.

"Uh, sorry sir, but these marks stop right here. I don't understand why." The man looked completely confused.

Cody looked at the marks on the floor and told the man to step to the side, when the guy moved Cody lifted the tapestry. "What the fuck?" Cody said and ripped the wall hanging down to expose the solid wooden door. "Mason, over here," Cody yelled.

Mark had been in the kitchen and ran toward Cody's voice. "What do you have?" he asked.

"I'd say a hidden door to start with." He pointed to the tapestry "that covered the wall in front of this doorway."

"Hit that lever there, let's have a look," Mark said excitedly.

Cody hit the lever and the door scraped open. He looked back at Mark and then the two entered the small secret room.

"Would you look at this?" Cody said walking over to the occult book collection.

"Strange for sure, what's that smell?" Mark asked.

"I'd say urine if I had to guess," Cody told him "mixed in with Pine-Sol."

Lt. Washington entered the room "interesting friend you

have Mason," she said looking around.

"Acquaintance L.T., not friend. We merely attended school together. Where's Agent Marlowe?"

"He went to the car to get Ms. Erickson."

Mark sent the uniformed officer to find the FBI Agent. Cody found the book that Debbie had earmarked. He stood there and read quietly then whistled. "We got him, take a look at this." He handed the book to Mark.

Lt. Washington asked Cody to tell her what he'd found. He began explaining the ritual written in the book when Lee and Maria walked into the room.

Maria turned pale immediately upon entering the room, she felt sick to her stomach, and Lee noticed her paleness. "You alright?" he asked her.

She gulped hard trying to keep her lunch in her stomach and shook her head no. "I feel nauseous Lee, I need air." She turned and left the room.

Lee worried about her as he watched her leave, unsure if he should follow her or not. She waved her hand letting him know he should stay there. She continued outside as fast as she could. Dropping to her knees in the snow she sucked in fresh air rapidly.

The neighbors were out watching the commotion. Some of them were standing on their front porches while others formed a group across the street from the Lowery house.

Clara telling whoever would listen to her that whatever that boy did now would not surprise her. She further informed them how he had talked about his poor deceased mother right after her death and then the way he had walked away from her when she tried to give him her condolences.

Maria couldn't hold down her lunch any longer. She began retching in the yard. Ian came over to her and lightly rubbed her back "what did you feel in there?" he asked.

She shook her head and got sick again. She hated when

this happened to her, she hated feeling what someone else felt, but knew it was all part of the gift. When she finally felt able to speak she told him "I felt fear, and drugged maybe."

"Drugged?"

"Yes I think he drugged them. We have to find them quick or we're going to be too late Ian." She looked up at him.

He helped her up and she wiped the wetness at her knees. Gathering strength she said "let's go tell the others, we're wasting our time here."

Ian followed Maria back to the little hidden room. He listened as she explained to the others the need to get out of this house and find these women.

"Do you have any idea where we need to look?" Lt. Washington asked her.

"Not really, first I don't know the area, second I don't feel him so much as I do the women. Since they were more than likely unconscious when they left I have no idea."

"I know there are a ton of searchers in the Forest today. They are volunteers, John Bingham, and his friends got together. I seriously doubt Eugene can find a spot in the Forest to do anything today," Mark told them.

"We can leave the uniforms here to take care of processing the house, get your friend Mr. Bingham on the phone and find out if they are out searching and where. We need to figure this out quickly," Lt. Washington told Mark.

John and Matt walked into Tate's. They had been all over the Forest again today, as well as, all over Freetown proper. The volunteers filled the tables again as Maggie ran around making sure everyone had plenty to drink rather it was coffee, water, hot chocolate, or whatever they wanted. Some grumbled when they were informed if they wanted alcohol they had to pay for it.

Dave highly suggested anyone planning on continuing

the search this afternoon refrain from drinking alcoholic beverages.

John's phone rang and he answered it, but couldn't hear a word Mark said to him. After repeated tries to hear, he told Mark he would call him right back. He hung up and stuffed his phone in his pocket then scooped up his crutches making his way to the men's bathroom. Once inside he leaned against the wall and call Mark back.

"Sorry I had to find a quiet place, couldn't hear ya. What's up?" he asked when Mark answered.

"Where are you?" Mark practically shouted at him.

"Tate's"

"Good, listen are the volunteers out today?"

"They were, now we're all back at Tate's trying to warm up before we head out again. Why?"

"John, I need you to stay calm for me okay?"

John's heart jumped into his throat he choked his words around it "Chrissy? Did you find her? Oh my God, Mark, is she okay?"

"John, listen to me, no we haven't found her, but we believe we know who has her." He hesitated.

"Who?"

"No John, not yet, we need to know where your volunteers have been searching. Could save us a lot of time."

"All over the place Mark, fuck we've been everywhere. Who has Chrissy, Mark?"

"John, I told you I need you to stay calm and focus here, we have to get out there and find her, before it's too late. He's taken them somewhere John. He plans to kill them today. The only reason I'm telling you this is because we are friends and your volunteers can make a huge difference right now. Get them back out there and fast. I'll be in touch."

"You're really not going to tell me?" John was boiling, what the fuck, he thought.

"Nope not yet, come on pal let's get the Forest saturated with people. Now!" Mark hung up, he hated doing that to John, but he knew if he'd told him who it was John would kill Eugene before the law could stop him.

John hustled out of the restroom as fast as he could move on his crutches and through the throng of people. He reached Dave and Sam quickly. "Get them to shut up," he shouted at the men.

Dave blew a whistle with his fingers and got everyone quieted. John faced them, fighting to keep his tears in check he choked a bit then said "Mark Mason just called me. They know who has Chrissy and he believes whoever it is has taken them to the Forest to kill them. We need to get back out there and fast. I know some of you haven't had a chance to get warm or drink anything, but please I'm begging you." He couldn't say anything else.

Dave gave him a minute to pull himself together. He needed information so he would know where to send the searchers. Once John looked up and he knew he could talk Dave bombarded him with question after question.

FORTY-SIX

Eugene had Debbie tied to four stakes with her arms and legs stretched out in a spread eagle fashion. She was still unconscious as he stood there admiring her beauty. "This is such a waste of my talents." He told her even though she couldn't hear him. Shaking his head he left the dilapidated shack to retrieve Chrissy.

Hefting her out of the trunk partially carrying her and partially pulling her into the Shack, he dumped her onto the snowy earthen floor. Leaving her there he went to get the stakes to secure her. He had a spring in his step today even though his hip pained him. The idea of what he knew would be coming soon had him excited. Every fiber of his being seemed to anticipate the thrill of the kill.

He pounded a stake into the ground and dragged Chrissy over to it. Untying her hands he took the length of rope to secure her right wrist to the stake. Stretching her out, he measured for the second stake and pounded that one into the ground. Tying her left wrist to that stake he continued on to the two stakes to hold her legs.

Every strike of the hammer against the wooden stakes brought him closer to the edge of insanity. The intensity building inside him would soon be unleashed on the women, and he could barely control himself. He wanted to feel their terror, watch them suffer as he slowly sliced through their delicious bodies. The nefarious thoughts had him giggling while he pictured the whiteness of the snow turn hideously red with blood. He didn't need to drain their blood, or take any of their body parts with him. He would spill their blood into the snow covered floor and watch it soak in.

Going back to his car he removed his leather pouch containing his favorite tools. His depraved mind conjuring the screams he hoped to hear soon. Looking all around the area he made sure they were alone. Nothing moved as he held his breath listening and watching. He actually wondered where John and his precious volunteers were. Combing the Forest in Freetown no doubt he thought. Not even that far away, but still far enough they wouldn't hear the screams he would produce from these two lovely creatures very soon.

The volunteers scattered in all directions staying in their assigned groups. Dave and Jo tried to calm John, but he became inconsolable. Ordering Matt to take him back into the Forest he quickly crutched his way to the truck. Sam grabbed Matt's arm before he could make it out the front door. "Keep him busy and away from anywhere you think this wacko might be. If John gets his hands on the poor bastard he's a dead man."

Matt shook his head "I'll do my best." As he hurried out to the truck John began blowing the horn. Matt understood John's impatience, but that didn't help the irritation he felt raising his blood pressure.

"Come on man let's go," John shouted as Matt climbed behind the wheel.

Matt took a couple deep breaths as he started the truck. He couldn't jump down John's throat like he wanted to. He had to keep his anger in check. "I'm moving as fast as I can John, we'll get in the Forest just as fast as everyone else."

John knew he had been bossy and pushy, but right now he didn't really care. He wanted to get out there and find his wife still alive. He rested his hands on the dashboard as Matt took off.

"Where to?" Matt asked.

"Let's hit Copi Cut and drive slowly through the Forest."

"Sounds good, okay Copi Cut Road it is." Matt drove the speed limit, not trying to push John's buttons or anything he wanted them searching just as bad as John did, but Matt would do so safely.

John had the niggling feeling he wasn't remembering something he should be. He thought back to his and Mark's conversation when the fourth girl had been murdered. He pictured himself standing outside the store in the parking lot talking to Mark. Going over that conversation slowly in his mind, he knew he felt the same way that night. What am I forgetting? He asked himself.

The truck seemed to find every pot hole they came close to. The jarring ride, bounced his leg causing shooting pains and having it dangling down with all this searching caused it to swell so much, the pressure alone kept his anger fueled.

Matt enjoyed the fact John wasn't yelling out orders anymore. He knew his friend didn't mean to treat him the way he had, but Matt wasn't one easily pushed around. He held his temper pretty well considering he wanted to punch John in the face more than once already.

Driving through the Forest using Copi Cut Road they passed several volunteers on foot. Matt didn't envy them being out there in the cold. He knew they focused on the Freetown side of the Forest because all the murders had taken place on this side, but what if the killer knew they would be over here so he changed it up a bit? Matt was formulating this thought when John hit the dash board hard with his fist.

"Fuck! That's it!" John pulled his cell phone out and told Matt "head to the Shack and hurry."

Matt looked over at him, "the Shack?" he asked surprised "we've already checked that out."

John waited for Mark to answer his phone and pointed his finger in the direction of the Shack for Matt's benefit. "Mark, I'm on my way to the Shack. It's Eugene isn't it?"

Taken back for a second Mark answered "we think so, but the Shack? Why and how did you figure it's Eugene?"

"I remember one night on The Ledge we were all drinking and telling stories. Eugene said something about how cool it would be to actually perform occult killings at the Shack. Don't you remember? He sat there fantasizing about it for hours."

Matt's blood ran cold he could see the squirrely little man killing someone. He definitely came across being odd, different than most anyway.

"Shit you're right, how the hell did we forget that? Alright on my way and John, don't do anything until I get there you hear me?"

John didn't reply he hung up his phone. He was going to tear Eugene Lowery limb from limb when he got his hands on him. He promised himself he would have the pleasure of killing that little mother fucker with his bare hands.

Matt drove as fast as he dared with the condition of the road. "It's Eugene?"

"Yep and God help him when I get there, because no man will be able to stop me. You stay out of my way Matt. I don't want to hurt you."

Mark got on the radio and called for additional units from the Fall River Police Department, this wouldn't be his jurisdiction, but Lee could take it from here.

Eugene had a very sharp scalpel in his hand as she smacked first Debbie's face, then Chrissy's. "Wakie wakie, you don't want to sleep through this," he taunted them. Grabbing handfuls of snow he rubbed it into their faces, hoping the cold stuff would help in waking them.

Chrissy shook her head side to side struggling to wake up. Debbie simply moaned and didn't fight the sleepy feeling.

Eugene had left their clothing on and now he began to

wish he had them naked in the cold. "Come on Chrissy, that's right open them big beautiful eyes for me. I have a surprise for you." The sinister laugh was back and he used it loving the sound of it. "Debbie, wake the fuck up!" He ordered smashing snow into her face and grinding it in with his gloved hand.

Chrissy's eyes opened completely and she strained to see around her. The Shack was bright, but not as bright as stepping outside. The cold bit into her causing her to shiver uncontrollably. Tugging on her arms and legs shot fear straight through her, as she realized she was tied up. Only able to lift her head a little she figured out what was happening.

Eugene squatted between the two women, "happy to see you're awake, Chrissy. Debbie will be joining us in just a minute."

"What are you doing, Eugene? I thought we had an agreement?" Chrissy tugged hard at the rope holding her. She felt the burn in her wrist and knew fighting it was futile.

"You know that agreement wasn't feasible Chrissy, I can't let you two go." Seeing the fear she felt flash across her face he smiled, licking his thin lips, "don't worry this will all be over soon. I will console John when they find you two." His gaze held no emotion, nothing human looked back at her.

"I won't beg you. I won't feed your sickness, Eugene. You might as well just kill me now." She laid her head back in the snow and felt the tears slide down the sides of her face. Her heartbeat so hard she feared he could hear it. She didn't know if she could be this brave once he started cutting on her, but she would do her best not to give him any pleasure in killing her. She thought about John, her heart breaking for him. If there truly is an afterlife and she could stay with him she would, she thought. Closing her eyes she silently prayed for strength to endure what was to come without satisfying

Eugene with her screams of torture, she felt sure were coming soon. She prayed to die quickly.

Debbie heard Eugene from far away. She felt the painful slaps across her face and the cold water on her skin. Eugene pushed Debbie's eyelids open. "Wake up, you bitch," he ordered. Her eyes stung from the brightness that entered them and she moved her head away trying to turn her body, but something held her down. Struggling to wake up her mind screamed it's too cold.

Eugene losing patience quickly performed a quick slice across Debbie's forearm to help pull her from the drug induced sleepiness. He watched the blood slip down the side of her arm and drop into the snow. The redness crawled out like fingers finding its way through the whiteness.

Debbie opened her eyes wide when the pain sliced through her. She stared up at the most evil face she'd ever seen. "Eugene, what are you doing?" she asked still dazed.

"Wonderful, wonderful you're both awake now." He licked his lips missing the spittle gathering in the corners. "We're going to have some fun. As you can both tell you are outside, tied up, freezing, and unfortunately for you, at my mercy." His laughter echoed in the small building.

Standing, he backed up and stood at their feet so they could both see him clearly. Debbie looked at her bloody arm, then over at Chrissy, and back to Eugene, her mind up to par with the situation now. She made a conscious effort not to panic. "Keep him talking." Her guides quiet reassuring voice sounded in her ears. Yes, surely if they were outside during the daytime someone would come along soon. Out of the corner of her eye she saw movement and quickly turned her head. The old lady stood there looking at Eugene. Her face full of sadness as stared at her son.

Eugene held the scalpel up to raise the fear factor a bit, but before he could goad them with his instrument he noticed

Debbie looking the other way. "Ms. Milo, you may want to focus on me as I explain what we're doing out here."

Debbie slowly turned her gaze to him, "Uh Eugene, you have a visitor I think you may want to focus on her right now." Debbie smiled at the older woman.

"Tried to warn you young lady, but you wouldn't listen to me." The woman *tsk tsk'd* at Debbie.

Debbie laughed and said "Really is that what you call your harassment?"

Eugene watched her closely his skin began to crawl "Stop it. Stop it right now."

The older woman chuckled "he knows I'm here."

Debbie's eyes darted back and forth between the two "Is there anything you'd like to tell him before he kills me?"

Eugene stomped his foot "I said stop this, you're not talking to anyone you're just trying to freak me out."

Debbie giggled while the old woman had a laughing fit. Her sadness from a moment ago gone completely. "She finds you very funny, Eugene." Debbie looked over at him "you know it's your mother right?"

Chrissy enjoyed the fear on Eugene's face, oh how the tables turned she thought.

"No it's not, your just trying to buy time, but it's not going to work, Ms. Milo."

"Ask me something only your mother would know I'll prove to you she's here."

Eugene wasn't sure he wanted to play along, but what if his mother was here? He couldn't kill these women in front of his mother!

As he paced around Mrs. Lowery found his agitation amusing. She watched him struggle with the possibility of her being there. "Tell him I said to stop this nonsense and go home. Clean up that pig sty he calls his bedroom and wait for the law to come get him."

"You sure you want me to tell him that?" Debbie wasn't too keen to mention the police to Eugene.

"Yes, exactly like I said it." Mrs. Lowery winked at her "he'll know I'm here then."

"What? What did she say?" Eugene stopped pacing looking between Debbie and the spot Debbie kept looking at.

"She said for you to stop this nonsense and go home to clean up that pig sty you call your bedroom." Debbie watched the man squat down and huddle against the flimsy wall behind him.

"Tell him the rest missy," Mrs. Lowery told her.

Biting into her lip she told him the rest, "and she said you should wait for the law to come get you."

"Well shit," Chrissy said "you were doing good, till that lil tidbit, Debbie."

"She told me twice to say that. What am I supposed to do?"

The two women strained to lift their heads to see what Eugene was doing. He sat there twirling the scalpel and watching the light flicker off the blade. They looked at each other and then Debbie turned to Mrs. Lowery.

"He's fine let him stew for a few," the old woman told her "he knows what to do now."

Eugene knew what the psychic told him came from his mother. That's the same way she always talked to him. She always referred to his bedroom as a pig sty even after he'd spend hours cleaning it. She would expect him to turn himself over to the law, 'take your medicine son' popped through his mind.

His heart hammered hard against his chest wall. He felt sweat bead along his lip even in the bitter cold.

Looking at the spot where he knew his mother stood he felt her watching, waiting, for him to do as she said.

FORTY-SEVEN

The Fall River Police Department dispatched several cars to the Shack area. Sgt. Wilcox had been told to intercept Matt's truck, and then to stay in a holding pattern until Agent Marlowe got there.

Matt saw the flashing lights coming at him, he began slowing down. John noticed them too and panicked.

"Don't stop Matt, ram 'em if you have to. Get me to the Shack before he kills her." John wasn't thinking rationally.

"What? No John, I'm not going to ram a police car."

"We don't have time to waste we gotta get to the Shack, Matt." John pounded his fist on the dash

"Hold on John, let's see what's going on. May be they already have her safe and sound. I'm sure Mark called them." Matt stopped and rolled his window down as a policeman approached his truck.

"Good afternoon, I'm Sgt. Wilcox with the Fall River Police Department are you John Bingham?"

Matt shook his head no and thumbed towards John "that's John," he said leaning back to give the officer a view of the big angry man.

"We gotta go Officer, my wife is dying while we're sitting here." John went to push his door open.

"I understand Mr. Bingham, give us a minute sir, and we'll head to the Shack with you. Please stay in the vehicle." Sgt. Wilcox observed John pushing at the truck door.

"I'm not waiting I'll walk if I have to." John's blood pressure sky rocketed, "give you a minute? She might not have a fucking minute!"

"John, you have a broken leg for goodness sake, hold on

a minute isn't going to make a difference," Matt reasoned.

John felt rage surge "What? Are you fucking kidding me? It isn't going to make..."

Sgt. Wilcox knew he needed to get control, "sir listen to your friend here, Agent Marlowe should be here momentarily and we'll be moving to the Shack then."

"Agent who? Do what?" John asked confused and angry.

"Agent Marlowe sir, he's with the FBI."

John knew this had to be the guy working with Mark, how long would it take them to get here. He looked around wildly, waiting against his nature. "Get on that radio of yours and find out how long? I'm telling you we don't have time to waste," John shouted.

Chrissy laughed hysterically through her freezing shivers. She took a lot of delight in the fear smeared across Eugene's face. He didn't know rather to shit or go blind she thought to herself.

Debbie looked over at her friend worried she was losing her mind. She glared at Chrissy. When Chrissy finally noticed Debbie's strange look, "What?" she asked on a hiccup giggle.

Mrs. Lowery ignored the woman and kept her gaze on her son. He never failed to embarrass her. "He's pathetic, he knows I'm here and still refuses to acknowledge me. Tell him I'm upset with him. Tell him I said to go home right this minute."

Debbie looked over at the spirit "No way am I telling him that."

Eugene stopped twirling the scalpel and looked at her "no way you're not telling me what?" He wasn't sure he wanted to know, but fear made him ask.

Debbie chewed her lip some more "your Mom says you should go home right now, but you can't leave us here we'll freeze to death."

"What else did she say? There's more you're not telling me." He walked over to her and knelt down "tell me."

"That's it, that's what she said." Debbie could see how frightened Eugene felt, she began to feel fear crawl through her, the fingers of fear touched her very heart.

"I need her to leave, make her go away," he ordered quietly.

"Make her go away." Mrs. Lowery laughed "he's scared out of his britches."

"Yes he is," Debbie told her.

"Yes he is what?" Eugene inquired, tension tightening his chest.

"Scared, she noticed you're scared. She doesn't want you to kill anyone else she wants you to untie us and go home." Debbie held her breath.

"No, I can't let you go. Shit!" he got up and walked out.

"Stop using that potty mouthed language you little monster. Get back here!" Mrs. Lowery hated ignorance. "Tell him I said to get back here!"

Debbie didn't want him to come back and she was sick and tired of this lady lighting the wacko's fuse. "Help us hear lady, quit pushing his buttons. Tell me the right thing to say," she implored Mrs. Lowery.

The minutes ticked by as John watched the cars pulling up. He threw his cell phone onto the floor mat and slammed his fist into the dashboard when he saw the officers gathering around a tall, broad shouldered man.

Agent Marlowe began giving orders to both departments. Mark went to advise John and Matt on the game plan.

When Mark saw John's face he knew it wouldn't be long before his friend blew a gasket. Choosing his words carefully he said "take it easy big guy. We're going to be in time. I wanted to let you know what we're doing. We can't afford any mistakes during this take down."

"Mark, we're wasting time we gotta move," John shouted.

"I understand what you're saying believe me, but Lee has to have everyone on the same page."

"Lee? Who the fuck is Lee?"

"He's the FBI agent I've been telling you about. We know what we're doing, John. I know this is hard on you, but we could get one of them killed if this isn't done right. We have two different departments out here."

"Just let me go Mark, I'll handle this." John couldn't wait another minute.

"No, now you listen to me, John. You are not going to get out of this vehicle until we have Chrissy and Debbie safely out. You keep your head about you or I won't even let you get close to the Shack."

John looked directly at his lifelong friend. He knew Mark meant every word, but he couldn't believe how nonchalant he was acting. "Try and stop me Mark. Matt DRIVE!"

Matt continued to wait giving Mark time to get John under control. He hated what John had to go through, but he wasn't about to screw up the only chance they had at getting the women back safely. He killed the trucks engine, a loud signal to John he wasn't going anywhere.

Lee whistled to Mark "let's roll."

"Okay listen Matt, you follow the last car in. Keep him in the truck until you see me give the okay signal. You two got that?"

John flipped his middle finger up in Mark's direction. Matt acknowledge with a shake of his head.

Mark took off for his car.

John sat frozen, staring straight ahead. He hated not

being in control, this broken leg couldn't have come at a worse time. He knew what Mark and Matt were doing was the right thing, but he also knew Eugene wouldn't dare hurt Chrissy if he saw John coming at him.

Eugene heard the vehicles before he saw them. "Well guess I screwed up royally now," he had an urge to run to his car and try to get away. He felt his pocket for his keys, finding them he limped to his car.

He was driving out of sight into the trees to hide as the police cars turned into the open field next to the Shack.

"You're safe," Mrs. Lowery said fading away.

"What? Where are you going? What do you mean we're safe?" Debbie asked the mist fading before her.

Then she and Chrissy began hearing car doors slam shut, someone got on a P.A. system and ordered Eugene to come out with his hands up. Both women started to cry.

Chrissy shivered so hard from the cold. Hurting everywhere as relieve flooded through her body.

"Looks like the Cavalry has arrived," Debbie said, laying her head down in the cold snow. She was so damn cold. She wondered how long it would take to get the feeling in her fingers and toes back.

Once again the order had been given to come out hands up "Can't they see him out there?" Debbie asked looking at Chrissy.

"He's not in here, get in here and help us," Chrissy shouted.

Mark and several others came running into the Shack. When he saw them tied up he yelled for blankets and an ambulance. John came in struggling on his crutches in the slippery snow. He saw Chrissy and began to cry as he dropped down beside her while an officer untied her hands.

Mark looked at him and shook his head. He knew better

than to tell Matt to keep the big lug in the truck. He should've put an officer on him.

"It's okay, babe, I'm okay." She tried to comfort him.

He pulled his coat off, as soon as, she was untied he wrapped her in it then held on to her tightly. Both shook badly, her from the cold and him from relief.

Mark put a coat around Debbie and held her to him. She proceeded to cry like a baby.

Lee began giving orders for evidence collection. Maria stood outside the Shack and talked with Mrs. Lowery.

Ian watched Maria and wondered who she talked too. Looking around he noticed tire marks leading into the distant trees. He pretended not to notice in case Eugene watched from his vantage point. Nonchalantly Ian stepped to the doorway and waved Ricky over. He whispered to him and Ricky disappeared back inside the Shack.

The Task Force guys all huddled in a corner discussing Eugene while Ian kept an eye on the area. No way would he escape them out here.

After a brief discussion Sgt. Wilcox and his men pretended to leave, but actually went to block the only way out. Lt. Washington and her men got into their vehicles and drove to the trees to apprehend Eugene. Walking across, would make them sitting ducks if he had a gun, they planned their attack well.

EMS personnel loaded Chrissy and Debbie into the back of the ambulance while John insisted he ride with them, refusing to leave his wife's side.

Matt sat in his truck talking to Dave on his cell phone and heard the cheers go up from the volunteers present in the Forest, close enough to hear Dave's announcement.

Eugene huddled down in the driver seat of his car. He wondered if his mother watched over him. She had ruined everything he thought crying like a baby. Slumped so far down in the seat he couldn't see the officer's approach.

With the vehicle surrounded Mark opened the driver side door while Cody simultaneously opened the passenger side door. Eugene blubbering like a crazy person didn't offer any fight as Mark hauled him roughly out of the car.

"Can you see her too?" he asked.

Mark looked around "see who?"

"Mother, is she still here?"

The officer's looked at each other and started laughing at him. He hated to be laughed at. "She's here I tell you," he sobbed.

"Sure she is." Mark laughed "I don't care who's here, consider your sorry ass under arrest for kidnapping, assault with a deadly weapon and murder to start with. I'm sure we can find a lot more to tack on later. Alex read this sorry sonuvabitch his rights." Mark couldn't bear to touch the man any longer.

"Mark, Mark," Eugene shouted "Don't let them hurt me. Mark, Mark." He couldn't believe his friend left him high and dry.

Lee remained busy with the Fall River officers while Lt. Washington cleared her men out. The arrest actually made in Fall River had Ricky turning Eugene over to them.

After he was arraigned in the morning Freetown would take possession of him. Most of the charges would be from Freetown, although he now had charges in both jurisdictions. Mark knew they would agree to hold the trial in Freetown.

For now they would go back to the station, cuss, discuss, and put their reports in order. These charges and reports would be airtight. No way would this fucking sicko ever be a threat to another human being in the free world.

* * *

Debbie could feel the tingling in her hands and feet, the

blood flowing normal again. She waited for the emergency room doctor to make his or her appearance. The ambulance attendant cleansed and wrapper her arm and now she waited for the fun part, the stitches. Chrissy lay in a bed just behind the curtain. Debbie could hear John telling Chrissy how frantically everyone searched for them. He spoke loud enough to include Debbie in the conversation.

"Instead of telling everyone back here about our ordeal why don't you just push the curtain back and we can all see each other John," Debbie suggested. She loved his including her in their conversation even if she felt like a third wheel. Knowing they needed time alone, but being the great friends they were they wouldn't leave her on her own, alone.

John hobbled over to the curtain and pushed it back "sorry I didn't want to intrude on your privacy, but I wanted you to know we knew you were missing too." He smiled at her.

"We figured you would all know I was missing. At least when you guys tried to get a hold of me over Chrissy missing." Tears slid down her cheeks "I can't thank you guys enough, John."

"Hey hey, don't do that." He hated when women cried.

Chrissy felt bad that Debbie didn't have anyone over there to hold her and comfort her. She decided to lighten the mood "John, did Deb tell you it was Mrs. Lowery that actually saved us from that lunatic?"

John whirled around "what? No she didn't." He looked back at Debbie "so?"

Debbie started laughing "yeah she freaked him out by showing up. He couldn't kill us in front of his mother."

"I wondered why he wasn't in the Shack with you guys, I planned to ask later." He stood between the two beds and looked back and forth like he watched a tennis match. "Old lady Lowery made an appearance huh?"

"Yeah, actually she'd been visiting me for quite some time. I just never put two and two together. Trust me when I say she didn't make it apparent by any means either. She always said vague shit like 'you have to stop him' or 'he's evil,' when I tried to find out who he is she disappeared." Deb shook her head, "go figure she meant the serial killer."

Joellen could be heard from the desk area "where are they? I demand you tell me where they are right this minute."

John, Chrissy and Debbie busted out laughing and Jo heard them "never mind I'll find them on my own." She stormed off in their direction.

John pulled the curtain back and waved her in. Seeing both women lying in hospital beds brought tears to her eyes. She quickly hugged Chrissy then went to Debbie grabbing her tightly. "Thank God you're both alright," she said through her tears.

"We're fine Jo," Debbie reassured her.

"I just can't believe that little squirrel could pull this off. He didn't strike me as intelligent enough, let alone strong enough." Her rant ended as she heard a throat clearing behind her. Turning around she saw the cutest Doctor she'd seen in years.

"I don't mean to interrupt this reunion, but I understand this young lady needs some stitching up." His smile showed the biggest dimples Jo or Debbie had ever seen.

Joellen stood up making room for the doctor to get closer. "Of course, doctor…"

"Dr. McClain," he provided.

A young nurse entered the curtained off area and began opening drawers, piling things onto the small stainless steel table. Debbie looked away. She'd never had stitches before and felt apprehensive about being shot with a needle into the painful cut.

Chrissy winked at her then nodded toward the hunky

doctor, Debbie smiled at her embarrassed. Once the nurse had the tray completed she removed the wrap the ambulance guy had placed on Debbie's arm.

Dr. McClain stepped up to the tray and pulled on gloves. Smiling down at Debbie he picked up her arm taking a look "yep you definitely need stitches, Ms. Milo."

Debbie could feel the warmth of his hands through the thin Playtex gloves, "I've never had stitches before," she said nervously taking a deep breath.

"Nothing to it, you won't feel a thing after you get this." He held up the needle and pushed a bit of liquid out the tip. "You're going to feel a little pinch and that should be it." He looked at her. "Ready?"

Oh those dimples she thought "I guess I don't have much choice." She looked away.

Joellen stepped into her line of sight "you need a hand to hold?" She offered.

Debbie started to say no thank you just as Dr. Delicious stuck the needle in. She sucked in a breath and then felt numbness tingle through her arm.

"See not bad at all," he said to her. "This is quite a laceration, deep but not wide." He examined the cut pulling it open and pushing it closed.

"Don't tell me the facts Doc, just sew it up." Debbie felt woozy, needles always bothered her.

Dr. McClain laughed, cleared his throat again and said "yes ma'am."

John and Chrissy laughed while Joellen held Debbie's free hand.

FORTY-EIGHT

Sam insisted everyone come to Tate's the next evening. He and Maggie figured that would give Chrissy and Debbie time to get home, freshen up and relax before facing all the volunteers and friends that wanted to wish them well and see them with their own eyes.

When Dave told everyone the women had been found and they were safe Sam didn't waste any time. He pulled Maggie into a back room and asked her to marry him. Hell they'd known each other for years and after seeing what John went through he didn't want to waste another minute.

Maggie instantly accepted and further asked him what the hell had taken him so long to come to his senses.

Debbie had a date set up with Dr. Delicious, thanks to Joellen, but figured he wouldn't have given up on wearing her down even without Jo's help.

Chrissy and John snuggled on the sofa. He had a hard time taking his hands off of her, afraid she'd disappear again.

He told her about the volunteers that came out to help him, about how lost he felt not knowing where to look. He told her he quit taking his pain pills because he couldn't think properly while taking them.

She told him about the secret room, how Eugene left them in their own urine and starving for hours at a time.

Both were grateful he was behind bars, Chrissy because she didn't want anyone else to die at his hands, John because he wanted to kill him.

Swinging her legs to the floor Chrissy stood up. "I'm going to get a shower before Debbie gets here." She leaned forward and kissed John's mouth. "I've missed you love."

John grabbed her pulling her onto his lap. "Me, you, too!" He smiled.

Mark and Cody arrived at the Bingham house a little while later. Lee and Maria were already there. Maria and Debbie sat in the kitchen exchanging information about their psychic abilities.

A few members of N.E.P.R. showed up too. Jo, Vinny, Sue and Matt never bothered to wait for invitations to visit. Besides these women were, their family too.

Chrissy thanked the men again as she handed them a beer. "How is Lilly, Mark?"

"Terrific now that you and Debbie are home safe. You're going to see her tomorrow night at Tate's, I promise. She can't wait to see both of you."

"Great I can't wait to see her. I've missed her." She went over and sat on the arm of John's recliner. John put his hand on her thigh and rubbed, he needed to touch her constantly right now, still coping with how close he'd come to losing her.

"We're not here in any official capacity in case you're wondering," Mark told them. "We were glad to hear Debbie and Maria were getting acquainted. She has been an amazing help in all of this."

"How did you know Debbie and Maria would be here?" John asked surprised.

Lee cleared his throat "uh I called him. I know Mark wanted to talk to you guys on a personal basis. He had paperwork to complete and official business to handle before he could get away." He shrugged his shoulders "I hope you don't mind."

"Hell no, we don't mind," John said "actually I planned to call you, Mark, Chrissy and I want to know what happens now?"

400

"Now we wait for Fall River to arraign him in the morning, then we transport him back here. Freetown will more than likely handle the trial phase unless his attorney asks for a change in venue."

"A change in venue?" Chrissy sat up straight "what does that mean?"

"Means the trail and jury selection takes place in another city because he can't get a fair trial here. Nothing for you guys to worry about," Mark assured her.

"I just wish you all had let me kill that mother fucker. We don't have the death penalty here so he gets to live. Where's the justice for the poor women he murdered?" John couldn't keep his anger under control.

"No unfortunately we don't have the death penalty here, but trust me when I say he will never walk freely again. He will suffer in a very small cell," Cody eagerly put in.

"Suffer? Are you kidding me? He continues to breath while they don't, he gets to fantasize about the torture he put those poor women through. Suffer? Not likely." John was pissed.

"I hear you loud and clear Mr. Bingham, but you would feel worst right now if you had killed him. You're not a cold blooded killer and taking someone's life may seem inconsequential when we have what we believe to be good reason, but believe me when I tell you, you don't want to experience that." Cody knew firsthand what that felt like and didn't wish it on his worst enemy.

Mark debated telling John, Eugene probably killed Larry too.

"The bastard will probably plead insanity and not even see the inside of a prison." John glared at Cody.

Cody threw his hands up he wouldn't try to convince John that what they did was the right thing. He knew the guy was entitled to feel everything he felt. He also knew if

Eugene pled insanity it would be an even worst fate than the small cell scenario.

Mark knew John well and he knew the rage John held in check "I hope he does plead insanity that would be so much worse for him in the long run. Think about spending the rest of your life in an asylum poked and prodded daily, thinking yourself the only sane one in there and the loonies you'd have to contend with. No it would be no walk in the park my friend, it would be pure hell especially for someone like Eugene."

"I hope he suffers daily, I feel so badly for those poor girls and their families," Chrissy said.

"You know, Chrissy, you're going to have to talk about everything you went through. You and Debbie both over and over. The more you get it out the less you will hold onto," Lee told her.

"I'm sure we'll talk about it Agent Marlowe, I don't intend to give him any power over me or my feelings and thoughts. I am a survivor and so is Debbie."

"Debbie is what?" she asked walking into the middle of the conversation.

Vinny jumped up and held his hand up quieting everyone he said "you tell us, you're the psychic." He laughed.

"Ha ha, very funny, Vinny." She flipped him off.

"We're just talking about dealing with what you and I've been through Deb. Don't let Vinny twist your panties in a knot." She shook her head at Vinny.

"He wishes," Debbie said sticking her tongue out at him.

"Yes, I do." Vinny smiled.

John noticed Matt sitting quietly watching everyone. He felt bad for treating the man so badly the last couple of days. After Vinny and Debbie quit razzing each other he said "Matt, I owe you an apology." He watched surprise flicker across Matt's face. "I have been over bearing and demanding a lot. I know you held your temper and your tongue while dealing with me and I want you to know how grateful I am. You've been a great friend to me for a long time and I had no right taking it out on you."

Matt laughed "you don't know how close you came to getting punched in the face by me. You are such a bastard sometimes."

"Yeah I do, and yeah I am." Everyone laughed at the two men as John admitted this to Matt.

"And you Mark Mason, who the hell do you think could've kept this idiot in that truck, once he had the Shack in sight?" Matt asked looking at his friend.

"I know, trust me I thought about it after I saw John come into the Shack. I guess I just hoped he'd listen." He shrugged his shoulders and took a drink of his beer. "I'm glad Eugene wasn't in there when John came in. It wouldn't have been pretty."

John insisted he wanted to sleep upstairs tonight like a normal person. No more chair for him, he wanted to feel Chrissy tight against him all night.

She didn't argue at all, she needed him tonight. His strong arms holding her all night long would remind her she's home safe, and Eugene can't hurt her. She wondered how long her thoughts would lead back to Eugene, how long before she felt normal again?

Pulling a long cotton nightgown from her drawer she toyed with the idea of taking yet another shower. She'd already had two in the few, short hours she had been home. Fighting the urge to scrub herself clean again, she slipped the gown over her head and crawled in next to John.

"I saw the wheels turning a second ago, what're you thinking?" he asked her pulling her up against him.

"Nothing babe, good night." She turned her head back to give a quick kiss, but he wouldn't let it go that easy.

"Uhn uhn, you've got to talk to me, Chrissy, don't keep it bottled up inside." He gently turned her over to face him. "I'm a big boy I can take it." He leaned down and brushed her lips gently.

Laughing she said "it's nothing really I just thought about taking another shower. I promise to talk to you if I feel the need. I'm not keeping anything bottled up, now I need sleep." She turned over and snuggled back against him.

"Promise?" He didn't want to push her, but he wanted her to talk about it.

"Yes I promise." She cupped his face in her hands and took a long lingering kiss from him. "I love you John."

"I love you more."

"Not possible." She snuggled up tight against him. "Good night my love."

"Good night, Chrissy." He put his arm over her middle and held on.

Debbie lay in her cold bed alone. She envied Chrissy. She wished she had someone to hold her safely all night long. She snuggled down into the covers as Joellen and Sue's laughter came through the open doorway. They had insisted they stay with her, at least for tonight. She was thankful for good friends.

Her mind drifted back to Dr. Delicious. He had been so gentle with her while he stitched her up. Made her laugh at his jokes and then allowed Jo to prod him into asking her out.

She wondered if he believed in paranormal activity. Probably not, he was a man of science and they were very close minded.

Smiling to herself she thought it felt good to be in a bed, although the floor gave her Chrissy to cuddle with.

FORTY-NINE

Cindy and Maggie enjoyed the crowd tonight, they were all in good humor and the tension that filled the establishment just yesterday dissipated quickly. Sam was happy his bar was filled with paying customers.

Mark and Lilly showed up with the entire Task Force, Lee Marlowe and Maria Erickson, as well as Patricia.

When John, Chrissy, and Debbie came through the front door the bar erupted into laughter, cheers, hoot's and hollering. It was deafening. Dave did the finger whistle thing again after a couple minutes calming the crowd down.

Maggie had drinks on her tray for them cutting through the crowd to reach them. Setting the drinks on the table that had been reserved for the guests of honor she grabbed both women in a hug "I'm so glad you're home. We've missed the hell out of you guys.

After tears were wiped away and laughs were shared John stood up to thank each and every one of them that helped search, made and hung posters, phone calls, or whatever they did, he thanked them sincerely. Smiling down at his wife he took her hand and squeezed "I love you Christine," he told her loudly.

The group went crazy again, cheering and banging on the tables. Tonight was definitely a night of celebration.

After Chrissy and Debbie thanked everyone, people began to settle down and enjoy their time together. The Task Force officers didn't stay very long they were ready to get home and spend time with their families. Mark and Lee were the only two that remained.

Lilly and Mark shared their wonderful news with all of

their friends, together.

Chrissy happy as ever for her friends and all their good news slapped the table with her palm and said "Let me get this straight. Maggie, you and Sam are engaged, Lilly, you and Mark are going to be parents, Debbie, you have a date with Dr. McClain, a.k.a. Dr. Delicious, do I have this right so far?" Her serious face and demeanor had them all wondering what she was up to.

John didn't say a word. He thought she'd be happy for their friends, but she looked anything but happy.

Debbie smiled and said "so far it all sounds right to me."

Chrissy smiled at Debbie, silently thanking her for being the only one courageous enough to confirm everything. "So I guess this means happy ever after, right?"

Once again a hush went around the table no body sure what to say. Some wondered if the ordeal she had been through might have been more than she could handle. She certainly acted strange to all of them, except Debbie.

"Is there a problem with happy ever after, Chrissy?" Debbie boldly asked.

"You bet your sweet ass there is." She picked up her beer mug and downed the rest of it making them all wait. "I have a house full of ghost and you. I'm speaking to the members of N.E.P.R., better get off your lazy asses and do something about them."

The group cracked up laughing. John composed himself quicker than the rest "I guess she wants her happy ending too."

"Don't you worry about them girl, Maria and I are on it." Debbie reached across and squeezed Chrissy hand.

ABOUT THE AUTHOR

T. L. Jones lives in South East Texas with her husband, Dave. They have three grown children. She is a former police officer and uses this experience to bring thrilling, believable mysteries to her readers.

Along with a vivid imagination T. L. loves anything paranormal and participates when possible in paranormal investigations. T.L. is a member of East Texas Paranormal.

She has a passion for writing and developing intriguing characters for her books. When time and weather permits you will find her scuba diving with her husband.

T. L. is an avid reader and enjoys hearing from her readers.

ABOUT THE CO-AUTHOR

John Brightman is the founder of New England Paranormal Research, N.E.P.R.. John has been investigating the paranormal for nearly a decade.

John's childhood acted as the main inspiration, growing up in the Freetown State Forest, part of the Bridgewater Triangle of Massachusetts. Specializing in the infamous murder cases of cult ... Carl Drew, as well as, Mary Lou Arruda.

ptivate every audience with his macabre tales
nce.

:search and state-of-the-art precision to gather
m to being featured on shows like the Travel
nel, and even international shows in over a
rld-wide.
in several paranormal documentary productions,
historically haunted film project.

Made in the USA
Charleston, SC
13 March 2013